The World's Best Short Stories

Anthology & Criticism

Volume VIII

Places

THE WORLD'S BEST SERIES

The World's Best Short Stories

The World's Best Poetry

CoreFiche: *World's Best Drama*
Microfiche with companion reference

The World's Best Short Stories

Anthology & Criticism

Volume VIII

Places

Stories by Allen, Boccaccio, Cather, Harte, Hawthorne, Irving, James, Jewett, Kipling, London, Maupassant, Melville, Pliny the Younger, Poe, Sawyer, Thomas, Twain, Voltaire, Wharton

Prepared by
The Editorial Board

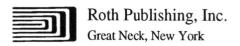

Roth Publishing, Inc.
Great Neck, New York

Contents

Preface

The World's Best Short Stories is designed to give both the serious student and the general reader a large selection and broad range of stories from around the world. Its ten volumes organize the stories into seven reader-friendly groupings:

Short Story Masters (Volumes I and II)
Famous Stories (Volume III)
Fables and Tales (Volume IV)
Mystery and Detection (Volume V)
Horror and Science Fiction (Volume VI)
Characters (Volume VII)
Places (Volume VIII)
Cultures (Volume IX)

Volume X is a research and reference guide and includes a cumulative index to all the volumes.

The arrangement of the stories suggests the multiple approaches for using these volumes. *Short Story Masters* focuses on the author; it contains stories that demonstrate the development of the short story as a conscious art form. *Famous Stories* is the volume to go to for well-known stories by authors who may or may not themselves be well-known. *Fables and Tales* includes fairy tales and other short non-realistic literature, as well as tales that are ancestors of the short story form. Volumes V and VI contain genre fiction; they act as a kind of counterpart to *Short Story Masters*. Whereas *Masters* places the short story in the tradition of an evolving art, these genre-centered volumes put it at the disposal of the general reader and the popular imagination. *Mystery and Detection* makes the case for a genre that has been continuously popular and critically treated since Poe, while *Horror and Science Fiction* looks at two different styles of fantastic literature--one finding its elements in the supernatural, the other in the superscientific.

The later volumes contain stories that are remarkable for a salient feature. The stories in *Characters* are portrait studies: their primary function is to examine the character of the hero or heroine. *Places* compiles stories that evoke a setting in a way that is memorable and important to the being of the story. Finally, *Cultures* uses ethnicity as its backdrop. It carries stories that are informed by their cultural setting.

The organization, variety, and breadth of **The World's Best Short Stories** makes it a unique anthology collection that can be used for study or read for pleasure.

Introduction

Perhaps influenced by Edgar Allan Poe's definition the modern reader has certain expectations from a short story. In his review of Hawthorne's *Twice Told Tales* Poe writes, "the unity of effect or impression is a point of the greatest importance. It is clear, moreover, that this unity cannot be thoroughly preserved in productions whose perusal cannot be completed at one sitting...And without unity of impression, the deepest effects cannot be brought about." To achieve this overall effect a short story must possess certain fundamental characteristics. A well-constructed short story should demonstrate a unity of characterization and theme through a setting of time, mood, or place.

Character portraits have a well-deserved place in the history of the short story. Finely plotted tales of sequential actions and reactions also are well appreciated. Many famous stories simply evoke an historical time, atmosphere or a psychological state. Authors often combine one or more of these elements. This volume will concern itself with place and demonstrate how place can overshadow other elements of the short story. Conversely, it will show place being used to reveal character, atmosphere, psychological state and historical time. The terms "place" and "setting" will be used interchangeably in this introduction. In other literary discussions the terms lieu or locale may also be used.

The Development of Setting in the Short Story

Setting has always been present in fiction as a backdrop which can take the reader to a different city, dwelling, or landscape. Occasionally setting has become more prominent in its role. It works in various ways, aside from just being an ornament, to enrich the telling of a short story. First let's briefly look at the presence of setting in the history of short fiction.

Setting has always played a role in short fiction although historically it is more often incidental. This can be seen in the great works of world literature that have contributed to the modern short story. Included in the great pieces of world fiction would be *The Arabian Nights* from India. Although it is a lengthy work the stories can stand alone. The earliest reference to this piece is 987 A.D. but it is believed to have been written much earlier. From Japan it would be necessary to mention *The Tale of Genji* as one of the earliest pieces of fiction. This too includes a series of tales which are often capable of being read as separate pieces. *The Tale of Genji* is dated in the early eleventh century. In both works setting is much less important than plot or characterization.

Both the Greeks and Romans contributed to the development of the short story. An example of the Greeks' contribution would be Homer's epic poem *The Odyssey*. Odysseus the hero travels on quests of adventure and battle that take the reader to various places but this is the extent of the use of setting. Several episodes of *The Odyssey* come very close to the modern short story form as is seen in the *Eumaeus' Tale* from *The Odyssey, Book XV* circa 1000 B.C. The island is described but setting is not the focus of attention nor is it used as a literary device. The Greeks were more often concerned with a great hero than with plot or setting. But a Roman work, a series of epistles written by Pliny the Younger circa 85 A.D., contains several portions that move towards the short story form. One section in particular narrates events that take place in a haunted house and it creates a powerful impression of setting. The locale of this story is a mansion, which is still appropriate in modern literature for a ghost story. The solitude of the place is equally apropos in terms of preparing the reader's expectations for such a ghastly event as the arrival of an evil ghost. The piece presented in this volume is filled with vivid details of the landscape of Pliny's villa in Tuscany. Although more a travelogue than a short story, it does provide an almost palpable sense of place. Near the end Pliny raises an interesting literary question that is germane to this volume. He wonders how much detail is necessary to convey a sense of place without losing a reader in minutiae.

Hebrew literature also possesses several pieces that enriched the development of the short story and setting as we know it. The best examples include *The Book of Jonah* and *The Book of Ruth*. Jonah's reconciliation with God occurs in the mouth of a whale, which is certainly an unexpected location. *The Book of Ruth* is meant to be an historical account that leads into the lineage of David. Here place is significant because where Ruth comes from in this story determines the action. Ruth's loyalty to her husband's family and clan signifies her willingness to self-sacrifice, to leave home behind and to do more of her share than necessary in the foreign village.

Among the earliest European stories written in the vernacular is *The Decameron* by Boccaccio (1313-1375). Boccaccio was a major contributor to the development of the short story. Most importantly, he was a humanist in that he believed that literature should recognize the conditions of men of all situations and backgrounds. He strung together a number of stories, narrated by different characters and told over a period of ten days (a technique that was adopted by Chaucer in *The Canterbury Tales* and by Hawthorne in *Tales of a Wayside Inn*). Boccaccio does pay significant attention to landscape and setting. He has unforgettable descriptions of palace gardens in which his characters have settled to relate stories to one another.

Although recognizably great fiction, none of the tales described above quite fit Poe's definition of a short story. The modern short story crystallizes in the 19th Century into the form that readers of today will find familiar.

Modern Literary Movements and Setting in the Short Story

Three major literary movements, Romanticism, Naturalism and Realism contributed to the growing importance of setting in prose literature. Romanticism, which developed during the late 18th and 19th Centuries in Europe, was a conscious revolt against Classicism. Classicism had rigid rules that required the writer to separate himself from emotion and subjectivity in order to focus on form. Romanticism permitted the artist to express emotion, elevate emotion over intellect, and focus on the individual. Everyday experience and common people were acceptable subjects. The Romantics believed in the essential goodness of humanity.

Romanticism was expressed in varying forms. For instance, Wordsworth's poetry was filled with descriptions of landscapes that came alive with his imaginative personification of nature to express his very personal feelings. He expressed a strong relationship between man and nature. Similarly the writings of Hawthorne and Melville often encompassed a transcendental element. Transcendentalists believed that God is immanent in man and nature and that individual intuition is the highest source of knowledge. This lends itself to the development of individualism and the rejection of traditional authority. It affects setting because for the first time personal expressions of feelings about surroundings was acceptable in literature.

Increased discoveries in science led to Realism, which asked artists to give an accurate depiction of their subject. Realism describes life without idealization. Arising in the 19th Century, among its most noted practitioners were Balzac and Howells. It is concerned with the common, everyday life of the middle and lower classes. Character is seen as a product of social factors and environment is an integral element of dramatic complications.

Naturalism was given its manifesto by Emile Zola in 1875 with his *Le Roman Experimental*. The writings of Darwin and Marx heavily influenced the movement, which has been described as Realism with a deterministic philosophy. It is similar to Realism in that it focuses on reality in terms of natural forces such as environment and physical needs and drives. It often depicts the harsher aspects of life. Naturalism is the result of a preoccupation with natural science. In its approach man is viewed as a minuscule part of a schematic yet cruel world. Thus, there could be no amicable relationship between the individual and his environment. Individuality suffers here because man becomes a mere pawn to superior forces. All action becomes involuntary. Hence setting gains importance.

Because of the brevity of the short story it is useful to use setting in more than one way. Most of the stories presented here do make use of more than one of the techniques under which they are grouped. But they are grouped under topics which refer to their predominant use of a particular literary device.

Setting Used to Create Tone and Atmosphere

Setting can be used to create a tone or an atmosphere by evoking certain emotions which can range from joy to terror. Edgar Allan Poe was a master of this technique and preferred to depict terror over other emotions. In his story *The Fall of the House of Usher*, he employs a number of devices to propel setting from its more traditional role as backdrop. One is the use of imagery to create atmosphere. The other is to use setting to develop characterization. The setting in this story is the mansion of Roderick Usher. Poe has developed a very vivid panorama of images which are used consistently throughout the story. The reader is drawn into "the mansion of gloom" and is never given a chance to escape from the clutches of his compelling, symbolic descriptions.

An eerie atmosphere is evoked through a description that incites uneasiness in the reader. This is achieved by describing the weather, the land and the mansion. The weather is said by the narrator to be "dull and dark" and he immediately feels a sense of gloom in response to his surroundings. He writes that there was "an atmosphere which had no affinity with the air of heaven, but which had reeked up from the decayed trees, and the gray wall, and the silent tarn - a pestilent and mystic vapor, dull sluggish, faintly discernible, and leaden hued." The narrator says, "I looked upon the scene before me - upon the mere house, and the simple landscape features of the domain - upon the bleak walls - upon the vacant eye-like windows... ." The house is described as if alive and in possession of sight. It is again given human characteristics when it is described as "the melancholy House of Usher." This atmosphere of gloom is a foreshadowing of the tragedy to come and a reflection of the dark and demented spirit of Roderick Usher.

Characterization is developed through these images by metaphor. Poe wants the reader to associate the characteristics of the mansion with Roderick Usher. The narrator states that the peasants have come to identify the House of Usher as both the place and as its inhabitants, the Usher family. Eventually the reader does the same. We are given a sense of decay and waste. Time wreaks havoc upon a once magnificent Gothic structure as well as upon Roderick Usher and the cataleptic Madeline. The portrayal of the decay of human life and spirit evokes in the reader the terror that Roderick Usher experiences because of his illness. Ultimately the story involves two deaths and the complete annihilation of Poe's architecture of the imagination, The House of Usher.

Setting as Symbol

Setting can function as a symbol. A place can represent an idea or feeling as in Willa Cather's *The Treasure of Far Island*. Far Island and its treasure represent the Eden-like world of childhood with its qualities of innocence, sense of wonder and feelings of completeness. We are introduced to Douglass, the protagonist, who is now an adult and a successful play-wright. He is returning to his hometown to visit his parents and in the forefront of his thoughts is his memory of Far Island and the treasure he hid there. Figuratively he has buried his childhood there, although literally he has buried trinkets. He still has a map leading to their location. He meets up with Margie, his childhood friend, who has grown into a beautiful woman. He convinces her to go with him to rediscover the treasure. Both think they have lost the magic of childhood only to find the magic of adulthood - love. They still use their imaginations to view their experiences through a veil of romance. The wonder of childhood need not be lost completely. It simply takes on a different form.

The last paragraph describes the island and represents a new beginning for the couple, "The locust chirped in the thicket: the setting sun threw a track of flame cross the water; the willows burned with fire and were not consumed; a glory was upon the sand and the river and upon the Silvery Beaches; and these two looked about over God's world and saw that it was good. In the western sky the palaces of crystal and gold were quenched in night, like the cities of old empires; and out of the east rose the same moon that has glorified all the romances of the world." Cather writes about the couple, "they had become as the gods, who dwell in their golden houses, recking little of the woes and labors of mortals, neither heeding any fall of rain or snow." So not only has Cather used the island to represent childhood, she has reflected the emotions of her characters in her descriptions of the island.

In *The Piazza* the narrator moves to a secluded country house that is rich in vistas of mountains, meadows, and wild flowers. In order to fully appreciate his view he builds a piazza in which to sit and look upon the countryside. But he begins to feel lonely and restless at his beautiful residence. He looks at the land and likens it to the ocean, "For not only do long ground swells roll the slanting grain and little wavelets of the grass ripple over upon the low piazza, as their beach, and the blown down of dandelions is wafted like the spray." He wishes it could carry him elsewhere and it figuratively does. One day he catches sight of a house on the mountain across the way. Despite the splendor of his haven the protagonist becomes restless for more. He imagines that fairies must inhabit the house across the way and for months he enjoys the fascination of the mysterious cottage. He believes that rainbows must end there and he is fascinated at the way light settles about the cottage. Finally he decides to set out to find something to add to his life, "I saw the golden mountain window, dazzling like a deep-sea dolphin. Fairies there, thought I once more, the queen of fairies at her fairy-window, at any rate, some glad mountain girl: it will do me good, it will cure this eagerness, to look on her. No more: I'll launch my yawl...and push away for fairyland, for rainbow's end, in fairyland."

He reaches the other side only to find a very sad and lonely girl living there who dreams of the happiness at the other house. Not knowing that her visitor is the owner of that cottage, she has similarly spent time dreaming of life on the mountain across the way. The narrator is driven by curiosity and loneliness and the girl is driven by her sadness and loneliness. The narrator realizes what he has at home and his restless spirit is quieted when he returns from the other mountain, "Enough. Launching my yawl no more for fairyland, I stick to the piazza. It is my box-royal...the scenery is magical - the illusion complete." This story quite effectively uses the houses as symbols of desired fulfillment.

Man's Relationship with Nature
and the Personification of Nature

In *Love of Life* Jack London gives a very realistic picture of the Canadian mountains. London sketches the terrain vividly and provides details of its skies, topography, and wildlife. Against this backdrop the author demonstrates how location in nature serves as the force behind character.

The protagonist remains unnamed. His identity is irrelevant. Lost in the wild, his sole interest is basic survival. The land determines his actions. After having been abandoned in this barren and cold wasteland he must struggle to find nourishment and keep conscious. His only hope is that he finds his way out of the ice desert. Injured and without adequate supplies his instinct is to survive. He is especially strong spirited. He continues to press forward even as thoughts of death creep into his mind. He contends with the land's adverse conditions and takes from it what he can. He subsists on berries and small animals.

The protagonist represents all men in their most primary state. Personality and societal role matter little. Although he has brief flashes of philosophical speculation, the protagonist is reduced to the level of a beast. His surroundings totally control his actions and reactions. Through setting London has demonstrated man's innate desire to survive and triumph over the most hopeless situations.

The Snow Story by Chauncey Thomas is much like Jack London's story *Love of Life* in the way that nature plays a primary role. But there are several additional touches in Thomas' story. For instance, Thomas not only gives a vivid description of the land but uses the picture to set emotional tones. He describes the Arctic with images of vibrancy and beauty, almost like a wintry wonderland, with the use of such phrases as "Airy crystals float as on the breath of polar fairies." He does this to show us how the protagonist, a mail carrier who travels on foot through the Arctic, is much a part of his surroundings. We can picture this man almost as a god at home in a high, remote crystalline land and we are made to understand his physical and spiritual strengths. But the tone changes to foreshadow his confrontation with Salardo the robber, and an approaching avalanche. A storm begins to rise and we are given such descriptions as "snow-sand cut his veil as if blown from a gun," and "The snow was as hard, sharp and glittering in the white night as the surface of broken steel...The ground ice cut like powdered glass shot from a battery."

There are also many instances of personification such as: "All nature was hushed as if frightened. A screeching eagle went flapping far away. From under the ruin a wolf howled dismally; then weaker and weaker - a piteous whine - and silence. The frozen wind went up a gulch of naked, fire-blackened pines crooning a requiem... it chilled the heart in icy triumph." Although nature temporarily triumphs, man is not quite the helpless pawn pictured by London. In Thomas' vision occasionally man can dominate nature through ingenuity.

Bret Harte's *The Outcasts of Poker Flat* is another story set in natural surroundings. Harte uses the setting not only to establish tone but also to reflect the characters' feelings. The regret of the outcasts over their misdeeds is reflected by nature itself. "It was one of the peculiarities of that mountain climate that its rays diffused a kindly warmth over the wintry landscape, as if in regretful commiseration of the past."

Setting as it Reveals a Region and Its Culture

Culture is not a primary concern in this volume. However, it is often relevant to setting since the discussion of a particular place can reveal the customs of its people. In these stories setting becomes a device to illustrate culture and values.

Rudyard Kipling's *The Miracle of Purun Bhagat* is an account of an Indian prime minister who belongs to the highest caste but decides to give up his public service and notoriety for less profitable pursuits. He gives up his successful career to take up "the begging-bowl and ochre-colored dress of a Sunnyasi, or holy man." He leaves the city for the countryside to fulfill his spiritual yearnings.

The journey of Purun Bhagat takes him through the farmlands and mountains of Tibet. Unlike *Love of Life* the land is portrayed as amicable.

It is a source of solace and spiritual knowledge for Purun Bhagat. Its bounty is described, "It was laid out like a map at his feet. He could see the evening gatherings, held on the circle of the threshing-floors because that was the only level ground; could see the wonderful unnamed green of the young rice, the indigo blues of the Indian corn, the dock-like patches of buckwheat, and, in its season, the red bloom of the amaranth, whose tiny seeds, being neither grain nor pulse, make a food than can be lawfully eaten by Hindus in time of fasts."

The protagonist's religiosity connects him to the land. As shown by his work as prime minister Purun Bhagat is a man of ideals. This is reinforced when he gives up a life of luxury. He has achieved a state of consciousness that allows him to be utterly serene. Nature and meditation allow him moments of transcendence when he forgets that he is of this life and trapped within a body,"...time stopped, and he, sitting at the mouth of the shrine, could not tell whether he were alive or dead: a man with control of his limbs or a part of the hills, and the clouds, and the shifting rain and sunlight." In order to achieve his religious goal he must feel at one with the land even if only for a brief period of time.

The reader not only learns of the holy man's life but also becomes aware of the values and beliefs of the Tibetan people. We discover that they are farmers. We are able to see how they revere a learned man, especially one who lives a spiritual life devoid of material possession and social concerns. Here setting is not only a backdrop but an important focal point for the protagonist's religious pursuits.

Washington Irving describes the setting of *The Legend of Sleepy Hollow* in minute detail including the land and the people of the region. In this way the story is much like Kipling's *The Miracle of Puran Bhagat*. With the beauty of upstate New York for a backdrop Irving explains how legends are perpetuated in this region. Most important to this setting of legend and superstition is Sleepy Hollow's seclusion. It exists untouched by the outside, changing world. The area itself is conducive to a belief in ghosts. "There was a contagion in the very air that blew from that haunted region: it breathed forth an atmosphere of dreams and fancies infecting all the land."

Irving details the basic workings of the community. The school master is housed by students' families. Dances are major social affairs. The people are religious with a susceptibility to superstitions and legend. They are farmers with little time for reading or learning. Irving shows how the nature of their work and the land they inhabit contributes to their superstitious ways. The Kipling story illustrates how setting can have a positive effect. Here we see the darker influence of setting.

In his story *King Solomon of Kentucky* James Lane Allen illustrates how setting can have both a positive and negative effect. He describes "a year of strange disturbances" in nature - droughts, frosts, swarms of locusts. But in the summer of 1833 the town of Lexington, "the Athens of the West," is far removed from such worries. Allen proceeds to paint a picture of an almost idyllic small town existence. Only the reprobate, Solomon, and the mostly unspoken threat of cholera mar the portrait. When the disease does strike the town Solomon's reformation provides both a personal and social redemption. Allen enhances the setting of this tale of the ante-bellum South by using dialect.

Setting as it Reveals Intellectual Climate

Henry James' *The Author of Beltraffio* can be viewed as allegorical from a number of perspectives - appearance versus reality, Aestheticism versus Puritanism, American idealism against Old World cynicism. In addition to its philosophical overtones there is, as there is in much of James' fiction, a deep, psychological element. Throughout the story James skillfully employs setting to reveal the philosophical and psychological differences among a famous author, his religious wife, their sickly child, and an American interloper.

Ostensibly the story is rather straightforward. The narrator, a young American writer, travels to England with the hope of meeting his hero, the famous and controversial author, Mark Ambient. Armed with a somewhat dated letter of introduction, he procures an invitation to Ambient's "cottage" in Surrey. There he meets the great *artiste*, his beautiful and very proper wife, their sickly but angelic child, and Ambient's eccentric, spinster sister. Long conversations in the drawing room are followed by long walks in the gardens and fields, candlelit dinners, and more long discussions on the nature of art and the art of nature. On a beautiful Sunday morning the child dies from a mysterious illness through the apparent, willful neglect of his mother.

The narrator describes the house and gardens in admiring tones. As befitting his name Ambient's personna pervades and surrounds all. "There was genius in his house too I thought when we got there; there was imagination in the carpets and curtains, in the pictures and books, in the garden behind it, where certain old brown walls were muffled in creepers that appeared to me to have been copied from a masterpiece..." By evoking the paintings of the pre-Raphaelites, James not only comments on Aestheticism but also allows the setting to foreshadow the denouement. "...the beautiful mother and beautiful child, interlaced there against a background of roses, a picture such as I doubtless shouldn't soon see again..." The narrator carries the religious allusion to its logical end when he observes, "...the mossy mottled garden-walls, where plum trees and pears, flattened and fastened upon the rusty bricks, looked like crucified figures with many arms."

Ever the master storyteller, James uses a setting of natural beauty and human artifice to illustrate the deadly intellectual and emotional conflict between husband and wife.

Setting as a Backdrop

Like Poe and James, Edith Wharton had more than a passing interest in the macabre. Although best known for her chronicles of society and its changing manners and mores, she also wrote some highly regarded tales of the supernatural.

In *The Eyes* Wharton employs a convention that can be traced from Boccaccio, to Chaucer, to the creation of Mary Shelley's *Frankenstein*, namely, a group of people spinning tales for their own entertainment. With a few deft sentences Wharton sets up the locale of the storytelling. "Seen through the haze of our cigars, and by the drowsy gleam of a coal fire, Culwin's library, with its oak walls and dark old bindings, made a good setting for such evocations..." Narrated almost entirely in the first person, the story does not depend on setting to produce its chilling effect, at least not setting as we have seen it used in other stories. Rather an hallucination, the ghostly blood-red eyes seen by Culwin, becomes part of the landscape of the story itself. As is appropriate in a ghost story an apparition becomes real not only to Culwin but to the reader as well.

In *Happiness*, Guy de Maupassant ironically contrasts the supposed civility of mainland France with the rugged terrain of Corsica. The initially snooty narrator views his journey to the island as something of a youthful lark. He looks at the locals with bemused indifference, almost as objects devoid of humanity. His viewpoint begins to change when he happens upon an elderly couple still very much in love. The wife was formerly a noblewoman, an acclaimed beauty of French society. The husband was a common foot soldier. Their love affair scandalized polite society and the couple fled France never to be seen again. Maupassant contrasts the barreness of the setting with the richness of the couple's happiness. He demonstrates how even in the most sterile surroundings good can be found.

Places of the Imagination

Although a writer may use imagination to bring a setting to life through personification or imagery, the place usually is of this world and very accessible to all readers. However writers sometimes find it necessary to create their own unique worlds. It may be needed to express some complex philosophical thought or may simply be a flight of fancy. Whatever the reason the writer's imagination can transport the reader to a world that is highly personal, somewhat familiar yet undoubtedly different.

Voltaire's *Micromegas* takes the reader into space, to the star Sirius and the planet Saturn. Apart from the scathing satire of contemporary events and society, Voltaire's writings always contained a moral thesis. Through the two aliens Voltaire is able to make a detached observation of earthlings. The opportunities for satirical comment are obvious. However Voltaire also is making a philosophical point about mankind's place in the world. *Micromegas* illustrates the entire littleness of man and man's world in reference to the universe as a whole. "Our life is a point, our duration a flash, our world an atom."

Mark Twain's story *Captain Stormfield's Visit to Heaven* deals with another place built with the imagination. Like Voltaire Twain was a master satirist. Unlike Voltaire he was the eternal optimist and leavened his satire with humor. While Voltaire's motto was "destroy the infamous thing," Twain's may well have been "the thing may be infamous, but it also can be saved."

The story reveals that there were other worlds saved by Christ and thus, heaven is populated by the spirits of earthlings and non-earthlings. To accomodate such a diverse population heaven is divided into different kingdoms. Stormfield's visit causes a stir among the heavenly clerks because he cannot quite remember from whence he came. The subsequent struggle to find the right kingdom for Stormfield allows Twain to make a number of humorous, satirical points about the nature of humanity. All ends well and Stormfield receives his harp, wings and halo. The simple point of the story is "...a man's got to be in his own heaven to be happy."

The City

Earlier we saw how Maupassant contrasted the mainland of France with the isolation of Corsica in *Happiness*. In her delightful little story, *Fame's Little Day*, Sarah Orne Jewett contrasts the rustic simplicity of Vermont with the urban hubbub of New York City.

In a slight variation of the city mouse and the country mouse, an elderly couple from Vermont arrive in New York to do business with buyers of the husband's maple syrup. They find the city intimidating and somewhat threatening. Their unease is heightened by a sense of inferiority to the New Yorkers. On a whim a young newspaper reporter writes a piece about their arrival in New York and they suddenly find themselves celebrities. Even so the elderly couple still long to return to Vermont. "They were both thinking of their gray farm-house high on a long western slope with the afternoon sun full in its face, the old barn, the pasture, the shaggy woods that stretched up the mountainside." Their trip to New York provides many great memories to bring home to Vermont but it also gives them an increased appreciation of home and a greater self-respect.

Time Period as an Element of Setting

A story can be set outside of the author's time in order to recreate a period. To do this it is necessary to describe the concerns and customs of the time period being portrayed. Research is of the utmost importance in order to provide an accurate historical picture. Nathanial Hawthorne consulted Strutt's *Book of English Sports and Pastimes* to help provide the background for his story of life in early New England, *The Maypole of Merrymount.* His story is woven around the May festivals that the settlers had brought from their native England. This setting is used to comment on Puritan austerity. Likewise in Ruth Sawyer's *The Princess and the Vagabone* the story is set during a time past. Set in Ireland the period details pervade this entertaining story. Both stories are captivating. Hawthorne provides a social commentary while bringing an early New England village to life. Sawyer creates rich characterizations and offers a rewarding view on the nature of love. In both pieces the time period assists character motivation as well as providing the reader with a fascinating look into times past.

Conclusion

Although a short story can exist without a focus on place, as we have seen setting undoubtedly can be used as a literary device to enhance the effect of a short story. A careful use of setting may sometimes even make all the difference between a travelogue and a short story. A travelogue may describe a place but if it does not metaphorically or otherwise touch upon emotion or psyche, it is then simply a depiction of one's observation without a subjective and personal dimension. When structuring the short story, a very concise and difficult form of literature, the modern writer must consider setting to be of the utmost importance.

Irena Spiegal

King Solomon of Kentucky

James Lane Allen

James Lane Allen (1849-1925), the youngest of seven children, was raised in the bluegrass region on a farm near Lexington, Kentucky. His early days were happy but after the Civil War his family suffered heavy financial losses. For years Allen knew poverty and hard work. He struggled to get an education. At about the age of ten he began attending a neighboring school. At seventeen he enrolled in Transylvania College, graduating with honors in 1872.

As a young man he taught Latin at local colleges in addition to spending time writing literary criticisms and fiction. He continued his studies and received his Master of Arts from Transylvania in 1877 and an honorary Master of Arts from Bethany College in 1880. In 1893 he left Kentucky and settled in New York where he concentrated on his writing.

Many of Allen's stories drew upon his experiences of growing up in the pre-Civil War South. His stories romanticized Kentucky. At a time when Realism was the predominant approach in literature Allen stood out with his adherence to Romanticism. Allen's writing also stirred up religious fundamentalists with his defense of Darwinism in his novel *The Reign of Law: A Tale of the Kentucky Hemp Fields* (1900). In addition he used his writing to comment on urban problems and World War One.

Among his best known works are *A Flute and Violin* (1891), *A Kentucky Cardinal* (1894), *The Choir Invisible* (1897), and *The Landmark* (1925), which was published posthumously.

IT HAD BEEN a year of strange disturbances--a desolating drought, a hurly-burly of destructive tempests, killing frosts in the tender valleys, mortal fevers in the tender homes. Now came tidings that all day the wail of myriads of locusts was heard in the green woods of Virginia and Tennessee; now that Lake Erie was blocked with ice on the very verge of summer, so that in the Niagara new rocks and islands showed their startling faces. In the Bluegrass Region of Kentucky countless caterpillars were crawling over the ripening apple orchards and leaving the trees as stark as when tossed in the thin air of bitter February days.

Then, flying low and heavily through drought and tempest and frost and plague, like the royal presence of disaster, that had been but heralded by its mournful train, came nearer and nearer the dark angel of the pestilence. M. Xaupi had given a great ball only the night before in the dancingrooms over the confectionery of M. Giron--that M. Giron who made the tall pyramids méringues and macaroons for wedding suppers, and spun around them a cloud of candied webbing as white and misty as the veil of the bride. It was the opening cotillon party of the summer. The men came in blue cloth coats with brass buttons, buff waistcoats, and laced ruffled shirts; the ladies came in white satins with ethereal silk overdresses, embroidered in the figure of a gold beetle or an oak leaf of green. The walls of the ballroom were painted to represent landscapes of blooming orangetrees, set here and there in clustering tubs; and the chandeliers and sconces were lighted with innumerable waxcandles, yellow and green and rose.

Only the day before, also, Clatterbuck had opened for the summer a new villa-house, six miles out in the country, with a dancingpavilion in a grove of maples and oaks, a pleasureboat on a sheet of crystal water, and a cellar stocked with old sherry, Sauterne, and Château Margaux wines, with anisette, "Perfect Love," and Guigholet cordials.

Down on Water Street, near where now stands a railway station, Hugh Lonney, urging that the fear of cholera was not the only incentive to cleanliness, had just fitted up a sumptuous bathhouse, where cold and shower baths might be had at twelve and a half cents each, or hot ones at three for half a dollar.

Yes, the summer of 1833 was at hand, and there must be new pleasures, new luxuries; for Lexington was the Athens of the West and the Kentucky Birmingham.

Old Peter Leuba felt the truth of this, as he stepped smiling out of his little musicstore on Main Street, and, rubbing his hands briskly together, surveyed once more his newlyarranged windows, in which were displayed gold and silver epaulets, bottles of Jamaica rum, garden seeds from Philadelphia, drums and guitars and harps. Dewees & Grant felt it in their drugstore on Cheapside, as they sent off a large order for calomel and superior Maccoboy, rappee, and Lancaster snuff. Bluff little Daukins Tegway felt it, as he hurried on the morning of that day to the office of the *Observer and Reporter*, and advertised that he would willingly exchange his beautiful assortment of painted muslins and Dunstable bonnets for flax and feathers. On the threshold he met a florid farmer, who had just offered ten dollars' reward for a likely runaway boy with a long fresh scar across his face; and tomorrow the paper would contain one more of those tragical little cuts, representing an African slave scampering away at the top of his speed, with a stick swung across his shoulder and a bundle dangling down his back. In front of Postlethwaite's Tavern, where now stands the Phoenix Hotel, a company of idlers, leaning back in Windsor chairs and planting their feet against the opposite wall on a level with their heads, smoked and chewed and yawned, as they discussed the administration of Jackson and arranged for the coming of Daniel Webster in June, when they would give him a great barbecue, and roast in his honor a buffalo bull taken from the herd embarked near Ashland. They hailed a passing merchant, who, however, would hear nothing of the bull, but fell to praising his Rocky Mountain beaver and Goose Creek salt; and another, who turned a dead ear to Daniel Webster, and invited them to drop in and examine his choice essences of peppermint, bergamot, and lavender.

But of all the scenes that might have been observed in Lexington on that day, the most remarkable occurred in front of the old courthouse at the hour of high noon. On the mellow stroke of the clock in the steeple above, the sheriff stepped briskly forth, closely followed by a man of powerful frame, whom he commanded to station himself on the pavement several feet off. A crowd of men and boys had already collected in anticipation, and others came quickly up as the clear voice of the sheriff was heard across the open public square and old marketplace.

He stood on the topmost of the courthouse steps, and for a moment looked down on the crowd with the usual air of official severity.

"Gentlemen," he then cried out sharply, "by an ordah of the cou't I now offah this man at public sale to the highes' biddah. He is ablebodied but lazy, without visible property or means of suppoht, an' of dissolute habits. He is therefoh adjudged guilty of high misdemeanahs, an' is to be sole into labah foh a twelvemonth. How much, then, am I offahed foh the vagrant ? How much am I offahed foh ole King Sol'mon ?"

Nothing was offered for old King Solomon. The spectators formed themselves into a ring around the big vagrant and settled down to enjoy the performance.

"Staht 'im, somebody."

Somebody started a laugh, which rippled around the circle.

The sheriff looked on with an expression of unrelaxed severity, but catching the eye of an acquaintance on the outskirts, he exchanged a lightning wink of secret appreciation. Then he lifted off his tight beaver hat, wiped out of his eyes a little shower of perspiration which rolled suddenly down from above, and warmed a degree to his theme.

"Come, gentlemen," he said, more suasively, "it's too hot to stan' heah all day. Make me an offah! You all know ole King Sol'mon; don't wait to be interduced. How much, then, to staht 'im? Say fifty dollahs! Twenty-five! Fifteen! Ten! Why, gentlemen! Not *ten* dollahs? Remembah this is the Bluegrass Region of Kentucky--the land of Boone an' Kenton, the home of Henry Clay!" he added, in an oratorical *crescendo.*

"He ain't wuth his victuals," said an oily little tavernkeeper, folding his arms restfully over his own stomach and cocking up one piggish eye into his neighbor's face. "He ain't wuth his 'taters."

"Buy 'im foh 'is rags!" cried a young law-student, with a Blackstone under his arm, to the town ragpicker opposite, who was unconsciously ogling the vagrant's apparel.

"I *might* buy 'im foh 'is *scalp,*" drawled a farmer, who had taken part in all kinds of scalp contests and was now known to be busily engaged in collecting crow scalps for a match soon to come off between two rival countries.

"I think I'll buy 'im foh a hatsign," said a manufacturer of tendollar Castor and Rhorum hats. This sally drew merry attention to the vagrant's hat, and the merchant felt rewarded.

"You'd bettah say the town ought to buy 'im an' put 'im up on top of the cou'thouse as a scarecrow foh the cholera," said some one else.

"What news of the cholera did the stagecoach bring this mohing?" quickly inquired his neighbor in his ear; and the two immediately fell into low, grave talk, forgot the auction, and turned away.

"Stop, gentlemen, stop!" cried the sheriff, who had watched the rising tide of goodhumor, and now saw his chance to float in on it with spreading sails. "You're runnin' the price in the wrong direction--down, not up. The law requires that he be sole to the highes' biddah, not the lowes'. As loyal citizens, uphole the constitution of the commonwealth of Kentucky an' make me an offah; the man is really a great bargain. In the first place, he would cos' his ownah little or nothin', because, as you see, he keeps himself in cigahs an' clo'es; then, his main article of diet is whisky--a supply of which he always has on han'. He don't even need a bed, foh you know he sleeps jus' as well on any doohstep; noh a chair, foh he prefers to sit roun' on the curbstones. Remembah, too, gentlemen, that ole King Sol'mon is a Virginian--from the same neighbouhhood as Mr. Clay. Remembah that he is well educated, that he is an *awful* Whig, an' that he has smoked mo' of the stumps of Mr. Clay's cigahs than any other man in existence. If you don't b'lieve *me*, gentlemen, yondah goes Mr. Clay now; call *him* ovah an' ask 'im foh yo'se'ves."

He paused, and pointed with his right forefinger towards Main Street, along which the spectators, with a sudden craning of necks, beheld the familiar figure of the passing statesman.

"But you don't need anybody to tell you these fac's, gentlemen," he continued. "You merely need to be reminded that ole King Sol'mon is no ohdinary man. Mo'ovah he has a kine heaht, he nevah spoke a rough wohd to anybody in this worl', an' he is as proud as Tecumseh of his good name an' charactah. An', gentlemen," he added, bridling with an air of mock gallantry and laying a hand on his heart, "if anythin' fu'thah is required in the way of a puffect encomium, we all know that there isn't anothah man among us who cuts as wide a swath among the ladies. The'foh, if you have any appreciation of virtue, any magnanimity of heaht, if you set a propah valuation upon the descendants of Virginia, that mothah of Presidents; if you believe in the pure laws of Kentucky as the pioneer bride of the Union; if you love America an' love the worl'-- make me a gen'rous, hightoned offah foh ole King Sol'mon !"

He ended his peroration amid a shout of laughter and applause, and, feeling satisfied that it was a good time for returning to a more practical treatment of his subject, proceeded in a sincere tone:

"He can easily earn from one to two dollahs a day, an' from three to six hundred a yeah. There's not anothah white man in town capable of doin' as much work. There's not a niggah han' in the hemp factories with such muscles an' such a chest. *Look* at 'em! An', if you don't b'lieve me, step fo'wahd and *feel* 'em. How much, then, is bid foh 'im ?"

"One dollah!" said the owner of a hemp factory, who had walked forward and felt the vagrant's arm, laughing, but coloring up also as the eyes of all were quickly turned upon him. In those days it was not an unheardof thing for the muscles of a human being to be thus examined when being sold into servitude to a new master.

"Thank you!" cried the sheriff, cheerily. "One precinc' heard from! One dollah! I am offahes one dollah foh ole King Sol'mon. One dollah foh the king! Make it a half. One dollah an' a half. Make it a half. one dol-dol-dol-dollah !"

Two medical students, returning from lectures at the old Medical hall, now joined the group, and the sheriff explained:

"One dollah is bid foh the vagrant ole King Sol'mon, who is to be sole into labah foh a twelvemonth. Is there any othah bid? Are you all done? One dollah, once----"

"Dollah and a half," said one of the students, and remarked half jestingly under his breath to his companion, "I'll buy him on the chance of his dying. We'll dissect him."

"Would you own his body if he *should* die?"

"If he dies while bound to me, I'll arrange *that*."

"One dollah an' a half," resumed the sheriff; and falling into the tone of a facile auctioneer he rattled on:

"One dollah an' a half foh ole Sol'mon--sol, sol, sol,--do, re, mi, fa, sol--do, re, mi, fa, sol! Why, gentlemen, you can set the king to music!"

All this time the vagrant had stood in the centre of that close ring of jeering and humorous bystanders--a baffling text from which to have preached a sermon on the infirmities of our imperfect humanity. Some years before, perhaps as a masterstroke of derision, there had been given to him that title which could but heighten the contrast of his personality and estate with every suggestion of the ancient sacred magnificence; and never had the mockery seemed so fine as at this moment, when he was led forth into the streets to receive the lowest sentence of the law upon his poverty and dissolute idleness. He was apparently in the very prime of life--a striking figure, for nature at least had truly done some royal work on him. Over six feet in height, erect, with limbs well shaped and sinewy, with chest and neck full of the lines of great power, a large head thickly covered with long reddish hair, eyes blue, face beardless, complexion fair but discolored by low passions and excesses--such was old King Solomon. He wore a stiff, high, black Castor hat of the period, with the crown smashed in and the torn rim hanging down over one ear; a blackcloth coat in the old style, ragged and buttonless; a white cotton shirt with the broad collar crumpled, wide open at the neck and down his sunburnt bosom; blue jeans pantaloons, patched at the seat and the knees and ragged cotton socks that fell down over the tops of his dusty shoes which were open at the heels.

At the corner of his sensual mouth rested the stump of a cigar. Once during the proceedings he had produced another, lighted it, and continued quietly smoking. If he took to himself any shame as the central figure of this ignoble performance, no one knew it. There was something almost royal in his unconcern. The humor, the badinage, the open contempt, of which he was the public target, fell thick and fast upon him, but as harmlessly as would balls of pith upon a coat of mail. In truth, there was that in his great, lazy, gentle, goodhumored bulk and bearing which made the gibes seem all but despicable. He shuffled from one foot to the other as though he found it a trial to stand up so long, but all the while looking the spectators full in the eyes without the least impatience. He suffered the man of the factory to walk round him and push and pinch his muscles as calmly as though he had been the show bull at a country fair. Once only, when the sheriff had pointed across the street at the figure of Mr. Clay, he had looked quickly in that direction with a kindling light in his eye and a passing flush on his face. For the rest, he seemed like a man who has drained his cup of human life and has nothing left him but to fill again and drink without the least surprise or eagerness.

The bidding between the man of the factory and the student had gone slowly on. The price had reached ten dollars. The heat was intense, the sheriff tired. Then something occurred to revivify the scene. Across the marketplace and towards the steps of the courthouse there suddenly came trundling along in breathless haste a huge old negress, carrying on one arm a large shallow basket containing apple crablanterns and fresh gingerbread. With a series of halfarticulate grunts and snorts she approached the edge of the crowd and tried to force her way through. She coaxed, she begged, she elbowed and pushed and scolded, now laughing, and now with the passion of tears in her thick, excited voice. All at once, catching sight of the sheriff, she lifted one ponderous brown arm, naked to the elbow, and waved her hand to him above the heads of those in front.

"Hole on, marster! Hole on!" she cried, in a tone of humorous entreaty. "Don't knock 'im off till I come! Gim *me* a bid at 'im!"

The sheriff paused and smiled. The crowd made way tumultuously, with broad laughter and comment.

"Stan' aside theah an' let Aun' Charlotte in!"

"Now you'll see biddin'!"

"Get out of the way foh Aun' Charlotte!"

"Up, my free niggah! Hurrah foh Kentucky!"

A moment more and she stood inside the ring of spectators, her basket on the pavement at her feet, her hands plumped akimbo into her fathomless sides, her head up, and her soft, motherly eyes turned eagerly upon the sheriff. Of the crowd she seemed unconscious, and on the vagrant before her she had not cast a single glance.

She was dressed with perfect neatness. A red and yellow Madras kerchief was bound about her head in a high coil, and another was crossed over the bosom of her stiffly starched and smoothly ironed blue cottonade dress. Rivulets of perspiration ran down over her nose, her temples, and around her ears, and disappeared mysteriously in the creases of her brown neck. A single drop accidentally hung glistening like a diamond on the circlet of one of her large brass ear-rings.

The sheriff looked at her a moment, smiling, but a little disconcerted. The spectacle was unprecedented.

"What do you want heah, Aun' Charlotte?" he asked, kindly. "You can't sell yo' pies an' gingerbread heah."

"I don' *wan'* sell no pies en gingerbread," she replied, contemptuously. "I wan' bid on *him*," and she nodded sidewise at the vagrant.

"White folks allers sellin' niggahs to wuk fuh *dem*; I gwine buy a white man to wuk fuh *me*. En he gwine t' git a mighty hard mistiss, you heah *me*!"

The eyes of the sheriff twinkled with delight.

"Ten dollahs is offahed foh ole King Sol'mon. Is theah any othah bid? Are you all done?"

"'Leben," she said.

Two young ragamuffins crawled among the legs of the crowd up to her basket and filched pies and cake beneath her very nose.

"Twelve!" cried the student, laughing.

"Thirteen!" she laughed too, but her eyes flashed.

" *You are bidding against a niggah,*" whispered the student's companion in his ear.

"So I am; let's be off," answered the other, with a hot flush on his proud face.

Thus the sale was ended, and the crowd variously dispersed. In a distant corner of the courtyard the ragged urchins were devouring their unexpected booty. The old negress drew a red handkerchief out of her bosom, untied a knot in a corner of it, and counted out the money to the sheriff. Only she and the vagrant were now left on the spot.

"You have bought me. What do you want me to do?" he asked quietly.

"Lohd, honey!" she answered, in a low tone of affectionate chiding, "I don' wan' you to do *nothin'!* I wuzn' gwine t' 'low dem white folks to buy you. Dey'd wuk you till you dropped dead. You go 'long en do ez you please."

She gave a cunning chuckle of triumph in thus setting at naught the end of justice, and, in a voice rich and musical with affection, she said, as she gave him a little push: "you bettah be gittin' out o' dis blazin' sun. G' on home! I be 'long by away."

I turned and moved slowly away in the direction of Water Street, where she lived; and she, taking up her basket, shuffled across the market place towards Cheapside, muttering to herself the while:

"you some mighty nigh gittin' dah too late, foolin' 'long wid dese pies. Seing *him* ca'se he don' wuk! Umph! If all de men in dis town dat don' wuk wuz to be tuk up en sole, d' wouldn' be 'nough money in de town to buy um! Don' I see 'em settin' 'roun' dese taverns f'om mohnin' till night."

She snorted out her indignation and disgust, and sitting down on the sidewalk, under a Lombardy poplar, uncovered her wares and kept the flies away with a locust bough, not discovering in her alternating good and ill humor, that half of them had been filched by her old tormentors.

This was the memorable scene enacted in Lexington on that memorable day of the year 1833--a day that passed so briskly. For whoever met and spoke together asked the one question: Will the cholera come to Lexington? And the answer always gave a nervous haste to business--a keener thrill to pleasure. It was of the cholera that the negro woman heard two sweet passing ladies speak as she spread her wares on the sidewalk. They were on their way to a little picturegallery just opened opposite M. Giron's ballroom, and in one breath she heard them discussing their toilets for the evening and in the next several portraits by Jouett.

So the day passed, the night came on, and M. Xaupi gave his brilliant ball. Poor old Xaupi--poor little Frenchman! whirled as a gamin of Paris through the mazes of the Revolution, and lately come all the way to Lexington to teach the people how to dance. Hop about blithely on thy dry legs, basking this night in the waxen radiance of manners and melodies and graces! Where will be thy tunes and airs tomorrow! Ay, smile and prompt away! On and on! Swing corners, ladies and gentlemen! Form the basket! Hands all round! While the bows were still darting across the strings, out of the low, red east there shot a long, tremulous bow of light up towards the zenith. And then, could human sight have beheld the invisible, it might have seen hovering over the town, over the ballroom, over M. Xaupi, the awful presence of the plague.

But knowing nothing of this, the heated revellers went merrily home in the chill air of the red and saffron dawn. And knowing nothing of it also, a man awakened on the doorstep of a house opposite the ballroom, where he had long since fallen asleep. His limbs were cramped and a shiver ran through his frame. Staggering to his feet, he made his way down to the house of Free Charlotte, mounted to his room by means of a stairway opening on the street, threw off his outer garments, kicked off his shoes, and taking a bottle from a closet pressed it several times to his lips with long outward breaths of satisfaction. Then, casting his great white bulk upon the bed, in a minute more he had sunk into a heavy sleep--the usual drunken sleep of old King Solomon.

He, too, had attended M. Xaupi's ball, in his own way and in his proper character, being drawn to the place for the pleasure of seeing the fine ladies arrive and float in, like large white moths of the summer night, of looking in through the open windows at the manycolored waxen lights and the snowy arms and shoulders, of having blown out to him the perfume and the music; not worthy to go in, being the lowest of the low, but attending from a doorstep of the street opposite--with a certain rich passion in his nature for splendor and revelry and sensuous beauty.

About 10 o'clock the sunlight entered through the shutters and awoke him. He threw one arm up over his eyes to intercept the burning rays. As he lay outstretched and stripped of grotesque rags, it could be better seen in what a mould nature had cast his figure. His breast, bare and tanned, was barred by full, arching ribs and knotted by crossing muscles; and his shirtsleeve, falling away to the shoulder from his bent arm, revealed its crowded muscles in the high relief of heroic bronze. For, although he had been sold as a vagrant, old King Solomon had in earlier years followed the trade of a digger of cellars, and the strenuous use of mattock and spade had developed every sinew to the utmost. His whole person, now half naked and in repose, was full of the suggestions of unspent power. Only his face, swollen and red, only his eyes, bloodshot and dull, bore the impress of wasted vitality. There, all too plainly stamped, were the passions long since raging and still on fire.

The sunlight had stirred him to but a low degree of consciousness, and some minutes passed before he realized that a stifling, resinous fume impregnated the air. He sniffed it quickly; through the window seemed to come the smell of burning tar. He sat up on the edge of the bed and vainly tried to clear his thoughts.

The room was a clean but poor habitation--uncarpeted, whitewashed, with a piece or two of the cheapest furniture, and a row of pegs on one wall, where usually hung those tattered coats and pantaloons, miscellaneously collected, that were his purple and fine linen. He turned his eyes in this direction now and noticed that his clothes were missing. The old shoes had disappeared from their corner; the cigar stumps, picked up here and there in the streets according to his wont, were gone from the mantelpiece. Near the door was a large bundle tied up in a sheet. In a state of bewilderment, he asked himself what it all meant. Then a sense of the silence in the street below possessed him. At this hour he was used to hear noises enough--from Hugh Lonney's new bathhouse on one side, from Harry Sikes's barber shop on the other.

A mysterious feeling of terror crept over and helped to sober him. How long had he lain asleep? By degrees he seemed to remember that two or three times he had awakened far enough to drink from the bottle under his pillow, only to sink again into heavier stupefaction. By degrees, too, he seemed to remember that other things had happened--a driving of vehicles this way and that, a hurrying of people along the street. He had thought it the breakingup of M. Xaupi's ball. More than once had not some one shaken and tried to arouse him? Through the wall of Harry Sikes's barber shop had he not heard cries of pain--sobs of distress?

He staggered to the window, threw open the shutters, and, kneeling at the sill, looked out. The street was deserted. The houses opposite were closed. Cats were sleeping in the silent doorways. But as he looked up and down he caught sight of people hurrying along crossstreets. From a distant lumber yard came the muffled sound of rapid hammerings. On the air was the faint roll of vehicles--the hush and the vague noises of a general terrifying commotion.

In the middle of the street below him a keg was burning, and, as he looked, the hoops gave way, the tar spread out like a stream of black lava, and a cloud of inky smoke and deepred furious flame burst upward through the sagging air. Just beneath the window a common cart had been backed close up to the door of the house. In it had been thrown a few small articles of furniture, and on the bottom bedclothes had been spread out as if for a pallet. While he looked old Charlotte hurried out with a pillow.

He called down to her in a strange, unsteady voice:

"What is the matter? What are you doing, Aunt Charlotte?"

She uttered a cry, dropped the pillow, and stared up at him. Her face looked dry and wrinkled.

"My God! De chol'ra's in town! I'm waitin' on you! Dress, en come down en fetch de bun'le by de dooh." And she hurried back into the house.

But he continued leaning on his folded arms, his brain stunned by the shock of the intelligence. Suddenly he leaned far out and looked down at the closed shutters of the barber shop. Old Charlotte reappeared.

"Where is Harry Sikes?" he asked.

"Dead en buried."

"When did he die?"

"Yestidd'y evenin'."

"What day is this?"

"Sadd'y."

M. Xaupi's ball had been on Thursday evening. That night the cholera had broken out. He had lain in his drunken stupor ever since. Their talk had lasted but a minute, but she looked up anxiously and urged him

"D' ain' no time to was'e, honey! D' ain' no time to was'e. I done got dis cyart to tek you 'way in, en I be ready to start in a minute. Put yo' clo'es on en bring de bun'le wid all yo' yudder things in it."

With incredible activity she climbed into the cart and began to roll up the bedclothes. In reality she had made up her mind to put him into the cart, and the pallet had been made for him to lie and finish his drunken sleep on, while she drove him away to a place of safety.

Still he did not move from the windowsill. He was thinking of Harry Sikes, who had shaved him many a time for nothing. Then he suddenly called down to her:

"Have many died of the cholera? Are there many cases in town?"

She went on with her preparations and took no notice of him. He repeated the question. She got down quickly from the cart and began to mount the staircase. He went back to bed, pulled the sheet up over him, and propped himself up among the pillows. Her soft, heavy footsteps slurred on the stairway as though her strength were failing, and as soon as she entered the room she sank into a chair, overcome with terror. He looked at her with a sudden sense of pity.

"Don't be frightened," he said, kindly. "It might only make it the worse for you."

"I can't he'p it, honey," she answered, wringing her hands and rocking herself to and fro; "de ole niggah can' he'p it. If de Lohd jes spah me to git out'n dis town wid you! Honey, ain' you able to put on yo' clo'es?"

"You've tied them all up in the sheet."

"De Lohd he'p crazy ole niggah!"

She started up and tugged at the bundle, and laid out a suit of his clothes, if things so incongruous could be called a suit.

"Have many people died of the cholera?"

"Dey been dyin' like sheep ev' since yestidd'y mohnin'--all day, en all las' night, en dis mohnin'! De man he done lock up de huss, en dey been buryin' 'em in cyarts. En de gravediggah he done run away, en hit look like d' ain' nobody to dig de graves."

She bent over the bundle, tying again the four corners of the sheet. Through the window came the sound of the quick hammers driving nails. She threw up her arms into the air, and then seizing the bundle dragged it rapidly to the door.

"You heah dat? Dey nailin' up cawfins in de lumbahyahd! Put on yo' clo'es, honey, en come on."

A resolution had suddenly taken shape in his mind.

"Go on away and save your life. Don't wait for me; I'm not going. And goodbye, Aunt Charlotte, in case I don't see you any more. You've been very kind to me--kinder than I deserved. Where have you put my mattock and spade?"

He said this very quietly, and sat up on the edge of the bed, his feet hanging down, and his hand stretched out towards her.

"Honey" she explained, coaxingly, from where she stood, "can't you sobar up a little en put on yo' clo'es? I gwine to tek you 'way to de country. You don' wan' no tools. You can' dig no cellahs now. De chol'ra's in town en de people's dyin' like sheep."

"I expect they will need me," he answered.

She perceived now that he was sober. For an instant her own fear was forgotten in an outburst of resentment and indignation.

"Dig graves fuh 'em, when dey put you up on de block en sell you same ez you wuz a niggah! Dig graves fuh 'em, when dey allers callin' you names on de street en makin' fun o' you !"

"They are not to blame. I have brought it on myself."

"But we can' stay heah en die o' de chol'ra!"

"You mustn't stay. You must go away at once."

"But if I go, who gwine tek cyah o' *you?*"

"Nobody."

She came quickly across the room to the bed, fell on her knees, clasped his feet to her breast, and looked up into his face with an expression of imploring tenderness. Then, with incoherent cries and with sobs and tears, she pleaded with him--pleaded for dear life; his and her own.

It was a strange scene. What historian of the heart will ever be able to do justice to those peculiar ties which bound the heart of the negro in years gone by to a race of not always worthy masters? This old Virginia nurse had known King Solomon when he was a boy playing with her young master, till that young master died on the way to Kentucky.

At the death of her mistress she had become free with a little property. By thrift and industry she had greatly enlarged this. Years passed and she became the only surviving member of the Virginian household, which had emigrated early in the century to the Bluegrass Region. The same wave of emigration had brought in old King Solomon from the same neighborhood. As she had risen in life, he had sunk. She sat on the sidewalks selling her fruits and cakes; he sat on the sidewalks more idle, more ragged and dissolute. On no other basis than these facts she began to assume a sort of maternal pitying care of him, patching his rags, letting him have money for his vices, and when, a year or two before, he had ceased working almost entirely, giving him a room in her house and taking in payment what he chose to pay.

He brushed his hand quickly across his eyes as she knelt before him now, clasping his feet to her bosom. From coaxing him as an intractable child she had, in the old servile fashion, fallen to imploring him, with touching forgetfulness of their real relations:

"O my marseter! O my marseter Solomon! Go 'way en save yo' life, en tek yo' po'ole niggah wid you!"

But his resolution was formed, and he refused to go. A hurried footstep paused beneath the window and a loud voice called up. The old nurse got up and went to the window. A man was standing by the cart at her door.

"For God's sake, let me have this cart to take my wife and little children away to the country! There is not a vehicle to be had in town. I will pay you--" He stopped, seeing the distress on her face.

"Is he dead?" he asked, for he knew of her care of old King Solomon.

"He *will* die!" she sobbed. "Tilt de t'ings out on de pavement. I gwine t' stay wid 'im en tek cyah o' 'im."

A little later, dressed once more in grotesque rags and carrying on his shoulder a rusty mattock and a rusty spade, old King Solomon appeared in the street below and stood looking up and down it with an air of anxious indecision. Then shuffling along rapidly to the corner of Mill Street, he turned up towards Main.

Here a full sense of the terror came to him. A man, hurrying along with his head down, ran full against him and cursed him for the delay:

"Get out of my way, you old beast!" he cried. "If the cholera would carry you off, it would be a blessing to the town."

Two or three little children, already orphaned and hungry, wandered past, crying and wringing their hands. A crowd of negro men with the muscles of athletes, some with naked arms, some naked to the waist, their eyes dilated, their mouths hanging open, sped along in tumultuous disorder. The plague had broken out in the hemp factory and scattered them beyond control.

He grew suddenly faint and sick. His senses swam, his heart seemed to cease beating, his tongue burned, his throat was dry, his spine like ice. For a moment the contagion of deadly fear overcame him, and, unable to stand, he reeled to the edge of the sidewalk and sat down.

Before him along the street passed the flying people--men on horseback with their wives behind and children in front, families in carts and wagons, merchants in twowheeled gigs and sulkies. A huge red and yellow stagecoach rolled ponderously by, filled within, on top, in front, and behind with a company of riotous students of law and of medicine. A rapid chorus of voices shouted to him as they passed:

"Goodbye, Solomon!"

"The cholera'll have you befoah sunset!"

"Better be diggin' yoah grave, Solomon! That'll be yoah last cellah."

"Dig us a big wine cellah undah the Medical Hall while we are away."

"And leave yo' body there! We want yo' skeleton."

"Goodbye, old Solomon!

A wretched carry-all passed with a household of more wretched women; their tawdry and gay attire, their haggard and painted and ghastly faces, looking horrible in the blaze of the pitiless sunlight. They, too simpered and hailed him and spent upon him their hardened and damaged badinage. Then there rolled by a highswung carriage, with the most luxurious of cushions, upholstered with morocco, with a coat-of-arms, a driver and a footman in livery, and drawn by sparkling, prancing horses. Lying back on the satin cushions a fine gentleman; at the window of the carriage two rosy children, who pointed their fingers at the vagrant and turned and looked into their father's face, so that he leaned forward, smiled, leaned back again, and was whirled away to a path of safety.

Thus they passed him, as he sat down on the sidewalk--even physicians from their patients, pastors from their stricken flocks. Why should not he flee? He had no ties, except the faithful affection of an old negress. Should he not at least save her life by going away, seeing that she would not leave him?

"The orphaned children wandered past again, sobbing more wearily. He called them to him.

"Why do you not go home? Where is your mother?" he asked.

"She is dead in the house," they answered; "and no one has come to bury her."

Slowly down the street was coming a short funeral train. It passed--a rude cortège: a common cart, in the bottom of which rested a box of plain boards containing the body of the old French dancingmaster; walking behind it, with a cambric handkerchief to his eyes, the old French confectioner; at his side, wearing the robes of his office and carrying an umbrella to ward off the burning sun, the beloved Bishop Smith; and behind them, two by two and with linked arms, perhaps a dozen men, most of whom had been at the ball.

No head was lifted or eye turned to notice the vagrant seated on the sidewalk. But when the train had passed he rose, laid his mattock and spade across his shoulder, and, stepping out into the street, fell into line at the end of the procession.

They moved down Short Street to the old buryingground, where the Baptist churchyard is today. As they entered it, two gravediggers passed out and hurried away. Those before them had fled. They had been at work but a few hours. Overcome with horror at the sight of thedead arriving more and more rapidly, they, too, deserted that post of peril. No one was left. Here and there in the churchyard could be seen bodies awaiting interment. Old King Solomon stepped quietly forward and, getting down into one of the halffinished graves, began to dig.

The vagrant had happened upon an avocation.

All summer long, Clatterbuck's dancingpavilion was as silent in its grove of oaks as a temple of the Druids, and his pleasureboat nestled in its moorings, with no hand to feather an oar in the little lake. All summer long, no athletic young Kentuckians came to bathe their white bodies in Hugh Lonney's new bathhouse for twelve and a half cents, and no one read Daukins Tegway's advertisement that he was willing to exchange his Dunstable bonnets for flax and feathers. The likely runaway boy, with a long, fresh scar across his face, was never found, nor the buffalo bull roasted for Daniel Webster, and Peter Leuba's guitars were never thrummed on any moonlit verandas. Only Dewees and Grant were busy, dispensing, not snuff but calomel.

Grass grew in the deserted streets. Gardens became little wildernesses of rank weeds and riotous creepers. Around shut windowlattices roses clambered and shed their perfume into the poisoned air, or dropped their faded petals to strew the echoless thresholds. In darkened rooms family portraits gazed on sad vacancy or looked helplessly down on rigid sheeted forms.

In the trees of poplar and locust along the streets the unmolested birds built and brooded. The oriole swung its hempen nest from a bough over the door of the spidertenanted factory, and in front of the old Medical Hall the blue-jay shot up his angry crest and screamed harshly down at the passing bier. In a cage hung against the wall of a house in a retired street a mockingbird sung, beat its breast against the bars, sung more passionately, grew silent and dropped dead from its perch, never knowing that its mistress had long since become a clod to its fullthroated requiem.

Famine lurked in the wake of the pestilence. Markets were closed. A few shops were kept open to furnish necessary supplies. Now and then some old negro might have been seen, driving a meatwagon in from the country, his nostrils stuffed with white cotton saturated with camphor. Oftener the only visible figure in the streets was that of a faithful priest going about among his perishing fold, or that of the bishop moving hither and thither on his ceaseless ministrations.

But over all the ravages of that terrible time there towered highest the solitary figure of that powerful gravedigger, who, nerved by the spectacle of the common misfortune, by one heroic effort rose for the time above the wrecks of his own nature. In the thick of the plague, in the very garden spot of the pestilence, he ruled like an unterrified king. Through days unnaturally chill with grey cloud and drizzling rain, or unnaturally hot with the fierce sun and suffocating damps that appeared to steam forth from subterranean cauldrons, he worked unfaltering, sometimes with a helper, sometimes with none. There were times when, exhausted, he would lie down in the halfdug graves and there sleep until able to go on; and many a midnight found him under the spectral moon, all but hidden by the rank nightshade as he bent over to mark out the lines of one of those narrow mortal cellars.

Nature soon smiles upon her own ravages and strews our graves with flowers, not as memories, but for other flowers when the spring returns.

It was one cool, brilliant morning late in that autumn. The air blew fresh and invigorating, as though on the earth there were no corruption, no death. Far southward had flown the plague. A spectator in the open court-square might have seen many signs of life returning to the town. Students hurried along, talking eagerly. Merchants met for the first time and spoke of the winter trade. An old negress, gayly and neatly dressed, came into the marketplace, and sitting down on a sidewalk displayed her yellow and red apples and fragrant gingerbread. She hummed to herself an old cradlesong, and in her soft, motherly black eyes shone a mild, happy radiance. A group of young ragamuffins eyed her longingly from a distance. Court was to open for the first time since the spring. The hour was early, and one by one the lawyers passed slowly in. On the steps of the courthouse three men were standing: Thomas Brown, the sheriff, old Peter Leuba, who had just walked over from his musicstore on Main Street; and little M. Giron, the French confectioner. Each wore mourning on his hat, and their voices were low and grave.

"Gentlemen," the sheriff was saying, "it was on this very spot the day befoah the cholera broke out that I sole 'im as a vagrant. An' I did the meanes' thing a man can evah do. I hel' 'im up to public ridicule foh his weakness an' made spoht of 'is infirmities. I laughed at 'is povahty an' 'is ole clo'es. I delivahed on 'im as complete an oration of sarcastic detraction as I could prepare on the spot, out of my own meanness an' with the vulgah sympathies of the crowd. Gentlemen, if I only had that crowd heah now, an' old King Sol'mon standin' in the midst of it, that I might ask 'im to accept a humble public apology, offahed from the heaht of one who feels himself unworthy to shake 'is han'! But, gentlemen, that crowd will nevah reassemble. Neahly ev'ry man of them is dead, an' Ole King Sol'mon buried them."

"He buried my friend Adolphe Xaupi," said François Giron, touching his eyes with his handkerchief.

"There is a case of my best Jamaica rum for him whenever he comes for it," said old Leuba, clearing his throat.

"But gentlemen, while we are speakin' of ole King Sol'mon we ought not to fohget who it is that has suppohted 'im. Yondah she sits on the sidewalk, sellin' 'er apples an' gingerbread."

The three men looked in the direction indicated.

"Heah comes old King Sol'mon now," exclaimed the sheriff.

Across the open square the vagrant was seen walking, slowly along with his habitual air of quiet, unobtrusive preoccupation. A minute more and he had come over and passed into the courthouse by a side door.

"Is Mr. Clay to be in court today?"

"He is expected, I think."

"Then let's go in; there will be a crowd."

"I don't know; so many are dead."

They turned and entered and found seats as quietly as possible; for a strange and sorrowful hush brooded over the courtroom. Until the bar assembled, it had not been realized how many were gone. The silence was that of a common overwhelming disaster. No one spoke with his neighbor, no one observed the vagrant as he entered and made his way to a seat on one of the meanest benches, a little apart from the others. He had not sat there since the day of his indictment for vagrancy. The judge took his seat and, making a great effort to control himself, passed his eyes slowly over the courtroom. All at once he caught sight of old King Solomon sitting against the wall in an obscure corner; and before any one could know what he was doing, he hurried down and walked up to the vagrant and grasped his hand. He tried to speak, but could not. Old King Solomon had buried his wife and daughter--buried them one clouded midnight, with no one present but himself.

Then the oldest member of the bar started up and followed the example; and then the other members, rising by a common impulse, filed slowly back and one by one wrung that hard and powerful hand. After them came the other persons in the courtroom. The vagrant, the grave-digger, had risen and stood against the wall, at first with a white face and a dazed expression, not knowing what it meant; afterwards, when he understood it, his head dropped suddenly forward and his tears fell thick and hot upon the hands that he could not see. And his were not the only tears. Not a man in the long file but paid his tribute of emotion as he stepped forward to honor that image of sadly eclipsed but still effulgent humanity. It was not grief, it was not gratitude, nor any sense of making reparation for the past. It was the softening influence of an act of heroism, which makes every man feel himself a brother hand in hand with every other-- such power has a single act of moral greatness to reverse the relations of men, lifting up one, and bringing all others to do him homage.

It was the coronation scene in the life of old King Solomon of Kentucky.

Day the Fifth

Giovanni Boccaccio

Giovanni Boccaccio (1313-1375) is best known for his masterpiece *The Decameron* (1353). This work is esteemed for its portrayal of life in 14th Century Italy and its variety of incidents and characters.

Born out of wedlock in Italy, Boccaccio spent his childhood with his father in Tuscany and Florence. While still quite young he was sent to Naples to study business. He eventually abandoned his studies to pursue his love of literature.

When Boccaccio was in Naples he met Maria d'Aquino. His love for her became an obsession but she died in 1348 of the Black Plague. Maria became the impetus of Boccaccio's earliest writings. She inspired one story in particular, *Amorosa Fiammetta*, one of the first works to treat the psychology of character.

Boccaccio became good friends with Petrarch, who had an enthusiasm for sacred works. Petrarch's influence inspired Boccaccio to abandon his work in the vernacular and turn to Latin. By now with his literary career waning Boccaccio embraced other scholarly pursuits; one being a translation of Homer.

HERE BEGINNETH THE FIFTH DAY OF THE DECAMERON WHEREIN UNDER THE GOVERNANCE OF FIAMMETTA IS DIS-COURSED OF THAT WHICH HATH HAPPILY BETIDED LOVERS AFTER SUNDRY CRUEL AND MISFORTUNATE ADVENTURES

THE EAST WAS already all white and the rays of the rising sun had made it light through all our hemisphere, when Fiammetta, allured by the sweet song of the birds, that blithely chanted the first hour of the day upon the branches, arose and let call all the other ladies and the three young men; then, with leisured pace descending into the fields, she went a-pleas-uring with her company about the ample plain upon the dewy grasses, discoursing with them of one thing and another, until the sun was some-what risen, when, feeling that its rays began to grow hot, she turned their steps to their abiding-place. There, with excellent wines and confections, she let restore the light fatigue had and they disported themselves in the delightsome garden until the eating hour, which being come and everything made ready by the discreet seneschal, they sat blithely down to meat, such being the queen's pleasure, after they had sung sundry roundelays and a ballad or two. Having dined orderly and with mirth, not unmindful of their wonted usance of dancing, they danced sundry short dances to the sound of songs and tabrets, after which the queen dismissed them all until the hour of slumber should be past. Accordingly, some betook themselves to sleep, whilst others addressed themselves anew to their diversion about the fair garden; but all, according to the wonted fashion, assembled together again, a little after none, near the fair fountain, whereas it pleased the queen. Then she, having seated herself in the chief room, looked towards Pamfilo and smilingly charged him make a beginning with the fairfortuned stories; whereto he willingly addressed himself and spoke as follows:

THE FIRST STORY

CIMON, LOVING, WAXETH WISE AND CARRIETH OFF TO SEA IPHGENIA HIS MISTRESS. BEING CAST INTO PRISON AT RHODES, HE IS DELIVERED THENCE BY LYSIMACHUS AND IN CONCERT WITH HIM CARRIETH OFF IPHIGENIA AND CASSANDRA ON THEIR WEDDINGDAY, WITH WHOM THE TWAIN FLEE INTO CRETE, WHERE THE TWO LADIES BECOME THEIR WIVES AND WHENCE THEY ARE PRESENTLY ALL FOUR RECALLED HOME

"Many stories, delightsome ladies, apt to give beginning to so glad a day as this will be, offer themselves unto me to be related; whereof one is the most pleasing to my mind, for that thereby, beside the happy issue which is to mark this day's discourses, you may understand how holy, how puissant and how full of all good is the power of Love, which many, unknowing what they say, condemn and vilify with great unright; and this, an I err not, must needs be exceeding pleasing to you, for that I believe you all to be in love.

There was, then, in the island of Cyprus, (as we have read aforetime in the ancient histories of the Cypriots,) a very noble gentleman, by name Aristippus, who was rich beyond any other of the country in all temporal things and might have held himself the happiest man alive, had not fortune made him woeful in one only thing, to wit, that amongst his other children he had a son who overpassed all the other youths of his age in stature and goodliness of body, but was a hopeless dullard and well nigh an idiot. His true name was Galesus, but for that neither by toil of teacher nor blandishment nor beating of his father nor study nor endeavour of whatsoever other had it been found possible to put into his head any inkling of letters or good breeding and that he had a rough voice and an uncouth and manners more befitting a beast than a man, he was of well nigh all by way of mockery called Cimon, which in their tongue signified as much as brute beast in ours. His father brooked his wasted life with the most grievous concern and having presently given over all hope of him, he bade him begone to his country house and there abide with his husbandmen, so he might not still have before him the cause of his chagrin; the which was very agreeable to Cimon, for that the manners and usages of clowns and churls were much more to his liking than those of the townsfolk.

Cimon, then, betaking himself to the country and there employing himself in the things that pertained thereto, it chanced one day, awhile after noon, as he passed from one farm to another, with his staff on his shoulder, that he entered a very fair coppice which was in those parts and which was then all in leaf, for that it was the month of May. Passing therethrough, he happened (even as his fortune guided him thither) upon a little mead compassed about with very high trees, in one corner whereof was a very clear and cool spring, beside which he saw a very fair damsel asleep upon the green grass, with so thin a garment upon her body that it hid well nigh nothing of her snowy flesh. She was covered only from the waist down with a very white and light coverlet; and at her feet slept on like wise two women and a man, her servants. When Cimon espied the young lady, he halted and leaning upon his staff, fell, without saying a word, to gazing most intently upon her with the utmost admiration, no otherwise than as he had never yet seen a woman's form, whilst in his rude breast, wherein for a thousand lessonings no least impression of civil pleasance had availed to penetrate, he felt a thought awaken which intimated to his gross and material spirit that this maiden was the fairest thing that had been ever seen of any living soul. Thence he proceeded to consider her various parts, commending her hair, which he accounted of gold, her brow, her nose, her mouth, her throat and her arms, and above all her breast, as yet but little upraised,--and grown of a sudden from a churl a judge of beauty, he ardently desired in himself to see the eyes, which, weighed down with deep sleep, she kept closed. To this end, he had it several times in mind to awaken her; but, for that she seemed to him beyond measure fairer than the other women aforetime seen of him, he misdoubted him she must be some goddess. Now he had wit enough to account things divine worthy of more reverence than those mundane; wherefore he forbore, waiting for her to awake of herself; and albeit the dèlay seemed overlong to him, yet, taken as he was with an unwonted pleasure, he knew not how to tear himself away.

It befell, then, that, after a long while, the damsel, whose name was Iphigenia, came to herself, before any of her people, and opening her eyes, saw Cimon (who, what for his fashion and uncouthness and his father's wealth and nobility, was known in a manner to every one in the country) standing before her, leant on his staff, marvelled exceedingly and said, 'Cimon, what goest thou seeking in this wood at this hour?' He made her no answer, but, seeing her eyes open, began to look steadfastly upon them, himseeming there proceeded thence a sweetness which fulfilled him with a pleasure such as he had never before felt. The young lady, seeing this, began to misdoubt her lest his so fixed looking upon her should move his rusticity to somewhat that might turn to her shame; wherefore, calling her women, she rose up, saying, 'Cimon, abide with God.' To which he replied, 'I will begone with thee'; and albeit the young lady, who was still in fear of him, would have declined his company, she could not win to rid herself of him till he had accompanied her to her own house.

Thence he repaired to his father's house [in the city,] and declared to him that he would on no wise consent to return to the country; the which was irksome enough to Aristippus and his kinsfolk; nevertheless they let him be, awaiting to see what might be the cause of his change of mind. Love's arrow having, then, through Iphigenia's beauty, penetrated into Cimon's heart, whereinto no teaching had ever availed to win an entrance, in a very brief time, proceeding from one idea to another, he made his father marvel and all his kinsfolk and every other that knew him. In the first place he besought his father that he would cause him go bedecked with clothes and every other thing, even as his brothers, the which Aristippus right gladly did. Then, consorting with young men of condition and learning the fashions and carriage that behoved unto gentlemen and especially unto lovers, he first, to the utmost wonderment of every one, in a very brief space of time, not only learned the first [elements of] letters, but became very eminent among the students of philosophy, and after (the love which he bore Iphigenia being the cause of all this) he not only reduced his rude and rustical manner of speech to seemliness and

civility, but became a past master of song and sound and exceeding expert
and doughty in riding and martial exercises, both by land and by sea. In
short, not to go recounting every particular of his merits, the fourth year
was not accomplished from the day of his first falling in love, ere he was
grown the sprightliest and most accomplished gentleman of all the young
men in the island of Cyprus, ay, and the best endowed with every
particular excellence. What, then, charming ladies, shall we say of Cimon? Certes, none other thing than that the lofty virtues implanted by
heaven in his generous soul had been bounden with exceeding strong
bonds of jealous fortune and shut in some straitest corner of his heart, all
which bonds Love, as a mightier than fortune, broke and burst in sunder
and in its quality of awakener and quickener of drowsed and sluggish wits,
urged forth into broad day light the virtues aforesaid, which had till then
been overdarkened with a barbarous obscurity, thus manifestly discovering from how mean a room it can avail to uplift those souls that are subject
unto it and to what an eminence it can conduct them with its beams.

Although Cimon, loving Iphigenia as he did, might exceed in certain
things, as young men in love very often do, nevertheless Aristippus,
considering that Love had turned him from a dunce into a man, not only
patiently bore with the extravagances into which it might whiles lead him,
but encouraged him to ensue its every pleasure. But Cimon, (who refused
to be called Galesus, remembering that Iphigenia had called him by the
former name,) seeking to put an honourable term to his desire, once and
again caused essay Cipseus, Iphigenia's father, so he should give him his
daughter to wife; but Cipseus still answered that he had promised her to
Pasimondas, a young nobleman of Rhodes, to whom he had no mind to
fail of his word. The time coming for the covenanted nuptials of Iphigenia
and the bridegroom having sent for her, Cimon said in himself, 'Now, O
Iphigenia, is the time to prove how much thou art beloved of me. By thee
am I become a man and so I may but have thee, I doubt not to become
more glorious than any god; and for certain I will or have thee or die."

Accordingly, having secretly recruited certain young noblemen who
were his friends and let privily equip a ship with everything apt for naval
battle, he put out to sea and awaited the vessel wherein Iphigenia was to
be transported to her husband in Rhodes. The bride, after much honour
done of her father to the bridegroom's friends, took ship with the latter,
who turned their prow towards Rhodes and departed. On the following
day, Cimon, who slept not, came out upon them with his ship and cried
out, in a loud voice, from the prow, to those who were on board

Iphigenia's vessel, saying, 'Stay, strike your sails or look to be beaten and sunken in the sea.' Cimon's adversaries had gotten up their arms on deck and made ready to defend themselves; whereupon he, after speaking the words aforesaid, took a grapplingiron and casting it upon the poop of the Rhodians, who were making off at the top of their speed, made it fast by main force to the prow of his own ship. Then, bold as a lion, he leapt on board their ship, without waiting for any to follow him, as if he held them all for nought, and Love spurring him, he fell upon his enemies with marvellous might, cutlass in hand, striking now this one and now that and hewing them down like sheep.

The Rhodians, seeing this, cast down their arms and all as with one voice confessed themselves prisoners; whereupon quoth Cimon to them, 'Young men, it was neither lust of rapine nor hate that I had against you made me depart Cyprus to assail you, arms in hand, in mid sea. That which moved me thereunto was the desire of a thing which to have gotten is a very grave matter to me and to you a very light one to yield me in peace; it is, to wit, Iphigenia, whom I loved over all else and whom, availing not to have of her father on friendly and peaceful wise, Love hath constrained me to win from you as an enemy and by force of arms. Wherefore I mean to be to her that which your friend Pasimondas should have been. Give her to me, then, and begone and God's grace go with you.'

The Rhodians, more by force constrained than of freewill, surrendered Iphigenia, weeping, to Cimon, who, seeing her in tears, said to her, 'Noble Lady, be not disconsolate; I am thy Cimon, who by long love have far better deserved to have thee than Pasimondas by plighted faith.' Thereupon he caused carry her aboard his own ship and returning to his companions, let the Rhodians go, without touching aught else of theirs. Then, glad beyond any man alive to have gotten so dear a prey, after devoting some time to comforting the weeping lady, he took counsel with his comrades not to return to Cyprus at that present; wherefore, of one accord, they turned the ship's head towards Crete, where well nigh every one, and especially Cimon, had kinsfolk, old and new, and friends in plenty and where they doubted not to be in safety with Iphigenia. But fortune the unstable, which had cheerfully enough vouchsafed unto Cimon the acquisition of the lady, suddenly changed the inexpressible joyance of the enamoured youth into sad and bitter mourning; for it was not four full told hours since he had left the Rhodians when the night (which Cimon looked to be more delightsome than any he had ever known) came on and with it a very troublous and tempestuous shift of weather, which filled all the sky with clouds and the sea with ravening winds, by reason whereof none could see what to do or whither to steer, nor could any even keep the deck to do any office.

How sore concerned was Cimon for this it needeth not to ask; himseemed the gods had vouchsafed him his desire but to make death the more grievous to him, whereof, with out that, he had before recked little. His comrades lamented on like wise, but Iphigenia bewailed herself over all, weeping sore and fearing every stroke of the waves; and in her chagrin she bitterly cursed Cimon's love and blamed his presumption, avouching that the tempest had arisen for none other thing but that the gods chose not that he, who would fain against their will have her to wife, should avail to enjoy his presumptuous desire, but, seeing her first die, should after himself perish miserably.

Amidst such lamentations and others yet more grievous, the wind waxing hourly fiercer and the seamen knowing not what to do, they came, without witting whither they went or availing to change their course, near to the island of Rhodes, and unknowing that it was Rhodes, they used their every endeavour to get to land thereon, an it were possible, for the saving of their lives. In this fortune was favourable to them and brought them into a little bight of the sea, where the Rhodians whom Cimon had let go had a little before arrived with their ship; nor did they perceive that they had struck the island of Rhodes till the dawn broke and made the sky somewhat clearer, when they found themselves maybe a bowshot distant from the ship left of them the day before. At this Cimon was beyond measure chagrined and fearing lest that should betide them which did in very deed ensue, bade use every endeavour to issue thence and let fortune after carry them whither it should please her, for that they could be nowhere in worse case than there. Accordingly, they made the utmost efforts to put to sea, but in vain; for the wind blew so mightily against them that not only could they not avail to issue from the little harbour, but whether they would or no, it drove them ashore.

No sooner were they come thither than they were recognized by the Rhodian sailors, who had landed from their ship, and one of them ran nimbly to a village hard by, whither the young Rhodian gentlemen had betaken themselves, and told the latter that, as luck would have it, Cimon and Iphigenia were come thither aboard their ship, driven, like themselves, by stress of weather. They, hearing this, were greatly rejoiced and repairing in all haste to the seashore, with a number of the villagers, took Cimon, together with Iphigenia and all his company, who had now landed and taken counsel together to flee into some neighbouring wood, and carried them to the village. The news coming to Pasimondas, he made his complaint to the senate of the island and according as he had ordered it with them, Lysimachus, in whom the chief magistracy of the Rhodians was for that year vested, coming thither from the city with a great company of menatarms, haled Cimon and all his men to prison. On such wise did the wretched and lovelorn Cimon lose his Iphigenia, scantwhile before won of him, without having taken of her more than a kiss or two; whilst she herself was received by many noble ladies of Rhodes and comforted as well for the chagrin had of her seizure as for the fatigue suffered by reason of the troubled sea; and with them she abode against the day appointed for her nuptials.

As for Cimon and his companions, their lives were granted them, in consideration of the liberty given by them to the young Rhodians the day before,--albeit Pasimondas used his utmost endeavour to procure them to be put to death,-- and they were condemned to perpetual prison, wherein, as may well be believed, they abode woebegone and without hope of any relief. However, whilst Pasimondas, as most he might, hastened the preparations for his coming nuptials, fortune, as if repenting her of the sudden injury done to Cimon, brought about a new circumstance for his deliverance, the which was on this wise. Pasimondas had a brother called Ormisdas, less in years, but not in merit, than himself, who had been long in treaty for the hand of a fair and noble damsel of the city, by name Cassandra, whom Lysimachus ardently loved, and the match had sundry times been broken off by divers untoward accidents. Now Pasimondas, being about to celebrate his own nuptials with the utmost splendour, bethought himself that it were excellently well done if he could procure Ormisdas likewise to take wife on the same occasion, not to resort afresh to expense and festival making. Accordingly, he took up again the parleys with Cassandra's parents and brought them to a successful issue; where-fore he and his brother agreed, in concert with them, that Ormisdas should take Cassandra to wife on the same day whenas himself took Iphigenia.

Lysimachus hearing this, it was beyond measure displeasing to him, for that he saw himself bereaved of the hope which he cherished, that, an Ormisdas took her not, he should certainly have her. However, like a wise man, he kept his chagrin hidden and fell to considering on what wise he might avail to hinder this having effect, but could see no way possible save the carrying her off. This seemed easy to him to compass for the office which he held, but he accounted the deed far more dishonourable than if he had not held the office in question. Ultimately, however, after long deliberation, honour gave place to love and he determined, come what might of it, to carry off Cassandra. Then, bethinking himself of the company he must have and the course he must hold to do this, he remembered him of Cimon, whom he had in prison with his comrades, and concluded that he might have no better or trustier companion than Cimon in this affair.

Accordingly, that same night he had him privily into his chamber and proceeded to bespeak him on this wise: 'Cimon, like as the gods are very excellent and bountiful givers of things to men, even so are they most sagacious provers of their virtues, and those, whom they find resolute and constant under all circumstances, they hold deserving, as the most worthy, of the highest recompenses. They have been minded to have more certain proof of thy worth than could be shown by thee within the limits of thy father's house, whom I know to be abundantly endowed with riches; wherefore, first, with the poignant instigations of love they brought thee from a senseless animal to be a man, and after with foul fortune and at this present with prison dour, they would fain try if thy spirit change not from that which it was, whenas thou wast scantwhile glad of the gotten prize. If that be the same as it was erst, they never yet vouchsafed thee aught so gladsome as that which they are presently prepared to bestow on thee and which, so thou mayst recover thy wonted powers and resume thy whilom spirit, I purpose to discover to thee.

Pasimondas, rejoicing in thy misadventure and a diligent promoter of thy death, bestirreth himself as most he may to celebrate his nuptials with thine Iphigenia, so therein he may enjoy the prize which fortune first blithely conceded thee and after, growing troubled, took from thee of a sudden. How much this must grieve thee, an thou love as I believe, I know by myself, to whom Ormisdas his brother prepareth in one same day to do a like injury in the person of Cassandra, whom I love over all else. To escape so great an unright and annoy of fortune, I see no way left open of her to us, save the valour of our souls and the might of our right hands, wherein it behoveth us take our swords and make us a way to the carrying off of our two mistresses, thee for the second and me for the first time. If, then, it be dear to thee to have again--I will not say thy liberty, whereof methinketh thou reckest little without thy lady, but--thy mistress, the gods have put her in thy hands, an thou be willing to second me in my emprize.'

All Cimon's lost spirit was requickened in him by these words and he replied, without overmuch consideration, 'Lysimachus, thou canst have no stouter or trustier comrade than myself in such an enterprise, an that be to ensue thereof for me which thou avouchest; wherefore do thou command me that which thou deemest should be done of me, and thou shalt find thyself wonderpuissantly seconded.' Then said Lysimachus, 'On the third day from this the newmarried wives will for the first time enter their husbands' houses, whereinto thou with thy companions armed and I with certain of my friends, in whom I put great trust, will make our way towards nightfall and snatching up our mistresses out of the midst of the guests, will carry them off to a ship, which I have caused secretly equip, slaying whosoever shall presume to offer opposition.' The device pleased Cimon and he abode quiet in prison until the appointed time.

The weddingday being come, great and magnificent was the pomp of the festival and every part of the two brothers' house was full of mirth and merrymaking; whereupon Lysimachus, having made ready everything needful, divided Cimon and his companions, together with his own friends, all armed under their clothes, into three parties and having first kindled them to his purpose with many words, secretly despatched one party to the harbour, so none might hinder their going aboard the ship, whenas need should be. Then, coming with the other twain, when as it seemed to him time, to Pasimondas his house, he left one party of them at the door, so as none might shut them up therewithin or forbid them the issue, and with Cimon and the rest went up by the stairs. Coming to the saloon where the newwedded brides were seated orderly at meat with many other ladies, they rushed in upon them and overthrowing the tables, took each his mistress and putting them in the hands of their comrades, bade straightway carry them to the ship that was in waiting. The brides fell aweeping and shrieking, as did likewise the other ladies and the servants, and the whole house was of a sudden full of clamour and lamentation.

Cimon and Lysimachus and their companions, drawing their swords, made for the stairs, without any opposition, all giving way to them, and as they descended, Pasimondas presented himself before them, with a great cudgel in his hand, being drawn thither by the outcry; but Cimon dealt him a swashing blow on the head and cleaving it sheer in sunder, laid him dead at his feet. The wretched Ormisdas, running to his brother's aid, was on like wise slain by one of Cimon's strokes, and divers others who sought to draw nigh them were in like manner wounded and beaten off by the companions of the latter and Lysimachus, who, leaving the house full of blood and clamour and weeping and woe, drew together and made their way to the ship with their prizes, unhindered of any. Here they embarked with their mistresses and all their companions, the shore being now full of armed folk come to the rescue of the ladies, and thrusting the oars into the water, made off, rejoicing, about their business. Coming presently to Crete, they were there joyfully received by many, both friends and kinsfolk, and espousing their mistresses with great pomp, gave themselves up to the glad enjoyment of their purchase. Loud and long were the clamours and differences in Cyprus and in Rhodes by reason of their doings; but, ultimately, their friends and kinsfolk, interposing in one and the other place, found means so to adjust matters that, after some exile, Cimon joyfully returned to Cyprus with Iphigenia, whilst Lysimachus on like wise returned to Rhodes with Cassandra, and each lived long and happily with his mistress in his own country."

The Treasure of Far Island

Willa Cather

Willa Cather (1873-1947) was born in 1873 in Back Creek Valley, Virginia. For an unknown reason her date of birth is recorded as 1876 on her tombstone. It is surmised that she instructed Edith Lewis, her companion, to put this date on her stone.

Cather grew up in Virginia among green hills and tall trees, but moved to the plains of Nebraska with her family when she was ten years old. Although she was unhappy about moving, she would later draw upon her experiences on the prairie to write many of her short stories and novels.

Her neighbors in Nebraska were immigrants from different countries, and they shared their life stories with her. They told about the struggles and hard work that they had endured in their countries and on the Nebraskan prairie. The impressions that these people made on Cather are described in her characterization of them in several of her stories.

Cather did not enroll in elementary school. Instead she was taught to read and write at home. She did attend the Red Cloud High School and developed an appreciation for the classics. After graduation she entered the University of Nebraska and, through reviews and essays for the *Nebraska State Journal*, developed the skills she needed to write short stories, poetry, and novels.

In 1905, after publishing her first collection of short stories, *The Troll Garden*, Cather was offered an editorial position with *McClure's* magazine. She worked as an editor and journalist for six years until Sarah Orne Jewett encouraged Cather to pursue her writing career full time.

Willa Cather's most reprinted stories are *Paul's Case* and *Neighbor Rosicky*. Her most acclaimed novels are *O'Pioneers* (1913), *My Antonia* (1918), *One of Ours* (1922), and *Death Comes to the Archbishop* (1927).

> *Dark brown is the river,*
> *Golden is the sand;*
> *It flows along forever,*
> *With trees on either hand.*
>
> *--Robert Louis Stevenson*

32

FAR ISLAND IS an oval sand bar, half a mile in length and perhaps a hundred yards wide, which lies about two miles up from Empire City in a turbid little Nebraska river. The island is known chiefly to the children who dwell in that region, and generation after generation of them have claimed it; fished there, and pitched their tents under the great arched tree, and built camp fires on its level, sandy outskirts. In the middle of the island, which is always above water except in flood time, grow thousands of yellowgreen creek willows and cottonwood seedlings, brilliantly green, even when the hottest winds blow, by reason of the surrounding moisture. In the summer months, when the capricious stream is low, the children's empire is extended by many rods, and a long irregular beach of white sand is exposed along the east coast of the island, never out of the water long enough to acquire any vegetation, but dazzling white, ripple marked, and full of possibilities for the imagination. The island is NoMan's-Land; every summer a new chief claims it and it has been called by many names; but it seemed particularly to belong to the two children who christened it Far Island, partially because they were the original discoverers and claimants, but more especially because they were of that favored race whom a New England sage called the true landlords and sealords of the world.

One afternoon, early in June, the Silvery Beaches of Far Island were glistening in the sun like pounded glass, and the same slanting yellow rays that scorched the sand beat upon the windows of the passenger train from the East as it swung into the Republican Valley from the uplands. Then a young man dressed in a suit of gray tweed changed his seat in order to be on the side of the car next the river. When he crossed the car several women looked up and smiled, for it was with a movement of boyish abandon and an audible chuckle of delight that he threw himself into the seat to watch for the shining curves of the river as they unwound through the trees. He was sufficiently distinguished in appearance to interest even tired women at the end of a long, sultry day's travel. As the train rumbled over a trestle built above a hollow grown up with sunflowers and ironweed, he sniffed with delight the rank odor, familiar to the prairiebred man, that is exhaled by such places as evening approaches. "Ha," he murmured under his breath, "there's the white chalk cliff where the Indians used to run the buffalo over Bison Leap--we kids called it--the remote sea wall of the boy world. I'm getting home sure enough. And heavens! there's the island, Far Island, the Ultima Thule; and the arched tree, and Spy Glass Hill, and the Silvery Beaches; my heart's going like a boy's. 'Once on a day he sailed away, over the sea to Skye.'"

He sat bolt upright with his lips tightly closed and his chest swelling, for he was none other than the original discoverer of the island, Douglass Burnham, the playwright--our only playwright, certain critics contend-- and, for the first time since he left it a boy, he was coming home. It was only twelve years ago that he had gone away, when Pagie and Temp and Birkner and Shorty Thompson had stood on the station siding and waved him goodbye, while he shut his teeth to keep the tears back; and now the train bore him up the old river valley, though the meadows where he used to hunt for cattails, along the streams where he had paddled his canvas boat, and past the willowgrown island where he had buried the pirate's treasure--a man with a man's work done and the world well in hand. Success had never tasted quite so sweet as it tasted then. The whistle sounded, the brakemen called Empire City, and Douglass crossed to the other side of the car and looked out toward the town, which lay half a mile up from the station on a low range of hills, half hidden by the tall cottonwood trees that still shaded its streets. Down the curve of the track he could see the old railroad "eating house," painted the red Burlington color; on the hill above the town the standpipe towered up from the treetops. Douglass felt the years dropping away from him. The train stopped. Waiting on the platform stood his father and a tall spare man, with a straggling colorless beard, whose dejected stoop and shapeless hat and illfitting clothes were in themselves both introduction and biography. The narrow chest, long arms, and skinny neck were not to be mistaken. It was Rhinehold Birkner, old Rhine who had not been energetic enough to keep up his father's undertaking business, and who now sold sewing machines and parlor organs in a feeble attempt to support an invalid wife and ten children, all colorless and narrow chested like himself. Douglass sprang from the platform and grasped his father's hand.

"Hello, father, hello, Rhine, where are the other fellows? Why, that's so, you must be the only one left. Heavens! how we *have* scattered. What a lot of talking we two have got before us."

Probably no event had transpired since Rhine's first baby was born that had meant so much to him as Douglass's return, but he only chuckled, putting his limp, rough hand into the young man's smooth, warm one, and ventured.

"Jest the same old coon, Doug."

"How's mother, father?" Douglass asked as he hunted for his checks.

"She's well, son, but she thought she couldn't leave supper to come down to meet you. She has been cooking pretty much all day and worrying for fear the train would be late and your supper would spoil."

"Of course she has. When I am elected to the Academy mother will worry about my supper." Douglass felt a trifle nervous and made a dash for the shabby little street car which ever since he could remember had been drawn by mules that wore jingling bells on their collars.

A silence settled down over the occupants of the car as the mules trotted off. Douglass felt that his father stood somewhat in awe of him, or at least in awe of that dread Providence which ordered such dark things as that a hardheaded, moneysaving realestate man should be the father of a whitefingered playwright who spent more on his fads in a year than his father had saved by the thrift of a lifetime. All the hundred things Douglass had had to say seemed congested upon his tongue, and though he had a good measure of that cheerful assurance common to young people whom the world has made much of, he felt a strange embarrassment in the presence of this angular graywhiskered man who used to warm his jacket for him in the hayloft.

His mother was waiting for him under the bittersweet vines on the porch, just where she had always stood to greet him when he came home for his college vacations, and, as Douglass had lived in a world where the emotions are cultivated and not despised, he was not ashamed of the lump that rose in his throat when he took her in his arms. She hurried him out of the dark into the parlor lamplight and looked him over from head to foot to assure herself that he was still the handsomest of men, and then she told him to go into her bedroom to wash his face for supper. She followed him, unable to take her eyes from this splendid creature whom all the world claimed but who was only hers after all. She watched him take off his coat and collar, rejoicing in the freshness of his linen and the whiteness of his skin; even the color of his silk suspenders seemed a matter of importance to her.

"Douglass," she said impressively, "Mrs. Governor gives a reception for you tomorrow night, and I have promised her that you will read some selections from your plays."

This was a matter which was very near Mrs. Burnham's heart. Those dazzling first nights and receptions and author's dinners which happened out in the great world were merely hearsay, but it was a proud day when her son was held in honor by the women of her own town, of her own church; women she had shopped and marketed and gone to sewing circle with, women whose cakes and watermelon pickles won premiums over hers at the county fair.

"Read?" ejaculated Douglass, looking out over the towel and pausing in his brisk rubbing, "why, mother, dear, I can't read, not any more than a John rabbit. Besides, plays aren't meant to be read. Let me give them one of my old stunts; 'The Polish Boy' or 'Regulus to the Carthaginians.'"

"But you must do it, my son; it won't do to disappoint Mrs. Governor. Margie was over this morning to see about it. She has grown into a very pretty girl." When his mother spoke in that tone Douglass acquiesced, just as naturally as he helped himself to her violet water, the same kind, he noticed, that he used to covertly sprinkle on his handkerchief when he was primping for Sunday school after she had gone to church.

"Mrs. Governor still leads the pack, then? What a civilizing influence she has been in this community. Taught most of us all the manners we ever knew. Little Margie has grown up pretty, you say? Well, I should never have thought it. How many boys have I slugged for yelling 'Reddy, go dye your hair green' at her. She was not an indifferent slugger herself and never exactly stood in need of masculine protection. What a wild Indian she was! Game, clear through, though! I never found such a mind in a girl. But *is* she a girl? I somehow always fancied she would grow up a man--and a ripping fine one. Oh, I see you are looking at me hard! No, mother, the girls don't trouble me much." His eyes met hers laughingly in the glass as he parted his hair. "You spoiled me so outrageously that women tell me frankly I'm a selfish cad and they will have none of me."

His mother handed him his coat with a troubled glance. "I was afraid, my son, that some of those actresses--"

The young man laughed outright. "Oh, never worry about them, mother. Wait till you've seen them at rehearsals in soiled shirtwaists wearing out their antiques and doing what they call 'resting' their hair. Poor things! They have to work too hard to bother about being attractive."

He went out into the dining room where the table was set for him just as it had always been when he came home on that same eight o'clock train from college. There were all his favorite viands and the old family silver spread on the white cloth with the maidenhair fern pattern, under the soft lamplight. It had been years since he had eaten by the mild light of a kerosene lamp. By his plate stood his own glass that his grandmother had given him with "For a Good Boy" ground on the surface which was dewy from the ice within. The other glasses were unclouded and held only fresh water from the pump, for his mother was very economical about ice and held the most exaggerated views as to the pernicious effects of ice water on the human stomach. Douglass only got it because he was the first dramatist of the country and a great man. When he decided that he would like a cocktail and asked for whiskey, his mother dealt him out a niggardly tablespoonful, saying, "That's as much as you ought to have at your age, Douglass." When he went out into the kitchen to greet the old servant and get some ice for his drink, his mother hurried after him crying with solicitude.

"I'll get the ice for you, Douglass. Don't you go into the refrigerator; you always leave the ice uncovered and it wastes."

Douglass threw up his hands, "Mother, whatever I may do in the world I shall never be clever enough to be trusted with that refrigerator. 'Into all the chambers of the palace mayest thou go, save into this thou shalt not go.'" And now he knew he was at home, indeed, for his father stood chuckling in the doorway, washing his hands from the milking, and the old servant threw her apron over her head to stop her laughter at this strange reception of a celebrity. The memory of his luxurious rooms in New York, where he lived when he was an artist, faded dim; he was but a boy again in his father's house and must not keep supper waiting.

The next evening Douglass with resignation accompanied his father and mother to the reception given in his honor. The town had advanced somewhat since his day; and he was amused to see his father appear in an apology for a frock coat and a black tie, such as Kentucky politicians wear. Although people wore frock coats nowadays they still walked to receptions, and as Douglass climbed the hill the whole situation struck him as farcical. He dropped his mother's arm and ran up to the porch with his hat in his hand, laughing. "Margie!" he called, intending to dash through the house until he found her. But in the vestibule he bumped up against something large and splendid, then stopped and caught his breath. A woman stood in the dark by the hall lamp with a lighted match in her hand. She was in white and very tall. The match burned but a moment; a moment the light played on her hair, red as Etruscan gold and piled high above the curve of the neck and head; a moment upon the oval chin, the lips curving upward and red as a crimson cactus flower; the deep, gray, fearless eyes; the white shoulders framed about with darkness. Then the match went out, leaving Douglass to wonder whether, like Anchises, he had seen the vision that should forever blind him to the beauty of mortal women.

"I beg your pardon," he stammered, backing toward the door, "I was looking for Miss Van Dyck. Is she--" Perhaps it was a mere breath of stifled laughter, perhaps it was a recognition by some sense more trustworthy than sight and subtler than mind; but there seemed a certain familiarity in the darkness about him, a certain sense of the security and peace which one experiences among dear and intimate things, and with widening eyes he said softly,

"Tell me, is this Margie?"

There was just a murmur of laughter from the tall, white figure. "I was going to be presented to you in the most proper form, and now you've spoiled it all. How are you, Douglass, and did you get a whipping this time? You've played hooky longer than usual. Ten years, isn't it?" She put out her hand in the dark and he took it and drew it through his arm.

"No, I didn't get a whipping, but I may get worse. I wish I'd come back five years ago. I would if I had known he said promptly.

The reading was just as stupid as he had said it would be, but his audience enjoyed it and he enjoyed his audience. There was the old deacon who had once caught him in his watermelon patch and set the dog on him; the president of the W.C.T.U., with her memorable black lace shawl and cane, who still continued to send him temperance tracts, mindful of the hundredth sheep in the parable; his old Sunday school teacher, a good man of limited information who never read anything but his Bible and *Teacher's Quarterly,* and who had once hung a cheap edition of *Camille* on the church Christmas tree for Douglass, with an inscription on the inside to the effect that the fear of the Lord is the beginning of Wisdom. There was the village criminal lawyer, one of those brilliant wrecks sometimes found in small towns, who, when he was so drunk he could not walk, used to lie back in his office chair and read Shakespeare by the hour to a little barefoot boy. Next him sat the rich banker who used to offer the boys a quarter to hitch up his horse for him, and then drive off, forgetting all about the quarter. Then there were fathers and mothers of Douglass's old clansmen and vassals who were scattered all over the world now. After the reading Douglass spent half an hour chatting with nice tiresome old ladies who reminded him of how much he used to like their teacakes and cookies, and answering labored compliments with genuine feeling. Then he went with a clear conscience and light heart whither his eyes had been wandering ever since he had entered the house.

"Margie, I needn't apologize for not recognizing you, since it was such an involuntary compliment. However did you manage to grow up like this? Was it boarding school that did it? I might have recognized you with your hair down, and oh, I'd know you anywhere when you smile! The teeth are just the same. Do you still crack nuts with them?"

"I haven't tried it for a long time. How remarkably little the years change you, Douglass. I haven't seen you since the night you brought out *The Clover Leaf,* and I heard your curtain speech. Oh, I was very proud of our Pirate Chief!"

Douglass sat down on the piano stool and looked searchingly into her eyes, which met his with laughing frankness.

"What! you were in New York then and didn't let me know? There was a day when you wouldn't have treated me so badly. Didn't you want to see me just a little bit--out of curiosity?"

"Oh, I was visiting some school friends who said it would be atrocious to bother you, and the newspapers were full of interesting details about your being so busy that you ate and got shaved at the theatre. Then one's time isn't one's own when one is visiting, you know." She saw the hurt expression on his face and repented, adding gayly, "But I may as well confess that I kept a sharp lookout for you on the street, and when I did meet you you didn't know me."

"And you didn't stop me? That's worse yet. How in Heaven's name was I to know you? Accost a goddess and say, 'Oh yes, you used to be a Pirate Chief and wear a butcher knife in your belt.' But I hadn't grown into an Apollo, save the mark! and you knew me well enough. I couldn't have passed you like that in a strange land."

"No, you do your duty by your countrymen, Douglass. You haven't grown haughty. One by one our old townspeople go out to see the world and bring us back tales of your glory. What unpromising specimens have you not dined and wined in New York! Why even old Skin Jackson, when he went to New York to have his eyes treated, you took to the Waldorf and to the Player's Club, where he drank with the Immortals. How do you have the courage to do it? *Did* he wear those dreadful gold nugget shirt studs that he dug up in Colorado when we were young?"

"Even the same, Margie, and he scored a hit with them. But you are dodging the point. When and where did you see me in New York?"

"Oh, it was one evening when you were crossing Madison Square. You were probably going to the theatre for Flashingham and Miss Grew were with you and you seemed in a hurry." Margie wished now that she had not mentioned the incident. "I remember that was the time I so deeply offended your mother on my return by telling her that Miss Grew had announced her engagement to you. How did it come out? She certainly did announce it."

"Doubtless, but it was entirely a misunderstanding on the lady's part. We never were anything of the sort," said Douglass impatiently. "That is a disgusting habit of Edith's; she announces a new engagement every fortnight as mechanically as the butler announces dinner. About once a month she calls the dear Twelfth Night girls together to a solemn high tea and gently breaks the news of a new engagement, and they kiss and cry over her ant say the things they have said a dozen times before and go away tittering. Why she has been engaged to every society chap in New York and to the whole Milton family, with the possible exception of Sir Henry, and her papa has cabled his blessing all over the known world to her. But it is a waste of time to talk about such nonsense; don't let's," he urged.

"I think it is very interesting; I don't indulge in weekly engagements myself. But there is one thing I want to know, Douglass; I want to know how you did it."

"Did what?"

Margie threw out her hands with an impetuous gesture. "Oh, all of it, all the wonderful things you have done. You remember that night when we lay on the sand bar--"

"The Uttermost Desert," interrupted Douglass softly.

"Yes, the Uttermost Desert, and in the light of the driftwood fire we planned the conquest of the world? Well, other people plan, too, and fight and suffer and fail the world over, and a very few succeed at the bitter end when they are old and it is no longer worth while. But you have done it as they used to do it in the fairy tales, without soiling your golden armor, and I can't find one line in your face to tell me that you have suffered or found life bitter to your tongue. How have you cheated fate?"

Douglass looked about him and saw that the guests had thronged about the punchbowl, and his mother, beaming in her new black satin, was relating touching incidents of his infancy to a group of old ladies. He leaned forward, clasped his hands between his knees, and launched into an animated description of how his first play, written at college, had taken the fancy of an old school friend of his father's who had turned manager. The second, a political farce, had put him firmly on his feet. Then followed his historical drama, *Lord Fairfax,* in which he had at first failed completely. He told her of those desperate days in New York when he would draw his blinds and work by lamplight until he was utterly exhausted, of how he fell ill and lost the thread of his play and used to wander about the streets trying to beat it out of the paving stones when the very policemen who jostled him on the crossings knew more about *Lord Fairfax* than he.

As he talked he felt the old sense of power, lost for many years; the power of conveying himself wholly to her in speech, of awakening in her mind every tint and shadow and vague association that was in his at the moment. He quite forgot the beauty of the woman beside him in the exultant realization of comradeship, the egotistic satisfaction of being wholly understood. Suddenly he stopped short.

"Come, Margie, you're not playing fair, you're telling me nothing about yourself. What plays have you been playing? Pirate or enchanted princess or sleeping beauty or Helen of Troy, to the disaster of men?"

Margie sighed as she awoke out of the fairyland. Doug's tales were as wonderful as ever.

"Oh, I stopped playing long ago. I have grown up and you have not. Some one has said that is wherein geniuses are different; they go on playing and never grow up. So you see you're only a case of arrested development, after all."

"I don't believe it, you play still, I can see it in your eyes. And don't say genius to me. People say that to me only when they want to be disagreeable or tell me how they would have written my plays. The word is my bogie. But tell me, are the cattails ripe in the Salt Marshes, and will your mother let you wade if the sun is warm, and do the winds still smell sharp with salt when they blow through the mists at night?"

"Why, Douglass, did the wind always smell salty to you there too? It does to me yet, and you know there isn't a particle of salt there. Why did we ever name them the Salt Marshes?"

"Because they *were* the Salt Marshes and couldn't have had any other name any more than the Far Island could. I went down to those pestiferous Maremma marshes in Italy to see whether they would be as real as our marshes, but they were not real at all; only miles and miles of bog. And do the nightingales still sing in the grove?"

"Yes. Other people call them ring doves--but they still sing there."

"And you still call them nightingales to yourself and laugh at the density of big people?"

"Yes, sometimes."

Later in the evening Douglass found another opportunity, and this time he was fortunate enough to encounter Margie alone as she was crossing the veranda.

"Do you know why I have come home in June, instead of July as I had intended, Margie? Well, sit down and let me tell you. They don't need you in there just now. About a month ago I changed my apartment in New York, and as I was sorting over my traps I came across a box of childish souvenirs. Among them was a faded bit of paper on which a map was drawn with elaborate care. It was the map of an island with curly blue lines all around it to represent water, such as we used always to draw around the continents in our geography class. On the west coast of the island a red sword was sticking upright in the earth. Beneath this scientific drawing was an inscription to the effect that *'whoso should dig twelve paces west of the huge fallen tree, in direct line with the path made by the setting sun on the water on the tenth day of June, should find the great treasure and his heart's desire!'*"

Margie laughed and applauded gently with her hands. "And so you have come to dig for it; some two thousand miles almost. There's a dramatic situation for you. I have my map still, and I've often contemplated going down to Far Island and digging, but it wouldn't have been fair, for the treasure was really yours, after all."

"Well, you are going now, and on the tenth day of June, that's next Friday, for that's what I came home for, and I had to spoil the plans and temper of a manager and all his company to do it."

Nonsense, there are too many mosquitoes on Far Island and I mind them more than I used to. Besides there are no good boats like the *Jolly Roger* nowadays."

"We'll go if I have to build another *Jolly Roger*. You can't make me believe you are afraid of mosquitoes. I know too well the mettle of your pasture. Please do, Margie, Please." He used his old insidious coaxing tone.

"Douglass, you have made me do dreadful things enough by using that tone of voice to me. I believe you used to hypnotize me. Will you never, never grow up?"

"Never so long as there are pirate's treasures to dig for and you will play with me, Margie. Oh, I wish I had some of the cake that Alice ate in Wonderland and could make you a little girl again."

That night, after the household was asleep, Douglass went out for a walk about the old town, treading the ways he had trod when he was a founder of cities and a leader of hosts. But he saw few of the old landmarks, for the blaze of Etruscan gold was in his eyes, and he felt as a man might feel who in some sleepy humdrum Italian village had unearthed a new marble goddess, as beautiful as she of Milo; and he felt as a boy might feel who had lost all his favorite marbles and his best pea shooter and the dog that slept with him, and had found them all again. He tried to follow, step by step, the wonderful friendship of his childhood.

A child's normal attitude toward the world is that of the artist, pure and simple. The rest of us have to do with the solids of this world, whereas only their form and color exist for the painter. So, in every wood and street and building there are things, not seen of older people at all, which make up their whole desirableness or objectionableness to children. There are maps and pictures formed by cracks in the walls of bare and unsightly sleeping chambers which make them beautiful; smooth places on the lawn where the grass is greener than anywhere else and which are good to sit upon; trees which are valuable by reason of the peculiar way in which the branches grow, and certain spots under the scrub willows along the creek which are in a manner sacred, like the sacrificial groves of the Druids, so that a boy is almost afraid to walk there. Then there are certain carpets which are more beautiful than others, because with a very little help from the imagination they become the rose garden of the Thousand and One Nights; and certain couches which are peculiarly adapted for playing Sindbad in his days of ease, after the toilsome voyages were over. A child's standard of value is so entirely his own, and his peculiar part and possessions in the material objects around him are so different from those of his elders, that it may be said his rights are granted by a different lease. To these two children the entire external world, like the people who dwelt in it, had been valued solely for what they suggested to the imagination, and people and places alike were merely stage properties, contributing more or less to the intensity of their inner life.

Green leaves a-floating

Castles of the foam,

Boats of mine a-boating

When will all come home?"

sang Douglass as they pulled from the mill wharf out into the rapid current of the river, which that morning seemed the most beautiful and noble of rivers, an enchanted river flowing peacefully out of Arcady with the Happy Isles somewhere in the distance. The ripples were touched with silver and the sky was as blue as though it had been made today; the cow bells sounded faintly from the meadows along the shore like the bells of fairy cities ringing on the day the prince errant brought home his bride; the meadows that sloped to the water's edge were the greenest in all the world because they were the meadows of the long ago; and the flowers that grew there were the freshest and sweetest of growing things because once, long ago in the golden age, two children had gathered other flowers like them, and the beauties of vanished summers were everywhere. Douglass sat in the end of the boat, his back to the sun and his straw hat tilted back on his head, pulling slowly and feeling that the day was fine rather than seeing it; for his eyes were fixed upon his helmsman in the other end of the boat, who sat with her hat in her lap, shading her face with a white parasol, and her wonderful hair piled high on her head like a helmet of gleaming bronze.

Of all the possessions of their childhood's Wonderland, Far Island had been dearest; it was graven on their hearts as Calais was upon Mary Tudor's. Long before they had set foot upon it the island was the goal of their loftiest ambitions and most delightful imaginings. They had wondered what trees grew there and what delightful spots were hidden away under the matted grapevines. They had even decided that a race of kindly dwarfs must inhabit it and had built up a civilization and historic annals for these imaginary inhabitants, surrounding the sand bar with all the mystery and enchantment which was attributed to certain islands of the sea by the mariners of Greece. Douglass and Margie had sometimes found it expedient to admit other children into their world, but for the most part these were but hewers of wood and drawers of water, who helped to shift the scenery and construct the balcony and place the king's throne, and were no more in the atmosphere of the play than were the supers who watched Mr. Keane's famous duel with Richmond. Indeed Douglass frequently selected the younger and more passive boys for his vassals on the principle that they did as they were bid and made no trouble. But there is something of the explorer in the least imaginative of boys, and when

Douglass came to the building of his famous boat, the *Jolly Roger,* he found willing hands to help him. Indeed the sawing and hammering, the shavings and cut fingers and blood blisters fell chiefly to the lot of dazzled lads who claimed no part in the craft, and who gladly trotted and sweated for their board and keep in this fascinating play world which was so much more exhilarating than any they could make for themselves.

"Think of it, Margie, we are really going back to the island after so many years, just you and I, the captain and his mate. Where are the other gallant lads that sailed with us then?"

"Where are the snows of yester' year?" sighed Margie softly. "It is very sad to grow up."

"Sad for them, yes. But we have never grown up, you know, we have only grown more considerate of our complexions," nodding at the parasol. "What a little mass of freckles you used to be, but I liked you freckled, too. Let me see: old Temp is commanding a regiment in the Philippines, and Bake has a cattle ranch in Wyoming, Mac is a government clerk in Washington, Jim keeps his father's hardware store, poor Ned and Shorty went down in a catboat on the Hudson while they were at college (I went out to hunt for the bodies, you know), and old Rhine is selling sewing machines; he never did get away at all, did he?"

"No, not for any length of time. You know it used to frighten Rhine to go to the next town to see a circus. He went to Arizona once for his lungs, but his family never could tell where he was for he headed all his letters 'Empire City, Nebraska,' for habit."

"Oh, that's delightful, Margie, you must let me use that. Rhine would carry Empire City through Europe with him and never know he was out of it. Have I told you about Pagie? Well, you know Pagie is travelling for a, New York tailoring house and I let his people make some clothes for me that I had to give to Flashingham's valet. When he first came to town he tried to be gay, with his fond mother's prayers still about him, a visible nimbus, and the Sunday school boy written all over his open countenance and downy lip and large, white butter teeth. But I know, at heart, he still detested naughty words and whiskey made him sick. One day I was standing at the Hoffman House bar with some fellows, when a slender youth, who looked like a nice girl masquerading as a rake, stepped up and ordered a claret and seltzer. The whine was unmistakable. I turned and said, even before I had looked at him squarely, 'Oh, Pagie! if your mother saw you here!'"

"Poor Pagie! I'll warrant he would rather have had bread and sugar. Do you remember how, at the Sunday school concerts on Children's Day, you and Pagie and Shorty and Temp used to stand in a row behind the flowerwreathed pulpit rail, all in your new roundabout suits with large silk bows tied under your collars, your hands behind you, and assure us with sonorous voices that you would come rejoicing bringing in the sheaves? Somehow, even then, I never doubted that you would do it."

The keel grated on the sand and Douglass sprang ashore and gave her his hand.

"Descend, O Miranda, upon your island! Do you know, Margie, it makes me seem fifteen again to feel this sand crunching under my feet. I wonder if I ever again shall feel such a thrill of triumph as I felt when I first leaped upon this sand bar? None of my first nights have given me anything like it. Do you remember *really,* and did you feel the same?"

"Of course I remember, and I knew that you were playing a double role that day, and that you were really the trailbreaker and worldfinder inside of the pirate all the while. Here are the same ripple marks on the Silvery Beaches, and here is the great arched tree, let's run for it." She started fleetly across the glittering sand and Douglass fell behind to watch with immoderate joy that splendid, generous body that governed itself so well in the open air. There was a wholesomeness of the sun and soil in her that was utterly lacking in the women among whom he had lived for so long. She had preserved that strength of arm and freedom of limb that had made her so fine a playfellow, and which modern modes of life have wellnigh robbed the world of altogether. Surely, he thought, it was like that that Diana's women sped after the stag down the slopes of Ida, with shouting and bright spear. She caught an overhang branch and swung herself upon the embankment and, leaning against the trunk of a tree, awaited him flushed and panting, her bosom rising and falling with her quick drawn breaths.

"Why did you close the tree behind you, Margie? I have always wanted to see just how Dryads keep house," he exclaimed, brushing away a dried leaf that had fallen on her shoulder.

"Don't strain your inventive powers to make compliments, Douglass; this is your vacation and you are to rest your imagination. See, the willows have scarcely grown at all. I'm sure we shall hear Pagie whimpering over there on the Uttermost Desert where we marooned him, or singing hymns to keep up his courage. Now for the Huge Fallen Tree. Do you suppose the floods have moved it?"

They struck through the dense willow thicket, matted with fragrant wild grapevines which Douglass beat down with his spade, and came upon the great white log, the bleached skeleton of a tree, and found the cross hacked upon it, the rough gashes of the hatchet now worn smooth by the wind and rain and the seething of spring freshets. Near the cross were cut the initials of the entire pirate crew; some of them were cut on gravestones now. The scrub willows had grown over the spot where they had decided the treasure must lie, and together they set to work to break them away. Douglass paused more than once to watch the strong young creature beside him, outlined against the tender green foliage, reaching high and low and snapping the withes where they were weakest. He was still wondering whether it was not all a dream picture, and was half afraid that his man would call him to tell him that some piqued and faded woman was awaiting him at the theatre to quarrel about her part.

"Still averse to manual labor, Douglass?" she laughed as she turned to bend a tall sapling. "The most remarkable thing about your enthusiasm was that you had only to sing of the glories of toil to make other people do all the work for you."

"No, Margie, I was thinking very hard indeed--about the Thracian women when they broke the boughs wherewith they flayed unhappy Orpheus."

"Now, Douglass, you'll spoil the play. A sentimental pirate is impossible. Pagie was a sentimental pirate and that was what spoiled him. A little more of this and I will maroon you upon the Uttermost Desert."

Douglass laughed and settled himself back among the green boughs and gazed at her with the abandoned admiration of an artist contemplating a masterpiece.

When they came to the digging of the treasure a little exertion was enough to unearth what had seemed hidden so fabulously deep in olden time. The chest was rotten and fell apart as the spade struck it, but the glass jar was intact, covered with sand and slime. Douglass spread his handkerchief upon the sand and weighted the corners down with pebbles and upon it poured the treasure of Far Island. There was the manuscript written in blood, a confession of fantastic crimes, and the Spaniard's heart in a bottle of alcohol, and Temp's Confederate bank notes, damp and grewsome to the touch, and Pagie's rare tobacco tags, their brilliant colors faded entirely away, and poor Shorty's bars of tinfoil dull and eaten with rust.

"And, Douglass," cried Maggie, "there is your father's silver ring that was made from a nugget; he whipped you for burying it. You remember it was given to a Christian knight by an English queen, and when he was slain before Jerusalem a Saracen took it and we killed the Saracen in the desert and cut off his finger to get the ring. It is strange how those wild imaginings of ours seem, in retrospect, realities, things that I actually lived through. I suppose that in cold fact my life was a good deal like that of other little girls who grow up in a village; but whenever I look back on it, it is all exultation and romance--sea fights and splendid galleys and Roman triumphs and brilliant caravans winding through the desert."

"To people who live by imagination at all, that is the only life that goes deep enough to leave memories. We were artists in those days, creating for the day only; making epics sung once and then forgotten, building empires that set with the sun. Nobody worked for money then, and nobody worked for fame, but only for the joy of the doing. Keats said the same thing more elegantly in his May Day Ode, and we were not so unlike those Hellenic poets who were content to sing to the shepherds and forget and be forgotten, 'rich in the simple worship of a day.'"

"Why, Douglass," she cried as she bent her face down to the little glass jar, "it was really our childhood that we buried here, never guessing what a precious thing we were putting under the ground. That was the real treasure of Far Island, and we might dig up the whole island for it but all the king's horses and all the king's men could not bring it back to us. That voyage we made to bury our trinkets, just before you went away to school, seems like unconscious symbolism, and somehow it stands out from all the other good times we knew then as the happiest of all." She looked off where the setting sun hung low above the water.

"Shall I tell you why, Margie? That was the end of our childhood, and there the golden days died in a blaze of glory, passed in music out of sight. That night, after our boat had drifted away from us, when we had to wade down the river hand in hand, we two, and the noises and the coldness of the water frightened us, and there were quicksands and sharp rocks and deep holes to shun, and terrible things lurking in the woods on the shore, you cried in a different way from the way you sometimes cried when you hurt yourself, and I found that I loved you afraid better than I had ever loved you fearless, and in that moment we grew up, and shut the gates of Eden behind us, and our empire was at an end."

"And now we are only kings in exile," sighed Margie softly, "who wander back to look down from the mountain tops upon the happy land we used to rule."

Douglass took her hand gently; "If there is to be any Eden on earth again for us, dear, we must make it with our two hearts."

There was a sudden brightness of tears in her eyes, and she drew away from him. "Ah, Douglass, you are determined to spoil it all. It is you who have grown up and taken on the ways of the world. The play is at an end for me." She tried to rise, but he held her firmly.

"From the moment I looked into your eyes in the vestibule that night we have been parts of the same dream again. Why, Margie, we have more romance behind us than most men and women ever live."

Margie's face grew whiter, but she pushed his hand away and the look in her eyes grew harder. "This is only a new play, Douglass, and you will weary of it tomorrow. I am not so good at playing as I used to be. I am no longer content with the simple worship of a day."

In her touch, in her white face, he divined the greatness of what she had to give. He bit his lip and answered, "I think you owe me more confidence than that, if only for the sake of those days when we trusted each other entirely. "

She turned with a quick flash of remorseful tenderness, as she used to do when she hurt him at play. "I only want to keep you from hurting us both, Douglass. We neither of us could go on feeling like this. It's only the dregs of the old enchantment. Things have always come easily to you, I know, for at your birth nature and fortune joined to make you great. But they do not come so to me; I should wake and weep."

"Then weep, my princess, for I will wake you now!"

The fire and fancy that had so bewitched her girlhood that no other man had been able to dim the memory of it came furiously back upon her, with arms that were new and strange and strong, and with tenderness stranger still in this wild fellow of dreams and jests; and all her vows never to grace another of his Roman triumphs were forgotten.

"You are right, Margie; the pirate play is ended and the time has come to divide the prizes, and I choose what I chose fifteen years ago. Out of the spoils of a lifetime of crime and bloodshed I claimed only the captive princess, and I claim her still. I have sought the world over for her, only to find her at last in the land of lost content."

Margie lifted her face from his shoulder, and, after the manner of women of her kind, she played her last card rhapsodically. "And she, O Douglass! the years she has waited have been longer than the waiting of Penelope, and she has woven a thousand webs of dreams by night and torn them asunder by day, and looked out across the Salt Marshes for the night train, and still you did not come. I was only your pensioner like Shorty and Temp and the rest, and I could not play anything alone. You took my world with you when you went and left me only a village of mud huts and loneliness."

As her eyes and then her lips met his in the dying light, he knew that she had caught the spirit of the play, and that she would ford the river by night with him and never be afraid.

The locust chirped in the thicket; the setting sun threw a track of flame across the water; the willows burned with fire and were not consumed; a glory was upon the sand and the river and upon the Silvery Beaches; and these two looked about over God's world and saw that it was good. In the western sky the palaces of crystal and gold were quenched in night, like the cities of old empires; and out of the east rose the same moon that has glorified all the romances of the world--that lighted Paris over the blue Ægean and the feet of young Montague to the Capulets' orchard. The dinner hour in Empire City was long past, but the two upon the island wist naught of these things, for they had become as the gods, who dwell in their golden houses, recking little of the woes and labors of mortals, neither heeding any fall of rain or snow.

The Outcasts of Poker Flat

Bret Harte

Bret Harte (1839-1902), noted for *The Luck of Roaring Camp and Other Stories* published in 1870, was a master of the short story form.

Born in Albany, New York, his father, a college professor, was intent on Harte receiving a traditional college education. It never materialized. After his father's death he moved to California with his mother to join his older brother who had caught gold fever. The people in the gold camps and the landscape of the Sierra Nevada mountains afforded Harte an abundance of ideas for his stories. At eighteen, he became a compositor for a newspaper and eventually the editor. He served as a United States consul in Germany from 1878 to 1885. His collected journalistic writings include *Colonel Starbottle's Client* (1892), and *The Bell-Ringer of Angels* (1894).

Harte's stories, poems, and novels, depicting the background of a region became known as "local color." As a writer Harte is best remembered for his ability to capture the essence of an era in American history.

AS MR. JOHN OAKHURST, gambler, stepped into the main street of Poker Flat on the morning of the 23d of November, 1850, he was conscious of a change in its moral atmosphere since the preceding night. Two or three men, conversing earnestly together, ceased as he approached and exchanged significant glances. There was a Sabbath lull in the air, which, in a settlement unused to Sabbath influences, looked ominous.

Mr. Oakhurst's calm, handsome face betrayed small concern in these indications. Whether he was conscious of any predisposing cause was another question. "I reckon they're after somebody," he reflected; "likely it's me." He returned to his pocket the handkerchief with which he had been whipping away the red dust of Poker Flat from his neat boots, and quietly discharged his mind of any further conjecture.

In point of fact, Poker Flat was "after somebody." It had lately suffered the loss of several thousand dollars, two valuable horses, and a prominent citizen. It was experiencing a spasm of virtuous reaction, quite as lawless and ungovernable as any of the acts that had provoked it. A secret committee had determined to rid the town of all improper persons. This was done permanently in regard of two men who were then hanging from the boughs of a sycamore in the gulch, and temporarily in the banishment of certain other objectionable characters. I regret to say that some of these were ladies. It is but due to the sex, however, to state that their impropriety was professional, and it was only in such easily established standards of evil that Poker Flat ventured to sit in judgment.

Mr. Oakhurst was right in supposing that he was included in this category. A few of the committee had urged hanging him as a possible example and a sure method of reimbursing themselves from his pockets of the sums he had won from them. "It's agin justice," said Jim Wheeler, "to let this yer young man from Roaring Camp--an entire stranger-- carry away our money." But a crude sentiment of equity residing in the breasts of those who had been fortunate enough to win from Mr. Oakhurst overruled this narrower local prejudice.

Mr. Oakhurst received his sentence with philosophic calmness, none the less coolly that he was aware of the hesitation of his judges. He was too much of a gambler not to accept fate. With him life was at best an uncertain game, and he recognized the usual percentage in favor of the dealer.

A body of armed men accompanied the deported wickedness of Poker Flat to the outskirts of the settlement. Besides Mr. Oakhurst, who was known to be a coolly desperate man, and for whose intimidation the armed escort was intended, the expatriated party consisted of a young woman familiarly known as "The Duchess;" another who had won the title of "Mother Shipton;" and "Uncle Billy," a suspected sluice-robber and confirmed drunkard. The cavalcade provoked no comments from the spectators, nor was any word uttered by the escort. Only when the gulch which marked the uttermost limit of Poker Flat was reached, the leader spoke briefly and to the point. The exiles were forbidden to return at the peril of their lives.

As the escort disappeared, their pentup feelings found vent in a few hysterical tears from the Duchess, some bad language from Mother Shipton, and a Parthian volley of expletives from Uncle Billy. The philosophic Oakhurst alone remained silent. He listened calmly to Mother Shipton's desire to cut somebody's heart out, to the repeated statements of the Duchess that she would die in the road, and to the alarming oaths that seemed to be bumped out of Uncle Billy as he rode forward. With the easy good humor characteristic of his class, he insisted upon exchanging his own riding-horse, "FiveSpot," for the sorry mule which the Duchess rode. But even this act did not draw the party into any closer sympathy. The young woman readjusted her somewhat draggled plumes with a feeble, faded coquetry; Mother Shipton eyed the possessor of "FiveSpot" with malevolence, and Uncle Billy included the whole party in one sweeping anathema.

The road to Sandy Bar--a camp that, not having as yet experienced the regenerating influences of Poker Flat, consequently seemed to offer some invitation to the emigrants--lay over a steep mountain range. It was distant a day's severe travel. In that advanced season the party soon passed out of the moist, temperate regions of the foothills into the dry, cold, bracing air of the Sierras. The trail was narrow and difficult. At noon the Duchess, rolling out of her saddle upon the ground, declared her intention of going no farther, and the party halted.

The spot was singularly wild and impressive. A wooded amphitheater, surrounded on three sides by precipitous cliffs of naked granite, sloped gently toward the crest of another precipice that overlooked the valley. It was, undoubtedly, the most suitable spot for a camp, had camping been advisable. But Mr. Oakhurst knew that scarcely half the journey to Sandy Bar was accomplished, and the party were not equipped or provisioned for delay. This fact he pointed out to his companions curtly, with a philosophic commentary on the folly of "throwing up their hand before the game was played out." But they were furnished with liquor, which in this emergency stood them in place of food, fuel, rest, and prescience. In spite of his remonstrances, it was not long before they were more or less under its influence. Uncle Billy passed rapidly from a bellicose state into one of stupor, the Duchess became maudlin, and Mother Shipton snored. Mr. Oakhurst alone remained erect, leaning against a rock, calmly surveying them.

Mr. Oakhurst did not drink. It interfered with a profession which required coolness, impassiveness, and presence of mind, and, in his own language, he "couldn't afford it." As he gazed at his recumbent fellow exiles, the loneliness begotten of his pariah trade, his habits of life, his very vices, for the first time seriously oppressed him. He bestirred himself in dusting his black clothes, washing his hands and face, and other acts characteristic of his studiously neat habits, and for a moment forgot his annoyance. The thought of deserting his weaker and more pitiable companions never perhaps occurred to him. Yet he could not help feeling the

want of that excitement which, singularly enough, was most conducive to
that calm equanimity for which he was notorious. He looked at the
gloomy walls that rose a thousand feet sheer above the circling pines
around him, at the sky ominously clouded, at the valley below, already
deepening into shadow; and doing so, suddenly he heard his own name
called.

A horseman slowly ascended the trail. In the fresh, open face of the
newcomer Mr. Oakhurst recognized Tom Simson, otherwise known as
"The Innocent," of Sandy Bar. He had met him some months before over
a "little game," and had, with perfect equanimity, won the entire fortune-
-amounting to some forty dollars--of that guileless youth. After the game
was finished, Mr. Oakhurst drew the youthful speculator behind the door
and thus addressed him: "Tommy, you're a good little man, but you can't
gamble worth a cent. Don't try it over again." He then handed him his
money back, pushed him gently from the room, and so made a devoted
slave of Tom Simson.

There was a remembrance of this in his boyish and enthusiastic
greeting of Mr. Oakhurst. He had started, he said, to go to Poker Flat to
seek his fortune. "Alone?" No, not exactly alone; in fact (a giggle), he had
run away with Piney Woods. Didn't Mr. Oakhurst remember Piney? She
that used to wait on the table at the Temperance House? They had been
engaged a long time, but old Jake Woods had objected, and so they had
run away, and were going to Poker Flat to be married, and here they were.
And they were tired out, and how lucky it was they had found a place to
camp, and company. All this the Innocent delivered rapidly, while Piney,
a stout comely damsel of fifteen, emerged from behind the pinetree, where
she had been blushing unseen, and rode to the side of her lover.

Mr. Oakhurst seldom troubled himself with sentiment, still less with
propriety; but he had a vague idea that the situation was not fortunate. He
retained, however, his presence of mind sufficiently to kick Uncle Billy,
who was about to say something, and Uncle Billy was sober enough to
recognize in Mr. Oakhurst's kick a superior power that would not bear
trifling. He then endeavored to dissuade Tom Simson from delaying
further, but in vain. He even pointed out the fact that there was no
provision, nor means of making a camp. But, unluckily, the Innocent met
this objection by assuring the party that he was provided with an extra
mule loaded with provisions, and by the discovery of a rude attempt at a
log house near the trail. "Piney can stay with Mrs. Oakhurst," said the
Innocent, pointing to the Duchess, "and I can shift for myself."

Nothing but Mr. Oakhurst's admonishing foot saved Uncle Billy from bursting into a roar of laughter. As it was, he felt compelled to retire up the canon until he could recover his gravity. There he confided the joke to the tall pinetrees, with many slaps of his leg, contortions of his face, and the usual profanity. But when he returned to the party, he found them seated by a fire--for the air had grown strangely chill and the sky overcast--in apparently amicable conversation. Piney was actually talking in an impulsive girlish fashion to the Duchess, who was listening with an interest and animation she had not shown for many days. The Innocent was holding forth, apparently with equal effect, to Mr. Oakhurst and Mother Shipton, who was actually relaxing into amiability. "Is this yer a d--d picnic?" said Uncle Billy, with inward scorn, as he surveyed the sylvan group, the glancing firelight, and the tethered animals in the foreground. Suddenly an idea mingled with the alcoholic fumes that disturbed his brain. It was apparently of a jocular nature, for he felt impelled to slap his leg again and cram his fist into his mouth.

As the shadows crept slowly up the mountain, a slight breeze rocked the tops of the pinetrees and moaned through their long and gloomy aisles. The ruined cabin, patched and covered with pine boughs, was set apart for the ladies. As the lovers parted, they unaffectedly exchanged a kiss, so honest and sincere that it might have been heard above the swaying pines. The frail Duchess and the malevolent Mother Shipton were probably too stunned to remark upon this last evidence of simplicity, and so turned without a word to the hut. The fire was replenished, the men lay down before the door, and in a few minutes were asleep.

Mr. Oakhurst was a light sleeper. Toward morning he awoke benumbed and cold. As he stirred the dying fire, the wind, which was now blowing strongly, brought to his cheek that which caused the blood to leave it,--snow!

He started to his feet with the intention of awakening the sleepers, for there was no time to lose. But turning to where Uncle Billy had been lying, he found him gone. A suspicion leaped to his brain, and a curse to his lips. He ran to the spot where the mules had been tethered--they were no longer there. The tracks were already rapidly disappearing in the snow.

The momentary excitement brought Mr. Oakhurst back to the fire with his usual calm. He did not waken the sleepers. The Innocent slumbered peacefully, with a smile on his goodhumored, freckled face; the virgin Piney slept beside her frailer sisters as sweetly as though attended by celestial guardians; and Mr. Oakhurst, drawing his blanket over his shoulders, stroked his mustaches and waited for the dawn. It came slowly in a whirling mist of snowflakes that dazzled and confused the eye. What could be seen of the landscape appeared magically changed. He looked over the valley, and summed up the present and future in two words, "Snowed in!"

A careful inventory of the provisions, which, fortunately for the party, had been stored within the hut, and so escaped the felonious fingers of Uncle Billy, disclosed the fact that with care and prudence they might last ten days longer. "That is," said Mr. Oakhurst *sotto voce* to the Innocent, "if you're willing to board us. If you ain't--and perhaps you'd better not--you can wait till Uncle Billy gets back with provisions." For some occult reason, Mr. Oakhurst could not bring himself to disclose Uncle Billy's rascality, and so offered the hypothesis that he had wandered from the camp and had accidentally stampeded the animals. He dropped a warning to the Duchess and Mother Shipton, who of course know the facts of their associate's defection. "They'll find out the truth about us *all* then they find out anything," he added significantly, "and there's no good frightening them now."

Tom Simson not only put all his worldly store at the disposal of Mr. Oakhurst, but seemed to enjoy the prospect of their enforced seclusion. "We'll have a good camp for a week, and then the snow'll melt, and we'll all go back together." The cheerful gayety of the young man and Mr. Oakhurst's calm infected the others. The Innocent, with the aid of pine boughs, extemporized a thatch for the roofless cabin, and the Duchess directed Piney in the rearrangement of the interior with a taste and tact that opened the blue eyes of that provincial maiden to their fullest extent. "I reckon now you're used to fine things at Poker Flat," said Piney. The Duchess turned away sharply to conceal something that reddened her cheeks through their professional tint, and Mother Shipton requested Piney not to "chatter." But when Mr. Oakhurst returned from a weary search for the trail, he heard the sound of happy laughter echoed from the rocks. He stopped in some alarm, and his thoughts first naturally reverted to the whiskey, which he had prudently cached. "And yet it don't some-how sound like whiskey," said the gambler. It was not until he caught sight of the blazing fire through the still blinding storm, and the group around it, that he settled to the conviction that it was "square fun."

Whether Mr. Oakhurst had cached his cards with the whiskey as something debarred the free access of the community, I cannot say. It was certain that, in Mother Shipton's words, he "didn't say 'cards' once" during that evening. Happily the time was beguiled by an accordion, produced somewhat ostentatiously by Tom Simson from his pack. Notwithstanding some difficulties attending the manipulation of this instrument, Piney Woods managed to pluck several reluctant melodies from its keys, to an accompaniment by the Innocent on a pair of bone castanets. But the crowning festivity of the evening was reached in a rude campmeeting hymn, which the lovers, joining hands, sang, with great earnestness and vociferation. I fear that a certain defiant tone and Covenanter's swing to its chorus, rather than any devotional quality, caused it speedily to infect the others, who at last joined in the refrain:--

"I'm proud to live in the service of the Lord,

And I'm bound to die in His army."

The pines rocked, the storm eddied and whirled above the miserable group, and the flames of their altar leaped heavenward, as if in token of the vow.

At midnight the storm abated, the rolling clouds parted, and the stars glittered keenly above the sleeping camp. Mr. Oakhurst, whose professional habits had enabled him to live on the smallest possible amount of sleep, in dividing the watch with Tom Simson somehow managed to take upon himself the greater part of that duty. He excused himself to the Innocent by saying that he had "often been a week without sleep." "Doing what?" asked Tom. "Poker!" replied Oakhurst sententiously. "When a man gets a streak of luck,--nigger-luck,--he don't get tired. The luck gives in first. Luck," continued the gambler reflectively, "is a mighty queer thing. All you know about it for certain is that it's bound to change. And it's finding out when it's going to change that makes you. We've had a streak of bad luck since we left Poker Flat,--you come along, and slap you get into it, too. If you can hold your cards right along you're all right. For," added the gambler with cheerful irrelevance--

" 'I'm proud to live in the service of the Lord,

And I'm bound to die in His army.' "

The third day came, and the sun, looking through the whitecurtained valley, saw the outcasts divide their slowly decreasing store of provisions for the morning meal. It was one of the peculiarities of that mountain climate that its rays diffused a kindly warmth over the wintry landscape, as if in regretful commiseration of the past. But it revealed drift on drift of snow piled high around the hut,--a hopeless, uncharted, trackless sea of white lying below the rocky shores to which the castaways still clung.

Through the marvelously clear air the smoke of the pastoral village of Poker Flat rose miles away. Mother Shipton saw it, and from a remote pinnacle of her rocky fastness hurled in that direction a final malediction. It was her last vituperative attempt, and perhaps for that reason was invested with a certain degree of sublimity. It did her good, she privately informed the Duchess. "Just you go out there and cuss, and see." She then set herself to the task of amusing "the child," as she and the Duchess were pleased to call Piney. Piney was no chicken, but it was a soothing and original theory of the pair thus to account for the fact that she didn't swear and wasn't improper.

When night crept up again through the gorges, the reedy notes of the accordion rose and fell in fitful spasms and longdrawn gasps by the flickering campfire. But music failed to fill entirely the aching void left by insufficient food, and a new diversion was proposed by Piney,--storytelling. Neither Mr. Oakhurst nor his female companions caring to relate their personal experiences, this plan would have failed too, but for the Innocent. Some months before he had chanced upon a stray copy of Mr. Pope's ingenious translation of the Iliad. He now proposed to narrate the principal incidents of that poem--having thoroughly mastered the argument and fairly forgotten the words--in the current vernacular of Sandy Bar. And so for the rest of that night the Homeric demigods again walked the earth. Trojan bully and wily Greek wrestled in the winds, and the great pines in the canon seemed to bow to the wrath of the son of Peleus. Mr. Oakhurst listened with quiet satisfaction. Most especially was he interested in the fate of "Ashheels," as the Innocent persisted in denominating the "swiftfooted Achilles."

So, with small food and much of Homer and the accordion, a week passed over the heads of the outcasts. The sun again forsook them, and again from leaden skies the snowflakes were sifted over the land. Day by day closer around them drew the snowy circle, until at last they looked from their prison over drifted walls of dazzling white, that towered twenty feet above their heads. It became more and more difficult to replenish their fires, even from the fallen trees beside them, now half hidden in the drifts. And yet no one complained. The lovers turned from the dreary prospect and looked into each other's eyes, and were happy. Mr. Oakhurst settled himself coolly to the losing game before him. The Duchess, more cheerful than she had been, assumed the care of Piney. Only Mother Shipton--once the strongest of the party--seemed to sicken and fade. At midnight on the tenth day she called Oakhurst to her side. "I'm going," she said, in a voice of querulous weakness, "but don't say anything about it. Don't waken the kids. Take the bundle from under my head, and open it." Mr. Oakhurst did so. It contained Mother Shipton's rations for the last week, untouched. "Give 'em to the child," she said, pointing to the sleeping Piney. "You've starved yourself," said the gambler. "That's what they call it," said the woman querulously, as she lay down again, and, turning her face to the wall, passed quietly away.

The accordion and the bones were put aside that day, and Homer was forgotten. When the body of Mother Shipton had been committed to the snow, Mr. Oakhurst took the Innocent aside, and showed him a pair of snowshoes, which he had fashioned from the old packsaddle. "There's one chance in a hundred to save her yet," he said, pointing to Piney; "but it's there," he added, pointing toward Poker Flat. "If you can reach there in two days she's safe." "And you?" asked Tom Simson. "I'll stay here," was the curt reply.

The lovers parted with a long embrace. "You are not going, too?" said the Duchess, as she saw Mr. Oakhurst apparently waiting to accompany him. "As far as the canon," he replied. He turned suddenly and kissed the Duchess, leaving her pallid face aflame, and her trembling limbs rigid with amazement.

Night came, but not Mr. Oakhurst. It brought the storm again and the whirling snow. Then the Duchess, feeding the fire, found that some one had quietly piled beside the hut enough fuel to last a few days longer. The tears rose to her eyes, but she hid them from Piney.

The women slept but little. In the morning, looking into each other's faces, they read their fate. Neither spoke, but Piney, accepting the position of the stronger, drew near and placed her arm around the Duchess's waist. They kept this attitude for the rest of the day. That night the storm reached its greatest fury, and, rending asunder the protecting vines, invaded the very hut.

Toward morning they found themselves unable to feed the fire, which gradually died away. As the embers slowly blackened, the Duchess crept closer to Piney, and broke the silence of many hours: "Piney, can you pray?" "No, dear," said Piney simply. The Duchess, without knowing exactly why, felt relieved, and, putting her head upon Piney's shoulder, spoke no more. And so reclining, the younger and purer pillowing the head of her soiled sister upon her virgin breast, they fell asleep.

The wind lulled as if it feared to waken them. Feathery drifts of snow, shaken from the long pine boughs, flew like white winged birds, and settled about them as they slept. The moon through the rifted clouds looked down upon what had been the camp. But all human stain, all trace of earthly travail, was hidden beneath the spotless mantle mercifully flung from above.

They slept all that day and the next, nor did they waken when voices and footsteps broke the silence of the camp. And when pitying fingers brushed the snow from their wan faces, you could scarcely have told from the equal peace that dwelt upon them which was she that had sinned. Even the law of Poker Flat recognized this, and turned away, leaving them still locked in each other's arms.

But at the head of the gulch, on one of the largest pinetrees, they found the deuce of clubs pinned to the bark with a bowieknife. It bore the following, written in pencil in a firm hand:--

BENEATH THIS TREE

LIES THE BODY

OF

JOHN OAKHURST

WHO HAD A STREAK OF BAD LUCK

ON THE 23D OF NOVEMBER 1850,

AND

HANDED IN HIS CHECK

ON THE 7TH DECEMBER, 1850.

And pulseless and cold, with a Derringer by his side and a bullet in his heart, though still calm as in life, beneath the snow lay he who was at once the strongest and yet the weakest of the outcasts of Poker Flat.

The Maypole of Merry Mount

Nathaniel Hawthorne

Nathaniel Hawthorne (1804-1864) is credited with writing the first American symbolic novel, *The Scarlet Letter,* published in 1850. Contrary to the popular legend that Hawthorne was a recluse, he was actively involved as a public servant. Having studied to be an historian, he acquired the foundation that he needed to set out on a writing career.

After graduating from Bowdoin College he lived quietly in Salem collecting information on the history and spiritual temper of Colonial New England. In 1828 Hawthorne completed his first novel *Fanshawe,* on Bowdoin life, and in 1832 he published his first short story, *The Token.* In 1837 he published the anthology, *Twice Told Tales.*

After marrying Sophia Peabody in 1842 he lived in the Old Manse in Concord. In 1846 he wrote *Mosses from an Old Manse*, which was published serially and as a volume. At this time his success was still minimal and he returned to Salem as a surveyor. It was not until after he published *The Scarlet Letter* in 1850 that he gained recognition as an accomplished writer and achieved economic success.

In 1852 Hawthorne settled in Wayside, Concord, his permanent home. It was at this time that he wrote the novels *The House of the Seven Gables* (1851), *The Blithedale Romance* (1852), and several collections of tales.

Hawthorne's other works include *The Life of Franklin Pierce* (1852), and *The Marble Faun* (1860).

There is an admirable foundation for a philosophic romance in the curious history of the early settlement of Mount Wollaston, or Merry Mount. In the slight sketch here attempted, the facts, recorded on the grave pages of our New England annalists have wrought themselves, almost spontaneously, into a sort of allegory. The masques, mummeries, and festive customs, described in the text, are in accordance with the manners of the age. Authority on these points may be found in Strutt's Book of English Sports and Pastimes.

BRIGHT WERE THE days at Merry Mount, when the Maypole was the banner staff of that gay colony! They who reared it, should their banner be triumphant were to pour sunshine over New England's rugged hills and scatter flower seeds throughout the soil. Jollity and gloom were contending for an empire. Midsummer eve had come, bringing deep verdure to the forest, and roses in her lap, of a more vivid hue than the tender buds of Spring. But May, or her mirthful spirit, dwelt all the year round at Merry Mount, sporting with the Summer months, and revelling with Autumn, and basking in the glow of Winter's fireside. Through a world of toil and care she flitted with a dreamlike smile, and came hither to find a home among the lightsome of Merry Mount.

Never had the Maypole been so gayly decked as at sunset on midsummer eve. This venerated emblem was a pinetree, which had preserved the slender grace of youth, while it equalled the loftiest height of the old wood monarchs. From its top streamed a silken banner, colored like the rainbow. Down nearly to the ground the pole was dressed with birchen boughs, and others of the liveliest green, and some with silvery leaves, fastened by ribbons that fluttered in fantastic knots of twenty different colors, but no sad ones. Garden flowers, and blossoms of the wilderness, laughed gladly forth amid the verdure, so fresh and dewy that they must have grown by magic on that happy pine-tree. Where this green and flowery splendor terminated, the shaft of the Maypole was stained with the seven brilliant hues of the banner at its top. On the lowest green bough hung an abundant wreath of roses, some that had been gathered in the sunniest spots of the forest, and others, of still richer blush, which the colonists had reared from English seed. O, people of the Golden Age, the chief of your husbandry was to raise flowers!

But what was the wild throng that stood hand in hand about the Maypole? It could not be that the fauns and nymphs, when driven from their classic groves and homes of ancient fable, had sought refuge, as all the persecuted did, in the fresh woods of the West. These were Gothic monsters, though perhaps of Grecian ancestry. On the shoulders of a comely youth uprose the head and branching antlers of a stag; a second, human in all other points, had the grim visage of a wolf; a third, still with the trunk and limbs of a mortal man, showed the beard and horns of a venerable he-goat. There was the likeness of a bear erect, brute in all but his hind legs, which were adorned with pink silk stockings. And here again, almost as wondrous, stood a real bear of the dark forest, lending each of his fore paws to the grasp of a human hand, and as ready for the dance as any in that circle. His inferior nature rose half way, to meet his companions as they stooped. Other faces wore the similitude of man or woman, but distorted or extravagant, with red noses pendulous before their mouths, which seemed of awful depth, and stretched from ear to ear in an eternal fit of laughter. Here might be seen the Salvage Man, well known in heraldry, hairy as a baboon, and girdled with green leaves. By his side, a noble figure, but still a counterfeit, appeared an Indian hunter, with feathery crest and wampum belt. Many of this strange company wore fools-caps, and had little bells appended to their garments, tinkling with a silvery sound, responsive to the inaudible music of their gleesome spirits. Some youths and maidens were of soberer garb, yet well maintained their places in the irregular throng by the expression of wild revelry upon their features. Such were the colonists of Merry Mount, as they stood in the broad smile of sunset round their venerated Maypole.

Had a wanderer, bewildered in the melancholy forest, heard their mirth, and stolen a half-affrighted glance, he might have fancied them the crew of Comus, some already transformed to brutes, some midway between man and beast, and the others rioting in the flow of tipsy jollity that foreran the change. But a band of Puritans, who watched the scene, invisible themselves, compared the masques to those devils and ruined souls with whom their superstition peopled the black wilderness.

Within the ring of monsters appeared the two airiest forms that had ever trodden on any more solid footing than a purple and golden cloud. One was a youth in glistening apparel, with a scarf of the rainbow pattern crosswise on his breast. His right hand held a gilded staff, the ensign of high dignity among the revellers, and his left grasped the slender fingers of a fair maiden, not less gayly decorated than himself. Bright roses glowed in contrast with the dark and glossy curls of each, and were scattered round their feet, or had sprung up spontaneously there. Behind this lightsome couple, so close to the Maypole that its boughs shaded his jovial face, stood the figure of an English priest, canonically dressed, yet decked with flowers, in heathen fashion, and wearing a chaplet of the native vine leaves. By the riot of his rolling eye, and the pagan decorations of his holy garb, he seemed the wildest monster there, and the very Comus of the crew.

"Votaries of the Maypole," cried the flower-decked priest, "merrily, all day long, have the woods echoed to your mirth. But be this your merriest hour, my hearts! Lo, here stand the Lord and Lady of the May, whom I, a clerk of Oxford, and high priest of Merry Mount, am presently to join in holy matrimony. Up with your nimble spirits, ye morris-dancers, green men, and glee maidens, bears and wolves, and horned gentlemen! Come; a chorus now, rich with the old mirth of Merry England, and the wilder glee of this fresh forest; and then a dance, to show the youthful pair what life is made of, and how airily they should go through it! All ye that love the Maypole, lend your voices to the nuptial song of the Lord and Lady of the May!"

This wedlock was more serious than most affairs of Merry Mount, where jest and delusion, trick and fantasy, kept up a continual carnival. The Lord and Lady of the May, though their titles must be laid down at sunset, were really and truly to be partners for the dance of life, beginning the measure that same bright eve. The wreath of roses, that hung from the lowest green bough of the Maypole, had been twined for them, and would be thrown over both their heads, in symbol of their flowery union. When the priest had spoken, therefore, a riotous uproar burst from the rout of monstrous figures.

"Begin you the stave, reverend Sir," cried they all; "and never did the woods ring to such a merry peal as we of the Maypole shall send up!"

Immediately a prelude of pipe, cithern, and viol, touched with practised minstrelsy, began to play from a neighboring thicket, in such a mirthful cadence that the boughs of the Maypole quivered to the sound. But the May Lord, he of the gilded staff, chancing to look into his Lady's eyes, was wonder struck at the almost pensive glance that met his own.

"Edith, sweet Lady of the May," whispered he reproachfully, "is yon wreath of roses a garland to hang above our graves, that you look so sad? O, Edith, this is our golden time! Tarnish it not by any pensive shadow of the mind; for it may be that nothing of futurity will be brighter than the mere remembrance of what is now passing."

"That was the very thought that saddened me! How came it in your mind too?" said Edith, in a still lower tone than he, for it was high treason to be sad at Merry Mount. "Therefore do I sigh amid this festive music. And besides, dear Edgar, I struggle as with a dream, and fancy that these shapes of our jovial friends are visionary, and their mirth unreal, and that we are no true Lord and Lady of the May. What is the mystery in heart?"

Just then, as if a spell had loosened them, down came a little shower of withering rose leaves from the Maypole. Alas, for the young lovers! No sooner had their hearts glowed with real passion than they were sensible of something vague and unsubstantial in their former pleasures, and felt a dreary presentiment of inevitable change. From the moment that they truly loved, they had subjected themselves to earth's doom of care and sorrow, and troubled joy, and had no more a home at Merry Mount. That was Edith's mystery. Now leave we the priest to marry them, and the masquers to sport round the Maypole, till the last sunbeam be withdrawn from its summit, and the shadows of the forest mingle gloomily in the dance. Meanwhile, we may discover who these gay people were.

Two hundred years ago, and more, the old world and its inhabitants became mutually weary of each other. Men voyaged by thousands to the West: some to barter glass beads, and such like jewels, for the furs of the Indian hunter; some to conquer virgin empires; and one stern band to pray. But none of these motives had much weight with the colonists of Merry Mount. Their leaders were men who had sported so long with life, that when Thought and Wisdom came, even these unwelcome guests were led astray by the crowd of vanities which they should have put to flight. Erring Thought and perverted wisdom were made to put on masques, and play the fool. The men of whom we speak, after losing the heart's fresh gayety, imagined a wild philosophy of pleasure, and came hither to act out their latest day-dream. They gathered followers from all that giddy tribe whose whole life is like the festal days of soberer men. In their train were minstrels, not unknown in London streets: wandering players, whose theaters had been the halls of noblemen; mummers, rope-dancers, and mountebanks, who would long be missed at wakes, church ales, and fairs; in a word, mirth makers of every sort, such as abounded in that age, but now began to be discountenanced by the rapid growth of Puritanism. Light had their footsteps been on land, and as lightly they came across the sea. Many had been maddened by their previous troubles into a gay despair; others were as madly gay in the flush of youth, like the May Lord and his Lady; but whatever might be the quality of their mirth, old and young were gay at Merry Mount. The young deemed themselves happy. The elder spirits, if they knew that mirth was but the counterfeit of happiness, yet followed the false shadow willfully, because at least her garments glittered brightest. Sworn triflers of a lifetime, they would not venture among the sober truths of life not even to be truly blest.

All the hereditary pastimes of Old England were transplanted hither. The King of Christmas was duly crowned, and the Lord of Misrule bore potent sway. On the Eve of St. John, they felled whole acres of the forest to make bonfires, and danced by the blaze all night, crowned with garlands, and throwing flowers into the flame. At harvest time, though their crop was of the smallest, they made an image with the sheaves of Indian corn, and wreathed it with autumnal garlands, and bore it home triumphantly. But what chiefly characterized the colonists of Merry Mount was their veneration for the Maypole. It has made their true history a poet's tale. Spring decked the hallowed emblem with the young blossoms and fresh green boughs; Summer brought roses of the deepest blush, and the perfected foliage of the forest; Autumn enriched it with that red and yellow gorgeousness which converts each wildwood leaf into a painted flower; and Winter silvered it with sleet, and hung it round with icicles, till it flashed in the cold sunshine, itself a frozen sunbeam. Thus each alternate season did homage to the Maypole, and paid it a tribute of its own richest splendor. Its votaries danced round it, once, at least, in every month; sometimes they called it their religion, or their altar; but always, it was the banner staff of Merry Mount.

Unfortunately, there were men in the new world of a sterner faith than these Maypole worshippers. Not far from Merry Mount was a settlement of Puritans, most dismal wretches, who said their prayers before daylight, and then wrought in the forest or the cornfield till evening made it prayer time again. Their weapons were always at hand to shoot down the straggling savage. When they met in conclave, it was never to keep up the old English mirth, but to hear sermons three hours long, or to proclaim bounties on the heads of wolves and the scalps of Indians. Their festivals were fast days, and their chief pastime the singing of psalms. Woe to the youth or maiden who did but dream of a dance! The selectman nodded to the constable; and there sat the light-heeled reprobate in the stocks; or if he danced it was round the whipping-post, which might be termed the Puritan Maypole.

A party of these grim Puritans, toiling through the difficult woods, each with a horseload of iron armor to burden his footsteps, would sometimes draw near the sunny precincts of Merry Mount. There were the silken colonists, sporting round their Maypole; perhaps teaching a bear to dance, or striving to communicate their mirth to the grave Indian; or masquerading in the skins of deer and wolves, which they had hunted for that especial purpose. Often, the whole colony were playing at blindman's buff, magistrates and all, with their eyes bandaged, except a single scapegoat, whom the blinded sinners pursued by the tinkling of the bells at his garments. Once, it is said, they were seen following a flower-decked corpse, with merriment and festive music, to his grave. But did the dead man laugh? In their quietest time, they sang ballads and told tales, for the edification of their pious visitors; or perplexed them with juggling tricks; or grinned at them through horse collars; and when sport itself grew wearisome, they made game of their own stupidity, and began a yawning match. At the very least of these enormities, the men of iron shook their heads and frowned so darkly that the revellers looked up, imagining that a momentary cloud had overcast the sunshine, which was to be perpetual there. On the other hand, the Puritans affirmed that, when a psalm was pealing from their place of worship, the echo which the forest sent them back seemed often like the chorus of a jolly catch, closing with a roar of laughter. Who but the fiend, and his bond slaves, the crew of Merry Mount, had thus disturbed them? In due time, a feud arose, stern and bitter on one side, and as serious on the other as anything could be among such light spirits as had sworn allegiance to the Maypole. The future complexion of New England was involved in this important quarrel. Should the grizzly saints establish their jurisdiction over the gay sinners, then would their spirits darken all the clime, and make it a land of clouded visages, of hard toil, of sermon and psalm forever. But should the banner staff of Merry Mount be fortunate, sunshine would break upon the hills, and flowers would beautify the forest, and late posterity do homage to the Maypole.

After these authentic passages from history, we return to the nuptials of the Lord and Lady of the May. Alas! we have delayed too long, and must darken our tale too suddenly. As we glance again at the Maypole, a solitary sunbeam is fading from the summit, and leaves only a faint, golden tinge blended with the hues of the rainbow banner. Even that dim light is now withdrawn, relinquishing the whole domain of Merry Mount to the evening gloom, which has rushed so instantaneously from the black surrounding woods. But some of these black shadows have rushed forth in human shape.

Yes, with the setting sun, the last day of mirth had passed from Merry Mount. The ring of gay masquers was disordered and broken; the stag lowered his antlers in dismay; the wolf grew weaker than a lamb; the bells of the morris-dancers tinkled with tremulous affright. The Puritans had played a characteristic part in the Maypole mummeries. Their darksome figures were intermixed with the wild shapes of their foes, and made the scene a picture of the moment, when waking thoughts start up amid the scattered fantasies of a dream. The leader of the hostile party stood in the centre of the circle, while the route of monsters cowered around him, like evil spirits in the presence of a dread magician. No fantastic foolery could look him in the face. So stern was the energy of his aspect, that the whole man, visage, frame, and soul, seemed wrought of iron, gifted with life and thought, yet all of one substance with his headpiece and breastplate. It was the Puritan of Puritans; it was Endicott himself!

"Stand off, priest of Baal!" said he, with a grim frown, and laying no reverent hand upon the surplice. "I know thee, Blackstone! Thou art the man who couldst not abide the rule even of thine own corrupted church, and hast come hither to preach iniquity, and to give example of it in thy life. But now shall it be seen that the Lord hath sanctified this wilderness for peculiar people. Woe unto them that would defile it! And first, for this flower-decked abomination, the altar of thy worship!"

And with his keen sword Endicott assaulted the hallowed Maypole. Nor long did it resist his arm. It groaned with a dismal sound; it showered leaves and rosebuds upon the remorseless enthusiast; and finally, with all its green boughs and ribbons and flowers, symbolic of departed pleasures, down fell the banner staff of Merry Mount. As it sank, tradition says, the evening sky grew darker, and the woods threw forth a more sombre shadow.

"There," cried Endicott, looking triumphantly on his work, "there lies the only Maypole in New England! The thought is strong within me that, by its fall, is shadowed forth the fate of light and idle mirth makers, amongst us and our posterity. Amen, saith John Endicott."

"Amen!" echoed his followers.

But the votaries of the Maypole gave one groan for their idol. At the sound, the Puritan leader glanced at the crew of Comus, each a figure of broad mirth, yet, at this moment, strangely expressive of sorrow and dismay.

"Valiant captain," quoth Peter Palfrey, the Ancient of the band, "what order shall be taken with the prisoners?"

"I thought not to repent me of cutting down a Maypole," replied Endicott, "yet now I could find in my heart to plant it again, and give each of these bestial pagans one other dance round their idol. It would have served rarely for a whipping-post!"

"But there are pine-trees enow," suggested the lieutenant.

"True, good Ancient," said the leader. "Wherefore, bind the heathen crew, and bestow on them a small matter of stripes apiece, as earnest of our future justice. Set some of the rogues in the stocks to rest themselves, so soon as Providence shall bring us to one of our own well-ordered settlements, where such accommodations may be found. Further penalties, such as branding and cropping of ears, shall be thought of hereafter."

"How many stripes for the priest?" inquired Ancient Palfrey.

"None as yet," answered Endicott, bending his iron frown upon the culprit. "It must be for the Great and General Court to determine, whether stripes and long imprisonment, and other grievous penalty, may atone for his transgressions. Let him look to himself! For such as violate our civil order, it may be permitted us to show mercy. But woe to the wretch that troubleth our religion!"

"And this dancing bear," resumed the officer. "Must he share the stripes of his fellows?"

"Shoot him through the head!" said the energetic Puritan. "I suspect witchcraft in the beast."

"Here be a couple of shining ones," continued Peter Palfrey, pointing his weapon at the Lord and Lady of May. "They seem to be of high station among these misdoers. Methinks their dignity will not be fitted with less than a double share of stripes."

Endicott rested on his sword, and closely surveyed the dress and aspect of the hapless pair. There they stood, pale, downcast, and apprehensive. Yet there was an air of mutual support, and of pure affection, seeking aid and giving it, that showed them to be man and wife, with the sanction of a priest upon their love. The youth, in the peril of the moment, had dropped his gilded staff, and thrown his arm about the Lady of the May, who leaned against his breast, too lightly to burden him, but with weight enough to express that their destinies were linked together, for good or evil. They looked first at each other, and then into the grim captain's face. There they stood, in the first hour of wedlock, while the idle pleasures, of which their companions were the emblems, had given place to the sternest cares of life, personified by the dark Puritans. But never had their youthful beauty seemed so pure and high as when its glow was chastened by adversity.

"Youth," said Endicott, "ye stand in an evil case thou and thy maiden wife. Make ready presently, for I am minded that ye shall both have a token to remember your wedding day!"

"Stern man," cried the May Lord, "how can I move thee? Were the means at hand, I would resist to the death. Being powerless, I entreat! Do with me as thou wilt, but let Edith go untouched!"

"Not so," replied the immitigable zealot. "We are not wont to show an idle courtesy to that sex, which requireth the stricter discipline. What sayest thou, maid? Shall thy silken bridegroom suffer thy share of the penalty, besides his own?"

"Be it death," said Edith, "and lay it all on me!"

Truly, as Endicott had said, the poor lovers stood in a woful case. Their foes were triumphant, their friends captive and abased, their home desolate, the benighted wilderness around them, and a rigorous destiny, in the shape of the Puritan leader, their only guide. Yet the deepening twilight could not altogether conceal that the iron man was softened; he smiled at the fair spectacle of early love; he almost sighed for the inevitable blight of early hopes.

"The troubles of life have come hastily on this young couple," observed Endicott. "We will see how they comport themselves under their present trials ere we burden them with greater. If, among the spoil, there be any garments of a more decent fashion, let them be put upon this May Lord and his Lady, instead of their glistening vanities. Look to it, some of you."

"And shall not the youth's hair be cut?" asked Peter Palfrey, looking with abhorrence at the lovelock and long glossy curls of the young man.

"Crop it forthwith, and that in the true pumpkinshell fashion," answered the captain. "Then bring them along with us, but more gently than their fellows. There be qualities in the youth, which may make him valiant to fight, and sober to toil, and pious to pray; and in the maiden, that may fit her to become a mother in our Israel, bringing up babes in better nurture than her own hath been. Nor think ye, young ones, that they are the happiest, even in our lifetime of a moment, who misspend it in dancing round a Maypole!"

And Endicott, the severest Puritan of all who laid the rock foundation of New England, lifted the wreath of roses from the ruin of the Maypole, and threw it, with his own gauntleted hand, over the heads of the Lord and Lady of the May. It was a deed of prophecy. As the moral gloom of the world overpowers all systematic gayety, even so was their home of wild mirth made desolate amid the sad forest. They returned to it no more. But as their flowery garland was wreathed of the brightest roses that had grown there, so, in the tie that united them, were intertwined all the purest and best of their early joys. They went heavenward, supporting each other along the difficult path which it was their lot to tread, and never wasted one regretful thought on the vanities of Merry Mount.

1836   *Twice-Told Tales*

The Legend of Sleepy Hollow

Washington Irving

Washington Irving (1783-1859) is one of the first American writers to create fiction that was intended for entertainment. His predecessors were proponents of literature that was both didactic and utilitarian. He is best remembered for the short stories *Rip Van Winkle* and *The Legend of Sleepy Hollow*.

Irving was the son of a successful New York merchant and was the youngest of eleven children. When he was sixteen he was given the opportunity to study law. At the age of twenty-three he was admitted to the New York Bar.

When Irving was nineteen he published a series of satiric articles in *The Morning Chronicle* under the pseudonym Jonathan Oldstyle. Meanwhile he read voraciously, studied, roamed the Hudson Valley, toured Europe, and was supported by his family's wealth. Later on, until its failure, he went to work in the family business. Although the failure placed family responsibilities in his hands, he still continued writing and completed *The Sketch-Book of Geoffrey Crayon* (1819). The book was an international success and he continued with his writing and resumed his travels.

From 1826 to 1829 he served as a diplomat in Spain, and from 1829 to 1831 he served as secretary of American Legation in London. Irving declined a nomination to Congress and an opportunity to run for mayor of New York. He refused the chance to become President Van Buren's Secretary of the Navy, choosing instead to begin work on *The Life of George Washington* (1855).

> *"A pleasing land of drowsy head it was*
> *Of dreams that wave before the half-shut eye;*
> *And of gay castles in the clouds that pass,*
> *Forever flushing round a summer sky."*
>   *--Castle of Indolence*

IN THE BOSOM of one of those spacious coves which indent the eastern shore of the Hudson, at that broad expansion of the river denominated by the ancient Dutch navigators the Tappaan Zee, and where they always prudently shortened sail and implored the protection of St. Nicholas when they crossed, there lies a small market town or rural port, which by some is called Greensburgh, but which is more generally and properly known by the name of Tarry Town.

This name was given it, we are told, in former days, by the good housewives of the adjacent country, from the inveterate propensity of their husbands to linger about the village tavern on market days. Be that as it may, I do not vouch for the fact, but merely advert to it, for the sake of being precise and authentic. Not far from this village, perhaps about three miles, there is a little valley or rather lap of land among high hills, which is one of the quietest places in the whole world. A small brook glides through it, with just murmur enough to lull one to repose, and the occasional whistle of a quail, or tapping of a woodpecker, is almost the only sound that ever breaks in upon the uniform tranquillity.

I recollect that, when a stripling, my first exploit in squirrel-shooting was in a grove of tall walnuttrees that shades one side of the valley. I had wandered into it at noon-time, when all nature is peculiarly quiet, and was startled by the roar of my own gun, as it broke the sabbath stillness around and was prolonged and reverberated by the angry echoes. If ever I should wish for a retreat whither I might steal from the world and its distractions, and dream quietly away the remnant of a troubled life, I know of none more promising than this little valley.

From the listless repose of the place and the peculiar character of its inhabitants, who are descendants from the original Dutch settlers, this sequestered glen has long been known by the name of Sleepy Hollow, and its rustic lads are called the Sleepy Hollow Boys throughout all the neighboring country. A drowsy, dreamy influence seems to hang over the land and to pervade the very atmosphere. Some say that the place was bewitched by a high German doctor, during the early days of the settlement; others, that an old Indian chief, the prophet or wizard of his tribe, held his powwows there before the country was discovered by Master Hendrick Hudson. Certain it is, the place still continues under the sway of some witching power that holds a spell over the minds of the good people, causing them to walk in a continual reverie. They are given to all kinds of marvelous beliefs; are subject to trances and visions, and frequently see strange sights, and hear music and voices in the air.

The whole neighborhood abounds with local tales, haunted spots, and twilight superstitions; stars shoot and meteors glare oftener across the valley than in any other part of the country, and the nightmare, with her whole nine fold, seems to make it the favorite scene of her gambols.

The dominant spirit, however, that haunts this enchanted region and seems to be commander-in-chief of all the powers of the air, the apparition of a figure on horseback without a head. It is said by some to be the ghost of a Hessian trooper, whose head had been carried away by a cannon-ball in some nameless battle during the revolutionary war, and who is ever and anon seen by the country folk, hurrying along in the gloom of night, as if on the wings of the wind. His haunts are not confined to the valley, but extend at times to the adjacent roads, and especially to the vicinity of a church that is at no great distance. Indeed, certain of the most authentic historians of those parts, who have been careful in collecting and collating the floating facts concerning this specter, allege that, the body of the trooper having been buried in the churchyard, the ghost rides forth to the scene of battle in mighty quest of his head, and that the rushing speed with which he sometimes passes along the hollow like a midnight blast is owing to his being belated and in a hurry to get back to the churchyard before daybreak.

Such is the general purport of this legendary superstition, which has furnished materials for many a wild story in that region of shadows, and the specter is known at all the country firesides by the name of The Headless Horseman of Sleepy Hollow.

It is remarkable that the visionary propensity I have mentioned is not confined to the native inhabitants of the valley, but is unconsciously imbibed by every one who resides there for a time. However wide awake they may have been before they entered that sleepy region, they are sure, in a little time, to inhale the witching influence of the air, and begin to grow imaginative--to dream dreams and see apparitions.

I mention this peaceful spot with all possible laud; for it is in such little retired Dutch valleys, found here and there embosomed in the great State of New York, that population, manners and customs remain fixed, while the great torrent of migration and improvement, which is making such incessant changes in other parts this restless country, sweeps by them unobserved. They are like those little nooks of still water which border a rapid stream, where we may see the straw and bubble riding quietly at anchor, or slowly revolving in their mimic harbor, undisturbed by the rush of the passing current. Tho many years have elapsed since I trod the drowsy shades of Sleepy Hollow, yet I question whether I should not still find the same trees and the same families vegetating in its sheltered bosom.

In this byplace of nature there abode, in a remote period of American history, that is to say, some thirty years since, a worthy wight of the name of Ichabod Crane, who sojourned, or, as he expressed it, "tarried," in Sleepy Hollow, for the purpose of instructing the children of the vicinity. He was a native of Connecticut, a State which supplies the Union with pioneers for the mind as well as for the forest, and sends forth yearly its legions of frontier woodmen and country schoolmasters.

The cognomen of Crane was not inapplicable to his person. He was tall, but exceedingly lank, with narrow shoulders, long arms and legs, hands that dangled a mile out of his sleeves, feet that might have served for shovels, and his whole frame most loosely hung together. His head was small and flat at top, with huge ears, large green glassy eyes, and a long snipe nose, so that it looked like a weathercock perched upon his spindle neck to tell which way the wind blew. To see him striding along the profile of a hill on a windy day, with his clothes bagging and fluttering about him, one might have mistaken him for the genius of famine descending upon the earth, or some scarecrow eloped from a cornfield.

His schoolhouse was a low building of one large room, rudely constructed of logs, the windows partly glazed and partly patched with leaves of copybooks. It was most ingeniously secured at vacant hours by a withe twisted in the handle of the door, and stakes set against the windowshutters; so that, tho a thief might get in with perfect ease, he would find some embarrassment in getting out--an idea most probably borrowed by the architect, Yost Van Houten, from the mystery of an eelpot. The schoolhouse stood in a rather lonely but pleasant situation, just at the foot of a woody hill, with a brook running close by and a formidable birch-tree growing at one end of it. From hence the low murmur of his pupils' voices, conning over their lessons, might be heard of a drowsy summer's day, like the hum of a beehive; interrupted now and then by the authoritative voice of the master in the tone of menace or command; or, peradventure, by the appalling sound of the birch, as he urged some tardy loiterer along the flowery path of knowledge. Truth to say, he was a conscientious man, that ever bore in mind the golden maxim, "spare the rod and spoil the child."--Ichabod Crane's scholars certainly were not spoiled.

I would not have it imagined, however, that he was one of those cruel potentates of the school who joy in the smart of their subjects; on the contrary, he administered justice with discrimination rather than severity, taking the burden off the backs of the weak and laying it on those of the strong. Your mere puny stripling, that winced at the least flourish of the rod, was passed by with indulgence; but the claims of justice were satisfied by inflicting a double portion on some little, tough, wrongheaded, broad-skirted Dutch urchin, who sulked and swelled and grew dogged and sullen beneath the birch. All this he called "doing his duty by their parents"; and he never inflicted a chastisement without following it by the assurance, so consolatory to the smarting urchin, that "he would remember it and thank him for it the longest day he had to live."

When school hours were over, he was even the companion and playmate of the larger boys; and on holy-day afternoons would convoy some of the smaller ones home, who happened to have pretty sisters, or good housewives for mothers, noted for the comforts of the cupboard. Indeed, it behooved him to keep on good terms with his pupils. The revenue arising from his school was small, and would have been scarcely sufficient to furnish him with daily bread, for he was a huge feeder, and, tho lank, had the dilating powers of an anaconda; but to help out his maintenance, he was, according to country custom in those parts, boarded and lodged at the houses of the farmers whose children he instructed. With these he lived successively a week at a time, thus going the rounds of the neighborhood with all his worldly effects tied up in a cotton handkerchief.

That all this might not be too onerous on the purses of his rustic patrons, who are apt to consider the costs of schooling a grievous burden and schoolmasters as mere drones, he had various ways of rendering himself both useful and agreeable. He assisted the farmers occasionally in the lighter labors of their farms; helped to make hay; mended the fences; took the horses to water; drove the cows from pasture, and cut wood for the winter fire. He laid aside, too, all the dominant dignity and absolute sway with which he lorded it in his little empire, the school, and became wonderfully gentle and ingratiating. He found favor in the eyes of the mothers, by petting the children, particularly the youngest; and like the lion bold, which whilom so magnanimously the lamb did hold, he would sit with a child on one knee and rock a cradle with his foot for whole hours together.

In addition to his other vocations, he was the singing-master of the neighborhood, and picked up many bright shillings by instructing the young folks in psalmody. It was a matter of no little vanity to him on Sundays to take his station in front of the church gallery, with a band of chosen singers; where, in his own mind, he completely carried away the palm from the parson. Certain it is, his voice resounded far above all the rest of the congregation, and there are peculiar quavers still to be heard in that church, and which may even be heard half a mile off, quite to the opposite side of the mill-pond, on a still Sunday morning, which are said to be legitimately descended from the nose of Ichabod Crane. Thus by divers little makeshifts, in that ingenious way which is commonly denominated "by hook and by crook," the worthy pedagog got on tolerably enough, and was thought, by all who understood nothing of the labor of head-work, to have a wonderfully easy life of it.

The schoolmaster is generally a man of some importance in the female circle of a rural neighborhood; being considered a kind of idle gentleman-like personage, of vastly superior taste and accomplishments to the rough country swains, and, indeed, inferior in learning only to the parson. His appearance, therefore, is apt to occasion some little stir at the teatable of a farmhouse and the addition of a supernumerary dish of cakes or sweetmeats, or, peradventure, the parade of a silver teapot. Our man of letters, therefore, was peculiarly happy in the smiles of all the country damsels. How he would figure among them in the churchyard, between services on Sundays! gathering grapes for them from the wild vines that overrun the surrounding trees; reciting for their amusement all the epitaphs on the tombstones, or sauntering, with a whole bevy of them, along the banks of the adjacent mill-pond; while the more bashful country bumpkins hung sheepishly back, envying his superior elegance and address.

From his half itinerant life, also, he was a kind of traveling gazette, carrying the whole budget of local gossip from house to house, so that his appearance was always greeted with satisfaction. He was, moreover, esteemed by the women as a man of great erudition, for he had read several books quite through, and was a perfect master of Cotton Mather's "History of New England Witchcraft," in which, by the way, he most firmly and potently believed.

He was, in fact, an odd mixture of small shrewdness and simple credulity. His appetite for the marvelous, and his powers of digesting it, were equally extraordinary; and both had been increased by his residence in this spell-bound region. No tale was too gross or monstrous for his capacious swallow. It was often his delight, after his school was dismissed in the afternoon, to stretch himself on the rich bed of clover, bordering the little brook that whimpered by his schoolhouse, and there con over old Mather's direful tales, until the gathering dusk of evening made the printed page a mere mist before his eyes. Then, as he wended his way, by swamp and stream and awful woodland, to the farmhouse where he happened to be quartered, every sound of nature, at that witching hour, fluttered his excited imagination: the moan of the whip-poor-will from the hillside; the boding cry of the tree-toad, that harbinger of storm; the dreary hooting of the screech-owl, or the sudden rustling in the thicket of birds frightened from their roost. The fireflies, too, which sparkled most vividly in the darkest places, now and then startled him, as one of uncommon brightness would stream across his path; and if, by chance, a huge blockhead of a beetle came winging his blundering flight against him, the poor varlet was ready to give up the ghost, with the idea that he was struck with a witch's token. His only resource on such occasions, either to drown thought or drive away evil spirits, was to sing psalm tunes; and the good people of Sleepy Hollow, as they sat by their doors of an evening, were often filled with awe at hearing his nasal melody, "in linked sweetness long drawn out," floating from the distant hill, or along the dusky road.

Another of his sources of fearful pleasure was to pass long winter evenings with the old Dutch wives, as they sat spinning by the fire, with a row of apples roasting and sputtering along the hearth, and listen to their marvelous tales of ghosts and goblins, and haunted fields and haunted brooks, and haunted bridges and haunted houses, and particularly of the headless horseman, or galloping Hessian of the Hollow, as they some-times called him. He would delight them equally by his anecdotes of witchcraft, and of the direful omens and portentous sights and sounds in the air, which prevailed in the earlier times of Connecticut; and would frighten them woefully with speculations upon comets and shooting stars, and with the alarming fact that the world did absolutely turn round, and that they were half the time topsyturvy!

But if there was a pleasure in all this, while snugly cuddling in the chimney corner of a chamber that was all of a ruddy glow from the crackling wood fire, and where, of course, no specter dared to show its face, it was dearly purchased by the terrors of his subsequent walk homeward. What fearful shapes and shadows beset his path, amid the dim and ghastly glare of a snowy night!--With what wistful look did he eye every trembling ray of light streaming across the waste fields from some distant window!--How often was he appalled, by some shrub covered with snow, which, like a sheeted specter, beset his very path!--How often did he shrink with curdling awe at the sound of his own steps on the frosty crust beneath his feet, and dread to look over his shoulder, lest he should behold some uncouth being tramping close behind him!--and how often was he thrown into complete dismay by some rushing blast, howling among the trees, in the idea that it was the galloping Hessian on one of his mighty scourings!

All these, however, were mere terrors of the night, fantoms of the mind, that walk in darkness: and tho he had seen many specters in his time, and had been more than once beset by Satan in divers shapes in his lonely perambulations, yet daylight put an end to all these evils; and he would have passed a pleasant life of it, in despite of the Devil and all his works, if his path had not been crossed by a being that causes more perplexity to mortal man than ghosts, goblins, and the whole race of witches put together; and that was--a woman.

Among the musical disciples who assembled, one evening in each week, to receive his instructions in psalmody, was Katrina Van Tassel, the daughter and only child of a substantial Dutch farmer. She was a blooming lass of fresh eighteen; plump as a partridge, ripe and melting and rosy-cheeked as one of her father's peaches, and universally famed, not merely for her beauty, but her vast expectations. She was withal a little of a coquet as might be perceived even in her dress, which was a mixture of ancient and modern fashions, as most suited to set off her charms. She wore the ornaments of pure yellow gold which her great-great-grand-mother had brought over from Saardam; the tempting stomacher of the olden time, and withal a provokingly short petticoat, to display the prettiest foot and ankle in the country round.

Ichabod Crane had a soft and foolish heart toward the sex; and it is not to be wondered at that so tempting a morsel soon found favor in his eyes, more specially after he had visited her in her paternal mansion. Old Baltus Van Tassel was a perfect picture of a thriving, contented, liberal-hearted farmer. He seldom, it is true, sent either his eyes or his thoughts beyond the boundaries of his own farm; but within these, everything was snug, happy, and well-conditioned. He was satisfied with his wealth, but not proud of it; and piqued himself upon the hearty abundance, rather than the style in which he lived. His stronghold situated on the banks of the Hudson, in one of those green, sheltered, fertile nooks in which the Dutch farmers are so fond of nestling. A great elm-tree spread its broad branches over it, at the foot of which bubbled up a spring of the softest and sweetest water, in a little well formed of a barrel, and then stole sparkling away through the grass, to a neighboring brook that babbled along among alders and dwarf willows. Hard by the farmhouse was a vast barn that might have served for a church, every window and crevice of which seemed bursting forth with the treasures of the farm; the flail was busily resounding within it from morning to night; swallows and martins skimmed twittering about the eaves; and rows of pigeons, some with one eye turned up, as if watching weather, some with their heads under their wings, or buried in their bosoms, and others, swelling, and cooing, and bowing about their dames, were enjoying the sunshine on the roof. Sleek, unwieldy porkers were grunting in the repose and abundance of their pens from whence sallied forth, now and then, troops of sucking pigs, as if to snuff the air. A stately squadron of snowy geese were riding in an adjoining pond, convoying whole fleets of ducks; regiments of turkeys were gobbling through the farmyard, and guineafowls fretting about it like ill-tempered housewives, with their peevish, discontented cry. Before the barn door strutted the gallant cock, that pattern of a husband, a warrior and a fine gentleman, clapping his burnished wings and crowing in the pride and gladness of his heart--sometimes tearing up the earth with his feet, and then generously calling his ever-hungry family of wives and children to enjoy the rich morsel which he had discovered.

The pedagog's mouth watered as he looked upon this sumptuous promise of luxurious winter fare. In his devouring mind's eye, he pictured to himself every roasting pig running about, with a pudding in its belly and an apple in its mouth; the pigeons were snugly put to bed in a comfortable pie and tucked in with a coverlet of crust; the geese were swimming in their own gravy, and the ducks pairing cosily in dishes, like snug married couples, with a decent competency of onion sauce. In the porkers he saw carved out the future sleek side of bacon and juicy relishing ham; not a turkey, but he beheld daintily trussed up, with its gizzard under its wing, and, peradventure, a necklace of savory sausages; and even bright chanticleer himself lay sprawling on his back, in a side dish, with uplifted claws, as if craving that quarter which his chivalrous spirit disdained to ask while living.

As the enraptured Ichabod fancied all this, and as he rolled his great green eyes over the fat meadow lands, the rich fields of wheat, of rye, of buckwheat and Indian corn, and the orchards burdened with ruddy fruit, which surrounded the warm tenement of Van Tassel, his heart yearned after the damsel who was to inherit these domains, and his imagination expanded with the idea how they might be readily turned into cash, and the money invested in immense tracts of wild land and shingle palaces in the wilderness. Nay, his busy fancy already realized his hopes, and presented to him the blooming Katrina, with a whole family of children mounted on the top of a wagon loaded with household trumpery, with pots and kettles dangling beneath; and he beheld himself bestriding a pacing mare, with a colt at her heels, setting out for Kentucky, Tennessee--or the Lord knows where!

When he entered the house, the conquest of his heart was complete. It was one of those spacious farmhouses, with highridged, but lowlysloping roofs, built in the style handed down from the first Dutch settlers. The low projecting eaves forming a piazza along the front capable of being closed up in bad weather. Under this were hung flails, harness, various utensils of husbandry, and nets for fishing in the neighboring river. Benches were built along the sides for summer use; and a great spinningwheel at one end and a churn at the other showed the various uses to which this important porch might be devoted. From this piazza the wonderful Ichabod entered the hall, which formed the center of the mansion, and the place of usual residence. Here, rows of resplendent pewter, ranged on a long dresser, dazzled his eyes. In one corner stood a huge bag of wool, ready to be spun; in another, a quantity of linseywoolsey just from the loom; ears of Indian corn and strings of dried applies and peaches hung in gay festoons along the walls, mingled with the gaud of red peppers; and a door left ajar gave him a peep into the best parlor, where the clawfooted chairs, and dark mahogany tables, shone like mirrors; andirons, with their accompanying shovel and tongs, glistened from their covert of asparagus tops; mock-oranges and conch shells decorated the mantelpiece; strings of various colored birds' eggs were suspended above it; a great ostrich egg was hung, from the center of the room, and a corner cupboard, knowingly left open, displayed immense treasures of old silver and wellmended china.

From the moment Ichabod laid his eyes upon these regions of delight, the peace of his mind was at an end, and his only study was how to gain the affections of the peerless daughter of Van Tassel. In this enterprise, however, he had more real difficulties than generally fell to the lot of a knighterrant of yore, who seldom had anything but giants, enchanters, fiery dragons, and such like easily conquered adversaries, to contend with; and had to make his way merely through gates of iron and brass and walls of adamant to the castlekeep, where the lady of his heart was confined; all which he achieved as easily as a man would carve his way to the center of a Christmas pie, and then the lady gave him her hand as a matter of course. Ichabod, on the contrary, had to win his way to the heart of a country coquet, beset with a labyrinth of whims and caprices, which were forever presenting new difficulties and impediments, and he had to encounter a host of fearful adversaries of real flesh and blood, the numerous rustic admirers who beset every portal to her heart; keeping a watchful and angry eye upon each other, but ready to fly out in the common cause against any new competitor.

Among these, the most formidable was a burly, roaring, roisterous blade, of the name of Abraham, or, according to the Dutch abbreviation, Brom Van Brunt, hero of the country round, which rung, with his feats of strength and hardihood. He was broad-shouldered and doublejointed, with short curly black hair, and a bluff, but not unpleasant countenance, having a mingled air of fun and arrogance. From his Herculean frame and great powers of limb, he had received the nickname of Brom Bones, by which he was universally known. He was famed for great knowledge and skill in horsemanship, being as dexterous on horseback as a Tartar. He was foremost at all races and cockfights, and with the ascendency which bodily strength always acquires in rustic life, was the umpire in all disputes, setting his hat on one side, and giving his decisions with an air and tone that admitted of no gainsay or appeal. He was always ready for either a fight or a frolic; had more mischief than illwill in his position; and, with all his overbearing roughness, there was a strong dash of waggish goodhumor at bottom. He had three or four boon companions of his own stamp, who regarded him as their model, and at the head of whom he scoured the country, attending every scene of feud or merriment for miles round. In cold weather, he was distinguished by a fur cap, surmounted with a flaunting fox's tail; and when the folks at a country gathering descried this wellknown crest at a distance, whisking about among a squad of hard riders, they always stood by for a squall. Sometimes his crew would be heard dashing along past the farmhouses at midnight, with whoop and halloo, like a troop of Don Cossacks, and the old dames, startled out of their sleep, would listen for a moment till the hurry-scurry had clattered by, and then exclaim, "Ay, there goes Brom Bones and his gang!" The neighbors looked upon him with a mixture of awe, admiration, and goodwill; and when any madcap prank or rustic brawl occurred in the vicinity, always shook their heads, and warranted Brom Bones was at the bottom of it.

This rantipole hero had for some time singled out the blooming Katrina for the object of his uncouth gallantries, and tho his amorous toyings were something like the gentle caresses and endearments of a bear, yet it was whispered that she did not altogether discourage his hopes. Certain it is, his advances were signals for rival candidates to retire, who felt no inclination to cross a lion in his amors, insomuch that when his horse was seen tied to Van Tassel's paling, on a Sunday night, a sure sign that his master was courting, or, as it is termed, "sparking," within, all other suitors passed by in despair and carried the war into other quarters.

Such was the formidable rival with whom Ichabod Crane had to contend, and considering all things, a stouter man than he would have shrunk from the competition, and a wiser man would have despaired. He had, however, a happy mixture of pliability and perseverance in his nature, he was in form and spirit like a supplejack--yielding, but tough; tho he bent, he never broke; and tho he bowed beneath the slightest pressure, yet, the moment it was away--jerk!--he was as erect and carried his head as high as ever.

To have taken the field openly against his rival would have been madness; for he was not a man to be thwarted in his amors, any more than that stormy lover, Achilles. Ichabod, therefore, made his advances in a quiet and gently insinuating manner. Under cover of his character of singing-master, he made frequent visits at the farmhouse; not that he had anything to apprehend from the meddlesome interference of parents, which is so often a stumblingblock in the path of lovers. Balt Van Tassel was an easy, indulsent soul; he loved his daughter better even than his pipe, and like a reasonable man, and an excellent father, let her have her way in everything. His notable little wife, too, had enough to do to attend to her housekeeping and manage the poultry; for, as she sagely observed, ducks and geese are foolish things, and must be looked after, but girls can take care of themselves. Thus, while the busy dame bustled about the house, or plied her spinningwheel at one end of the piazza, honest Balt would sit smoking his evening pipe at the other, watching the achievements of a little wooden warrior, who, armed with a sword in each hand, was most valiantly fighting the wind on the pinnacle of the barn. In the meantime, Ichabod would carry on his suit with the daughter by the side of the spring under the great elm, or sauntering along in the twilight, that hour so favorable to the lover's eloquence.

I profess not to know how women's hearts are wooed and won. To me they have always been matters of riddle and admiration. Some seem to have but one vulnerable point, or door of access; while others have a thousand avenues, and may be captured in a thousand different ways. It is a great triumph of skill to gain the former, but a still greater proof of generalship to maintain possession of the latter, for a man must battle for his fortress at every door and window. He that wins a thousand common hearts is therefore entitled to some renown; but he who keeps undisputed sway over the heart of a coquet, is indeed a hero. Certain it is, this was not the case with the redoubtable Brom Bones; and from the moment Ichabod Crane made his advances, the interests of the former evidently declined: his horse was no longer seen tied at the palings on Sunday nights, and a deadly feud gradually arose between him and the preceptor of Sleepy Hollow.

Brom, who had a degree of rough chivalry in his nature, would fain have carried matters to open warfare, and settled their pretensions to the lady according to the mode of those most concise and simple reasoners, the knightserrant of yore--by single combat; but Ichabod was too conscious of the superior might of his adversary to enter the lists against him; he had overheard the boast of Bones, that he would "double the schoolmaster up, and put him on a shelf"; and he was too wary to give him an opportunity. There was something extremely provoking in this obstinately pacific system; it left Brom no alternative but to draw upon the funds of rustic waggery in his disposition, and to play off boorish practical jokes upon his rival. Ichabod became the object of whimsical persecution to Bones and his gang of rough riders. They harried his hitherto peaceful domains; smoked out his singingschool, by stopping up the chimney; broke into the schoolhouse at night, in spite of its formidable fastenings of withe and window stakes, and turned everything topsyturvy; so that the poor schoolmaster began to think all the witches in the country held their meetings there. But what was still more annoying, Brom took all opportunities of turning him into ridicule in presence of his mistress, and had a scoundrel dog whom he taught to whine in the most ludicrous manner, and introduced as a rival of Ichabod's, to instruct her in psalmody.

In this way, matters went on for some time, without producing any material effect on the relative situations of the contending powers. On a fine autumnal afternoon, Ichabod, in pensive mood, sat enthroned on the lofty stool from whence he usually watched all the concerns of his little literary realm. In his hand he swayed a ferule, that scepter of despotic power; the birch of justice reposed on three nails, behind the throne, a constant terror to evil doers; while on the desk before him might be seen sundry contraband articles and prohibited weapons, detected upon the persons of idle urchins, such as halfmunched apples, pop-guns, whirligigs, flycages, and whole legions of rampant little paper gamecocks. Apparently there had been some appalling act of justice recently inflicted, for his scholars were all busily intent upon their books, or slyly whispering behind them with one eye kept upon the master; and a kind of buzzing stillness reigned throughout the schoolroom. It was suddenly interrupted by the appearance of a negro in towcloth jacket and trousers, a round crowned fragment of a hat, like the cap of Mercury, and mounted on the back of a ragged, wild, halfbroken colt, which he managed with a rope by way of halter. He came clattering up to the school door with an invitation to Ichabod to attend a merry-making, or "quilting frolic," to be held that evening at Mynheer Van Tassel's; and having delivered his message with that air of importance, and effort at fine language, which a negro is apt to display on petty embassies of the kind, he dashed over the brook, and, was seen scampering away up the hollow, full of the importance and hurry of his mission.

All was now bustle and hubbub in the late quiet schoolroom. The scholars were hurried through their lessons, without stopping at trifles; those who were nimble skipped over half with impunity, and those who were tardy had a smart application now and then in the rear, to quicken their speed, or help them over a tall word. Books were flung aside, without being put away on the shelves; inkstands were overturned, benches thrown down, and the whole school was turned loose an hour before the usual time; bursting forth like a legion of young imps, yelping and racketing about the green, in joy at their early emancipation.

The gallant Ichabod now spent at least an extra half-hour at his toilet, brushing and furbishing up his best, and indeed only suit of rusty black, and arranging his looks by a bit of broken lookingglass that hung up in the schoolhouse. That he might make his appearance before his mistress in the true style of a cavalier, he borrowed a horse from the farmer with whom he was domiciliated, a choleric old Dutchman, of the name of Hans Van Ripper, and thus gallantly mounted, issued forth like a knight-errant in quest of adventures. But it is meet I should, in the true spirit of romantic story, give some account of the looks and equipment of my hero and his steed. The animal he bestrode was a broken-down plow-horse that had outlived almost everything but his viciousness. He was gaunt and shagged, with a ewe neck and a head like a hammer; his rusty mane and tail were tangled and knotted with burrs; one eye had lost its pupil, and was glaring and spectral, but the other had the gleam of a genuine devil in it. Still he must have had fire and mettle in his day, if we may judge from his name, which was Gunpowder. He had, in fact, been a favorite steed of his master's, the choleric Van Ripper, who was a furious rider, and had infused, very probably, some of his own spirit into the animal; for, old and broken-down as he looked, there was more of the lurking devil in him than in any young filly in the country.

Ichabod was a suitable figure for such a steed. He rode with short stirrups, which brought his knees nearly up to the pommel of the saddle; his sharp elbows stuck out like grasshoppers'; he carried his whip perpendicularly in his hand, like a scepter, and as the horse jogged on, the motion of his arms was not unlike the flapping of a pair of wings. A small wool hat rested on the top of his nose, for so his scanty strip of forehead might be called, and the skirts of his black coat fluttered out almost to the horse's tail. Such was the appearance of Ichabod and his steed as they shambled out of the gate of Hans Van Ripper, and it was altogether such an apparition as is seldom to be met with in broad daylight.

It was, as I have said, a fine autumnal day; the sky was clear and serene, and nature wore that rich and golden livery which we always associate with the idea of abundance. The forests had put on their sober brown and yellow, while some trees of the tenderer kind had been nipped by the frosts into brilliant dyes of orange, purple, and scarlet. Streaming files of wild ducks began to make their appearance high in the air; the bark of the squirrel might be heard from the groves of beech and hickory-nuts, and the pensive whistle of the quail at intervals from the neighboring stubble-field.

The small birds were taking their farewell banquets. In the fulness of their revelry, they fluttered, chirping and frolicking, from bush to bush and tree to tree, capricious from the very profusion and variety around them. There was the honest cock-robin, the favorite game of stripling sportsmen, with its loud querulous note, and the twittering blackbirds flying in sable clouds; and the golden-winged woodpecker, with his crimson crest, his broad black gorget and splendid plumage; and the cedar-bird, with its redtipped wings and yellowtipped tail, and its little monteiro cap of feathers; and the blue jay, that noisy coxcomb, in his gay light blue coat and white underclothes, screaming and chattering, nodding, and bobbing, and bowing, and pretending to be on good terms with every songster of the grove.

As Ichabod jogged slowly on his way, his eye, ever open to every symptom of culinary abundance, ranged with delight over the treasures of jolly autumn. On all sides he beheld vast store of apples, some hanging in oppressive opulence on the trees, some gathered into baskets and barrels for the market, others heaped up in rich piles for the ciderpress. Further on he beheld great fields of Indian corn, with its golden ears peeping from their leafy coverts and holding out the promise of cakes and hastypudding; and the yellow pumpkins lying beneath them, turning up their fair round bellies to the sun, and giving ample prospects of the most luxurious of pies; and anon he passed the fragrant buckwheat fields, breathing the odor of the beehive, and as he beheld them, soft anticipations stole over his mind of dainty slapjacks, wellbuttered, and garnished with honey or treacle, by the delicate little dimpled hand of Katrina Van Tassel.

Thus feeding his mind with many sweet thoughts and "sugared suppositions," he journeyed along the sides of a range of hills which look out upon some of the goodliest scenes of the mighty Hudson. The sun gradually wheeled his broad disk down into the west. The wide bosom of the Tappaan Zee lay motionless and glassy, excepting that here and there a gentle undulation waved and prolonged the blue shadow of the distant mountain. A few amber clouds floated in the sky, without a breath of air to move them. The horizon was of a fine golden tint, changing gradually into a pure apple green, and from that into the deep blue of the midheaven. A slanting ray lingered on the woody crests of the precipices that overhung some parts of the river, giving greater depth to the dark gray and purple of their rocky sides. A sloop was loitering in the distance, dropping slowly down with the tide, her sail hanging uselessly against the mast; and as the reflection of the sky gleamed along the still water, it seemed as if the vessel was suspended in the air.

It was toward evening that Ichabod arrived at the castle of the Heer Van Tassel, which he found thronged with the pride and flower of the adjacent country. Old farmers, a spare leathernfaced race, in homespun coats and breeches, blue stockings, huge shoes, and magnificent pewter buckles. Their brisk, withered little dames, in close crimped caps, longwaisted gowns, homespun petticoats, with scissors and pincushions, and gay calico pockets hanging on the outside. Buxom lasses, almost as antiquated as their mothers, except where a straw hat, a fine ribbon, or perhaps a white frock, gave symptoms of city innovations. The sons in short squareskirted coats, with rows of stupendous brass buttons, and their hair generally cued in the fashion of the times, especially if they could procure an eelskin for the purpose, it being esteemed throughout that country as a potent nourisher and strengthener of the hair.

Brom Bones, however, was the hero of the scene, having come to the gathering on his favorite steed Daredevil, a creature, like himself, full of mettle and mischief, and which no one but himself could manage. He was, in fact, noted for preferring vicious animals, given to all kinds of tricks which kept the rider in constant risk of his neck, for he held a tractable well-broken horse as unworthy of a lad of spirit.

Fain would I pause to dwell upon the world of charms that burst upon the enraptured gaze of my hero, as he entered the state parlor of Van Tassel's mansion. Not those of the bevy of buxom lasses, with their luxurious display of red and white, but the ample charms of a genuine Dutch country teatable, in the sumptuous time of autumn. Such heapedup platters of cakes of various and almost indescribable kinds, known only to experienced Dutch housewives! There was the doughty doughnut, the tender olykoek, and crisp and crumbling cruller; sweet cakes and short cakes, ginger cakes and honey cakes, and the whole family of cakes. And then there were apple pies, and peach pies, and pumpkin pies; besides slices of ham and smoked beef; and moreover delectable dishes of pre- served plums, and peaches, and pears, and quinces; not to mention broiled shad and roasted chickens; together with bowls of milk and cream, all mingled higgledypiggledy, pretty much as I have enumerated them, with the motherly teapot sending up its clouds of vapor from the midst-- Heaven bless the mark! I want breath and time to discuss this banquet as it deserves, and am too eager to get on with my story. Happily, Ichabod Crane was not in so great a hurry as his historian, but did ample justice to every dainty.

He was a kind and thankful creature, whose heart dilated in proportion as his skin was filled with good cheer, and whose spirits rose with eating, as some men's do with drink. He could not help, too, rolling his large eyes round him as he ate, and chuckling with the possibility that he might one day be lord of all this scene of almost unimaginable luxury and splendor. Then, he thought, how soon he'd turn his back upon old the schoolhouse; snap his fingers in the face of Hans Van Ripper, and every other niggardly patron, and kick any itinerant pedagog out of doors that should dare to call him comrade!

Old Baltus Van Tassel moved about among his guests with a face dilated with content and goodhumor, round and jolly as the harvest moon. His hospitable attentions were brief, but expressive, being confined to a shake of the hand, a slap on the shoulder, a loud laugh, and a pressing invitation to "fall to and help themselves."

And now the sound of the music from the common room, or hall, summoned to the dance. The musician was an old grayheaded negro, who had been the itinerant orchestra of the neighborhood for more than half a century. His instrument was as old and battered as himself. The greater part of the time he scraped away on two or three strings, accompanying every movement of the bow with a motion of the head; bowing almost to the ground, and stamping with his foot whenever a fresh couple were to start.

Ichabod prided himself upon his dancing as much as upon his vocal powers. Not a limb, not a fiber about him was idle; and to have seen his loosely hung frame in full motion, and clattering about the room, you would have thought St. Vitus himself, that blessed patron of the dance, was figuring before you in person. He was the admiration of all the negroes; who, having gathered, of all ages and sizes, from the farm and the neighborhood, stood forming a pyramid of shining black faces at every door and window, gazing with delight at the scene, rolling their white eyeballs, and showing grinning rows of ivory from ear to ear. How could the flogger of urchins be otherwise than animated and joyous?--the lady of his heart was his partner in the dance, and smiling graciously in reply to all his amorous oglings; while Brom Bones, sorely smitten with love and jealousy, sat brooding by himself in one corner.

When the dance was at an end, Ichabod was attracted to a knot of the sager folks, who, with Old Van Tassel, sat smoking at one end of the piazza, gossiping over former times, and drawling out long stories about the war.

This neighborhood, at the time of which I am speaking, was one of those highly favored places which abound with chronicle and great men. The British and American line had run near it during the war; it had, therefore, been the scene of marauding, and infested with refugees, cowboys, and all kind of border chivalry. Just sufficient time had elapsed to enable each storyteller to dress up his tale with a little becoming fiction, and, in the indistinctness of his recollection, to make himself the hero of every exploit.

There was the story of Doffue Martling, a large blue-bearded Dutchman, who had nearly taken a British frigate with an old iron ninepounder from a mud breastwork, only that his gun burst at the sixth discharge. And there was an old gentleman who shall be nameless, being too rich a mynheer to be lightly mentioned, who, in the battle of White Plains, being an excellent master of defense, parried a musketball with a smallsword, insomuch that he absolutely felt it whiz round the blade and glance off at the hilt; in proof of which he was ready at any time to show the sword, with the hilt a little bent. There were several more that had been equally great in the field, not one of whom but was persuaded that he had a considerable hand in bringing the war to a happy termination.

But all these were nothing to the tales of ghosts and apparitions that succeeded. The neighborhood is rich in legendary treasures of the kind. Local tales and superstitions thrive best in these sheltered longsettled retreats; but are trampled under foot by the shifting throng that forms the population of most of our country places. Besides, there is no encouragement for ghosts in most of our villages, for they have scarcely had time to finish their first nap, and turn themselves in their graves, before their surviving friends have traveled away from the neighborhood: so that when they turn out at night to walk their rounds, they have no acquaintance left to call upon. This is perhaps the reason why we so seldom hear of ghosts except in our long-established Dutch communities.

The immediate cause, however, of the prevalence of supernatural stories in these parts was doubtless owing to the vicinity of Sleepy Hollow. There was a contagion in the very air that blew from that haunted region; it breathed forth an atmosphere of dreams and fancies infecting all the land. Several of the Sleepy Hollow people were present at Van Tassel's, and, as usual, were doling out their wild and wonderful legends. Many dismal tales were told about funeral trains, and mourning cries and wailings heard and seen about the great tree where the unfortunate Major André was taken, and which stood in the neighborhood. Some mention was made also of the woman in white, that haunted the dark glen at Raven Rock, and was often, heard to shriek on winter nights before a storm, having perished there in the snow. The chief part of the stories, however, turned upon the favorite specter of Sleepy Hollow, the headless horseman, who had been heard several times of late, patrolling the country, and, it is said, tethered his horse nightly among the graves the churchyard.

The sequestered situation of this church seems almost to have made it a favorite haunt of troubled spirits. It stands on a knoll, surrounded by locust trees and lofty elms, from among which its decent, whitewashed walls shine modestly forth, like Christian purity, beaming through the shades of retirement. A gentle slope descends from it to a silver sheet of water, bordered by high trees, between which peeps may be caught at the blue hills of the Hudson. To look upon its grassgrown yard, where the sunbeams seem to sleep so quietly, one would think that there at least the dead might rest in peace. On one side of the church extends a wide woody dell, along which raves a large brook among broken rocks and trunks of fallen trees. Over a deep black part of the stream, not far from the church, was formerly thrown a wooden bridge; the road that led to it, and the bridge itself, were thickly shaded by overhanging trees, which cast a gloom about it, even in daytime; but occasioned a fearful darkness at night. Such was one of the favorite haunts of the headless horseman, and the place where he was most frequently encountered. The tale was told of old Brouwer, a most heretical disbeliever in ghosts, how he met the horseman returning from his foray into Sleepy Hollow, and was obliged to get up behind him; how they galloped over bush and brake, over hill and swamp, until they reached the bridge; when the horseman suddenly turned into a skeleton, threw old Brouwer into the brook, and sprang away over the treetops with a clap of thunder.

This story was immediately matched by a thrice marvelous adventure of Brom Bones, who made light of the galloping Hessian as an arrant jockey. He affirmed that, on returning one night from the neighboring village of Sing Sing, he had been overtaken by this midnight trooper; that he had offered to race with him for a bowl of punch, and should have won it too, for Daredevil beat the goblin horse all hollow, but just as they came to the church bridge the Hessian bolted, vanished in a flash of fire

All these tales, told in that drowsy undertone with which men talk in the dark, the countenance of the listeners only now and then receiving a casual gleam from the glare of a pipe, sunk deep in the mind of Ichabod. He repaid them in kind with large extracts from his invaluable author, Cotton Mather, and added many marvelous events that had taken place in his native State of Connecticut, and fearful sights which he had seen in his nightly walks about Sleepy Hollow.

The revel now gradually broke up. The old farmers gathered together their families in their wagons, and were heard for some time rattling along the hollow roads, and over the distant hills. Some of the damsels mounted on pillions behind their favorite swains, and their lighthearted laughter, mingled with the clatter of hoofs, echoed along the silent woodlands, sounding fainter and fainter, until they gradually died away--and the late scene of noise and frolic was all silent and deserted. Ichabod only lingered behind, according to the custom of country lovers, to have a têteàtête with the heiress, fully convinced that he was now on the high road to success. What passed at this interview I will not pretend to say, for in fact I do not know. Something, however, I fear me, must have gone wrong, for he certainly sallied forth, after no very great interval, with an air quite desolate and chapfallen.--Oh, these women! these women! Could that girl have been playing off any of her coquettish tricks?--Was her encouragement of the poor pedagog all a mere sham to secure her conquest of his rival?--Heaven only knows, not I!--Let it suffice to say, Ichabod stole forth with the air of one who had been sacking a henroost, rather than a fair lady's heart. Without looking to the right or left to notice the scene of rural wealth on which he had so often gloated, he went straight to the stable, and with several hearty cuffs and kicks roused his steed most uncourteously from the comfortable quarters in which he was soundly sleeping, dreaming of mountains of corn and oats, and whole valleys of timothy and clover.

It was the very witching time of night that Ichabod, heavy-hearted and crestfallen, pursued his travel homeward, along the sides of the lofty hills which rise above Tarry Town, and which he had traversed so cheerily in the afternoon. The hour was as dismal as himself. Far below him the Tappaan Zee spread its dusky and indistinct waste of waters, with here and there the tall mast of a sloop, riding quietly at anchor under the land. In the dead hush of midnight he could even hear the barking of the watchdog from the opposite shore of the Hudson; but it was so vague and faint as only to give an idea of his distance from this faithful companion of man. Now and then, too, the longdrawn crowing of a cock, accidentally awakened, would sound far, far off, from some farmhouse away among the hills--but it was like a dreaming sound in his ear. No signs of life occurred near him, but occasionally the melancholy chirp of a cricket, or perhaps the guttural twang of a bullfrog from a neighboring marsh, as if sleeping uncomfortably, and turning suddenly in his bed.

All the stories of ghosts and goblins that he had heard in the afternoon now came crowding upon his recollection. The night grew darker and darker, the stars seemed to sink deeper in the sky, and driving clouds occasionally hid them from his sight. He had never felt so lonely and dismal. He was moreover, approaching the very place where many of the scenes of the ghost stories had been laid. In the center of the road stood an enormous tulip tree, which towered like a giant above all the other trees of the neighborhood, and formed a kind of landmark. Its limbs were gnarled and fantastic, large enough to form trunks for ordinary trees, twisting down almost to the earth, and rising again into the air. It was connected with the tragical story of the unfortunate André, who had been taken prisoner hard by; and was universally known by the name of Major André's tree. The common people regarded it with a mixture of respect and superstition, partly out of sympathy for the fate of its illstarred namesake, and partly from the tales of strange sights and doleful lamentations told concerning it.

As Ichabod approached this fearful tree he began to whistle; he thought his whistle was answered: it was but a blast sweeping sharply through the dry branches. As he approached a little nearer, he thought he saw something white hanging in the midst of the tree: he paused, and ceased whistling; but, on looking more narrowly, perceived that it was a place where the tree had been scathed by lightning and the white wood laid bare. Suddenly he heard a groan--his teeth chattered, and his knees smote against the saddle: it was but the rubbing of one huge bough upon another, as they were swayed about by the breeze. He passed the tree in safety, but new perils lay before him.

About two hundred yards from the tree a small brook crossed the road, and ran into a marshy and thickly wooded glen known by the name of Wiley's Swamp. A few rough logs, laid side by side, served for a bridge over this stream. On that side of the road where the brook entered the wood a group of oaks and chestnuts, matted thick with wild grapevines, threw a cavernous gloom over it. To pass this bridge was the severest trial. It was at this identical spot that the unfortunate André was captured, and under the covert of those chestnuts and vines were the sturdy yeomen concealed who surprised him. This has ever since been considered a haunted stream, and fearful are the feelings of a schoolboy who has to pass it alone after dark.

As he approached the stream his heart began to thump; he summoned up, however, all his resolution, gave his horse half a score of kicks in the ribs, and attempted to dash briskly across the bridge; but instead of starting forward, the perverse old animal made a lateral movement, and ran broadside against the fence. Ichabod, whose fears increased with the delay, jerked the reins on the other side, and kicked lustily with the contrary foot. It was all in vain; his steed started, it is true, but it was only to plunge to the opposite side of the road into a thicket of brambles and alder bushes. The schoolmaster now bestowed both whip and heel upon the starveling ribs of old Gunpowder, who dashed forward, snuffing and snorting, but came to a stand just by the bridge with a suddenness that had nearly sent his rider sprawling over his head. Just at this moment a plashy tramp by the side of the bridge caught the sensitive ear of Ichabod. In the dark shadow of the grove, on the margin of the brook, he beheld something huge, misshapen, black and towering. It stirred not, but seemed gathering up in the gloom, like some gigantic monster ready to spring upon the traveler.

The hair of the affrighted pedagog rose upon his head with terror. What was to be done? To turn and fly was now too late; and besides, what chance was there of escaping ghost or goblin, if such it was, which could ride upon the wings of the wind? Summoning therefore, a show of courage, he demanded in stammering accents--"Who are you?" He received no reply. He repeated his demand in a still more agitated voice. Still there was no answer. Once more he cudgeled the sides of the inflexible Gunpowder, and shutting his eyes, broke forth with involuntary fervor into a psalm tune. Just then the shadowy object of alarm put itself in motion, and with a scramble and a bound stood at once in the middle of the road. Tho the night was dark and dismal, yet the form of the unknown might now in some degree be ascertained. He appeared to be a horseman of large dimensions, and mounted on a black horse of powerful frame. He made no offer of molestation or sociability, but kept aloof on one side of the road, jogging along on the blind side of old Gunpowder, who had now got over his fright and waywardness.

Ichabod, who had no relish for this strange midnight companion, and bethought himself of the adventure of Brom Bones with the galloping Hessian, now quickened his steed, in hopes of leaving him behind. The stranger, however, quickened his horse to an equal pace. Ichabod pulled up, and fell into a walk, thinking to lag behind--the other did the same. His heart began to sink within him; he endeavored to resume his psalm tune, but his parched tongue clove to the roof of his mouth, and he could not utter a stave. There was something in the moody and dogged silence of this pertinacious companion that was mysterious and appalling. It was soon fearfully accounted for. On mounting a rising ground, which brought the figure of his fellowtraveler in relief against the sky, gigantic in height, and muffled in a cloak, Ichabod was horrorstruck, on perceiving that he was headless! but his horror was still more increased, on observing that the head, which should have rested on his shoulders, was carried before him on the pommel of his saddle! His terror rose to desperation; he rained a shower of kicks and blows upon Gunpowder, hoping, by a sudden movement, to give his companion the slip--but the specter started full jump with him. Away, then, they dashed through thick and thin; stones flying and sparks flashing at every bound. Ichabod's flimsy garments fluttered in the air, as he stretched his long lank body away over his horse's head, in the eagerness of his flight.

They had now reached the road which turns off to Sleepy Hollow; but Gunpowder, who seemed possessed with a demon, instead of keeping up it, made an opposite turn, and plunged headlong downhill to the left. This road leads through a sandy hollow, shaded by trees for about a quarter of a mile, where it crosses the bridge famous in goblin story; and just beyond swells the green knoll on which stands the whitewashed church.

As yet the panic of the steed had given his unskillful rider an apparent advantage in the chase; but just as he had got halfway through the hollow, the girths of the saddle gave way, and he felt it slipping from under him. He seized it by the pommel, and endeavored to hold it firm, but in vain; and had just time to save himself by clasping old Gunpowder round the neck, when the saddle fell to the earth, and he heard it trampled under foot by his pursuer. For a moment the terror of Hans Van Ripper's wrath passed across is his mind--for it was his Sunday saddle; but this was no time for petty fears: the goblin was hard on his haunches; and (unskillful rider that he was!) he had much ado to maintain his seat; sometimes slipping on one side, sometimes on another, and sometimes jolted the high ridge of his horse's backbone, with a violence that he verily feared would cleave him asunder.

An opening in the trees now cheered him with the hopes that the church bridge was at hand. The wavering reflection of a silver star in the bosom of the brook told him that he was not mistaken. He saw the walls of the church dimly glaring under the trees beyond. He recollected the place where Brom Bones's ghostly competitor had disappeared. "If I can but reach that bridge," thought Ichabod, "I am safe." Just then he heard the black steed panting and blowing close behind him; he even fancied that he felt his hot breath. Another convulsive kick in the ribs, and old Gunpowder sprung upon the bridge; he thundered over the resounding planks; he gained the opposite side, and now Ichabod cast a look behind to see if his pursuer should vanish, according to rule, in a flash of fire and brimstone. Just then he saw the goblin rising in his stirrups, and in the very act of hurling his head at him. Ichabod endeavored to dodge the horrible missile, but too late. It encountered his cranium with a tremendous crash--he was tumbled headlong into the dust, and Gunpowder, the black steed, and the goblin rider, passed by like a whirlwind.

The next morning the old horse was found without his saddle, and with the bridle under his feet, soberly cropping the grass at his master's gate. Ichabod did not make his appearance at breakfast--dinnerhour came, but no Ichabod. The boys assembled at the schoolhouse, and strolled idly about the banks of the brook; but no schoolmaster. Hans Van Ripper now began to feel some uneasiness about the fate of poor Ichabod, and his saddle. An inquiry was set on foot, and after diligent investigation they came upon his traces. In one part of the road leading to the church was found the saddle trampled in the dirt; the tracks of horses' hoofs deeply dented in the road, and evidently at furious speed, were traced to the bridge, beyond which, on the bank of a broad part of the brook, where the water ran deep and black, was found the hat of the unfortunate Ichabod, and close beside it a shattered pumpkin.

The brook was searched, but the body of the schoolmaster was not to be discovered. Hans Van Ripper, as executor of his estate, examined the bundle which contained all his worldly effects. They consisted of two shirts and a half; two stocks for the neck; a pair or two of worsted stockings; an old pair of corduroy smallclothes; a rusty razor; a book of psalm tunes full of dog's ears; and a broken pitchpipe. As to the books and furniture of the schoolhouse, they belonged to the community, excepting Cotton Mather's "History of Witchcraft," a New England Almanac, and a book of dreams and fortunetelling; in which last was a sheet of foolscap much scribbled and blotted, by several fruitless attempts to make a copy of verses in honor of the heiress of Van Tassel. These magic books and the poetic scrawl were forthwith consigned to the flames by Hans Van Ripper; who, from that time forward, determined to send his children no more to school; observing that he never knew any good come of this same reading and writing. Whatever money the schoolmaster possessed, and he had received his quarter's pay but a day or two before, he must have had about his person at the time of his disappearance.

The mysterious event caused much speculation at the church on the following Sunday. Knots of gazers and gossips were collected in the churchyard, at the bridge, and at the spot where the hat and pumpkin had been found. The stories of Brouwer, of Bones, and a whole budget of others, were called to mind; and when they had diligently considered them all, and compared them with the symptoms of the present case, they shook their heads, and came to the conclusion that Ichabod had been carried off by the galloping Hessian. As he was a bachelor, and in nobody's debt, nobody troubled his head any more about him! the school was removed to a different quarter of the Hollow, and another pedagog reigned in his stead.

It is true, an old farmer, who had been down to New York on a visit several years after, and from whom this account of the ghostly adventure was received, brought me the intelligence that Ichabod Crane was still alive; that he had left the neighborhood partly through fear of the goblin and Hans Van Ripper, and partly in mortification at having been suddenly dismissed by the heiress; that he had changed his quarters to a distant part of the country; had kept school and studied law at the same time; had been admitted to the bar; turned politician; electioneered; written for the newspapers; and finally had been made a Justice of the Ten Pound Court. Brom Bones too, who, shortly after his rival's disappearance, conducted the, blooming Katrina in triumph to the altar, was observed to look exceedingly knowing whenever the story of Ichabod was related, and always burst into a hearty laugh at the mention of the pumpkin; which led some to suspect that he knew more about the matter than he chose to tell.

The old country wives, however, who are the best judges of these matters, maintain to this day that Ichabod was spirited away by supernatural means; and it is a favorite story often told about the neighborhood round the winter evening fire. The bridge became more than ever the object of superstitious awe; and that may be the reason why the road has been altered of late years, so as to approach the church by the border of the millpond. The schoolhouse being deserted, soon fell to decay, and was reported to be haunted by the ghost of the unfortunate pedagog; the plowboy, loitering homeward of a still summer evening, has often fancied his voice at a distance chanting a melancholy psalm tune among the tranquil solitudes of Sleepy Hollow.

POSTSCRIPT

FOUND IN THE HANDWRITING OF MR. KNICKERBOCKER

The preceding Tale is given, almost in the precise words in which I heard it related at a Corporation meeting of the ancient city of the Manhattoes, at which were present many of its sagest and most illustrious burghers. The narrator was a pleasant, shabby, gentlemanly old fellow in pepperandsalt clothes, with a sadly humorous face; and one whom I strongly suspected of being poor--he made such efforts to be entertaining. When his story was concluded there was much laughter and approbation, particularly from two or three deputy aldermen, who had been asleep the greater part of the time. There was, however, one tall, drylooking old gentleman, with beetling eyebrows, who maintained a grave and rather severe face throughout; now and then folding his arms, inclining his head, and looking down upon the floor, as if turning a doubt over in his mind.

He was one of your wary men, who never laugh but upon good grounds--when they have reason and the law on their side. When the mirth of the rest of the company had subsided, and silence was restored, he leaned one arm on the elbow of his chair, and sticking the other akimbo, demanded, with a slight but exceedingly sage motion of the head and contraction of the brow, what was the moral of the story, and what it went to prove.

The storyteller, who was just putting a glass of wine to his lips, as a refreshment after his toils, paused for a moment, looked at his inquirer with an air of infinite deference, and lowering the glass slowly to the table, observed that the story was intended most logically to prove:

"That there is no situation in life but has its advantages and pleasures--provided we will but take a joke as we find it;

"That, therefore, he that runs races with goblin troopers is likely to have rough riding of it;

"Ergo, for a country schoolmaster to be refused the hand of a Dutch heiress is a certain step to high preferment in the State."

The cautious old gentleman knit his brows tenfold closer after this explanation, being sorely puzzled by the ratiocination of the syllogism; while, methought, the one in the pepperandsalt eyed him with something of a triumphant leer. At length he observed, that all this was very well, but still he thought the story a little on the extravagant--there were one or two points on which he had his doubts:

"Faith, sir," replied the storyteller, "as to that matter, I don't believe onehalf of it myself."

D. K.

The Author of Beltraffio

Henry James

Henry James (1843-1916) successfully mastered the craft of the short story and the novel. He is noted for his portrayal of the conflict between American and European cultures. Some of his greatest works include *The Americans, Portrait of a Lady,* and the short stories, *Daisy Miller, The Beast in the Jungle,* and *The Turn of the Screw.*

James was born in New York City in 1843, the brother of well-known psychologist and philosopher William James. James was influenced by his father's interest in philosophy, theology, and the cultural life in New York and abroad. James received his early education in England, Switzerland, France, and Germany, all of which bustled with intellectual activity. He briefly studied painting, which may have sharpened his visual perception, resulting in the highly detailed settings in his writing.

James began studying law at Harvard when he was nineteen but continued to work on his writing. Two years later his unsigned story *A Tragedy of Error* appeared in *Continental Monthly.* A year later his stories began to be published in *The Atlantic Monthly.* In 1875 he published his first collection of stories, *A Passionate Pilgrim and Other Tales.*

In the early part of his writing career he spent much time in Paris where he became acquainted with the naturalists Flaubert and Turgenev. Their influence on James' style is seen in his adoption of the idea that the writer is a researcher into life. However, he did not accept the idea that man is left to the whim of chance. This sense of determinism set him apart from the naturalists.

James experimented with psychological devices that developed the portrayal of character and influenced: D. H. Lawrence, James Joyce, Joseph Conrad, Edith Wharton, Virginia Woolf, Willa Cather, and T. S. Elliot.

MUCH AS I WISHED to see him I had kept my letter of introduction three weeks in my pocketbook. I was nervous and timid about meeting him - conscious of youth and ignorance, convinced that he was tormented by strangers and especially by my country-people, and not exempt from the suspicion that he had the irritability as well as the dignity of genius.

Moreover, the pleasure, if it should occur - for I could scarcely believe it was near at hand - would be so great that I wished to think of it in advance, to feel it there against my breast, not to mix it with satisfactions more superficial and usual. In the little game of new sensations that I was playing with my ingenuous mind I wished to keep my visit to the author of 'Beltraffio' as a trumpcard. It was three years after the publication of that fascinating work, which I had read over five times and which now, with my riper judgement, I admire on the whole as much as ever. This will give you about the date of my first visit of any duration - to England; for you will not have forgotten the commotion, I may even say the scandal, produced by Mark Ambient's masterpiece. It was the most complete presentation that had yet been made of the gospel of art; it was a kind of aesthetic warcry. People had endeavoured to sail nearer to 'truth' in the cut of their sleeves and the shape of their sideboards; but there had not as yet been, among English novels, such an example of beauty of execution and 'intimate' importance of theme. Nothing had been done in that line from the point of view of art for art. That served me as a fond formula, I may mention, when I was twentyfive; how much it still serves I won't take upon myself to say especially as the discerning reader will be able to judge for himself. I had been in England, briefly, a twelvemonth before the time to which I began by alluding, and had then learned that Mr Ambient was in distant lands was making a considerable tour in the East; so that there was nothing to do but to keep my letter till I should be in London again. It was of little use to me to hear that his wife had not left England and was, with her little boy, their only child, spending the period of her husband's absence a good many months at a small place they had down in Surrey. They had a house in London, but actually in the occupation of other persons. All this I had picked up, and also that Mrs Ambient was charming my friend the American poet, from whom I had my introduction, had never seen her, his relations with the great man confined to the exchange of letters; but she wasn't, after all, though she had lived so near the rose, the author of 'Beltraffio', and I didn't go down into Surrey to call on her. I went to the Continent, spent the following winter in Italy and returned to London in May. My visit to Italy had opened my eyes to a good many things, but to nothing more than the beauty of certain pages in the works of Mark Ambient. I carried his productions about in my trunk they are not, as you know, very numerous, but he had preluded to 'Beltraffio' by some exquisite things and I used to read them over in the evening at the inn. I used profoundly to reason that the man who drew those characters and wrote that style understood what he saw and knew what he was doing. This is my sole ground for mentioning my winter in Italy. He had been there much in former years he was saturated with what painters call the 'feeling' of that classic land. He expressed the charm of the old hillcities of Tuscany, the look of certain lonely grassgrown places which, in the past, had echoed with life; he understood the great artists, he understood the spirit of the Renaissance; he understood everything. The scene of one of his earlier novels was laid in Rome, the scene of another in Florence, and I had moved through these cities in company with the figures he set so firmly on their feet. This is why I was now so much happier even than before in the prospect of making his acquaintance.

At last, when I had dallied with my privilege long enough, I dispatched to him the missive of the American poet. He had already gone out of town; he shrank from the rigour of the London 'season', and it was his habit to migrate on the first of June. Moreover I had heard he was this year hard at work on a new book, into which some of his impressions of the East were to be wrought, so that he desired nothing so much as quiet days. That knowledge, however, didn't prevent me *cet âge est sans pitié* - from sending with my friend's letter a note of my own, in which I asked his leave to come down and see him for an hour or two on some day to be named by himself. My proposal was accompanied with a very frank expression of my sentiments, and the effect of the entire appeal was to elicit from the great man the kindest possible invitation. He would be delighted to see me, especially if I should turn up on the following Saturday and would remain till the Monday morning. We would take a walk over the Surrey commons, and I could tell him all about the other great man, the one in America. He indicated to me the best train, and it may be imagined whether on the Saturday afternoon I was punctual at Waterloo. He carried his benevolence to the point of coming to meet me at the little station at which I was to alight, and my heart beat very fast as I saw his handsome face, surmounted with a soft wideawake and which I knew by a photograph long since enshrined on my mantelshelf, scanning the carriagewindows as the train rolled up. He recognised me as infallibly as I had recognised himself; he appeared to know by instinct how a young American of critical pretensions, rash youth, would look when much divided between eagerness and modesty. He took me by the hand and smiled at me and said: 'You must be a *you*, I think!' and asked if I should mind going on foot to his house, which would take but a few minutes. I remember feeling it a piece of extraordinary affability that he should give directions about the conveyance of my bag; I remember feeling altogether very happy and rosy, in fact quite transported, when he laid his hand on my shoulder as we came out of the station.

I surveyed him, askance, as we walked together; I had already, I had indeed instantly, seen him as all delightful. His face is so well known that I needn't describe it; he looked to me at once an English gentleman and a man of genius, and I thought that a happy combination. There was a brush of the Bohemians in his fineness; you would easily have guessed his belonging to the artist guild. He was addicted to velvet jackets, to cigarettes, to loose shirtcollars, to looking a little dishevelled. His features, which were firm but not perfectly regular, are fairly enough represented in his portraits; but no portrait I have seen gives any idea of his expression. There were innumerable things in it, and they chased each other in and out of his face. I have seen people who were grave and gay in quick alternation; but Mark Ambient was grave and gay at one and the same moment. There were other strange oppositions and contradictions in his slightly faded and fatigued countenance. He affected me somehow as at once fresh and stale, at once anxious and indifferent. He had evidently had an active past, which inspired one with curiosity; yet what was that compared to his obvious future? He was just enough above middle height to be spoken of as tall, and rather lean and long in the flank. He had the friendliest frankest manner possible, and yet I could see it cost him something. It cost him small spasms of the selfconsciousness that is an Englishman's last and dearest treasure the thing he pays his way through life by sacrificing small pieces of even as the gallant but moneyless adventurer in 'Quentin Durward' broke off links of his brave gold chain. He had been thirtyeight years old at the time 'Beltraffio' was published. He asked me about his friend in America, about the length of my stay in England, about the last news in London and the people I had seen there; and I remember looking for the signs of genius in the very form of his questions and thinking I found it. I liked his voice as if I were somehow myself having the use of it.

There was genius in his house too I thought when we got there; there was imagination in the carpets and curtains, in the pictures and books, in the garden behind it, where certain old brown walls were muffled in creepers that appeared to me to have been copied from a masterpiece of one of the preRaphaelites. That was the way many things struck me at that time, in England as reproductions of something that existed primarily in art or literature. It was not the picture, the poem, the fictive page, that

seemed to me a copy; these things were the originals, and the life of happy
and distinguished people was fashioned in their image. Mark Ambient
called his house a cottage, and I saw afterwards he was right; for if it
hadn't been a cottage it must have been a villa, and a villa, in England at
least, was not a place in which one could fancy him at home. But it was,
to my vision, a cottage glorified and translated; it was a palace of art, on
a slightly reduced scale and might besides have been the dearest haunt of
the old English *genius loci*. It nestled under a cluster of magnificent
beeches, it had little creaking lattices that opened out of, or into, pendent
mats of ivy, and gables, and old red tiles, as well as a general aspect of
being painted in watercolours and inhabited by people whose lives would
go on in chapters and volumes. The lawn seemed to me of extraordinary
extent, the gardenwalls of incalculable height, the whole air of the place
delightfully still, private, proper to itself. 'My wife must be somewhere
about,' Mark Ambient said as we went in. 'We shall find her perhaps
we've about an hour before dinner. She may be in the garden. I'll show
you my little place.'

We passed through the house and into the grounds, as I should have
called them, which extended into the rear. They covered scarce three or
four acres, but, like the house, were very old and crooked and full of traces
of long habitation, with inequalities of level and little flights of steps
mossy and cracked were these which connected the different parts with
each other. The limits of the place, cleverly dissimulated, were muffled in
the great verdurous screens. They formed, as I remember, a thick loose
curtain at the further end, in one of the folds of which, as it were, we
presently made out from afar a little group. 'Ah there she is!' said Mark
Ambient; 'and she has got the boy.' He noted that last fact in a slightly
different tone from any in which he yet had spoken. I wasn't fully aware
of this at the time, but it lingered in my ear and I afterwards understood
it.

'Is it your son?' I enquired, feeling the question not to be brilliant.

'Yes, my only child. He's always in his mother's pocket. She coddles
him too much.' It came back to me afterwards too the sound of these
critical words. They weren't petulant; they expressed rather a sudden
coldness, a mechanical submission. We went a few steps further, and then
he stopped short and called the boy, beckoning to him repeatedly.

'Dolcino, come and see your daddy!' There was something in the way
he stood still and waited that made me think he did it for, a purpose. Mrs
Ambient had her arm round the child's waist, and he was leaning against

her knee; but though he moved at his father's call she gave no sign of releasing him. A lady, apparently a neighbour, was seated near her, and before them was a gardentable on which a teaservice had been placed.

Mark Ambient called again, and Dolcino struggled in the maternal embrace; but, too tightly held, he after two or three fruitless efforts jerked about and buried his head deep in his mother's lap. There was a certain awkwardness in the scene; I thought it odd Mrs Ambient should pay so little attention to her husband. But I wouldn't for the world have betrayed my thought and, to conceal it, I began loudly to rejoice in the prospect of our having tea in the garden. 'Ah she won't let him come!' said my host with a sigh; and we went our way till we reached the two ladies. He mentioned my name to his wife, and I noticed that he addressed her as 'My dear,' very genially, without a trace of resentment at her detention of the child. The quickness of the transition made me vaguely ask myself if he were perchance henpecked a shocking surmise which I instantly dismissed. Mrs Ambient was quite such a wife as I should have expected him to have; slim and fair, with a long neck and pretty eyes and an air of good breeding. She shone with a certain coldness and practised in intercourse a certain bland detachment, but she was clothed in gentleness as in one of those vaporous redundant scarves that muffle the heroines of Gainsborough and Romney. She had also a vague air of race, justified by my afterwards learning that she was 'connected with the aristocracy'. I have seen poets married to women of whom it was difficult to conceive that they should gratify the poetic fancy women with dull faces and glutinous minds, who were none the less, however, excellent wives. But there was no obvious disparity in Mark Ambient's union. My hostess so far as she could be called so delicate and quiet, in a white dress, with her beautiful child at her side, was worthy of the author of a work so distinguished as 'Beltraffio'. Round her neck she wore a black velvet ribbon, of which the long ends, tied behind, hung down her back, and to which, in front, was attached a miniature portrait of her little boy. Her smooth shining hair was confined in a net. She gave me an adequate greeting and Dolcino I thought this small name of endearment delightful took advantage of her getting up to slip away from her and go to his father, who seized him in silence and held him high for a long moment, kissing him several times.

I had lost no time in observing that the child, not more than seven years old, was extraordinarily beautiful. He had the face of an angel the eyes, the hair, the smile of innocence, the more than mortal bloom. There was something that deeply touched, that almost alarmed, in his beauty, composed, one would have said, of elements too fine and pure for the breath of this world. When I spoke to him and he came and held out his hand and smiled at me I felt a sudden strange pity for him quite as if he had been an orphan or a changeling or stamped with some social stigma. It was impossible to be in fact more exempt from these misfortunes, and yet, as one kissed him, it was hard to keep from murmuring all tenderly 'Poor little devil!' though why one should have applied this epithet to a living cherub is more than I can say. Afterwards indeed I knew a trifle better; I grasped the truth of his being too fair to live, wondering at the same time that his parents shouldn't have guessed it and have been in proportionate grief and despair. For myself I had no doubt of his evanescence, having already more than once caught in the fact the particular infant charm that's as good as a deathwarrant.

The lady who had been sitting with Mrs Ambient was a jolly ruddy personage in velveteen and limp feathers, whom I guessed to be the vicar's wife our hostess didn't introduce me and who immediately began to talk to Ambient about chrysanthemums. This was a safe subject, and yet there was a certain surprise for me in seeing the author of 'Beltraffio' even in such superficial communion with the Church of England. His writings implied so much detachment from that institution, expressed a view of life so profane, as it were, so independent and so little likely in general to be thought edifying, that I should have expected to find him an object of horror to vicars and their ladies of horror repaid on his own part by any amount of effortless derision. This proved how little I knew as yet of the English people and their extraordinary talent for keeping up their forms, as well as of some of the mysteries of Mark Ambient's hearth and home. I found afterwards that he had, in his study, between nervous laughs and free cigarpuffs, some wonderful comparisons for his clerical neighbours; but meanwhile the chrysanthemums were a source of harmony, as he and the vicaress were equally attached to them, and I was surprised at the knowledge they exhibited of this interesting plant. The lady's visit, however, had presumably been long, and she presently rose for departure and kissed Mrs Ambient. Mark started to walk with her to the gate of the grounds, holding Dolcino by the hand.

'Stay with me, darling,' Mrs Ambient said to the boy, who had surrendered himself to his father.

Mark paid no attention to her summons, but Dolcino turned and looked at her in shy appeal. 'Can't I go with papa?'

'Not when I ask you to stay with me.'

'But please don't ask me, mamma,' said the child in his small clear new voice.

'I must ask you when I want you. Come to me, dearest.' And Mrs Ambient, who had seated herself again, held out her long slender slightly too osseous hands.

Her husband stopped, his back turned to her, but without releasing the child. He was still talking to the vicaress, but this good lady, I think, had lost the thread of her attention. She looked at Mrs Ambient and at Dolcino, and then looked at me, smiling in a highly amused cheerful manner and almost to a grimace.

'Papa,' said the child, 'mamma wants me not to go with you.

'He's very tired he has run about all day. He ought to be quiet till he goes to bed. Otherwise he won't sleep.' These declarations fell successively and very distinctly from Mrs Ambient's lips.

Her husband, still without turning round, bent over the boy and looked at him in silence. The vicaress gave a genial irrelevant laugh and observed that he was a precious little pet. 'Let him choose,' said Mark Ambient. 'My dear little boy, will you go with me or will you stay with your mother?'

'Oh it's a shame!' cried the vicar's lady with increased hilarity.

'Papa, I don't think I can choose,' the child answered, making his voice very low and confidential. 'But I've been a great deal with mamma today,' he then added.

'And very little with papa! My dear fellow, I think you *have* chosen!' On which Mark Ambient walked off with his son, accompanied by reechoing but inarticulate comments from my fellow visitor.

His wife had seated herself again, and her fixed eyes, bent on the ground, expressed for a few moments so much mute agitation that anything I could think of to say would be but a false note. Yet she none the less quickly recovered herself, to express the sufficiently civil hope that I didn't mind having had to walk from the station. I reassured her on this point, and she went on: 'We've got a thing that might have gone for you, but my husband wouldn't order it.' After which and another longish pause, broken only by my plea that the pleasure of a walk with our friend would have been quite what I would have chosen, she found for reply: 'I believe the Americans walk very little.'

'Yes, we always run,' I laughingly allowed.

She looked at me seriously, yet with an absence in her pretty eyes. 'I suppose your distances are so great.'

'Yes, but we break our marches! I can't tell you the pleasure to me of finding myself here,' I added. 'I've the greatest admiration for Mr Ambient.'

'He'll like that. He likes being admired.'

'He must have a very happy life then. He has many worshippers.'

'Oh yes, I've seen some of them,' she dropped, looking away, very far from me, rather as if such a vision were before her at the moment. It seemed to indicate, her tone, that the sight was scarcely edifying, and I guessed her quickly enough to be in no great intellectual sympathy with the author of 'Beltraffio'. I thought the fact strange, but somehow, in the glow of my own enthusiasm, didn't think it important: it only made me wish rather to emphasise that homage.

'For me, you know,' I returned doubtless with a due *suffisance* - 'he's quite the greatest of living writers.'

'Of course I can't judge. Of course he's very clever,' she said with a patient cheer.

'He's nothing less than supreme, Mrs Ambient! There are pages in each of his books of a perfection classing them with the greatest things. Accordingly for me to see him in this familiar way, in his habit as he lives, and apparently to find the man as delightful as the artist well, I can't tell you how much too good to be true it seems and how great a privilege I think it.' I knew I was gushing, but I couldn't help it, and what I said was a good deal less than what I felt. I was by no means sure I should dare to say even so much as this to the master himself, and there was a kind of rapture in speaking it out to his wife which was not affected by the fact that, as a wife, she appeared peculiar. She listened to me with her face grave again and her lips a little compressed, listened as if in no doubt, of course, that her husband was remarkable, but as if at the same time she had heard it frequently enough and couldn't treat it as stirring news. There was even in her manner a suggestion that I was so young as to expose myself to being called forward an imputation and a word I had always loathed; as well as a hinted reminder that people usually got over their early extravagance. 'I assure you that for me this is a redletter day,' I added.

She didn't take this up, but after a pause, looking round her, said abruptly and a trifle dryly: 'We're very much afraid about the fruit this year.'

My eyes wandered to the mossy mottled gardenwalls, where plumtrees and pears, flattened and fastened upon the rusty bricks, looked like crucified figures with many arms. 'Doesn't it promise well?'

'No, the trees look very dull. We had such late frosts.'

Then there was another pause. She addressed her attention to the opposite end of the grounds, kept it for her husband's return with the child. 'Is Mr Ambient fond of gardening?' it occurred to me to ask, irresistibly impelled as I felt myself, moreover, to bring the conversation constantly back to him.

'He's very fond of plums,' said his wife.

'Ah well then I hope your crop will be better than you fear. It's a lovely old place,' I continued. 'The whole impression's that of certain places he has described. Your house is like one of his pictures.'

She seemed a bit frigidly amused at my glow. 'It's a pleasant little place. There are hundreds like it.'

'Oh it has his *tone*,' I laughed, but sounding my epithet and insisting on my point the more sharply that my companion appeared to see in my appreciation of her simple establishment a mark of mean experience.

It was clear I insisted too much. 'His tone?' she repeated with a harder look at me and a slightly heightened colour.

'Surely he has a tone, Mrs Ambient.'

'Oh yes, he has indeed! But I don't in the least consider that I'm living in one of his books at all. I shouldn't care for that in the least,' she went on with a smile that had in some degree the effect of converting her really sharp protest into an insincere joke. 'I'm afraid I'm not very literary. And I'm not artistic,' she stated.

'I'm very sure you're not ignorant, not stupid,' I ventured to reply, with the accompaniment of feeling immediately afterwards that I had been both familiar and patronising. My only consolation was in the sense that she had begun it, had fairly dragged me into it. She had thrust forward her limitations.

'Well, whatever I am I'm very different from my husband. If you like him you won't like me. You needn't say anything. Your liking me isn't in the least necessary!'

'Don't defy me!' I could but honourably make answer.

She looked as if she hadn't heard me, which was the best thing she could do; and we sat some time without further speech. Mrs Ambient had evidently the enviable English quality of being able to be mute without unrest. But at last she spoke she asked me if there seemed many people in town. I gave her what satisfaction I could on this point, and we talked a little of London and of some of its characteristics at that time of the year. At the end of this I came back irrepressibly to Mark.

'Doesn't he like to be there now? I suppose he doesn't find the proper quiet for his work. I should think his things had been written for the most part in a very still place. They suggest a great stillness following on a kind of tumult. Don't you think so?' I laboured on. 'I suppose London's a tremendous place to collect impressions, but a refuge like this, in the country, must be better for working them up. Does he get many of his impressions in London, should you say?' I proceeded from point to point in this malign enquiry simply because my hostess, who probably thought me an odious chattering person, gave me time; for when I paused - I've not represented my pauses - she simply continued to let her eyes wander while her long fair fingers played with the medallion on her neck. When I stopped altogether, however, she was obliged to say something, and what she said was that she hadn't the least idea where her husband got his impressions. This made me think her, for a moment, positively disagreeable; delicate and proper and rather aristocratically fine as she sat there. But I must either have lost that view a moment later or been goaded by it to further aggression, for I remember asking her if our great man were in a good vein of work and when we might look for the appearance of the book on which he was engaged. I've every reason now to know that she found me insufferable.

She gave a strange small laugh as she said; 'I'm afraid you think I know much more about my husband's work than I do. I haven't the least idea what he's doing,' she then added in a slightly different, that is a more explanatory, tone and as if from a glimpse of the enormity of her confession. 'I don't read what he writes.'

She didn't succeed, and wouldn't even had she tried much harder, in making this seem to me anything less than monstrous. I stared at her and I think I blushed. 'Don't you admire his genius? Don't you admire "Beltraffio"?'

She waited, and I wondered what she could possibly say. She didn't speak, I could see, the first words that rose to her lips; she repeated what she had said a few minutes before. 'Oh of course he's very clever!' And with this she got up; our two absentees had reappeared.

Mrs Ambient left me and went to meet them; she stopped and had a few words with her husband that I didn't hear and that ended in her taking the child by the hand and returning with him to the house. Her husband joined me in a moment, looking, I thought, the least bit conscious and constrained, and said that if I would come in with him he would show me my room. In looking back upon these first moments of my visit I find it important to avoid the error of appearing to have at all fully measured his situation from the first or made out the signs of things mastered only afterwards. This later knowledge throws a backward light and makes me forget that, at least on the occasion of my present reference - I mean that first afternoon - Mark Ambient struck me as only enviable. Allowing for this he must yet have failed of much expression as we walked back to the house, though I remember well the answer he made to a remark of mine on his small son.

'That's an extraordinary little boy of yours. I've never seen such a child.'

'Why,' he asked while we went, 'do you call him extraordinary?'

'He's so beautiful, so fascinating. He's like some perfect little work of art.'

He turned quickly in the passage, grasping my arm. 'Oh don't call him that, or you'll - you'll !' But in his hesitation he broke off suddenly, laughing at my surprise. Immediately afterwards, however, he added: 'You'll make his little future very difficult.'

I declared that I wouldn't for the world take any liberties with his little future - it seemed to me to hang by threads of such delicacy. I should only be highly interested in watching it.

'You Americans are very keen,' he commented on this. 'You notice more things than we do.'

'Ah if you want visitors who aren't struck with you,' I cried, 'you shouldn't have asked me down here!'

He showed me my room, a little bower of chintz, with open windows where the light was green, and before he left me said irrelevantly: 'As for my small son, you know, we shall probably kill him between us before we've done with him!' And he made this assertion as if he really believed it, without any appearance of jest, his fine nearsighted expressive eyes looking straight into mine.

'Do you mean by spoiling him?'

'No, by fighting for him!'

'You had better give him to me to keep for you,' I said. 'Let me remove the apple of discord!'

It was my extravagance of course, but he had the air of being perfectly serious. 'It would be quite the best thing we could do. I should be all ready to do it.'

'I'm greatly obliged to you for your confidence.'

But he lingered with his hands in his pockets. I felt as if within a few moments I had, morally speaking, taken several steps nearer to him. He looked weary, just as he faced me then, looked preoccupied and as if there were something one might do for him. I was terribly conscious of the limits of my young ability, but I wondered what such a service might be, feeling at bottom nevertheless that the only thing I could do for him was to like him. I suppose he guessed this and was grateful for what was in my mind, since he went on presently: 'I haven't the advantage of being an American, but I also notice a little, and I've an idea that' - here he smiled and laid his hand on my shoulder 'even counting out your nationality you're not destitute of intelligence. I've only known you half an hour, but -!' For which again he pulled up. 'You're very young after all.'

'But you may treat me as if I could understand you!' I said; and before he left me to dress for dinner he had virtually given me a promise that he would.

When I went down into the drawingroom - I was very punctual - I found that neither my hostess nor my host had appeared. A lady rose from the sofa, however, and inclined her head as I rather surprisedly gazed at her. 'I dare say you don't know me,' she said with the modern laugh. 'I'm Mark Ambient's sister.' Whereupon I shook hands with her, saluting her very low. Her laugh was modern - by which I mean that it consisted of the vocal agitation serving between people who meet in drawingrooms as the solvent of social disparities, the medium of transitions; but her appearance was - what shall I call it? - medieval. She was pale and angular, her long thin face was inhabited by sad dark eyes and her black hair intertwined with golden fillets and curious clasps. She wore a faded velvet robe which clung to her when she moved and was 'cut', as to the neck and sleeves, like the garments of old Italians. She suggested a symbolic picture, something akin even to Dürer's Melancholia, and was so perfect an image of a type which I, in my ignorance, supposed to be extinct, that while she rose before me I was almost as much startled as if I had seen a ghost. I afterwards concluded that Miss Ambient wasn't incapable of deriving pleasure from this weird effect, and I now believe that reflexion concerned in her having sunk again to her seat with her long lean but not ungraceful arms locked together in an archaic manner on her knees and her mournful eyes addressing me a message of intentness which foreshadowed what I was subsequently to suffer. She was a singular fatuous artificial creature, and I was never more than half to penetrate her motives and mysteries. Of one thing I'm sure at least: that they were considerably less insuperable than her appearance announced. Miss Ambient was a restless romantic disappointed spinster, consumed with the love of MichaelAngelesque attitudes and mystical robes; but I'm now convinced she hadn't in her nature those depths of unutterable thought which, when you first knew her, seemed to look out from her eyes and to prompt her complicated gestures. Those features in especial had a misleading eloquence; they lingered on you with a faroff dimness, an air of obstructed sympathy, which was certainly not always a key to the spirit of their owner; so that, of a truth, a young lady could scarce have been so dejected and disillusioned without having committed a crime for which she was consumed with remorse, or having parted with a hope that she couldn't sanely have entertained. She had, I believe, the usual allowance of rather vain motives: she wished to be looked at, she wished to be married, she wished to be thought original.

It cost me a pang to speak in this irreverent manner of one of Ambient's name, but I shall have still less gracious things to say before I've finished my anecdote, and moreover - I confess it - I owe the young lady a bit of a grudge. Putting aside the curious cast of her face she had no natural aptitude for an artistic development, had little real intelligence. But her affectations rubbed off on her brother's renown, and as there were plenty of people who darkly disapproved of him they could easily point to his sister as a person formed by his influence. It was quite possible to regard her as a warning, and she had almost compromised him with the world at large. He was the original and she the inevitable imitation. I suppose him scarce aware of the impression she mainly produced, beyond having a general idea that she made up very well as a Rossetti; he was used to her and was sorry for her, wishing she would marry and observing how she didn't. Doubtless I take her too seriously, for she did me no harm, though I'm bound to allow that I can only halfaccount for her. She wasn't so mystical as she looked, but was a strange indirect uncomfortable embarrassing woman. My story gives the reader at best so very small a knot to untie that I needn't hope to excite his curiosity by delaying to remark that Mrs Ambient hated her sisterinlaw. This I learned but later on, when other matters came to my knowledge. I mention it, however, at once, for I shall perhaps not seem to count too much on having beguiled him if I say he must promptly have guessed it. Mrs Ambient, a person of conscience, put the best face on her kinswoman, who spent a month with her twice a year; but it took no great insight to recognise the very different personal paste of the two ladies, and that the usual feminine hypocrisies would cost them on either side much more than the usual effort. Mrs Ambient, smoothhaired, thinlipped, perpetually fresh, must have regarded her crumpled and dishevelled visitor as an equivocal joke; she herself so the opposite of a Rossetti, she herself a Reynolds or a Lawrence, with no more farfetched note in her composition than a cold ladylike candour and a wellstarched muslin dress.

It was in a garment and with an expression of this kind that she made her entrance after I had exchanged a few words with Miss Ambient. Her husband presently followed her and, there being no other company, we went to dinner. The impressions I received at that repast are present to me still. The elements of oddity in the air hovered, as it were, without descending - to any immediate check of my delight. This came mainly of course from Ambient's talk, the easiest and richest I had ever heard. I mayn't say today whether he laid himself out to dazzle a rather juvenile pilgrim from over the sea; but that matters little - it seemed so natural to him to shine. His spoken wit or wisdom, or whatever, had thus a charm almost beyond his written; that is if the high finish of his printed prose be really, as some people have maintained, a fault. There was such a kindness in him, however, that I've no doubt it gave him ideas for me, or about me, to see me sit as openmouthed as I now figure myself. Not so the two ladies, who not only were very nearly dumb from beginning to end of the meal, but who hadn't even the air of being struck with such an exhibition of fancy and taste. Mrs Ambient, detached, and inscrutable, met neither my eye nor her husband's: she attended to her dinner, watched her servants, arranged the puckers in her dress, exchanged at wide intervals a remark with her sisterinlaw and, while she slowly rubbed her lean white hands between the courses, looked out of the window at the first signs of evening - the long June day allowing us to dine without candles. Miss Ambient appeared to give little direct heed to anything said by her brother; but on the other hand she was much engaged in watching its effect upon me. Her 'dieaway' pupils continued to attach themselves to my countenance, and it was only her air of belonging to another century that kept them from being importunate. She seemed to look at me across the ages, and the interval of time diminished for me the inconvenience. It was as if she knew in a general way that he must be talking very well, but she herself was so at home among such allusions that she had no need to pick them up and was at liberty to see what would become of the exposure of a candid young American to a high aesthetic temperature.

The temperature was aesthetic certainly, but it was less so than I could have desired, for I failed of any great success in making our friend abound about himself. I tried to put him on the ground of his own genius, but he slipped through my fingers every time and shifted the saddle on one or other of his contemporaries. He talked about Balzac and Browning, about what was being done in foreign countries, about his recent tour in the East and the extraordinary forms of life to be observed in that part of the world. I felt he had reasons for holding off from a direct profession of literary faith, a full consistency or sincerity, and therefore dealt instead with certain social topics, treating them with extraordinary humour and with a due play of that power of ironic evocation in which his books abound. He had a deal to say about London as London appears to the observer who has the courage of some of his conclusions during the highpressure time - from April to July - of its gregarious life. He flashed his faculty of playing with the caught image and liberating the wistful idea over the whole scheme of manners or conception of intercourse of his compatriots, among whom there were evidently not a few types for which he had little love. London in short was grotesque to him, and he made capital sport of it; his only allusion that I can remember to his own work was his saying that he meant some day to do an immense and general, a kind of epic, social satire. Miss Ambient's perpetual gaze seemed to put to me: 'Do you perceive how artistic, how very strange and interesting, we are? Frankly now is it possible to be *more* artistic, *more* strange and interesting, than this? You surely won't deny that we're remarkable.' I was irritated by her use of the plural pronoun, for she had no right to pair herself with her brother; and moreover of course I couldn't see my way to - at all genially - include Mrs Ambient. Yet there was no doubt they were, taken together, unprecedented enough, and, with all allowances, I had never been left, or condemned, to draw so many rich inferences.

After the ladies had retired my host took me into his study to smoke, where I appealingly brought him round, or so tried, to some disclosure of fond ideals. I was bent on proving I was worthy to listen to him, on repaying him for what he had said to me before dinner, by showing him how perfectly I understood. He liked to talk; he liked to defend his convictions and his honour (not that I attacked them); he liked a little perhaps - it was a pardonable weakness - to bewilder the youthful mind even while wishing to win it over. My ingenuous sympathy received at any rate a shock from three or four of his professions - he made me occasionally gasp and stare. He couldn't help forgetting, or rather couldn't know, how little, in another and dryer clime, I had ever sat in the school in which he was master; and he promoted me as at a jump to a sense of its penetralia. My trepidations, however, were delightful; they were just what I had hoped for, and their only fault was that they passed away too quickly; since I found that for the main points I was essentially, I was quite constitutionally, on Mark Ambient's 'side'. This was the taken stand of the artist to whom every manifestation of human energy was a thrilling spectacle and who felt for ever the desire to resolve his experience of life into a literary form. On that high head of the passion for form - the attempt at perfection, the quest for which was to his mind the real search for the holy grail - he said the most interesting, the most inspiring things. He mixed with them a thousand illustrations from his own life, from other lives he had known, from history and fiction, and above all from the annals of the time that was dear to him beyond all periods, the Italian cinquecento. It came to me thus that in his books he had uttered but half his thought, and that what he had kept back - from motives I deplored when I made them out later - was the finer, and braver part. It was his fate to make a great many still more 'prepared' people than me not inconsiderably wince; but there was no grain of bravado in his ripest things (I've always maintained it, though often contradicted), and at bottom the poor fellow, disinterested to his finger-tips and regarding imperfection not only as an aesthetic but quite also as a social crime, had an extreme dread of scandal. There are critics who regret that having gone so far he didn't go further; but I regret nothing - putting aside two or three of the motives I just mentioned - since he arrived at a noble rarity and I don't see how you can go beyond that. The hours I spent in his study - this first one and the few that followed it; they were not after all so numerous - seem to glow, as I look back on them, with a tone that is partly that of the brown old room, rich, under the shaded candle-light where we sat and smoked, with the dusky delicate bindings of valuable books; partly that of his voice, of which I still catch the echo, charged with the fancies and figures that came at his command. When we went back to the drawingroom we found Miss Ambient alone in possession and prompt to mention that her sisterinlaw had a quarter of an hour before been called by the nurse to see the child, who appeared rather unwell - a little feverish.

'Feverish! how in the world comes he to be feverish?' Ambient asked.

'He was perfectly right this afternoon.'

'Beatrice says you walked him about too much - you almost killed him.'

'Beatrice must be very happy - she has an opportunity to triumph!' said my friend with a bright bitterness which was all I could have wished it.

'Surely not if the child's ill,' I ventured to remark by way of pleading for Mrs Ambient.

'My dear fellow, you aren't married - you don't know the nature of wives!' my host returned with spirit.

I tried to match it. 'Possibly not; but I know the nature of mothers.'

'Beatrice is perfect as a mother,' sighed Miss Ambient quite tremendously and with her fingers interlaced on her embroidered knees.

'I shall go up and see my boy,' her brother went on. 'Do you suppose he's asleep?'

'Beatrice won't let you see him, dear' - as to which our young lady looked at me, though addressing our companion.

'Do you call that being perfect as a mother?' Ambient asked.

'Yes, from her point of view.'

'Damn her point of view!' cried the author of 'Beltraffio'. And he left the room; after which we heard him ascend the stairs.

I sat there for some ten minutes with Miss Ambient, and we naturally had some exchange of remarks, which began, I think, by my asking her what the point of view of her sisterinlaw could be.

'Oh it's so very odd. But we're so very odd altogether. Don't you find us awfully unlike others of our class? - which indeed mostly, in England, is awful. We've lived so much abroad. I adore "abroad". Have you people like us in America?'

'You're not all alike, you interesting three - or, counting Dolcino, four - surely, surely; so that I don't think I understand your question. We've no one like your brother - I may go so far as that.'

'You've probably more persons like his wife,' Miss Ambient desolately smiled.

'I can tell you that better when you've told me about her point of view.'

'Oh yes - oh yes. Well,' said my entertainer, 'she doesn't like his ideas. She doesn't like them for the child. She thinks them undesirable.'

Being quite fresh from the contemplation of some of Mark Ambient's *arcana* I was particularly in a position to appreciate this announcement. But the effect of it was to make me, after staring a moment, burst into laughter which I instantly checked when I remembered the indisposed child above and the possibility of parents nervously or fussily anxious.

'What has that infant to do with ideas?' I asked. 'Surely he can't tell one from another. Has he read his father's novels?'

'He's very precocious and very sensitive, and his mother thinks she can't begin to guard him too early.' Miss Ambient's head drooped a little to one side and her eyes fixed themselves on futurity. Then of a sudden came a strange alteration; her face lighted to an effect more joyless than any gloom, to that indeed of a conscious insincere grimace, and she added: 'When one has children what one writes becomes a great responsibility.'

'Children are terrible critics,' I prosaically answered. 'I'm really glad I haven't any.'

'Do you also write then? And in the same style as my brother? And do you like that style? And do people appreciate it in America? I don't write, but I think I feel.' To these and various other enquiries and observations my young lady treated me till we heard her brother's step in the hall again and Mark Ambient reappeared. He was so flushed and grave that I supposed he had seen something symptomatic in the condition of his child. His sister apparently had another idea; she gazed at him from afar - as if he had been a burning ship on the horizon - and simply murmured 'Poor old Mark!'

'I hope you're not anxious,' I as promptly pronounced.

'No, but I'm disappointed. She won't let me in. She has locked the door, and I'm afraid to make a noise.' I dare say there might have been a touch of the ridiculous in such a confession, but I liked my new friend so much that it took nothing for me from his dignity. 'She tells me - from behind the door - that she'll let me know if he's worse.'

'It's very good of her,' said Miss Ambient with a hollow sound.

I had exchanged a glance with Mark in which it's possible he read that my pity for him was untinged with contempt, though I scarce know why he should have cared; and as his sister soon afterwards got up and took her bedroom candlestick he proposed we should go back to his study. We sat there till after midnight; he put himself into his slippers and an old velvet jacket, he lighted an ancient pipe, but he talked considerably less than before. There were longish pauses in our communion, but they only made me feel we had advanced in intimacy. They helped me further to understand my friend's personal situation and to imagine it by no means the happiest possible. When his face was quiet it was vaguely troubled, showing, to my increase of interest - if that was all that was wanted! - that for him too life was the same struggle it had been for so many another man of genius. At last I prepared to leave him, and then, to my ineffable joy, he gave me some of the sheets of his forthcoming book - which, though unfinished, he had indulged in the luxury, so dear to writers of delibera-tion, of having 'set up', from chapter to chapter, as he advanced. These early pages, the *prémices* in the language of letters, of that new fruit of his imagination, I should take to my room and look over at my leisure. I was in the act of leaving him when the door of the study noiselessly opened and Mrs Ambient stood before us. She observed us a moment, her candle in her hand, and then said to her husband that as she supposed he hadn't gone to bed she had come down to let him know Dolcino was more quiet and would probably be better in the morning. Mark Ambient made no reply; he simply slipped past her in the doorway, as if for fear she might seize him in his passage, and bounded upstairs to judge for himself of his child's condition. She looked so frankly discomfited that I for a moment believed her about to give him chase. But she resigned herself with a sigh and her eyes turned, ruefully and without a ray, to the lamplit room where various book, at which I had been looking were pulled out of their places on the shelves and the fumes of tobacco hung in midair. I bade her goodnight and then, without intention, by a kind of fatality, a perversity that had already made me address her overmuch on that question of her husband's powers, I alluded to the precious proofsheets with which Ambient had entrusted me and which I nursed there under my arm. 'They're the opening chapters of his new book,' I said. 'Fancy my satisfaction at being allowed to carry them to my room!'

She turned away, leaving me to take my candlestick from the table in the hall; but before we separated, thinking it apparently a good occasion to let me know once for all - since I was beginning, it would seem, to be quite 'thick' with my host - that there was no fitness in my appealing to her for sympathy in such a case; before we separated, I say, she remarked to me with her quick fine wellbred inveterate curtness: 'I dare say you attribute to me ideas I haven't got. I don't take that sort of interest in my husband's proofsheets. I consider his writings most objectionable!'

I had an odd colloquy the next morning with Miss Ambient, whom I found strolling in the garden before breakfast. The whole place looked as fresh and trim, amid the twitter of the birds, as if, an hour before, the housemaids had been turned into it with their dustpans and featherbrushes. I almost hesitated to light a cigarette and was doubly startled when, in the act of doing so, I suddenly saw the sister of my host, who had, at the best, something of the weirdness of an apparition, stand before me. She might have been posing for her photograph. Her sadcoloured robe arranged itself in serpentine folds at her feet; her hands locked themselves listlessly together in front; her chin rested on a cinquecento ruff. The first thing I did after bidding her goodmorning was to ask her for news of her little nephew - to express the hope she had heard he was better. She was able to gratify this trust she - spoke as if we might expect to see him during the day. We walked through the shrubberies together and she gave me further light on her brother's household, which offered me an opportunity to repeat to her what his wife had so startled and distressed me with the night before. *Was* it the sorry truth that she thought his productions objectionable?

'She doesn't usually come out with that so soon!' Miss Ambient returned in answer to my breathlessness.

'Poor lady,' I pleaded, 'she saw I'm a fanatic.'

'Yes, she won't like you for that. But you mustn't mind, if the rest of us like you! Beatrice thinks a work of art ought to have a "purpose". But she's a charming woman - don't you think her charming? I find in her quite the grand air.'

'She's very beautiful,' I produced with an effort; while I reflected that though it was apparently true that Mark Ambient was mismated it was also perceptible that his sister was perfidious. She assured me her brother and his wife had no other difference but this one - that she thought his writings immoral and his influence pernicious. It was a fixed idea; she was afraid of these things for the child. I answered that it was in all conscience enough, the trifle of a woman's regarding her husband's mind as a well of corruption, and she seemed much struck with the novelty of my remark. 'But there hasn't been any of the sort of trouble that there so often is among married people,' she said. 'I suppose you can judge for yourself that Beatrice isn't at all - well, whatever they call it when a woman kicks over! And poor Mark doesn't make love to other people either. You might think he would, but I assure you he doesn't. All the same of course, from her point of view, you know, she has a dread of my brother's influence on the child - on the formation of his character, his "ideals", poor little brat, his principles. It's as if it were a subtle poison or a contagion - something that would rub off on his tender sensibility when his father kisses him or holds him on his knee. If she could she'd prevent Mark from even so much as touching him. Every one knows it - visitors see it for themselves; so there's no harm in my telling you. Isn't it excessively odd? It comes from Beatrice's being so religious and so tremendously moral - so *à cheval* on fifty thousand *riguardi*. And then of course we mustn't forget,' my companion added, a little unexpectedly, to this polyglot proposition, 'that some of Mark's ideas are - well, really - rather impossible, don't you know?'

I reflected as we went into the house, where we found Ambient unfolding **The Observer** at the breakfasttable, that none of them were probably quite so 'impossible, don't you know?' as his sister. Mrs Ambient, a little 'the worse', as was mentioned, for her ministrations, during the night to Dolcino, didn't appear at breakfast. Her husband described her however as hoping to go to church. I afterwards learnt that she did go, but nothing naturally was less on the cards than that we should accompany her. It was while the churchbell droned near at hand that the author of 'Beltraffio' led me forth for the ramble he had spoken of in his note. I shall attempt here no record of where we went or of what we saw. We kept to the fields and copses and commons, and breathed the same sweet air as the nibbling donkeys and the browsing sheep, whose woolliness seemed to me, in those early days of acquaintance with English objects, but part of the general texture of the small dense landscape, which looked as if the harvest were gathered by the shears and with all nature bleating and braying for the violence. Everything was full of expression for Mark Ambient's visitor - from the big bandylegged geese whose whiteness was a 'note' amid all the tones of green as they wandered beside a neat little oval pool, the foreground of a thatched and whitewashed inn, with a grassy approach and a pictorial sign - from these humble wayside animals to the crests of high woods which let a gable or a pinnacle peep here and there and looked even at a distance like trees of good company, conscious of an individual profile. I admired the hedgerows, I plucked the fainthued heather, and I was for ever stopping to say how charming I thought the threadlike footpaths across the fields, which wandered in a diagonal of finer grain from one smooth stile to another. Mark Ambient was abundantly goodnatured and was as much struck, dear man, with some of my observations as I was with the literary allusions of the landscape. We sat and smoked on stiles, broaching paradoxes in the decent English air; we took short cuts across a park or two where the bracken was deep and my companion nodded to the old woman at the gate; we skirted rank coverts which rustled here and there as we passed, and we stretched ourselves at last on a heathery hillside where if the sun wasn't too hot neither was the earth too cold, and where the country lay beneath us in a rich blue mist. Of course I had already told him what I thought of his new novel, having the previous night read every word of the opening chapters before I went to bed.

'I'm not without hope of being able to make it decent enough,' he said as I went back to the subject while we turned up our heels to the sky. 'At least the people who dislike my stuff - and there are plenty of them, I believe - will dislike this thing (if it does turn out well) most.' This was the first time I had heard him allude to the people who couldn't read him - a class so generally conceived to sit heavy on the consciousness of the man of letters. A being organised for literature as Mark Ambient was must certainly have had the normal proportion of sensitiveness, of irritability; the artistic *ego,* capable in some cases of such monstrous development, must have been in his composition sufficiently erect and active. I won't therefore go so far as to say that he never thought of his detractors or that he had any illusions with regard to the number of his admirers - he could never so far have deceived himself as to believe he was popular, but I at least then judged (and had occasion to be sure later on) that stupidity ruffled him visibly but little, that he had an air of thinking it quite natural he should leave many simple folk, tasting of him, as simple as ever he found them, and that he very seldom talked about the newspapers, which, by the way, were always even abnormally vulgar about him. Of course he may have thought them over - the newspapers - night and day; the only point I make is that he didn't show it; while at the same time he didn't strike one as a man actively on his guard. I may add that, touching his hope of making the work on which he was then engaged the best of his books, it was only partly carried out. That place belongs incontestably to 'Beltraffio', in spite of the beauty of certain parts of its successor. I quite believe, however, that he had at the moment of which I speak no sense of having declined; he was in love with his idea, which was indeed magnificent, and though for him, as I suppose for every sane artist, the act of execution had in it as much torment as joy, he saw his result grow like the crescent of the young moon and promise to fill the disk. 'I want to be truer than I've ever been,' he said, settling himself on his back with his hands clasped behind his head; 'I want to give the impression of life itself. No, you may say what you will, I've always arranged things too much, always smoothed them down and rounded them off and tucked them in - done everything to them that life doesn't do. I've been a slave to the old superstitions.'

'You a slave, my dear Mark Ambient? You've the freest imagination of our day!'

'All the more shame to me to have done some of the things I have! The reconciliation of the two women in "Natalina", for instance, which could never really have taken place. That sort of thing's ignoble - I blush when I think of it! This new affair must be a golden vessel, filled with the purest distillation of the actual; and oh how it worries me, the shaping of the vase, the hammering of the metal! I have to hammer it so fine, so smooth; I don't do more than an inch or two a day. And all the while I have to be so careful not to let a drop of the liquor escape! When I see the kind of things Life herself, the brazen hussy, does, I despair of ever catching her peculiar trick. She has an impudence, Life! If one risked a fiftieth part of the effects she risks! It takes ever so long to believe it. You don't know yet, my dear youth. It isn't till one has been watching her some forty years that one finds out half of what she's up to! Therefore one's earlier things must inevitably contain a mass of rot. And with what one sees, on one side, with its tongue in its cheek, defying one to be real enough, and on the other the *bonnes gens*,' rolling up their eyes at one's cynicism, the situation has elements of the ludicrous which the poor reproducer himself is doubtless in a position to appreciate better than any one else. Of course one mustn't worry about the *bonnes gens*,' Mark Ambient went on while my thoughts reverted to his ladylike wife as interpreted by his remarkable sister.

'To sink your shaft deep and polish the plate through which people look into it - that's what your work consists of,' I remember ingeniously observing.

'Ah polishing one's plate - that's the torment of execution!' he exclaimed, jerking himself up and sitting forward. 'The effort to arrive at a surface, if you think anything of that decent sort necessary - some people don't, happily for them! My dear fellow, if you could see the surface I dream of as compared with the one with which I've to content myself. Life's really too short for art - one hasn't time to make one's shell ideally hard. Firm and bright, firm and bright is very well to say - the devilish thing has a way sometimes of being bright, and even of being hard, as mere tough frozen pudding is hard, without being firm. When I rap it with my knuckles it doesn't give the right sound. There are horrible sandy stretches where I've taken the wrong turn because I couldn't for the life of me find the right. If you knew what a dunce I am sometimes! Such things figure to me now base pimples and ulcers on the brow of beauty!'

'They're very bad, very bad,' I said as gravely as I could.

'Very bad? They're the highest social offence I know; it ought - it absolutely ought; I'm quite serious - to be capital. If I knew I should be publicly thrashed else I'd manage to find the true word. The people who can't - some of them don't so much as know it when they see it - would shut their inkstands, and we shouldn't be deluged by this flood of rubbish!'

I shall not attempt to repeat everything that passed between us, nor to explain just how it was that, every moment I spent in his company, Mark Ambient revealed to me more and more the consistency of his creative spirit, the spirit in him that felt all life as plastic material. I could but envy him the force of that passion, and it was at any rate through the receipt of this impression that by the time we returned I had gained the sense of intimacy with him that I have noted. Before we got up for the homeward stretch he alluded to his wife's having once - or perhaps more than once - asked him whether he should like Dolcino to read 'Beltraffio'. He must have been unaware at the moment of all that this conveyed to me - as well doubtless of my extreme curiosity to hear what he had replied. He had said how much he hoped Dolcino would read *all* his works - when he was twenty; he should like him to know what his father had done. Before twenty it would be useless; he wouldn't understand them.

'And meanwhile do you propose to hide them - to lock them up in a drawer?' Mrs Ambient had proceeded.

'Oh no - we must simply tell him they're not intended for small boys. If you bring him up properly after that he won't touch them.'

To this Mrs Ambient had made answer that it might be very awkward when he was about fifteen, say; and I asked her husband if it were his opinion in general that young people shouldn't read novels.

'Good ones - certainly not!' said my companion. I suppose I had had other views, for I remember saying that for myself I wasn't sure it was bad for them if the novels were 'good' to the right intensity of goodness. 'Bad for *them,* I don't say so much!' my companion returned. 'But very bad, I'm afraid, for the poor dear old novel itself.' That oblique accidental allusion to his wife's attitude was followed by a greater breadth of reference as we walked home. 'The difference between us is simply the opposition between two distinct ways of looking at the world, which have never succeeded in getting on together, or in making any kind of common household, since the beginning of time. They've borne all sorts of names, and my wife would tell you it's the difference between Christian and Pagan. I may be a pagan, but I don't like the name; it sounds sectarian. She thinks me at any rate no better than an ancient Greek. It's the difference between making the most of life and making the least, so that you'll get another better one in some other time and place. Will it be a sin to make the most of that one too, I wonder; and shall we have to be bribed off in the future state as well as in the present? Perhaps I care too much for beauty - I don't know, I doubt if a poor devil *can*; I delight in it, I adore it, I think of it continually, I try to produce it, to reproduce it. My wife holds that we shouldn't cultivate or enjoy it without extraordinary precautions and reserves. She's always afraid of it, always on her guard. I don't know what it can ever have done to her, what grudge it owes her or what resentment rides. And she's so pretty too herself! Don't you think she's lovely? She was at any rate when we married. At that time I wasn't aware of that difference I speak of - I thought it all came to the same thing: in the end, as they say. Well, perhaps it will in the end. I don't know what the end will be. Moreover I care for seeing things as they are; that's the way I try to show them in any professed picture. But you mustn't talk to Mrs Ambient about things as they are. She has a mortal dread of things as they are.'

'She's afraid of them for Dolcino,' I said: surprised a moment afterwards at being in a position - thanks to Miss Ambient - to be so explanatory; and surprised even now that Mark shouldn't have shown visibly that he wondered what the deuce I knew about it. But he didn't; he simply declared with a tenderness that touched me: 'Ah nothing shall ever hurt him!'

He told me more about his wife before we arrived at the gate of home, and if he be judged to have aired overmuch his grievance I'm afraid I must admit that he had some of the foibles as well as the gifts of the artistic temperament; adding, however, instantly that hitherto, to the best of my belief, he had rarely let this particular cat out of the bag. 'She thinks me immoral - that's the long and short of it,' he said as we paused outside a moment and his hand rested on one of the bars of his gate; while his conscious expressive perceptive eyes - the eyes of a foreigner, I had begun to account them, much more than of the usual Englishman - viewing me now evidently as quite a familiar friend, took part in the declaration. 'It's very strange when one thinks it all over, and there's a grand comicality in it that I should like to bring out. She's a very nice woman, extraordinarily well-behaved, upright and clever and with a tremendous lot of good sense about a good many matters. Yet her conception of a novel - she has explained it to me once or twice, and she doesn't do it badly as exposition - is a thing so false that it makes me blush. It's a thing so hollow, so dishonest, so lying, in which life is so blinked and blinded, so dodged and disfigured, that it makes my ears burn. It's two different ways of looking at the whole affair,' he repeated, pushing open the gate. 'And they're irreconcileable!' he added with a sigh. We went forward to the house, but on the walk, halfway to the door, he stopped and said to me: 'If you're going into this kind of thing there's a fact you should know beforehand; it may save you some disappointment. There's a hatred of art, there's a hatred of literature - I mean of the genuine kind. Oh the shams - *those* they'll swallow by the bucket!' I looked up at the charming house, with its genial colour and crookedness, and I answered with a smile that those evil passions might exist, but that I should never have expected to find them there. 'Ah it doesn't matter after all,' he a bit nervously laughed; which I was glad to hear, for I was reproaching myself with having worked him up.

If I had it soon passed off, for at luncheon he was delightful; strangely delightful considering that the difference between himself and his wife was, as he had said, irreconcileable. He had the art, by his manner, by his smile, by his natural amenity, of reducing the importance of it in the common concerns of life; and Mrs Ambient, I must add, lent herself to this transaction with a very good grace. I watched her at table for further illustrations of that fixed idea of which Miss Ambient had spoken to me; for in the light of the united revelations of her sisterinlaw and her husband she had come to seem to me almost a sinister personage. Yet the signs of a sombre fanaticism were not more immediately striking in her than before; it was only after a while that her air of incorruptible conformity, her tapering monosyllabic correctness, began to affect me as in themselves a cold thin flame. Certainly, at first, she resembled a woman with as few passions as possible; but if she had a passion at all it would indeed be that of Philistinism. She might have been (for there are guardianspirits, I suppose, of all great principles) the very angel of the pink of propriety - putting the pink for a principle, though I'd rather put some dismal cold blue. Mark Ambient, apparently, ten years before, had simply and quite inevitably taken her for an angel, without asking himself for what. He had been right in calling my attention to her beauty. In looking for some explanation of his original surrender to her I saw more than before that she was, physically speaking, a wonderfully cultivated human plant - that he might well have owed her a brief poetic inspiration. It was impossible to be more propped and pencilled, more delicately tinted and petalled.

If I had had it in my heart to think my host a little of a hypocrite for appearing to forget at table everything he had said to me in our walk, I should instantly have cancelled such a judgement on reflecting that the good news his wife was able to give him about their little boy was ground enough for any optimistic reaction. It may have come partly too from a certain compunction at having breathed to me at all harshly on the cool fair lady who sat there - a desire to prove himself not after all so mismated. Dolcino continued to be much better, and it had been promised him he should come downstairs after his dinner. As soon as we had risen from our own meal Mark slipped away, evidently for the purpose of going to his child; and no sooner had I observed this than I became aware his wife had simultaneously vanished. It happened that Miss Ambient and I, both at the same moment, saw the tail of her dress whisk out of a doorway; an incident that led the young lady to smile at me as if I now knew all the secrets of the Ambients. I passed with her into the garden and we sat down on a dear old bench that rested against the west wall of the house. It was a perfect spot for the middle period of a Sunday in June, and its felicity seemed to come partly from an antique sundial which, rising in front of us and forming the centre of a small intricate parterre, measured the moments ever so slowly and made them safe for leisure and talk. The

garden bloomed in the suffused afternoon, the tall beeches stood still for
an example, and, behind and above us, a rosetree of many seasons,
clinging to the faded grain of the brick, expressed the whole character of
the scene in a familiar exquisite smell. It struck me as a place to offer
genius every favour and sanction - not to bristle with challenges and
checks. Miss Ambient asked me if I had enjoyed my walk with her brother
and whether we had talked of many things.

'Well, of most things,' I freely allowed, though I remembered we
hadn't talked of Miss Ambient.

'And don't you think some of his theories are very peculiar?'

'Oh I guess I agree with them all.' I was very particular, for Miss
Ambient's entertainment, to guess.

'Do you think art's everything?' she put to me in a moment.

'In art, of course I do!'

'And do you think beauty's everything?'

'Everything's a big word, which I think we should use as little as
possible. But how can we not want beauty?'

'Ah there you are!' she sighed, though I didn't quite know what she
meant by it. 'Of course it's difficult for a woman to judge how far to go,'
she went on. 'I adore everything that gives a charm to life. I'm intensely
sensitive to form. But sometimes I draw back - don't you see what I mean?
- I don't quite see where I shall be landed. I only want to be quiet, after
all,' Miss Ambient continued as if she had long been baffled at this modest
desire. 'And one must be good, at any rate, must not one?' she pursued
with a dubious quaver - an intimation apparently that what I might say one
way or the other would settle it for her. It was difficult for me to be very
original in reply, and I'm afraid I repaid her confidence with an unblush-
ing platitude. I remember moreover attaching to it an enquiry, equally
destitute of freshness and still more wanting perhaps in tact, as to whether
she didn't mean to go to church, since that was an obvious way of being
good. She made answer that she had performed this duty in the morning,
and that for her, of Sunday afternoons, supreme virtue consisted in
answering the week's letters. Then suddenly and without transition she
brought out: 'It's quite a mistake about Dolcino's being better. I've seen
him and he's not at all right.'

I wondered, and somehow I think I scarcely believed. 'Surely his
mother would know, wouldn't she?'

She appeared for a moment to be counting the leaves on one of the great beeches. 'As regards most matters one can easily say what, in a given situation, my sisterinlaw will, or would, do. But in the present case there are strange elements at work.'

'Strange elements? Do you mean in the constitution of the child?'

'No, I mean in my sisterinlaw's feelings.'

'Elements of affection of course; elements of anxiety,' I concurred. 'But why do you call them strange?'

She repeated my words. 'Elements of affection, elements of anxiety. She's very anxious.'

Miss Ambient put me indescribably ill at ease; she almost scared me, and I wished she would go and write her letters. 'His father will have seen him now,' I said, 'and if he's not satisfied he will send for the doctor.'

'The doctor ought to have been here this morning,' she promptly returned. 'He lives only two miles away.'

I reflected that all this was very possibly but a part of the general tragedy of Miss Ambient's view of things; yet I asked her why she hadn't urged that view on her sister-in-law. She answered me with a smile of extraordinary significance and observed that I must have very little idea of her 'peculiar' relations with Beatrice; but I must do her the justice that she re-enforced this a little by the plea that any distinguishable alarm of Mark's was ground enough for a difference of his wife's. He was always nervous about the child, and as they were predestined by nature to take opposite views, the only thing for the mother was to cultivate a false optimism. In Mark's absence and that of his betrayed fear she would have been less easy. I remembered what he had said to me about their dealings with their son - that between them they'd probably put an end to him; but I didn't repeat this to Miss Ambient: the less so that just then her brother emerged from the house, carrying the boy in his arms. Close behind him moved his wife, grave and pale; the little sick face was turned over Ambient's shoulder and towards the mother. We rose to receive the group, and as they came near us Dolcino twisted himself about. His enchanting eyes showed me a smile of recognition, in which, for the moment, I should have taken a due degree of comfort. Miss Ambient, however, received another impression, and I make haste to say that her quick sensibility, which visibly went out to the child, argues that in spite of her affectations she might have been of some human use. 'It won't do at all - it won't do at all,' she said to me under her breath. 'I shall speak to Mark about the Doctor.'

Her small nephew was rather white, but the main difference I saw in him was that he was even more beautiful than the day before. He had been dressed in his festal garments - a velvet suit and a crimson sash - and he looked like a little invalid prince too young to know condescension and smiling familiarly on his subjects.

'Put him down, Mark, he's not a bit at his ease,' Mrs Ambient said.

'Should you like to stand on your feet, my boy?' his father asked.

He made a motion that quickly responded. 'Oh yes; I'm remarkably well.'

Mark placed him on the ground; he had shining pointed shoes with enormous bows. 'Are you happy now, Mr Ambient?'

'Oh yes, I'm particularly happy,' Dolcino replied. But the words were scarce out of his mouth when his mother caught him up and, in a moment, holding him on her knees, took her place on the bench where Miss Ambient and I had been sitting. This young lady said something to her brother, in consequence of which the two wandered away into the garden together.

I remained with Mrs Ambient, but as a servant had brought out a couple of chairs I wasn't obliged to seat myself beside her. Our conversation failed of ease, and I, for my part, felt there would be a shade of hypocrisy in my now trying to make myself agreeable to the partner of my friend's existence. I didn't dislike her - I rather admired her; but I was aware that I differed from her inexpressibly. Then I suspected, what I afterwards definitely knew and have already intimated, that the poor lady felt small taste for her husband's so undisguised disciple; and this of course was not encouraging. She thought me an obtrusive and designing, even perhaps a depraved, young man whom a perverse Providence had dropped upon their quiet lawn to flatter his worst tendencies. She did me the honour to say to Miss Ambient, who repeated the speech, that she didn't know when she had seen their companion take such a fancy to a visitor; and she measured apparently my evil influence by Mark's appreciation of my society. I had a consciousness, not oppressive but quite sufficient, of all this; though I must say that if it chilled my flow of smalltalk it yet didn't prevent my thinking the beautiful mother and beautiful child, interlaced there against their background of roses, a picture such as I doubtless shouldn't soon see again. I was free, I supposed, to go into the house and write letters, to sit in the drawing-room, to repair to my own apartment and take a nap; but the only use I made of my freedom was to linger still in my chair and say to myself that the light hand of Sir Joshua might have painted Mark Ambient's wife and son. I found myself looking perpetually at the latter small mortal, who looked constantly back at me, and that was enough to detain me. With these vaguely - amused eyes he smiled, and I felt it an absolute impossibility to abandon a child with such an expression. His attention never strayed; it attached itself to my face as if among all the small incipient things of his nature throbbed a desire to say something to me. If I could have taken him on my own knee he perhaps would have managed to say it; but it would have been a critical matter to ask his mother to give him up, and it has remained a constant regret for me that on that strange Sunday afternoon I didn't even for a moment hold Dolcino in my arms. He had said he felt remarkably well and was especially happy; but though peace may have been with him as he pillowed his charming head on his mother's breast, dropping his little crimson silk legs from her lap, I somehow didn't think security was. He made no attempt to walk about; he was content to swing his legs softly and strike one as languid and angelic.

Mark returned to us with his sister; and Miss Ambient, repeating her mention of the claims of her correspondence, passed into the house. Mark came and stood in front of his wife, looking down at the child, who immediately took hold of his hand and kept it while he stayed. 'I think Mackintosh ought to see him,' he said; 'I think I'll walk over and fetch him.'

'That's Gwendolen's idea, I suppose,' Mrs Ambient replied very sweetly.

'It's not such an outoftheway idea when one's child's ill,' he returned.

'I'm not ill, papa; I'm much better now,' sounded in the boy's silver pipe.

'Is that the truth, or are you only saying it to be agreeable? You've a great idea of being agreeable, you know.'

The child seemed to meditate on this distinction, this imputation, for a moment; then his exaggerated eyes, which had wandered, caught my own as I watched him. 'Do *you* think me agreeable?' he enquired with the candour of his age and with a look that made his father turn round to me laughing and ask, without saying it, 'Isn't he adorable?'

'Then why don't you hop about, if you feel so lusty?' Ambient went on while his son swung his hand.

'Because mamma's holding me close!'

'Oh yes; I know how mamma holds you when I come near!' cried Mark with a grimace at his wife.

She turned her charming eyes up to him without deprecation or concession. 'You can go for Mackintosh if you like. I think myself it would be better. You ought to drive.'

'She says that to get me away,' he put to me with a gaiety that I thought a little false; after which he started for the Doctor's.

I remained there with Mrs Ambient, though even our exchange of twaddle had run very thin. The boy's little fixed white face seemed, as before, to plead with me to stay, and after a while it produced still another effect, a very curious one, which I shall find it difficult to express. Of course I expose myself to the charge of an attempt to justify by a strained logic after the fact a step which may have been on my part but the fruit of a native want of discretion; and indeed the traceable consequences of that perversity were too lamentable to leave me any desire to trifle with the question. All I can say is that I acted in perfect good faith and that Dolcino's friendly little gaze gradually kindled the spark of my inspiration. What helped it to glow were the other influences - the silent suggestive gardennook, the perfect opportunity (if it was not an opportunity for that it was an opportunity for nothing) and the plea I speak of, which issued from the child's eyes and seemed to make him say: 'The mother who bore me and who presses me here to her bosom - sympathetic little organism that I am - has really the kind of sensibility she has been represented to you as lacking, if you only look for it patiently and respectfully. How is it conceivable she shouldn't have it? How is it possible that I should have so much of it - for I'm quite full of it, dear strange gentleman - if it weren't also in some degree in her? I'm my great father's child, but I'm also my beautiful mother's, and I'm sorry for the difference between them!' So it shaped itself before me, the vision of reconciling Mrs Ambient with her husband, of putting an end to their ugly difference. The project was absurd of course, for had I not had his word for it - spoken with all the bitterness of experience - that the gulf dividing them was wellnigh bottomless? Nevertheless, a quarter of an hour after Mark had left us, I observed to my hostess that I couldn't get over what she had told me the night before about her thinking her husband's compositions 'objectionable.' I had been so very sorry to hear it, had thought of it constantly and wondered whether it mightn't be possible to make her change her mind. She gave me a great cold stare, meant apparently as an admonition to me to mind my business. I wish I had taken this mute counsel, but I didn't take it. I went on to remark that it seemed an immense pity so much that was interesting should be lost on her.

'Nothing's lost upon me,' she said in a tone that didn't make the contradiction less. 'I know they're very interesting.'

'Don't you like papa's books?' Dolcino asked, addressing his mother but still looking at me. Then he added to me: 'Won't you read them to me, American gentleman?'

'I'd rather tell you some stories of my own,' I said. 'I know some that are awfully good.'

'When will you tell them? Tomorrow?'

'Tomorrow with pleasure, if that suits you.'

His mother took this in silence. Her husband, during our walk, had asked me to remain another day; my promise to her son was an implication that I had consented, and it wasn't possible the news could please her. This ought doubtless to have made me more careful as to what I said next, but all I can plead is that it didn't. I soon mentioned that just after leaving her the evening before, and after hearing her apply to her husband's writings the epithet already quoted, I had on going up to my room sat down to the perusal of those sheets of his new book that he had been so good as to lend me. I had sat entranced till nearly three in the morning - I had read them twice over. 'You say you haven't looked at them. I think it's such a pity you shouldn't. Do let me beg you to take them up. They're so very remarkable. I'm sure they'll convert you. They place him in - really - such a dazzling light. All that's best in him is there. I've no doubt it's a great liberty, my saying all this; but pardon me, and *do* read them!'

'Do read them, mamma!' the boy again sweetly shrilled. 'Do read them!'

She bent her head and closed his lips with a kiss. 'Of course I know he has worked immensely over them,' she said; after which she made no remark, but attached her eyes thoughtfully to the ground. The tone of these last words was such as to leave me no spirit for further pressure, and after hinting at a fear that her husband mightn't have caught the Doctor I got up and took a turn about the grounds. When I came back ten minutes later she was still in her place watching her boy, who had fallen asleep in her lap. As I drew near she put her finger to her lips and a short time afterwards rose, holding him; it being now best, she said, that she should take him upstairs. I offered to carry him and opened my arms for the purpose; but she thanked me and turned away with the child in her embrace, his head on her shoulder. 'I'm very strong,' was her last word as she passed into the house, her slim flexible figure bent backward with the filial weight. So I never laid a longing hand on Dolcino.

I betook myself to Ambient's study, delighted to have a quiet hour to look over his books by myself. The windows were open to the garden; the sunny stillness, the mild light of the English summer, filled the room without quite chasing away the rich dusky tone that was a part of its charm and that abode in the serried shelves where old morocco exhaled the fragrance of curious learning, as well as in the brighter intervals where prints and medals and miniatures were suspended on a surface of faded stuff. The place had both colour and quiet; I thought it a perfect room for work and went so far as to say to myself that, if it were mine to sit and scribble in, there was no knowing but I might learn to write as well as the author of 'Beltraffio'. This distinguished man still didn't reappear, and I rummaged freely among his treasures. At last I took down a book that detained me a while and seated myself in a fine old leather chair by the window to turn it over. I had been occupied in this way for half an hour - a good part of the afternoon had waned - when I became conscious of another presence in the room and, looking up from my quarto, saw that Mrs Ambient, having pushed open the door quite again in the same noiseless way marking or disguising her entrance the night before, had advanced across the threshold. On seeing me she stopped; she had not, I think, expected to find me. But her hesitation was only of a moment; she came straight to her husband's writingtable as if she were looking for something. I got up and asked her if I could help her. She glanced about an instant and then put her hand upon a roll of papers which I recognised, as I had placed it on that spot at the early hour of my descent from my room.

'Is this the new book?' she asked, holding it up.

'The very sheets,' I smiled; 'with precious annotations.'

'I mean to take your advice' - and she tucked the little bundle under her arm. I congratulated her cordially and ventured to make of my triumph, as I presumed to call it, a subject of pleasantry. But she was perfectly grave and turned away from me, as she had presented herself, without relaxing her rigour; after which I settled down to my quarto again with the reflexion that Mrs Ambient was truly an eccentric. My triumph too suddenly seemed to me rather vain. A woman who couldn't unbend at a moment exquisitely indicated would never understand Mark Ambient. He came back to us at last in person, having brought the Doctor with him. 'He was away from home,' Mark said, 'and I went after him to where he was supposed to be. He had left the place, and I followed him to two or three others, which accounts for my delay.' He was now with Mrs Ambient, looking at the child, and was to see Mark again before leaving the house. My host noticed at the end of two minutes that the proofsheets of his new book had been removed from the table; and when I told him, in reply to his question as to what I knew about them, that Mrs Ambient had carried them off to read he turned almost pale with surprise. 'What has suddenly made her so curious?' he cried; and I was obliged to tell him that I was at the bottom of the mystery. I had had it on my conscience to assure her that she really ought to know of what her husband was capable. 'Of what I'm capable? Elle ne s'en doute que trop!'' said Ambient with a laugh; but he took my meddling very goodnaturedly and contented himself with adding that he was really much afraid she would burn up the sheets, his emendations and all, of which latter he had no duplicate. The Doctor paid a long visit in the nursery, and before he came down I retired to my own quarters, where I remained till dinnertime. On entering the drawingroom at this hour I found Miss Ambient in possession, as she had been the evening before.

'I was right about Dolcino,' she said, as soon as she saw me, with an air of triumph that struck me as the climax of perversity. 'He's really very ill.'

'Very ill! Why when I last saw him, at four o'clock, he was in fairly good form.'

'There has been a change for the worse, very sudden and rapid, and when the Doctor got here he found diphtheritic symptoms. He ought to have been called, as I knew, in the morning, and the child oughtn't to have been brought into the garden.'

'My dear lady, he was very happy there,' I protested with horror.

'He would be very happy anywhere. I've no doubt he's very happy now, with his poor little temperature-!' She dropped her voice as her brother came in, and Mark let us know that as a matter of course Mrs Ambient wouldn't appear. It was true the boy had developed diphtheritic symptoms, but he was quiet for the present and his mother earnestly watching him. She was a perfect nurse, Mark said, and Mackintosh would come back at ten. Our dinner wasn't very gay - with my host worried and absent; and his sister annoyed me by her constant tacit assumption, conveyed in the very way she nibbled her bread and sipped her wine, of having 'told me so.' I had had no disposition to deny anything she might have told me, and I couldn't see that her satisfaction in being justified by the event relieved her little nephew's condition. The truth is that, as the sequel was to prove, Miss Ambient had some of the qualities of the sibyl and had therefore perhaps a right to the sibylline contortions. Her brother was so preoccupied that I felt my presence an indiscretion and was sorry I had promised to remain over the morrow. I put it to Mark that clearly I had best leave them in the morning; to which he replied that, on the contrary, if he was to pass the next days in the fidgets my company would distract his attention. The fidgets had already begun for him, poor fellow; and as we sat in his study with our cigars after dinner he wandered to the door whenever he heard the sound of the Doctor's wheels. Miss Ambient, who shared this apartment with us, gave me at such moments significant glances; she had before rejoining us gone upstairs to ask about the child. His mother and his nurse gave a fair report, but Miss Ambient found his fever high and his symptoms very grave. The Doctor came at ten o'clock, and I went to bed after hearing from Mark that he saw no present cause for alarm. He had made every provision for the night and was to return early in the morning

I quitted my room as eight struck the next day and when I came downstairs saw, through the open door of the house, Mrs Ambient standing at the front gate of the grounds in colloquy with Mackintosh. She wore a white dressing-gown, but her shining hair was carefully tucked away in its net, and in the morning freshness, after a night of watching, she looked as much 'the type of the lady' as her sister-in-law had described her. Her appearance, I suppose, ought to have reassured me; but I was still nervous and uneasy, so that I shrank from meeting her with the necessary challenge. None the less, however, was I impatient to learn how the new day found him; and as Mrs Ambient hadn't seen me I passed into the grounds by a roundabout way and, stopping at a further gate, hailed the Doctor just as he was driving off. Mrs Ambient had returned to the house before he got into his cart.

'Pardon me, but as a friend of the family I should like very much to hear about the little boy.'

The stout sharp circumspect man looked at me from head to foot and then said: 'I'm sorry to say I haven't seen him.'

'Haven't seen him?'

'Mrs Ambient came down to meet me as I alighted, and told me he was sleeping so soundly, after a restless night, that she didn't wish him disturbed. I assured her I wouldn't disturb him, but she said he was quite safe now and she could look after him herself.'

'Thank you very much. Are you coming back?'

'No sir; I'll be hanged if I come back!' cried the honest practitioner in high resentment. And the horse started as he settled beside his man.

I wandered back into the garden, and five minutes later Miss Ambient came forth from the house to greet me. She explained that breakfast wouldn't be served for some time and that she desired a moment herself with the Doctor. I let her know that the good vexed man had come and departed, and I repeated to her what he had told me about his dismissal. This made Miss Ambient very serious, very serious indeed, and she sank into a bench, with dilated eyes, hugging her elbows with crossed arms. She indulged in many strange signs, she confessed herself immensely distressed, and she finally told me what her own last news of her nephew had been. She had sat up very late - after me, after Mark - and before going to bed had knocked at the door of the child's room, opened to her by the nurse. This good woman had admitted her and she had found him quiet, but flushed and 'unnatural,' with his mother sitting by his bed. 'She held his hand in one of hers,' said Miss Ambient, 'and in the other - what do you think? - the proofsheets of Mark's new book! She was reading them there intently: did you ever hear of anything so extraordinary? Such a very odd time to be reading an author whom she never could abide!' In her agitation Miss Ambient was guilty of this vulgarism of speech, and I was so impressed by her narrative that only in recalling her words later did I notice the lapse. Mrs Ambient had looked up from her reading with her finger on her lips - I recognised the gesture she had addressed me in the afternoon - and, though the nurse was about to go to rest, had not encouraged her sisterinlaw to relieve her of any part of her vigil. But certainly at that time the boy's state was far from reassuring - his poor little breathing so painful; and what change could have taken place in him in those few hours that would justify Beatrice in denying Mackintosh access? This was the moral of Miss Ambient's anecdote, the moral for herself at least. The moral for me, rather, was that it *was* a very singular

time for Mrs Ambient to be going into a novelist she had never appreciated and who had simply happened to be recommended to her by a young
American she disliked. I thought of her sitting there in the sickchamber in
the still hours of the night and after the nurse had left her, turning and
turning those pages of genius and wrestling with their magical influence.
I must be sparing of the minor facts and the later emotions of this
sojourn - it lasted but a few hours longer - and devote but three words to
my subsequent relations with Ambient. They lasted five years - till his
death - and were full of interest, of satisfaction and, I may add, of sadness.
The main thing to be said of these years is that I had a secret from him
which I guarded to the end. I believe he never suspected it, though of this
I'm not absolutely sure. If he had so much as an inkling the line he had
taken, the line of absolute negation of the matter to himself, shows an
immense effort of the will. I may at last lay bare my secret, giving it for
what it is worth; now that the main sufferer has gone, that he has begun
to be alluded to as one of the famous early dead and that his wife has
ceased to survive him; now too that Miss Ambient, whom I also saw at
intervals during the time that followed, has, with her embroideries and her
attitudes, her necromantic glances and strange intuitions, retired to a
Sisterhood, where, as I am told, she is deeply immured and quite lost to
the world.

Mark came in to breakfast after this lady and I had for some time been
seated there. He shook hands with me in silence, kissed my companion,
opened his letters and newspapers and pretended to drink his coffee. But
I took these movements for mechanical and was little surprised when he
suddenly pushed away everything that was before him and, with his head
in his hands and his elbows on the table, sat staring strangely at the cloth.

'What's the matter, *caro fratello mio*?' Miss Ambient quavered, peeping from behind the urn.

He answered nothing, but got up with a certain violence and strode to
the window. We rose to our feet, his relative and I, by a common impulse,
exchanging a glance of some alarm; and he continued to stare into the
garden. 'In heaven's name what has got possession of Beatrice?' he cried
at last, turning round on us a ravaged face. He looked from one of us to
the other - the appeal was addressed to us alike.

Miss Ambient gave a shrug. 'My poor Mark, Beatrice is always -
Beatrice!'

'She has locked herself up with the boy - bolted and barred the door. She refuses to let me come near him!' he went on.

'She refused to let Mackintosh see him an hour ago!' Miss Ambient promptly returned.

'Refused to let Mackintosh see him? By heaven I'll smash in the door!' And Mark brought his fist down upon the sideboard, which he had now approached, so that all the breakfastservice rang.

I begged Miss Ambient to go up and try to have speech of her sisterinlaw, and I drew Mark out into the garden. 'You're exceedingly nervous, and Mrs Ambient's probably right,' I there undertook to plead. 'Women know; women should be supreme in such a situation. Trust a mother - a devoted mother, my dear friend!' With such words as these I tried to soothe and comfort him, and, marvellous to relate, I succeeded, with the help of many cigarettes, in making him walk about the garden and talk, or suffer me at least to to so for near an hour. When about that time had elapsed his sister reappeared, reaching us rapidly and with a convulsed face while she held her hand to her heart.

'Go for the Doctor, Mark - go for the Doctor this moment!'

'Is he dying? Has she killed him?' my poor friend cried, flinging away his cigarette.

'I don't know what she has done! But she's frightened, and now she wants the Doctor.'

'He told me he'd be hanged if he came back!' I felt myself obliged to mention.

'Precisely - therefore Mark himself must go for him, and not a messenger. You must see him and tell him it's to save your child. The trap has been ordered - it's ready.'

'To save him? I'll save him, please God!' Ambient cried, bounding with his great strides across the lawn.

As soon as he had gone I felt I ought to have volunteered in his place, and I said as much to Miss Ambient; but she checked me by grasping my arm while we heard the wheels of the dogcart rattle away from the gate. 'He's off - he's off - and now I can think! To get him away - while I think - while I think!'

'While you think of what, Miss Ambient?'

'Of the unspeakable thing that has happened under this roof!'

Her manner was habitually that of such a prophetess of ill that I at first allowed for some great extravagance. But I looked at her hard, and the next thing felt myself turn white. 'Dolcino is dying then - he's dead?' 'It's too late to save him. His mother has let him die! I tell you that because you're sympathetic, because you've imagination,' Miss Ambient was good enough to add, interrupting my expression of horror. 'That's why you had the idea of making her read Mark's new book!'

'What has that to do with it? I don't understand you. Your accusation's monstrous.'

'I see it all - I'm not stupid,' she went on, heedless of my emphasis. 'It was the book that finished her - it was that decided her!'

'Decided her? Do you mean she has murdered her child?' I demanded, trembling at my own words.

'She sacrificed him; she determined to do nothing to make him live. Why else did she lock herself in, why else did she turn away the Doctor? The book gave her a horror; she determined to rescue him - to prevent him from ever being touched. He had a crisis at two o'clock in the morning. I know that from the nurse, who had left her then, but whom, for a short time, she called back. The darling got much worse, but she insisted on the nurse's going back to bed, and after that she was alone with him for hours.'

I listened with a dread that stayed my credence, while she stood there with her tearless glare. 'Do you pretend then she has no pity, that she's cruel and insane?'

'She held him in her arms, she pressed him to her breast, not to see him; but she gave him no remedies; she did nothing the Doctor ordered. Everything's there untouched. She has had the honesty not even to throw the drugs away!'

I dropped upon the nearest bench, overcome with my dismay - quite as much at Miss Ambient's horrible insistence and distinctness as at the monstrous meaning of her words. Yet they came amazingly straight, and if they did have a sense I saw myself too woefully figure in it. Had I been then a proximate cause -? 'You're a very strange woman and you say incredible things,' I could only reply.

She had one of her tragic headshakes. 'You think it necessary to protest, but you're really quite ready to believe me. You've received an impression of my sisterinlaw - you've guessed of what she's capable.'

I don't feel bound to say what concession on this score I made to Miss Ambient, who went on to relate to me that within the last halfhour Beatrice had had a revulsion, that she was tremendously frightened at what she had done; that her fright itself betrayed her; and that she would now give heaven and earth to save the child. 'Let us hope she will!' I said, looking at my watch and trying to time poor Ambient; whereupon my companion repeated all portentously 'Let us hope so!' When I asked her if she herself could do nothing, and whether she oughtn't to be with her sisterinlaw, she replied: 'You had better go and judge! She's like a wounded tigress!'

I never saw Mrs Ambient till six months after this, and therefore can't pretend to have verified the comparison. At the latter period she was again the type of the perfect lady. 'She'll treat him better after this,' I remember her sisterin-law's saying in response to some quick outburst, on my part, of compassion for her brother. Though I had been in the house but thirtysix hours this young lady had treated me with extraordinary confidence, and there was therefore a certain demand I might, as such an intimate, make of her. I extracted from her a pledge that she'd never say to her brother what she had just said to me, that she'd let him form his own theory of his wife's conduct. She agreed with me that there was misery enough in the house without her contributing a new anguish, and that Mrs Ambient's proceedings might be explained, to her husband's mind, by the extravagance of a jealous devotion. Poor Mark came back with the Doctor much sooner than we could have hoped, but we knew five minutes afterwards that it was all too late. His sole, his adored little son was more exquisitely beautiful in death than he had been in life. Mrs Ambient's grief was frantic; she lost her head and said strange things. As for Mark's - but I won't speak of that. *Basta, basta,* as he used to say. Miss Ambient kept her secret - I've already had occasion to say that she had her good points - but it rankled in her conscience like a guilty participation and, I imagine, had something to do with her ultimately retiring from the world. And, apropos of consciences, the reader is now in a position to judge of my compunction for my effort to convert my cold hostess. I ought to mention that the death of her child in some degree converted her. When the new book came out (it was long delayed) she read it over as a whole, and her husband told me that during the few supreme weeks before her death - she failed rapidly after losing her son, sank into a consumption and faded away at Mentone - she even dipped into the black 'Beltraffio'.

Fame's Little Day

Sarah Orne Jewett

Sarah Orne Jewett (1849-1909) was born in South Berwick, Maine. As a young child she accompanied her father, a distinguished physician, on his rounds to the rural areas surrounding South Berwick. She came to know his patients well and would later use her impressions of them to create some of her characters.

Jewett's father had a love of literature and was an avid book collector. His well-stocked library gave Jewett the opportunity to read many of the classics. She also came to admire Jane Austen, Honore Balzac, Aleksandr Turgenev, and Gustave Flaubert.

Jewett's first successful publication was her short story *Mr. Bruce*, which appeared in *The Atlantic Monthly.* Her first book *Deephaven* (1877) contained fictionalized sketches of her memories of Maine. The books immediate success placed her in the ranks of such authors as William Dean Howells and James Russell Lowell. Her stories were detailed studies of average people similar to Flaubert's. Her writing was admired by William James, Henry James, and Rudyard Kipling. At the 1901 commencement exercises at Bowdoin College she was awarded the degree of Doctor of Literature, the first ever to be awarded to a woman.

Jewett's best known fiction includes *A Country Doctor* (1884), *A Marsh Island* (1885), *A White Heron* (1886), *Tales of New England* (1890), and *The Country of the Pointed Firs* (1896).

NOBODY EVER KNEW, except himself, what made a foolish young newspaper reporter, who happened into a small old-fashioned hotel in New York, observe Mr. Abel Pinkham with deep interest, listen to his talk, ask a question or two of the clerk, and then go away and make up an effective personal paragraph for one of the morning papers. He must have had a heart full of fun, this young reporter, and something honestly rustic and pleasing must have struck him in the guest's demeanor, for there was a flavor in the few lines he wrote that made some of his fellows seize upon the little paragraph, and copy it, and add to it, and keep it moving. Nobody knows what starts such a thing in journalism, or keeps it alive after it is started, but on a certain Thursday morning the fact was made known to the world that among the notabilities then in the city, Abel Pinkham, Esquire, a distinguished citizen of Wetherford, Vermont, was visiting New York on important affairs connected with the maplesugar industry of his native State. Mr. Pinkham had expected to keep his visit unannounced, but it was likely to occasion much interest in business and civic circles. This was something like the way that the paragraph started; but here and there a kindred spirit of the original journalist caught it up and added discreet lines about Mr. Pinkham's probable stay in town, his occupation of an apartment on the fourth floor of the Ethan Allen Hotel, and other circumstances so uninteresting to the reading public in general that presently in the next evening edition, one city editor after another threw out the item, and the young journalists, having had their day of pleasure, passed on to other things.

Mr. and Mrs. Pinkham had set forth from home with many forebodings, in spite of having talked all winter about taking this journey as soon as the spring opened. They would have caught at any reasonable excuse for giving it up altogether, because when the time arrived it seemed so much easier to stay at home. Mrs. Abel Pinkham had never seen New York; her husband himself had not been to the city for a great many years; in fact, his reminiscences of the former visit were not altogether pleasant, since he had foolishly fallen into many snares, and been much gulled in his character of honest young countryman. There was a tarnished and worthless counterfeit of a large gold watch still concealed between the outer boarding and inner lath and plaster of the leanto bedroom which Mr. Abel Pinkham had occupied as a bachelor; it was not the only witness of his being taken in by city sharpers, and he had winced ever since at the thought of their wiles. But he was now a man of sixty, well-to-do, and of authority in town affairs; his children were all well married and settled in homes of their own, except a widowed daughter, who lived at home with her young son, and was her mother's lieutenant in household affairs.

The boy was almost grown, and at this season, when the maple sugar was all made and shipped, and it was still too early for spring work on the land, Mr. Pinkham could leave home as well as not, and here he was in New York, feeling himself to be a stranger and foreigner to city ways. If it had not been for that desire to appear well in his wife's eyes, which had buoyed him over the bar of many difficulties, he could have found it in his heart to take the next train back to Wetherford, Vermont, to be there rid of his best clothes and the stiff rim of his heavy felt hat. He could not let his wife discover that the noise and confusion of Broadway had the least power to make him flinch: he cared no more for it than for the woods in snowtime. He was as good as anybody, and she was better. They owed nobody a cent; and they had come on purpose to see the city of New York.

They were sitting at the breakfasttable in the Ethan Allen Hotel, having arrived at nightfall the day before. Mrs. Pinkham looked a little pale about the mouth. She had been kept awake nearly all night by the noise, and had enjoyed but little the evening she had spent in the stuffy parlor of the hotel, looking down out of the window at what seemed to her but garish scenes, and keeping a reproachful and suspicious eye upon some unpleasantly noisy young women of forward behavior who were her only companions. Abel himself was by no means so poorly entertained in the hotel office and smokingroom. He felt much more at home than she did, being better used to meeting strange men than she was to strange women, and he found two or three companions who had seen more than he of New York life. It was there, indeed, that the young reporter found him, hearty and country-fed, and loved the appearance of his best clothes, and the way Mr. Abel Pinkham brushed his hair, and loved the way that he spoke in a loud and manful voice the belief and experience of his honest heart.

In the morning at breakfasttime the Pinkhams were depressed. They missed their good bed at home; they were troubled by the roar and noise of the streets that hardly stopped over night before it began again in the morning. The waiter did not put what mind he may have had to the business of serving them; and Mrs. Abel Pinkham, whose cooking was the triumph of parish festivals at home, had her own opinion about the beefsteak. She was a woman of imagination, and now that she was fairly here, spectacles and all, it really pained her to find that the New York of her dreams, the metropolis of dignity and distinction, of wealth and elegance, did not seem to exist. These poor streets, these unlovely people, were the end of a great illusion. They did not like to meet each other's eyes, this worthy pair. The man began to put on an unbecoming air of assertion, and Mrs. Pinkham's face was full of lofty protest.

"My gracious me, Mary Ann! I *am* glad I happened to get the 'Tribune' this mornin'," said Mr. Pinkham, with sudden excitement. "Just you look here! I'd like well to know how they found out about our comin'!" and he handed the paper to his wife across the table. There--there 't is; right by my thumb," he insisted. "Can't you see it?" and he smiled like a boy as she finally brought her large spectacles to bear upon the important paragraph.

"I guess they think somethin' of us, if you don't think much o' them," continued Mr. Pinkham, grandly. "Oh, they know how to keep the run o' folks who are somebody to home! Draper and Fitch knew we was comin' this week: you know I sent word I was comin' to settle with them myself. I suppose they send folks round to the hotels, these newspapers, but I shouldn't thought there'd been time. Anyway, they've thought 't was worth while to put us in!"

Mrs. Pinkham did not take the trouble to make a mystery out of the unexpected pleasure. "I want to cut it out an' send it right up home to daughter Sarah," she said, beaming with pride, and looking at the printed names as if they were flattering photographs. "I think 't was most too strong to say we was among the notables. But there! 't is their business to dress up things, and they have to print somethin' every day. I guess I shall go up and put on my best dress," she added, inconsequently; "this one's kind of dusty; it's the same I rode in."

"Le' me see that paper again," said Mr. Pinkham jealously. "I didn't more 'n half sense it, I was so taken aback. Well, Mary Ann, you didn't expect you was goin' to get into the papers when you came away. *'Abel Pinkham, Esquire, of Wetherford, Vermont'*. It looks well, don't it? But you might have knocked me down with a feather when I first caught sight of them words."

"I guess I shall put on my other dress," said Mrs. Pinkham, rising, with quite a different air from that with which she had sat down to her morning meal. "This one looks a little out o' style, as Sarah said, but when I got up this mornin' I was so homesick it didn't seem to make any kind o' difference. I expect that saucy girl last night took us to be nobodies. I'd like to leave the paper round where she couldn't help seein' it."

"Don't take any notice of her," said Abel, in a dignified tone. "If she can't do what you want an' be civil, we'll go somewheres else. I wish I'd done what we talked of at first an' gone to the Astor House, but that young man in the cars told me 't was remote from the things we should want to see. The Astor House was the top o' everything when I was here last, but I expected to find some changes. I want you to have the best there is," he said, smiling at his wife as if they were just making their wedding journey. "Come, let's be stirrin'; 't is long past eight o'clock," and he ushered her to the door, newspaper in hand.

Later that day the guests walked up Broadway, holding themselves erect, and feeling as if every eye was upon them. Abel Pinkham had settled with his correspondents for the spring consignments of maple sugar, and a round sum in bank bills was stowed away in his breast pocket. One of the partners had been a Wetherford boy, so when there came a renewal of interest in maple sugar, and the best confectioners were ready to do it honor, the finest quality being at a large premium, this partner remembered that there never was any sugar made in Wetherford of such melting and delicious flavor as from the trees on the old Pinkham farm. He had now made a good bit of money for himself on this private venture, and was ready that morning to pay Mr. Abel Pinkham cash down, and to give him a handsome order for the next season for all he could make. Mr. Fitch was also generous in the matter of such details as freight and packing; he was immensely polite and kind to his old friends, and begged them to come out and stay with him and his wife, where they lived now, in a not far distant New Jersey town.

"No, no, sir," said Mr. Pinkham promptly. "My wife has come to see the city, and our time is short. Your folks 'll be up this summer, won't they? We'll wait an' visit then."

"You must certainly take Mrs. Pinkham up to the Park," said the commission merchant. "I wish I had time to show you round myself. I suppose you've been seeing some things already, haven't you? I noticed your arrival in the 'Herald.'"

"The 'Tribune' it was," said Mr. Pinkham, blushing through a smile and looking round at his wife.

"Oh no; I never read the 'Tribune,'" said Mr. Fitch. "There was quite an extended notice in my paper. They must have put you and Mrs. Pinkham into the 'Herald' too." And so the friends parted, laughing. "I am much pleased to have a call from such distinguished parties," said Mr. Fitch, by way of final farewell, and Mr. Pinkham waved his hand grandly in reply.

"Let's get the 'Herald,' then," he said, as they started up the street. "We can go an' sit over in that little square that we passed as we came along, and rest an' talk things over about what we'd better do this afternoon. I'm tired out atrampin' and standin'. I'd rather have set still while we were there, but he wanted us to see his store. Done very well, Joe Fitch has but 'tain't a business I should like."

There was a lofty look and sense of behavior about Mr. Pinkham of Wetherford. You might have thought him a great politician as he marched up Broadway, looking neither to right hand nor left. He felt himself to be a person of great responsibilities.

"I begin to feel sort of at home myself," said his wife, who always had a certain touch of simple dignity about her. "When we was comin' yesterday New York seemed to be all strange, and there wasn't nobody expectin' us. I feel now just as if I'd been here before."

They were now on the edge of the betterlooking part of the town; it was still noisy and crowded, but noisy with fine carriages instead of drays, and crowded with welldressed people. The hours for shopping and visiting were beginning, and more than one person looked with appreciative and friendly eyes at the comfortable pleasedlooking elderly man and woman who went their easily beguiled and loitering way. The pavement peddlers detained them, but the cabmen beckoned them in vain; their eyes were busy with the immediate foreground. Mrs. Pinkham was embarrassed by the recurring reflection of herself in the great windows.

I wish I had seen about a new bonnet before we came," she lamented. "They seem to be havin' on some o' their spring things."

Don't you worry, Mary Ann. I don't see anybody that looks any better than you do," said Abel, with boyish and reassuring pride.

Mr. Pinkham had now bought the "Herald," and also the "Sun," well recommended by an able newsboy, and presently they crossed over from that corner by the Fifth Avenue Hotel which seems like the very heart of New York, and found a place to sit down on the Square--an empty bench, where they could sit side by side and look the papers through, reading over each other's shoulder, and being impatient from page to page. The paragraph was indeed repeated, with trifling additions. Ederton of the "Sun" had followed the "Tribune" man's lead, and fabricated a brief interview, a, marvel of art and discretion, but so general in its allusions that it could create no suspicion; it almost deceived Mr. Pinkham himself, so that he found unaffected pleasure in the fictitious occasion, and felt as if he had easily covered himself with glory. Except for the bare fact of the interview's being imaginary, there was no discredit to be cast upon Mr. Abel Pinkham's having said that he thought the country near Wetherford looked well for the time of year, and promised a fair hay crop, and that his income was augmented onehalf to threefifths by his belief in the future of maple sugar. It was likely to be the great coming crop of the Green

Mountain State. Ederton suggested that there was talk of Mr. Pinkham's presence in the matter of a great maplesugar trust, in which much of the capital of Wall Street would be involved.

"How they do hatch up these things, don't they?" said the worthy man at this point. "Well, it all sounds well, Mary Ann."

"It says here that you are a very personable man," smiled his wife. "and have filled some of the most responsible town offices" (this was the turn taken by Goffey of the "Herald"). "Oh, and that you are going to attend the performance at Barnum's this evening, and occupy reserved seats. Why, I didn't know--who have you told about that?--who was you talkin' to last night, Abel?"

"I never spoke o' goin' to Barnum's to any livin' soul," insisted Abel, flushing. "I only thought of it two or three times to myself that perhaps I might go an' take you. Now that is singular; perhaps they put that in just to advertize the show."

Ain't it a kind of a low place for folks like us to be seen in?" suggested Mrs. Pinkham timidly. "People seem to be payin' us all this attention, an' I don't know's 't would be dignified for us to go to one o' them circus places."

"I don't care; we shan't live but once. I ain't comin' to New York an' confine myself to evenin' meetin's," answered Abel, throwing away discretion and morality together. "I tell you I'm goin' to spend this sugarmoney just as we've a mind to. You've worked hard, an' counted a good while on comin', and so've I; an' I ain't goin' to mince my steps an' pinch an' screw for nobody. I'm goin' to hire one o' them hacks an' ride up to the Park."

"Joe Fitch said we could go right up in one o' the elevated railroads for five cents, an' return when we was ready," protested Mary Ann, who had a thriftier inclination than her husband; but Mr. Pinkham was not to be let or hindered, and they presently found themselves going up Fifth Avenue in a somewhat battered open landau. The spring sun shone upon them, and the spring breeze fluttered the black ostrich tip on Mrs. Pinkham's durable winter bonnet, and brought the pretty color to her faded cheeks.

"There! this is something like. Such people as we are can't go meechin' round; it ain't expected. Don't it pay for a lot o' hard work?" said Abel; and his wife gave him a pleased look for her only answer. They were both thinking of their gray farmhouse high on a long western slope, with the afternoon sun full in its face, the old red barn, the pasture, the shaggy woods that stretched far up the mountain-side.

"I wish Sarah an' little Abel was here to see us ride by," said Mary Ann Pinkham, presently. "I can't seem to wait to have 'em get that newspaper. I'm so glad we sent it right off before we started this mornin'. If Abel goes to the postoffice comin' from school, as he always does, they'll have it to read tomorrow before suppertime."

This happy day in two plain lives ended, as might have been expected, with the great Barnum show. Mr. and Mrs. Pinkham found themselves in possession of countless advertizing cards and circulars next morning, and these added somewhat to their sense of responsibility. Mrs. Pinkham became afraid that the hotelkeeper would charge them double. "We've got to pay for it some way; there. I don't know but I'm more'n willin'," said the good soul. "I never did have such a splendid time in all my life. Findin' you so respected 'way off here is the best of anything; an' then seein' them dear little babies in their nice carriages, all along the streets and up to the Central Park! I never shall forget them beautiful little creatur's. And then the houses, an' the hosses, an' the store windows, an' all the rest of it! Well, I can't make any country pitcher hold no more, an' I want to get home an' think it over, goin' about my housework."

They were just entering the door of the Ethan Allen Hotel for the last time, when a young man met them and bowed cordially. He was the original reporter of their arrival, but they did not know it, and the impulse was strong within him to formally invite Mr. Pinkham to make an address before the members of the Produce Exchange on the following morning; but he had been a country boy himself, and their look of seriousness and selfconsciousness appealed to him unexpectedly. He wondered what effect this great experience would have upon their afterlife. The best fun, after all, would be to send marked copies of his paper and Ederton's to all the weekly newspapers in that part of Vermont. He saw before him the evidence of their happy increase of selfrespect, and he would make all their neighborhood agree to do them honor. Such is the dominion of the press.

"Who was that young man?--he kind of bowed to you," asked the lady from Wetherford, after the journalist had meekly passed; but Abel Pinkham, Esquire, could only tell her that he looked like a young fellow who was sitting in the office the evening that they came to the hotel. The reporter did not seem to these distinguished persons to be a young man of any consequence.

The Miracle of Purun Bhagat

Rudyard Kipling

Rudyard Kipling (1865-1936) employed a multitude of themes in his writing. His short fiction and poetry describe war, love, ghosts, duty, and honor. He even wrote animal fables and stories for children.

Kipling was born in Bombay, India. He was educated at the United Services College in England where he started his writing career. He contributed to the school paper and upon his return to India became a journalist for *The Civil and Military Gazette.*

Kipling's experiences of the social forces of Industrialism, Imperialism, the army and world travels were reflected in his writing. Kipling began writing stories when he was relatively young. However, his stories were not immediately accepted by publishers in the United States and England because the locales seemed too exotic. He portrayed characters with a hearty roughness and language that was not always genteel. This initial rejection by publishers did not sway him from continuing to write.

Kipling eventually gained acceptance in literary and academic circles. He received the Nobel Prize for Literature in 1907 and was the recipient of several honorable degrees.

Kipling's best known works are *The Jungle Book* (1894), *The Second Jungle Book* (1895), *Captains Courageous* (1897), *Kim* (1901), and *Just So Stories* (1902).

> *The night we felt the earth would move*
> *We stole and plucked him by the hand,*
> *Because we loved him with the love*
> *That knows but cannot understand.*
>
> *And when the roaring hillside broke,*
> *And all our world fell down in rain,*
> *We saved him, we the Little Folk;*
> *But lo! he does not come again!*
>
> *Mourn now, we saved him for the sake*
> *Of such poor love as wild ones may.*
> *Mourn ye! Our brother will not wake,*
> *And his own kind drive us away!*
>
> *Dirge of the Langurs.*

THERE WAS ONCE a man in India who was Prime Minister of one of the semiindependent native States in the northwestern part of the country. He was a Brahmin, so highcaste that caste ceased to have any particular meaning for him; and his father had been an important official in the gaycoloured tagrag and bobtail of an oldfashioned Hindu Court. But as Purun Dass grew up he felt that the old order of things was changing, and that if any one wished to get on in the world he must stand well with the English, and imitate all that the English believed to be good. At the same time a native official must keep his own master's favour. This was a difficult game, but the quiet, closemouthed young Brahmin, helped by a good English education at a Bombay University, played it coolly, and rose, step by step, to be Prime Minister of the kingdom. That is to say, he held more real power than his master, the Maharajah.

When the old king--who was suspicious of the English, their railways and telegraphs--died, Purun Dass stood high with his young successor, who had been tutored by an Englishman; and between them, though he always took care that his master should have the credit, they established schools for little girls, made roads and started State dispensaries and shows of agricultural implements, and published a yearly bluebook on the "Moral and Material Progress of the State," and the Foreign Office and the Government of India were delighted. Very few native States take up English progress altogether, for they will not believe, as Purun Dass showed he did, that what was good for the Englishman must be twice as good for the Asiatic. The Prime Minister became the honoured friend of Viceroys, and Governors, and Lieutenant-Governors, and medical missionaries, and common missionaries, and hardriding English officers who came to shoot in the State preserves, as well as of whole hosts of tourists who travelled up and down India in the cold weather, showing how things ought to be managed. In his spare time he would endow scholarships for the study of medicine and manufactures on strictly English lines, and write letters to the "Pioneer," the greatest Indian daily paper, explaining his master's aims and objects.

At last he went to England on a visit, and had to pay enormous sums to the priests when he came back; for even so highcaste a Brahmin as Purun Dass lost caste by crossing the black sea. In London he met and talked with every one worth knowing--men whose names go all over the world--and saw a great deal more than he said. He was given honorary degrees by learned universities, and he made speeches and talked of Hindu social reform to English ladies in evening dress, till all London cried, "This is the most fascinating man we have ever met at dinner since cloths were first laid."

When he returned to India there was a blaze of glory, for the Viceroy himself made a special visit to confer upon the Maharajah the Grand Cross of the Star of India--all diamonds and ribbons and enamel; and at the same ceremony, while the cannon boomed, Purun Dass was made a Knight Commander of the Order of the Indian Empire, so that his name stood Sir Purun Dass, K.C.I.E.

That evening, at dinner in the big Viceregal tent, he stood up with the badge and the collar of the Order on his breast, and replying to the toast of his master's health, made a speech few Englishmen could have bettered.

Next month, when the city had returned to its sunbaked quiet, he did a thing no Englishman would have dreamed of doing; for, so far as the world's affairs went, he died. The jewelled order of his knighthood went back to the Indian Government, and a new Prime Minister was appointed to the charge of affairs, and a great game of General Post began in all the subordinate appointments. The priests knew what had happened, and the people guessed; but India is the one place in the world where a man can do as he pleases and nobody asks why; and the fact that Dewan Sir Purun Dass, K.C.I.E., had resigned position, palace, and power, and taken up the beggingbowl and ochrecoloured dress of a Sunnyasi, or holy man, was considered nothing extraordinary. He had been, as the Old Law recommends, twenty years a youth twenty years a fighter,--though he had never carried a weapon in his life,--and twenty years head of a household. He had used his wealth and his power for what he knew both to be worth; he had taken honour when it came his way, he had seen men and cities far and near, and men and cities had stood up and honoured him. Now he would let these things go, as a man drops the cloak he no longer needs.

Behind him, as he walked through the city gates, an antelope skin and brasshandled crutch under his arm, and a beggingbowl of polished brown *cocodemer* in his hand, barefoot, alone, with eyes cast on the ground-- behind him they were firing salutes from the bastions in honour of his happy successor. Purun Dass nodded. All that life was ended; and he bore it no more illwill or goodwill than a man bears to a colourless dream of the night. He was a Sunnyasi--a houseless, wandering mendicant, depending on his neighbours for his daily bread; and so long as there is a morsel to divide in India, neither priest nor beggar starves. He had never in his life tasted meat, and very seldom eaten even fish. A fivepound note would have covered his personal expenses for food through any one of the many years in which he had been absolute master of millions of money. Even when he was being lionized in London he had held before him his dream of peace and quiet--the long, white, dusty Indian road, printed all over with bare feet, the incessant, slow-moving traffic, and the sharpsmelling wood smoke curling up under the figtrees in the twilight, where the wayfarers sit at their evening meal.

When the time came to make that dream true the Prime Minister took the proper steps, and in three days you might more easily have found a bubble in the trough of the long Atlantic seas than Purun Dass among the roving, gathering, separating millions of India.

At night his antelope skin was spread where the darkness overtook him--sometimes in a Sunnyasi monastery by the roadside; sometimes by a mudpillar shrine of Kala Pir, where the Jogis, who are another misty division of holy men, would receive him as they do those who know what castes and divisions are worth; sometimes on the outskirts of a little Hindu village, where the children would steal up with the food their parents had prepared; and sometimes on the pitch of the bare grazinggrounds, where the flame of his stick fire waked the drowsy camels. It was all one to Purun Dass--or Purun Bhagat, as he called himself now. Earth, people, and food were all one. But unconsciously his feet drew him away northward and eastward; from the south to Rohtak; from Rohtak to Kurnool; from Kurnool to ruined Samanah, and then up-stream along the dried bed of the Gugger river that fills only when the rain falls in the hills, till one day he saw the far line of the great Himalayas.

Then Purun Bhagat smiled, for he remembered that his mother was of Rajput Brahmin birth, from Kulu way--a Hillwoman, always homesick for the snows--and that the least touch of Hill blood draws a man at the end back to where he belongs.

"Yonder," said Purun Bhagat, breasting the lower slopes of the Sewaliks, where the cacti stand up like seven-branched candlesticks--"yonder I shall sit down and get knowledge"; and the cool wind of the Himalayas whistled about his ears as he trod the road that led to Simla.

The last time he had come that way it had been in state, with a clattering cavalry escort, to visit the gentlest and most affable of Viceroys; and the two had talked for an hour together about mutual friends in London, and what the Indian common folk really thought of things. This time Purun Bhagat paid no calls, but leaned on the rail of the Mall, watching that glorious view of the Plains spread out forty miles below, till a native Mohammedan policeman told him he was obstructing traffic; and Purun Bhagat salaamed reverently to the Law, because he knew the value of it, and was seeking for a Law of his own. Then he moved on, and slept that night in an empty hut at Chota Simla, which looks like the very last end of the earth, but it was only the beginning of his journey.

He followed the HimalayaThibet road, the little tenfoot track that is blasted out of solid rock, or strutted out on timbers over gulfs a thousand feet deep; that dips into warm, wet, shutin valleys, and climbs out across bare, grassy hillshoulders where the sun strikes like a burning-glass; or turns through dripping, dark forests where the treeferns dress the trunks from head to heel, and the pheasant calls to his mate. And he met Thibetan herdsmen with their dogs and flocks of sheep, each sheep with a little bag of borax on his back, and wandering woodcutters, and cloaked and blanketed Lamas from Thibet, coming into India on pilgrimage, and envoys of little solitary Hillstates, posting furiously on ringstreaked and piebald ponies, or the cavalcade of a Rajah paying a visit; or else for a long, clear day he would see nothing more than a black bear grunting and rooting below in the valley. When he first started, the roar of the world he had left still rang in his ears, as the roar of a tunnel rings long after the train has passed through; but when he had put the Mutteeanee Pass behind him that was all done, and Purun Bhagat was alone with himself walking, wondering, and thinking, his eyes on the ground, and his thoughts with the clouds.

One evening he crossed the highest pass he had met till then--it had been a two days' climb--and came out on a line of snowpeaks that banded all the horizon-- mountains from fifteen to twenty thousand feet high, looking almost near enough to hit with a stone, though they were fifty or sixty miles away. The pass was crowned with dense, dark forest--deodar, walnut, wild cherry, wild olive, and wild pear, but mostly deodar, which is the Himalayan cedar; and under the shadow of the deodars stood a deserted shrine to Kali--who is Durga, who is Sitala, who is sometimes worshipped against the smallpox.

Purun Dass swept the stone floor clean, smiled at the grinning statue, made himself a little mud fireplace at the back of the shrine, spread his antelope skin on a bed of fresh pineneedles, tucked his *bairagi*--his brasshandled crutch--under his armpit, and sat down to rest.

Immediately below him the hillside fell away, clean and cleared for fifteen hundred feet, where a little village of stonewalled houses, with roofs of beaten earth, clung to the steep tilt. All round it the tiny terraced fields lay out like aprons of patchwork on the knees of the mountain, and cows no bigger than beetles grazed between the smooth stone circles of the threshingfloors. Looking across the valley, the eye was deceived by the size of things, and could not at first realize that what seemed to be low scrub, on the opposite mountainflank, was in truth a forest of hundredfoot pines. Purun Bhagat saw an eagle swoop across the gigantic hollow, but the great bird dwindled to a dot ere it was halfway over. A few bands of scattered clouds strung up and down the valley, catching on a shoulder of the hills, or rising up and dying out when they were level with the head of the pass. And "Here shall I find peace," said Purun Bhagat.

Now, a Hill-man makes nothing of a few hundred feet up or down, and as soon as the villagers saw the smoke in the deserted shrine, the village priest climbed up the terraced hillside to welcome the stranger.

When he met Purun Bhagat's eyes--the eyes of a man used to control thousands--he bowed to the earth, took the beggingbowl without a word, and returned to the village, saying, "We have at last a holy man. Never have I seen such a man. He is of the Plains--but palecoloured--a Brahmin of the Brahmins." Then all the housewives of the village said, "Think you he will stay with us?" and each did her best to cook the most savory meal for the Bhagat. Hillfood is very simple, but with buckwheat and Indian corn, and rice and red pepper, and little fish out of the stream in the valley, and honey from the fluelike hives built in the stone walls, and dried apricots, and turmeric, and wild ginger, and bannocks of flour, a devout woman can make good things, and it was a full bowl that the priest carried to the Bhagat. Was he going to stay? asked the priest. Would he need a *chela*--a disciple--to beg for him? Had he a blanket against the cold weather? Was the food good?

Purun Bhagat ate, and thanked the giver. It was in his mind to stay. That was sufficient, said the priest. Let the beggingbowl be placed outside the shrine, in the hollow made by those two twisted roots, and daily should the Bhagat be fed; for the village felt honoured that such a man--he looked timidly into the Bhagat's face--should tarry among them.

That day saw the end of Purun Bhagat's wanderings. He had come to the place appointed for him--the silence and the space. After this, time stopped, and he, sitting at the mouth of the shrine, could not tell whether he were alive or dead; a man with control of his limbs, or a part of the hills, and the clouds, and the shifting rain and sunlight. He would repeat a Name softly to himself a hundred hundred times, till, at each repetition, he seemed to move more and more out of his body, sweeping up to the doors of some tremendous discovery; but, just as the door was opening, his body would drag him back, and, with grief, he felt he was locked up again in the flesh and bones of Purun Bhagat.

Every morning the filled beggingbowl was laid silently in the crutch of the roots outside the shrine. Sometimes the priest brought it; sometimes a Ladakhi trader, lodging in the village, and anxious to get merit, trudged up the path; but, more often, it was the woman who had cooked the meal overnight; and she would murmur hardly above her breath: "Speak for me before the gods, Bhagat. Speak for such a one, the wife of soandso!" Now and then some bold child would be allowed the honour, and Purun Bhagat would hear him drop the bowl and run as fast as his little legs could carry him, but the Bhagat never came down to the village. It was laid out like a map at his feet. He could see the evening gatherings, held on the circle of the threshing-floors because that was the only level ground; could see the wonderful unnamed green of the young rice, the indigo blues of the Indian corn, the docklike patches of buckwheat, and, in its season, the red bloom of the amaranth, whose tiny seeds, being neither grain nor pulse, make a food than can be lawfully eaten by Hindus in time of fasts.

When the year turned, the roofs of the huts were all little squares of purest gold, for it was on the roofs that they laid out their cobs of the corn to dry. Hiving and harvest, ricesowing and husking, passed before his eyes, all embroidered down there on the manysided plots of fields, and he thought of them all, and wondered what they all led to at the long last.

Even in populated India a man cannot a day sit still before the wild things run over him as though he were a rock; and in that wilderness very soon the wild things, who knew Kali's Shrine well, came back to look at the intruder. The *langurs,* the big graywhiskered monkeys of the Himalayas, were, naturally, the first, for they are alive with curiosity; and when they had upset the begging-bowl, and rolled it round the floor, and tried their teeth on the brasshandled crutch, and made faces at the antelope skin, they decided that the human being who sat so still was harmless. At evening, they would leap down from the pines, and beg with their hands for things to eat, and then swing off in graceful curves. They liked the warmth of the fire, too, and huddled round it till Purun Bhagat had to push them aside to throw on more fuel; and in the morning, as often as not, he would find a furry ape sharing his blanket. All day long, one or other of the tribe would sit by his side, staring out at the snows, crooning and looking unspeakably wise and sorrowful.

After the monkeys came the *barasingh,* that big deer which is like our red deer, but stronger. He wished to rub off the velvet of his horns against the cold stones of Kali's statue, and stamped his feet when he saw the man at the shrine. But Purun Bhagat never moved, and, little by little, the royal stag edged up and nuzzled his shoulder. Purun Bhagat slid one cool hand along the hot antlers, and the touch soothed the fretted beast, who bowed his head, and Purun Bhagat very softly rubbed and raveled off the velvet. Afterward, the *barasingh* brought his doe and fawn--gentle things that mumbled on the holy man's blanket--or would come alone at night, his eyes green in the fireflicker, to take his share of fresh walnuts. At last, the muskdeer, the shyest and almost the smallest of the deerlets, came, too, her big rabbity ears erect; even brindled, silent *mushicknabha* must needs find out what the light in the shrine meant, and drop out her mooselike nose into Purun Bhagat's lap, coming and going with the shadows of the fire. Purun Bhagat called them all "my brothers," and his low call of *"Bhai! Bhai!"* would draw them from the forest at noon if they were within earshot. The Himalayan black bear, moody and suspicious--Sona, who has the Vshaped white mark under his chin--passed that way more than once; and since the Bhagat showed no fear, Sona showed no anger, but watched him, and came closer, and begged a share of the caresses, and a dole of bread or wild berries. Often, in the still dawns, when the Bhagat would climb to the very crest of the pass to watch the red day walking along the peaks of the snows, he would find Sona shuffling and grunting at his heels, thrusting a curious forepaw under fallen trunks, and bringing it away with a *whoof* of impatience; or his early steps would wake Sona where he lay curled up, and the great brute, rising erect, would think to fight, till he heard the Bhagat's voice and knew his best friend.

Nearly all hermits and holy men who live apart from the big cities have the reputation of being able to work miracles with the wild things, but all the miracle lies in keeping still, in never making a hasty movement, and, for a long time, at least, in never looking directly at a visitor. The villagers saw the outline of the *barasingh* stalking like a shadow through the dark forest behind the shrine; saw the *minaul,* the Himalayan pheasant, blazing in her best colours before Kali's statue; and the *langurs* on their haunches, inside, playing with the walnut shells. Some of the children, too, had heard Sona singing to himself, bearfashion behind the fallen rocks, and the Bhagat's reputation as miracleworker stood firm.

Yet nothing was further from his mind than miracles. He believed that all things were one big Miracle, and when a man knows that much he knows something to go upon. He knew for a certainty that there was nothing great and nothing in little world: and day and night he strove to think out his way into the heart of things, back to the place whence his soul had come.

So thinking, his untrimmed hair fell down about his shoulders, the stone slab at the side of the antelope skin was dented into a little hole by the foot of his brasshandled crutch, and the place between the treetrunks, where the beggingbowl rested day after day, sunk and wore into a hollow almost as smooth as the brown shell itself; and each beast knew his exact place at the fire. The fields changed their colours with the seasons; the threshingfloors filled and emptied, and filled again and again; and again and again, when winter came, the *langurs* frisked among the branches feathered with light snow, till the mothermonkeys brought their sadeyed little babies up from the warmer valleys with the spring. There were few changes in the village. The priest was older, and many of the little children who used to come with the beggingdish sent their own children now; and when you asked of the villagers how long their holy man had lived in Kali's Shrine at the head of the pass, they answered. "Always."

Then came such summer rains as had not been known in the Hills for many seasons. Through three good months the valley was wrapped in cloud and soaking mist--steady, unrelenting downfall, breaking off into thundershower after thundershower. Kali's Shrine stood above the clouds for the most part, and there was a whole month in which the Bhagat never saw his village. It was packed away under a white floor of cloud that swayed and shifted and rolled on itself and bulged upward, but never broke from its piers--the streaming flanks of the valley.

All that time he heard nothing but the sound of a million little waters, overhead from the trees, and underfoot along the ground, soaking through the pineneedles, dripping from the tongues of draggled fern, and spouting in newly torn muddy channels down the slopes. Then the sun came out, and drew forth the good incense of the deodars and the rhododendrons, and that faroff, clean smell which the Hill people call "the smell of the snows." The hot sunshine lasted for a week, and then the rains gathered together for their last downpour, and the water fell in sheets that flayed off the skin of the ground and leaped back in mud. Purun Bhagat heaped his fire high that night, for he was sure his brothers would need warmth; but never a beast came to the shrine, though he called and called till he dropped asleep, wondering what had happened in the woods.

It was in the black heart of the night, the rain drumming like a thousand drums, that he was roused by a plucking at his blanket, and stretching out, felt the little hand of a *langur*. "It is better here than in the trees," he said sleepily, loosening a fold of blanket; "take it and be warm." The monkey caught his hand and pulled hard. "Is it food, then?" said Purun Bhagat. "Wait awhile, and I will prepare some." As he kneeled to throw fuel on the fire the *langur* ran to the door of the shrine, crooned, and ran back again, plucking at the man's knee.

"What is it? What is thy trouble, Brother?" said Purun Bhagat, for the *langur's* eyes were full of things that he could not tell. "Unless one of thy caste be in a trap-- and none set traps here--I will not go into that weather. Look, Brother, even the *barasingh* comes for shelter!"

The deer's antlers clashed as he strode into the shrine, clashed against the grinning statue of Kali. He lowered them in Purun Bhagat's direction and stamped uneasily, hissing through his halfshut nostrils.

"Hai! Hai! Hai!" said the Bhagat, snapping his fingers. "Is *this* payment for a night's lodging?" But the deer pushed him toward the door, and as he did so Purun Bhagat heard the sound of something opening with a sigh, and saw two slabs of the floor draw away from each other, while the sticky earth below smacked its lips.

"Now I see," said Purun Bhagat. "No blame to my brothers that they did not sit by the fire tonight. The mountain is falling. And yet--why should I go?" His eye fell on the empty beggingbowl, and his face changed. "They have given me good food daily since--since I came, and, if I am not swift, tomorrow there will not be one mouth in the valley. Indeed, I must go and warn them below. Back there, Brother! Let me get to the fire."

The *barasingh* backed unwillingly as Purun Bhagat drove a pine torch deep into the flame, twirling it till it was well lit. "Ah! He came to warn me," he said, rising. "Better than that we shall do; better than that. Out, now, and lend me thy neck, Brother, for I have but two feet."

He clutched the bristling withers of the *barasingh* with his right hand, held the torch away with his left, and stepped out of the shrine into the desperate night. There was no breath of wind, but the rain nearly drowned the flare as the great deer hurried down the slope, sliding on his haunches. As soon as they were clear of the forest more of the Bhagat's brothers joined them. He heard, though he could not see, the *langurs* pressing about him and behind them the *uhh! uhh!* of Sona. The rain matted his long white hair into ropes; the water splashed beneath his bare feet, and his yellow robe clung to his frail old body, but he stepped down steadily, leaning against the *barasingh*. He was no longer a holy man, but Sir Purun Dass, K.C.I.E., Prime Minister of no small State, a man accustomed to command, going out to save life. Down the steep, plashy path they poured all together, the Bhagat and his brothers, down and down till the deer's feet clicked and stumbled on the wall of a threshingfloor, and he snorted because he smelt Man. Now they were at the head of the one crooked village street, and the Bhagat beat with his crutch on the barred windows of the blacksmith's house as his torch blazed up in the shelter of the eaves. "Up and out!" cried Purun Bhagat; and he did not know his own voice, for it was years since he had spoken aloud to a man. "The hill falls! The hill is falling! Up and out, oh, you within!"

"It is our Bhagat," said the blacksmith's wife. "He stands among his beasts. Gather the little ones and give the call."

It ran from house to house, while the beasts, cramped in the narrow way, surged and huddled round the Bhagat, and Sona puffed impatiently.

The people hurried into the street--they were no more than seventy souls all told--and in the glare of the torches they saw their Bhagat holding back the terrified *barasingh* while the monkeys plucked piteously at his skirts, and Sona sat on his haunches and roared.

"Across the valley and up the next hill!" shouted Purun Bhagat. "Leave none behind! We follow!"

Then the people ran as only Hill folk can run, for they knew that in a landslip you must climb for the highest ground across the valley. They fled, splashing through the little river at the bottom, and panted up the terraced fields on the far side, while the Bhagat and his brethren followed. Up and up the opposite mountain they climbed, calling to each other by name--rollcall of the village-- and at their heels toiled the big *barasingh*, weighted by the failing strength of Purun Bhagat. At last the deer stopped in the shadow of a deep pinewood, five hundred feet up the hillside. His instinct, that had warned him of the coming slide, told him he would be safe here.

Purun Bhagat dropped fainting by his side, for the chill of the rain and that fierce climb were killing him; but first he called to the scattered torches ahead, "Stay and count your numbers"; then, whispering to the deer as he saw the lights gather in a cluster: "Stay with me, Brother. Stay--till--I--go!"

There was a sigh in the air that grew to a mutter, and a mutter that grew to a roar, and a roar that passed all sense of hearing, and the hillside on which the villagers stood was hit in the darkness, and rocked to the blow. Then a note as steady, deep, and true as the deep C of the organ drowned everything for perhaps five minutes, while the very roots of the pines quivered to it. It died away, and the sound of the rain falling on miles of hard ground and grass changed to the muffled drum of water on soft earth. That told its own tale.

Never a villager--not even the priest--was bold enough to speak to the Bhagat who had saved their lives. They crouched under the pines and waited till the day. When it came they looked across the valley and saw that what had been forest, and terraced field, and trackthreaded grazing-ground was one raw, red, fanshaped smear, with a few trees flung head-down on the scarp. That red ran high up the hill of their refuge, damming back the little river, which had begun to spread into a brickcoloured lake. Of the village, of the road to the shrine, of the shrine itself, and the forest behind, there was not trace. For one mile in width and two thousand feet in sheer depth the mountainside had come away bodily, planed clean from head to heel.

And the villagers, one by one, crept through the wood to pray before their Bhagat. They saw the *barasingh* standing over him, who fled when they came near, and they heard the *langurs* wailing in the branches, and Sona moaning up the hill; but their Bhagat was dead, sitting crosslegged, his back against a tree, his crutch under his armpit, and his face turned to the northeast.

The priest said: "Behold a miracle after a miracle, for in this very attitude must all Sunnyasis be buried! Therefore where he now is we will build the temple to our holy man."

They built the temple before a year was ended--a little stoneandearth shrine--and they called the hill the Bhagat's Hill, and they worship there with lights and flowers and offerings to this day. But they do not know that the saint of their worship is the late Sir Purun Dass, K.C.l.E., D.C.L., Ph. D., etc., once Prime minister of the progressive and enlightened State of Mohiniwala, and honorary or corresponding member of more learned and scientific societies than will ever do any good in this world or the next.

Love of Life

Jack London

Jack London (1876-1916), born John Griffith London, was a novelist and short story writer. An illegitimate child, London grew up along the Oakland waterfront in dire poverty. He was largely self-educated except for spending one semester at the University of California.

London demonstrated a strong sense of individualism at a young age and at seventeen he went to sea. By the age of twenty he had already been an oyster pirate, Klondike adventurer, and a vagabond. His hobo lifestyle exposed him to the cruelties of society and helped shape his socialist ideas. London joined the Klondike Gold Rush in 1897. His experiences in the rugged wilderness later surfaced in some of his most popular writings.

In 1900 London married Bess Maddern but they divorced in 1905. The same year he married Charmain Kittredge. After winning first prize for a descriptive essay he decided to make writing his career. In 1902 he published his first novel, *A Daughter of the Snows*, which brought him financial security. Despite his literary success London's past struggle with poverty had a lasting effect on him. Notwithstanding his strong streak of individualism he was a committed socialist. His later work expressed empathy for the poor, prophecies of world revolution and a belief in a utopian, socialist future.

London's fifty volumes of novels, short stories, and essays often show how man and beast are behaviorally alike and how both are subject to a harsh world.

His best known works are *The Call of the Wild* (1903), *The Sea Wolf* (1904), and *White Fang* (1906).

> *"This out of all will remain--*
> *They have lived and have tossed:*
> *So much of the game will be gain,*
> *Though the gold of the dice has been lost."*

THEY LIMPED PAINFULLY down the bank, and once the foremost of the two men staggered among the roughstrewn rocks. They were tired and weak, and their faces had the drawn expression of patience which comes of hardship long endured. They were heavily burdened with blanket packs which were strapped to their shoulders. Headstraps, passing across the forehead, helped support these packs. Each man carried a rifle. They walked in a stooped posture, the shoulders well forward, the head still farther forward, the eyes bent upon the ground.

"I wish we had just about two of them cartridges that's layin' in that cache of ourn," said the second man.

His voice was utterly and drearily expressionless. He spoke without enthusiasm; and the first man, limping into the milky stream that foamed over the rocks, vouchsafed no reply.

The other man followed at his heels. They did not remove their footgear, though the water was icy cold--so cold that their ankles ached and their feet went numb. In places the water dashed against their knees, and both men staggered for footing.

The man who followed slipped on a smooth boulder, nearly fell, but recovered himself with a violent effort, at the same time uttering a sharp exclamation of pain. He seemed faint and dizzy and put out his free hand while he reeled, as though seeking support against the air. When he had steadied himself he stepped forward, but reeled again and nearly fell. Then he stood still and looked at the other man, who had never turned his head.

The man stood still for fully a minute, as though debating with himself. Then he called out:

"I say, Bill, I've sprained my ankle."

Bill staggered on through the milky water. He did not look around. The man watched him go, and though his face was expressionless as ever, his eyes were like the eyes of a wounded deer.

The other man limped up the farther bank and continued straight on without looking back. The man in the stream watched him. His lips trembled a little, so that the rough thatch of brown hair which covered them was visibly agitated. His tongue even strayed out to moisten them.

"Bill!" he cried out.

It was the pleading cry of a strong man in distress, but Bill's head did not turn. The man watched him go, limping grotesquely and lurching forward with stammering gait up the slow slope toward the soft skyline of the lowlying hill. He watched him go till he passed over the crest and disappeared. Then he turned his gaze and slowly took in the circle of the world that remained to him now that Bill was gone.

Near the horizon the sun was smouldering dimly, almost obscured by formless mists and vapors, which gave an impression of mass and density without outline or tangibility. The man pulled out his watch, the while resting his weight on one leg. It was four o'clock, and as the season was near the last of July or first of August,--he did not know the precise date within a week or two,--he knew that the sun roughly marked the north-west. He looked to the south and knew that somewhere beyond those bleak hills lay the Great Bear Lake; also, he knew that in that direction the Arctic Circle cut its forbidding way across the Canadian Barrens. This stream in which he stood was a feeder to the Coppermine River, which in turn flowed north and emptied into Coronation Gulf and the Arctic Ocean. He had never been there, but he had seen it, once, on a Hudson Bay Company chart.

Again his gaze completed the circle of the world about him. It was not a heartening spectacle. Everywhere was soft skyline. The hills were all lowlying. There were no trees, no shrubs, no grasses--naught but a tremendous and terrible desolation that sent fear swiftly dawning into his eyes.

"Bill!" he whispered, once and twice; "Bill!"

He cowered in the midst of the milky water, as though the vastness were pressing in upon him with overwhelming force, brutally crushing him with its complacent awfulness. He began to shake as with an aguefit, till the gun fell from his hand with a splash. This served to rouse him. He fought with his fear and pulled himself together, groping in the water and recovering the weapon. He hitched his pack farther over on his left shoulder, so as to take a portion of its weight from off the injured ankle. Then he proceeded, slowly and carefully, wincing with pain, to the bank.

He did not stop. With a desperation that was madness, unmindful of the pain, he hurried up the slope to the crest of the hill over which his comrade had disappeared--more grotesque and comical by far than that limping, jerking comrade. But at the crest he saw a shallow valley, empty of life. He fought with his fear again, overcame it, hitched the pack still farther over on his left shoulder, and lurched on down the slope.

The bottom of the valley was soggy with water, which the thick moss held, spongelike, close to the surface. This water squirted out from under his feet at every step, and each time he lifted a foot the action culminated in a sucking sound as the wet moss reluctantly released its grip. He picked his way from muskeg to muskeg, and followed the other man's footsteps along and across the rocky ledges which thrust like islets through the sea of moss.

Though alone, he was not lost. Farther on he knew he would come to where dead spruce and fir, very small and weazened, bordered the shore of a little lake, the *titchinnichilie,* in the tongue of the country, the "land of little sticks." And into that lake flowed a small stream, the water of which was not milky. There was rushgrass on that stream--this he remembered well--but no timber, and he would follow it till its first trickle ceased at a divide. He would cross this divide to the first trickle of another stream, flowing to the west, which he would follow until it emptied into the river Dease, and here he would find a cache under an upturned canoe and piled over with many rocks. And in this cache would be ammunition for his empty gun, fishhooks and lines, a small net--all the utilities for the killing and snaring of food. Also, he would find flour,--not much,--a piece of bacon, and some beans.

Bill would be waiting for him there, and they would paddle away south down the Dease to the Great Bear Lake. And south across the lake they would go, ever south, till they gained the Mackenzie. And south, still south, they would go, while the winter raced vainly after them, and the ice formed in the eddies, and the days grew chill and crisp, south to some warm Hudson Bay Company post, where timber grew tall and generous and there was grub without end.

These were the thoughts of the man as he strove onward. But hard as he strove with his body, he strove equally hard with his mind, trying to think that Bill had not deserted him, that Bill would surely wait for him at the cache. He was compelled to think this thought, or else there would not be any use to strive, and he would have lain down and died. And as the dim ball of the sun sank slowly into the northwest he covered every inch--and many times--of his and Bill's flight south before the downcoming winter. And he conned the grub of the cache and the grub of the Hudson Bay Company post over and over again. He had not eaten for two days; for a far longer time he had not had all he wanted to eat. Often he stooped and picked pale muskeg berries, put them into his mouth, and chewed and swallowed them. A muskeg berry is a bit of seed enclosed in a bit of water. In the mouth the water melts away and the seed chews sharp and bitter. The man knew there was no nourishment in the berries, but he chewed them patiently with a hope greater than knowledge and defying experience.

At nine o'clock he stubbed his toe on a rocky ledge, and from sheer weariness and weakness staggered and fell. He lay for some time, without movement, on his side. Then he slipped out of the packstraps and clumsily dragged himself into a sitting posture. It was not yet dark, and in the lingering twilight he groped about among the rocks for shreds of dry moss. When he had gathered a heap he built a fire,--a smouldering, smudgy fire,--and put a tin pot of water on to boil.

He unwrapped his pack and the first thing he did was to count his matches. There were sixtyseven. He counted them three times to make sure. He divided them into several portions, wrapping them in oil paper, disposing of one bunch in his empty tobacco pouch, of another bunch in the inside band of his battered hat, of a third bunch under his shirt on the chest. This accomplished, a panic came upon him, and he unwrapped them all and counted them again. There were still sixtyseven.

He dried his wet footgear by the fire. The moccasins were in soggy shreds. The blanket socks were worn through in places, and his feet were raw and bleeding. His ankle was throbbing, and he gave it an examination. It had swollen to the size of his knee. He tore a long strip from one of his two blankets and bound the ankle tightly. He tore other strips and bound them about his feet to serve for both moccasins and socks. Then he drank the pot of water, steaming hot, wound his watch, and crawled between his blankets.

He slept like a dead man. The brief darkness around midnight came and went. The sun arose in the northeast--at least the day dawned in that quarter, for the sun was hidden by gray clouds.

At six o'clock he awoke, quietly lying on his back. He gazed straight up into the gray sky and knew that he was hungry. As he rolled over on his elbow he was startled by a loud snort, and saw a bull caribou regarding him with alert curiosity. The animal was not more than fifty feet away, and instantly into the man's mind leaped the vision and the savor of a caribou steak sizzling and frying over a fire. Mechanically he reached for the empty gun, drew a bead, and pulled the trigger. The bull snorted and leaped away, his hoofs rattling and clattering as he fled across the ledges.

The man cursed and flung the empty gun from him. He groaned aloud as he started to drag himself to his feet. It was a slow and arduous task. His joints were like rusty hinges. They worked harshly in their sockets, with much friction, and each bending or unbending was accomplished only through a sheer exertion of will. When he finally gained his feet, another minute or so was consumed in straightening up, so that he could stand erect as a man should stand.

He crawled up a small knoll and surveyed the prospect. There were no trees, no bushes, nothing but a gray sea of moss scarcely diversified by gray rocks, gray lakelets, and gray streamlets. The sky was gray. There was no sun nor hint of sun. He had no idea of north, and he had forgotten the way he had come to this spot the night before: But he was not lost. He knew that. Soon he would come to the land of the little sticks. He felt that it lay off to the left somewhere, not far--possibly just over the next low hill.

He went back to put his pack into shape for travelling. He assured himself of the existence of his three separate parcels of matches, though he did not stop to count them. But he did linger, debating, over a squat moosehide sack. It was not large. He could hide it under his two hands. He knew that it weighed fifteen pounds,--as much as all the rest of the pack,--and it worried him. He finally set it to one side and proceeded to roll the pack. He paused to gaze at the squat moosehide sack. He picked it up hastily with a defiant glance about him, as though the desolation were trying to rob him of it; and when he rose to his feet to stagger on into the day, it was included in the pack on his back.

He bore away to the left, stopping now and again to eat muskeg berries. His ankle had stiffened, his limp was more pronounced, but the pain of it was as nothing compared with the pain of his stomach. The hunger pangs were sharp. They gnawed and gnawed until he could not keep his mind steady on the course he must pursue to gain the land of little sticks. The muskeg berries did not allay this gnawing, while they made his tongue and the roof of his mouth sore with their irritating bite.

He came upon a valley where rock ptarmigan rose on whirring wings from the ledges and muskegs. Ker--ker--ker was the cry they made. He threw stones at them, but could not hit them. He placed his pack on the ground and stalked them as a cat stalks a sparrow. The sharp rocks cut through his pants' legs till his knees left a trail of blood; but the hurt was lost in the hurt of his hunger. He squirmed over the wet moss, saturating his clothes and chilling his body; but he was not aware of it, so great was his fever for food. And always the ptarmigan rose, whirring, before him, till their ker--ker--ker became a mock to him, and he cursed them and cried aloud at them with their own cry.

Once he crawled upon one that must have been asleep. He did not see it till it shot up in his face from its rocky nook. He made a clutch as startled as was the rise of the ptarmigan, and there remained in his hand three tailfeathers. As he watched its flight he hated it, as though it had done him some terrible wrong. Then he returned and shouldered his pack.

As the day wore along he came into valleys or swales where game was more plentiful. A band of caribou passed by, twenty and odd animals, tantalizingly within rifle range. He felt a wild desire to run after them, a certitude that he could run them down. A black fox came toward him, carrying a ptarmigan in his mouth. The man shouted. It was a fearful cry, but the fox, leaping away in fright, did not drop the ptarmigan.

Late in the afternoon he followed a stream, milky with lime, which ran through sparse patches of rushgrass. Grasping these rushes firmly near the root, he pulled up what resembled a young onionsprout no larger than a shinglenail. It was tender, and his teeth sank into it with a crunch that promised deliciously of food. But its fibers were tough. It was composed of stringy filaments saturated with water, like the berries, and devoid of nourishment. He threw off his pack and went into the rushgrass on hands and knees, crunching and munching, like some bovine creature.

He was very weary and often wished to rest--to lie down and sleep; but he was continually driven on--not so much by his desire to gain the land of little sticks as by his hunger. He searched little ponds for frogs and dug up the earth with his nails for worms, though he knew in spite that neither frogs nor worms existed so far north.

He looked into every pool of water vainly, until, as the long twilight came on, he discovered a solitary fish, the size of a minnow, in such a pool. He plunged his arm in up to the shoulder, but it eluded him. He reached for it with both hands and stirred up the milky mud at the bottom. In his excitement he fell in, wetting himself to the waist. Then the water was too muddy to admit of his seeing the fish, and he was compelled to wait until the sediment had settled.

The pursuit was renewed, till the water was again muddied. But he could not wait. He unstrapped the tin bucket and began to bale the pool. He baled wildly at first, splashing himself and flinging the water so short a distance that it ran back into the pool. He worked more carefully, striving to be cool, though his heart was pounding against his chest and his hands were trembling. At the end of half an hour the pool was nearly dry. Not a cupful of water remained. And there was no fish. He found a hidden crevice among the stones through which it had escaped to the adjoining and larger pool--a pool which he could not empty in a night and a day. Had he known of the crevice, he could have closed it with a rock at the beginning and the fish would have been his.

Thus he thought, and crumpled up and sank down upon the wet earth. At first he cried softly to himself, then he cried loudly to the pitiless desolation that ringed him around; and for a long time after he was shaken by great dry sobs.

He built a fire and warmed himself by drinking quarts of hot water, and made camp on a rocky ledge in the same fashion he had the night before. The last thing he did was to see that his matches were dry and to wind his watch. The blankets were wet and clammy. His ankle pulsed with pain. But he knew only that he was hungry, and through his restless sleep he dreamed of feasts and banquets and of food served and spread in all imaginable ways.

He awoke chilled and sick. There was no sun. The gray of earth and sky had become deeper, more profound. A raw wind was blowing, and the first flurries of snow were whitening the hilltops. The air about him thickened and grew white while he made a fire and boiled more water. It was wet snow, half rain, and the flakes were large and soggy. At first they melted as soon as they came in contact with the earth, but ever more fell, covering the ground, putting out the fire, spoiling his supply of mossfuel.

This was a signal for him to strap on his pack and stumble onward, he knew not where. He was not concerned with the land of little sticks, nor with Bill and the cache under the upturned canoe by the river Dease. He was mastered by the verb "to eat." He was hungermad. He took no heed of the course he pursued, so long as that course led him through the swale bottoms. He felt his way through the wet snow to the watery muskeg berries, and went by feel as he pulled up the rushgrass by the roots. But it was tasteless stuff and did not satisfy. He found a weed that tasted sour and he ate all he could find of it, which was not much, for it was a creeping growth, easily hidden under the several inches of snow.

He had no fire that night, nor hot water, and crawled under his blanket to sleep the broken hunger-sleep. The snow turned into a cold rain. He awakened many times to feel it falling on his upturned face. Day came--a gray day and no sun. It had ceased raining. The keenness of his hunger had departed. Sensibility, as far as concerned the yearning for food, had been exhausted. There was a dull, heavy ache in his stomach, but it did not bother him so much. He was more rational, and once more he was chiefly interested in the land of little sticks and the cache by the river Dease.

He ripped the remnant of one of his blankets into strips and bound his bleeding feet. Also, he recinched the injured ankle and prepared himself for a day of travel. When he came to his pack, he paused long over the squat moosehide sack, but in the end it went with him.

The snow had melted under the rain, and only the hilltops showed white. The sun came out, and he succeeded in locating the points of the compass, though he knew now that he was lost. Perhaps, in his previous days' wanderings, he had edged away too far to the left. He now bore off to the right to counteract the possible deviation from his true course.

Though the hunger pangs were no longer so exquisite, he realized that he was weak. He was compelled to pause for frequent rests, when he attacked the muskeg berries and rushgrass patches. His tongue felt dry and large, as though covered with a fine hairy growth, and it tasted bitter in his mouth. His heart gave him a great deal of trouble. When he had travelled a few minutes it would begin a remorseless thump, thump, thump, and then leap up and away in a painful flutter of beats that choked him and made him go faint and dizzy.

In the middle of the day he found two minnows in a large pool. It was impossible to bale it, but he was calmer now and managed to catch them in his tin bucket. They were no longer than his little finger, but he was not particularly hungry. The dull ache in his stomach had been growing duller and fainter. It seemed almost that his stomach was dozing. He ate the fish raw, masticating with painstaking care, for the eating was an act of pure reason. While he had no desire to eat, he knew that he must eat to live.

In the evening he caught three more minnows, eating two and saving the third for breakfast. The sun had dried stray shreds of moss, and he was able to warm himself with hot water. He had not covered more than ten miles that day; and the next day, travelling whenever his heart permitted him, he covered no more than five miles. But his stomach did not give him the slightest uneasiness. It had gone to sleep. He was in a strange country, too, and the caribou were growing more plentiful, also the wolves. Often their yelps drifted across the desolation, and once he saw three of them slinking away before his path.

Another night; and in the morning, being more rational, he untied the leather string that fastened the squat moosehide sack. From its open mouth poured a yellow stream of coarse golddust and nuggets. He roughly divided the gold in halves, caching one half on a prominent ledge, wrapped in a piece of blanket, and returning the other half to the sack. He also began to use strips of the one remaining blanket for his feet. He still clung to his gun, for there were cartridges in that cache by the river Dease.

This was a day of fog, and this day hunger awoke in him again. He was very weak and was afflicted with a giddiness which at times blinded him. It was no uncommon thing now for him to stumble and fall; and stumbling once, he fell squarely into a ptarmigan nest. There were four newly hatched chicks, a day old--little specks of pulsating life no more than a mouthful; and he ate them ravenously, thrusting them alive into his mouth and crunching them like eggshells between his teeth. The mother ptarmigan beat about him with great outcry. He used his gun as a club with which to knock her over, but she dodged out of reach. He threw stones at her and with one chance shot broke a wing. Then she fluttered away, running, trailing the broken wing, with him in pursuit.

The little chicks had no more than whetted his appetite. He hopped and bobbed clumsily along on his injured ankle, throwing stones and screaming hoarsely at times; at other times hopping and bobbing silently along, picking himself up grimly and patiently when he fell, or rubbing his eyes with his hand when the giddiness threatened to overpower him.

The chase led him across swampy ground in the bottom of the valley, and he came upon footprints in the soggy moss. They were not his own--he could see that. They must be Bill's. But he could not stop, for the mother ptarmigan was running on. He would catch her first, then he would return and investigate.

He exhausted the mother ptarmigan; but he exhausted himself. She lay panting on her side. He lay panting on his side, a dozen feet away, unable to crawl to her. And as he recovered she recovered, fluttering out of reach as his hungry hand went out to her. The chase was resumed. Night settled down and she escaped. He stumbled from weakness and pitched head foremost on his face, cutting his cheek, his pack upon his back. He did not move for a long while; then he rolled over on his side, wound his watch, and lay there until morning.

Another day of fog. Half of his last blanket had gone into footwrappings. He failed to pick up Bill's trail. It did not matter. His hunger was driving him too compellingly--only--only he wondered if Bill, too, were lost. By midday the irk of his pack became too oppressive. Again he divided the gold, this time merely spilling half of it on the ground. In the afternoon he threw the rest of it away, there remaining to him only the halfblanket, the tin bucket, and the rifle.

An hallucination began to trouble him. He felt confident that one cartridge remained to him. It was in the chamber of the rifle and he had overlooked it. On the other hand, he knew all the time that the chamber was empty. But the hallucination persisted. He fought it off for hours, then threw his rifle open and was confronted with emptiness. The disappointment was as bitter as though he had really expected to find the cartridge.

He plodded on for half an hour, when the hallucination arose again. Again he fought it, and still it persisted, till for very relief he opened his rifle to unconvince himself. At times his mind wandered farther afield, and he plodded on, a mere automaton, strange conceits and whimsicalities gnawing at his brain like worms. But these excursions out of the real were of brief duration, for ever the pangs of the hungerbite called him back. He was jerked back abruptly once from such an excursion by a sight that caused him nearly to faint. He reeled and swayed, doddering like a drunken man to keep from falling. Before him stood a horse. A horse! He could not believe his eyes. A thick mist was in them, intershot with sparkling points of light. He rubbed his eyes savagely to clear his vision, and beheld, not a horse, but a great brown bear. The animal was studying him with bellicose curiosity.

The man had brought his gun halfway to his shoulder before he realized. He lowered it and drew his huntingknife from its beaded sheath at his hip. Before him was meat and life. He ran his thumb along the edge of his knife. It was sharp. The point was sharp. He would fling himself upon the bear and kill it. But his heart began its warning thump, thump, thump. Then followed the wild upward leap and tattoo of flutters, the pressing as of an iron band about his forehead, the creeping of the dizziness into his brain.

His desperate courage was evicted by a great surge of fear. In his weakness, what if the animal attacked him? He drew himself up to his most imposing stature, gripping the knife and staring hard at the bear. The bear advanced clumsily a couple of steps, reared up, and gave vent to a tentative growl. If the man ran, he would run after him; but the man did not run. He was animated now with the courage of fear. He, too, growled, savagely, terribly, voicing the fear that is to life germane and that lies twisted about life's deepest roots.

The bear edged away to one side, growling menacingly, himself appalled by this mysterious creature that appeared upright and unafraid. But the man did not move. He stood like a statue till the danger was past, when he yielded to a fit of trembling and sank down into the wet moss.

He pulled himself together and went on, afraid now in a new way. It was not the fear that he should die passively from lack of food, but that he should be destroyed violently before starvation had exhausted the last particle of the endeavor in him that made toward surviving. There were the wolves. Back and forth across the desolation drifted their howls, weaving the very air into a fabric of menace that was so tangible that he found himself, arms in the air, pressing it back from him as it might be the walls of a windblown tent.

Now and again the wolves, in packs of two and three, crossed his path. But they sheered clear of him. They were not in sufficient numbers, and besides they were hunting the caribou, which did not battle, while this strange creature that walked erect might scratch and bite.

In the late afternoon he came upon scattered bones where the wolves had made a kill. The debris had been a caribou calf an hour before, squawking and running and very much alive. He contemplated the bones, cleanpicked and polished, pink with the celllife in them which had not yet died. Could it possibly be that he might be that ere the day was done! Such was life, eh? A vain and fleeting thing. It was only life that pained. There was no hurt in death. To die was to sleep. It meant cessation, rest. Then why was he not content to die?

But he did not moralize long. He was squatting in the moss, a bone in his mouth, sucking at the shreds of life that still dyed it faintly pink. The sweet meaty taste, thin and elusive almost as a memory, maddened him. He closed his jaws on the bones and crunched. Sometimes it was the bone that broke, sometimes his teeth. Then he crushed the bones between rocks, pounded them to a pulp, and swallowed them. He pounded his fingers, too, in his haste, and yet found a moment in which to feel surprise at the fact that his fingers did not hurt much when caught under the descending rock.

Came frightful days of snow and rain. He did not know when he made camp, when he broke camp. He travelled in the night as much as in the day. He rested wherever he fell, crawled on whenever the dying life in him flickered up and burned less dimly. He, as a man, no longer strove. It was the life in him, unwilling to die, that drove him on. He did not suffer. His nerves had become blunted, numb, while his mind was filled with weird visions and delicious dreams.

But ever he sucked and chewed on the crushed bones of the caribou calf, the least remnants of which he had gathered up and carried with him. He crossed no more hills or divides, but automatically followed a large stream which flowed through a wide and shallow valley. He did not see this stream nor this valley. He saw nothing save visions. Soul and body walked or crawled side by side, yet apart, so slender was the thread that bound them.

He awoke in his right mind, lying on his back on a rocky ledge. The sun was shining bright and warm. Afar off he heard the squawking of caribou calves. He was aware of vague memories of rain and wind and snow, but whether he had been beaten by the storm for two days or two weeks he did not know.

For some time he lay without movement, the genial sunshine pouring upon him and saturating his miserable body with its warmth. A fine day, he thought. Perhaps he could manage to locate himself. By a painful effort he rolled over on his side. Below him flowed a wide and sluggish river. Its unfamiliarity puzzled him. Slowly he followed it with his eyes, winding in wide sweeps among the bleak, bare hills, bleaker and barer and lowerlying than any hills he had yet encountered. Slowly, deliberately, without excitement or more than the most casual interest, he followed the course of the strange stream toward the skyline and saw it emptying into a bright and shining sea. He was still unexcited. Most unusual, he thought, a vision or a mirage--more likely a vision, a trick of his disordered mind. He was confirmed in this by sight of a ship lying at anchor in the midst of the shining sea. He closed his eyes for a while, then opened them. Strange how the vision persisted! Yet not strange. He knew there were no seas or ships in the heart of the barren lands, just as he had known there was no cartridge in the empty rifle.

He heard a snuffle behind him--a halfchoking gasp or cough. Very slowly, because of his exceeding weakness and stiffness, he rolled over on his other side. He could see nothing near at hand, but he waited patiently. Again came the snuffle and cough, and outlined between two jagged rocks not a score of feet away he made out the gray head of a wolf. The sharp ears were not pricked so sharply as he had seen them on other wolves; the eyes were bleared and bloodshot, the head seemed to droop limply and forlornly. The animal blinked continually in the sunshine. It seemed sick. As he looked it snuffled and coughed again.

This, at least, was real, he thought, and turned on the other side so that he might see the reality of the world which had been veiled from him before by the vision. But the sea still shone in the distance and the ship was plainly discernible. Was it reality, after all? He closed his eyes for a long while and thought, and then it came to him. He had been making north by east, away from the Dease Divide and into the Coppermine Valley. This wide and sluggish river was the Coppermine. That shining sea was the Arctic Ocean. That ship was a whaler, strayed east, far east, from the mouth of the Mackenzie, and it was lying at anchor in Coronation Gulf. He remembered the Hudson Bay Company chart he had seen long ago, and it was all clear and reasonable to him.

He sat up and turned his attention to immediate affairs. He had worn through the blanketwrappings, and his feet were shapeless lumps of raw meat. His last blanket was gone. Rifle and knife were both missing. He had lost his hat somewhere, with the bunch of matches in the band, but the matches against his chest were safe and dry inside the tobacco pouch and oil paper. He looked at his watch. It marked eleven o'clock and was still running. Evidently he had kept it wound.

He was calm and collected. Though extremely weak, he had no sensation of pain. He was not hungry. The thought of food was not even pleasant to him, and whatever he did was done by his reason alone. He ripped off his pants' legs to the knees and bound them about his feet. Somehow he had succeeded in retaining the tin bucket. He would have some hot water before he began what he foresaw was to be a terrible journey to the ship.

His movements were slow. He shook as with a palsy. When he started to collect dry moss, he found he could not rise to his feet. He tried again and again, then contented himself with crawling about on hands and knees. Once he crawled near to the sick wolf. The animal dragged itself reluctantly out of his way, licking its chops with a tongue which seemed hardly to have the strength to curl. The man noticed that the tongue was not the customary healthy red. It was a yellowish brown and seemed coated with a rough and halfdry mucus.

After he had drunk a quart of hot water the man found he was able to stand, and even to walk as well as a dying man might be supposed to walk. Every minute or so he was compelled to rest. His steps were feeble and uncertain, just as the wolfs that trailed him were feeble and uncertain; and that night, when the shining sea was blotted out by blackness, he knew he was nearer to it by no more than four miles.

Throughout the night he heard the cough of the sick wolf, and now and then the squawking of the caribou calves. There was life all around him, but it was strong life, very much alive and well, and he knew the sick wolf clung to the sick man's trail in the hope that the man would die first. In the morning, on opening his eyes, he beheld it regarding him with a wistful and hungry stare. It stood crouched, with tail between its legs, like a miserable and woebegone dog. It shivered in the chill morning wind, and grinned dispiritedly when the man spoke to it in a voice that achieved no more than a hoarse whisper.

The sun rose brightly, and all morning the man tottered and fell toward the ship on the shining sea. The weather was perfect. It was the brief Indian Summer of the high latitudes. It might last a week. To-morrow or next day it might be gone.

In the afternoon the man came upon a trail. It was of another man, who did not walk, but who dragged himself on all fours. The man thought it might be Bill, but he thought in a dull, uninterested way. He had no curiosity. In fact, sensation and emotion had left him. He was no longer susceptible to pain. Stomach and nerves had gone to sleep. Yet the life that was in him drove him on. He was very weary, but it refused to die. It was because it refused to die that he still ate muskeg berries and minnows, drank his hot water, and kept a wary eye on the sick wolf.

He followed the trail of the other man who dragged himself along, and soon came to the end of it--a few freshpicked bones where the soggy moss was marked by the footpads of many wolves. He saw a squat moosehide sack, mate to his own, which had been torn by sharp teeth. He picked it up, though its weight was almost too much for his feeble fingers. Bill had carried it to the last. Ha! ha! He would have the laugh on Bill. He would survive and carry it to the ship in the shining sea. His mirth was hoarse and ghastly, like a raven's croak, and the sick wolf joined him, howling lugubriously. The man ceased suddenly. How could he have the laugh on Bill if that were Bill; if those bones, so pinkywhite and clean, were Bill?

He turned away. Well, Bill had deserted him; but he would not take the gold, nor would he suck Bill's bones. Bill would have, though, had it been the other way around, he mused as he staggered on.

He came to a pool of water. Stooping over in quest of minnows, he jerked his head back as though he had been stung. He had caught sight of his reflected face. So horrible was it that sensibility awoke long enough to be shocked. There were three minnows in the pool, which was too large to drain; and after several ineffectual attempts to catch them in the tin bucket he forbore. He was afraid, because of his great weakness, that he might fall in and drown. It was for this reason that he did not trust himself to the river astride one of the many driftlogs which lined its sandspits.

That day he decreased the distance between him and the ship by three miles; the next day by two--for he was crawling now as Bill had crawled; and the end of the fifth day found the ship still seven miles away and him unable to make even a mile a day. Still the Indian Summer held on, and he continued to crawl and faint, turn and turn about; and ever the sick wolf coughed and wheezed at his heels. His knees had become raw meat like his feet, and though he padded them with the shirt from his back it was a red track he left behind him on the moss and stones. Once, glancing back, he saw the wolf licking hungrily his bleeding trail, and he saw sharply what his own end might be--unless--unless he could get the wolf. Then began as grim a tragedy of existence as was ever played--a sick man that crawled, a sick wolf that limped, two creatures dragging their dying carcasses across the desolation and hunting each other's lives.

Had it been a well wolf, it would not have mattered so much to the man; but the thought of going to feed the maw of that loathsome and all but dead thing was repugnant to him. He was finicky. His mind had begun to wander again, and to be perplexed by hallucinations, while his lucid intervals grew rarer and shorter.

He was awakened once from a faint by a wheeze close in his ear. The wolf leaped lamely back, losing its footing and falling in its weakness. It was ludicrous, but he was not amused. Nor was he even afraid. He was too far gone for that. But his mind was for the moment clear, and he lay and considered. The ship was no more than four miles away. He could see it quite distinctly when he rubbed the mists out of his eyes, and he could see the white sail of a small boat cutting the water of the shining sea. But he could never crawl those four miles. He knew that, and was very calm in the knowledge. He knew that he could not crawl half a mile. And yet he wanted to live. It was unreasonable that he should die after all he had undergone. Fate asked too much of him. And, dying, he declined to die. It was stark madness, perhaps, but in the very grip of Death he defied Death and refused to die.

He closed his eyes and composed himself with infinite precaution. He steeled himself to keep above the suffocating languor that lapped like a rising tide through all the wells of his being. It was very like a sea, this deadly languor, that rose and rose and drowned his consciousness bit by bit. Sometimes he was all but submerged, swimming through oblivion with a faltering stroke; and again, by some strange alchemy of soul, he would find another shred of will and strike out more strongly.

Without movement he lay on his back, and he could hear, slowly drawing near and nearer, the wheezing intake and output of the sick wolfs breath. It drew closer, ever closer, through an infinitude of time, and he did not move. It was at his ear. The harsh dry tongue grated like sandpaper against his cheek. His hands shot out--or at least he willed them to shoot out. The fingers were curved like talons, but they closed on empty air. Swiftness and certitude require strength, and the man had not this strength.

The patience of the wolf was terrible. The man's patience was no less terrible. For half a day he lay motionless, fighting off unconsciousness and waiting for the thing that was to feed upon him and upon which he wished to feed. Sometimes the languid sea rose over him and he dreamed long dreams; but ever through it all, waking and dreaming, he waited for the wheezing breath and the harsh caress of the tongue.

He did not hear the breath, and he slipped slowly from some dream to the feel of the tongue along his hand. He waited. The fangs pressed softly; the pressure increased; the wolf was exerting its last strength in an effort to sink teeth in the food for which it had waited so long. But the man had waited long, and the lacerated hand closed on the jaw. Slowly, while the wolf struggled feebly and the hand clutched feebly, the other hand crept across to a grip. Five minutes later the whole weight of the man's body was on top of the wolf. The hands had not sufficient strength to choke the wolf, but the face of the man was pressed close to the throat of the wolf and the mouth of the man was full of hair. At the end of half an hour the man was aware of a warm trickle in his throat. It was not pleasant. It was like molten lead being forced into his stomach, and it was forced by his will alone. Later the man rolled over on his back and slept.

There were some members of a scientific expedition on the whaleship *Bedford*. From the deck they remarked a strange object on the shore. It was moving down the beach toward the water. They were unable to classify it, and, being scientific men, they climbed into the whaleboat alongside and went ashore to see. And they saw something that was alive but which could hardly be called a man. It was blind, unconscious. It squirmed along the ground like some monstrous worm. Most of its efforts were ineffectual, but it was persistent, and it writhed and twisted and went ahead perhaps a score of feet an hour.

Three weeks afterward the man lay in a bunk on the whaleship *Bedford,* and with tears streaming down his wasted cheeks told who he was and what he had undergone. He also babbled incoherently of his mother, of sunny Southern California, and a home among the orange groves and flowers.

The days were not many after that when he sat at table with the scientific men and ship's officers. He gloated over the spectacle of so much food, watching it anxiously as it went into the mouths of others. With the disappearance of each mouthful an expression of deep regret came into his eyes. He was quite sane, yet he hated those men at mealtime. He was haunted by a fear that the food would not last. He inquired of the cook, the cabin boy, the captain, concerning the food stores. They reassured him countless times; but he could not believe them, and pried cunningly about the lazarette to see with his own eyes.

It was noticed that the man was getting fat. He grew stouter with each day. The scientific men shook their heads and theorized. They limited the man at his meals, but still his girth increased and he swelled prodigiously under his shirt.

The sailors grinned. They knew. And when the scientific men set a watch on the man, they knew too. They saw him slouch for'ard after breakfast, and, like a mendicant, with outstretched palm, accost a sailor. The sailor grinned and passed him a fragment of sea biscuit. He clutched it avariciously, looked at it as a miser looks at gold, and thrust it into his shirt bosom. Similar were the donations from other grinning sailors.

The scientific men were discreet. They let him alone. But they privily examined his bunk. It was lined with hardtack; the mattress was stuffed with hardtack; every nook and cranny was filled with hardtack. Yet he was sane. He was taking precautions against another possible famine--that was all. He would recover from it, the scientific men said; and he did, ere the *Bedford's* anchor rumbled down in San Francisco Bay.

Happiness

Guy de Maupassant

Maupassant (1850-1893) accomplished technical precision by controlling imagery and the structure of the scene in the short story and novella. Maupassant's writing portrayed the lives of the masses and he often wrote about the tragic lives of the common folk. Maupassant's primary mentors were Louis Bouillet, Gustave Flaubert, and Emile Zola.

Born into the Norman upper bourgeoisie of Rouen, it was here that Maupassant later met Flaubert and Bouillet, the poet. Bouillet guided him in his early literary pursuits but, after Bouillet's death in 1869 Maupassant began to study law in Paris. The Franco-Prussian War interrupted his studies and he served for a time in a Norman regiment. Unable to resume his studies after his family's business failed, he secured a post in the naval ministry.

In 1875 his first short story, *The Dead Hand,* was published in a local newspaper. Until his publication of *Roly-Poly* in 1880 Maupassant served his literary apprenticeship under Flaubert. While he moved slowly through the bureaucracy, he remained a conscientious worker at his post, continuing to write at home after work.

Maupassant was introduced to Emile Zola, the most successful literary person of his era, by Flaubert. With other young writers Maupassant attended meetings conducted by Zola to plan a volume of stories about the Franco-Prussian War. The volume, *Evening at Medan,* contained Maupassant's story, *Boule de Suif,* second in sequence to Zola's. It was highly commended by his peers. His success terminated his apprenticeship with Flaubert. Thereafter he followed Zola's school of Naturalism.

IT WAS TEATIME before the appearance of the lamps. The villa commanded the sea; the sun, which had disappeared, had left the sky all rosy from his passing -- rubbed, as it were, with golddust; and the Mediterranean, without a ripple, without a shudder, smooth, still shining under the dying day, seemed like a huge and polished metal plate.

179

Far off to the right the jagged mountains outlined their black profile on the paled purple of the west.

We talked of love, we discussed that old subject, we said again the things which we had said already very often. The sweet melancholy of the twilight made our words slower, caused a tenderness to waver in our souls; and that word, "love," which came back ceaselessly, now pronounced by a strong man's voice, now uttered by the frailtoned voice of a woman, seemed to fill the little *salon*, to flutter there like a bird, to hover there like a spirit.

Can one remain in love for several years in succession?

"Yes," maintained some.

"No," affirmed others.

We distinguished cases, we established limitations, we cited examples; and all, men and women, filled with rising and troubling memories, which they could not quote, and which mounted to their lips, seemed moved, and talked of that common, that sovereign thing, the tender and mysterious union of two beings, with a profound emotion and an ardent interest.

But all of a sudden some one, whose eyes had been fixed upon the distance, cried out:

"Oh! Look down there; what is it?"

On the sea, at the bottom of the horizon, loomed up a mass, gray, enormous, and confused.

The women had risen from their seats, and without understanding, looked at this surprising thing which they had never seen before.

Some one said:

"It is Corsica! You see it so two or three times a year, in certain exceptional conditions of the atmosphere, when the air is perfectly clear, and it is not concealed by those mists of seafog which always veil the distances."

We distinguished vaguely the mountain ridges, we thought we recognized the snow of their summits. And every one remained surprised, troubled, almost terrified, by this sudden apparition of a world, by this phantom risen from the sea. Maybe that those who, like Columbus, went away across undiscovered oceans had such strange visions as this.

Then said an old gentleman who had not yet spoken:

"See here: I knew in that island which raises itself before us, as if in person to answer what we said, and to recall to me a singular memory -- I knew, I say, an admirable case of love which was true, of love which, improbably enough, was happy.

"Here it is.

"Five years ago I made a journey in Corsica. That savage island is more unknown and more distant from us than America, even though you see it sometimes from the very coasts of France, as we have done today.

"Imagine a world which is still chaos, imagine a storm of mountains separated by narrow ravines where torrents roll; not a single plain, but immense waves of granite, and giant undulations of earth covered with brushwood or with high forests of chestnuttrees and pines. It is a virgin soil, uncultivated, desert, although you sometimes make out a village like a heap of rocks, on the summit of a mountain. No culture, no industries, no art. One never meets here with a morsel of carved wood, or a bit of sculptured stone, never the least reminder that the ancestors of these people had any taste, whether rude or refined, for gracious and beautiful things. It is this which strikes you the most in their superb and hard country: their hereditary indifference to that search for seductive forms which is called Art.

"Italy, where every palace, full of masterpieces, is a masterpiece itself: Italy, where marble, wood, bronze, iron, metals, and precious stones attest man's genius, where the smallest old things which lie about in the ancient houses reveal that divine care for grace -- Italy is for us the sacred country which we love, because she shows to us and proves to us the struggle, the grandeur, the power, and the triumph of the intelligence which creates.

And, face to face with her, the savage Corsica has remained exactly as in her earliest days. A man lives there in his rude house, indifferent to everything which does not concern his own bare existence or his family feuds. And he has retained the vices and the virtues of savage races; he is violent, malignant, sanguinary without a thought of remorse, but also hospitable, generous, devoted, simple, opening his door to passers-by, and giving his faithful friendship in return for the least sign of sympathy.

"So, for a month, I had been wandering over this magnificent island with the sensation that I was at the end of the world. No more inns, no taverns, no roads. You gain by mule-paths hamlets hanging up, as it were, on a mountain side, and commanding tortuous abysses whence of an evening you hear rising the steady sound, the dull and deep voice, of the torrent. You knock at the doors of the houses. You ask a shelter for the night and something to live on till the morrow. And you sit down at the humble board, and you sleep under the humble roof, and in the morning you press the extended hand of your host, who has guided you as far as the outskirts of the village.

"Now, one night, after ten hours' walking, I reached a little dwelling quite by itself at the bottom of a narrow valley which was about to throw itself into the sea a league farther on. The two steep slopes of the mountain, covered with brush, with fallen rocks and with great trees, shut in this lamentably sad ravine like two somber walls.

"Around the cottages were some vines, a little garden, and, farther off, several large chestnut-trees -- enough to live on; in fact, a fortune for this poor country.

"The woman who received me was old, severe, and neat -- exceptionally so. The man, seated on a straw chair, rose to salute me, then sat down again without saying a word. His companion said to me:

"'Excuse him; he is deaf now. He is eighty-two years old.'

"She spoke the French of France. I was surprised.

"I asked her:

"'You are not of Corsica?'

"She answered:

"'No; we are from the Continent. But we have lived here now fifty years.'

"A feeling of anguish and of fear seized me at the thought of those fifty years passed in this gloomy hole, so far from the cities where human beings dwell. An old shepherd returned, and we began to eat the only dish there was for dinner, a thick soup in which potatoes, lard, and cabbages had been boiled together.

"When the short repast was finished, I went and sat down before the door, my heart pinched by the melancholy of the mournful landscape, wrung by that distress which sometimes seizes travelers on certain sad evenings, in certain desolate places. It seems that everything is near its ending -- existence, and the universe itself. You perceive sharply the dreadful misery of life, the isolation of every one, the nothingness of all things and the black loneliness of the heart which nurses itself and deceives itself with dreams until the hour of death.

"The old woman rejoined me, and, tortured by that curiosity which ever lies at the bottom of the most resigned of souls:

"'So you come from France?' said she.

"'Yes; I'm traveling for pleasure.'

"'You are from Paris, perhaps?'

"'No, I am from Nancy.'

"It seemed to me that an extraordinary emotion agitated her. How I saw, or rather how I felt it, I do not know."

She repeated, in a slow voice:

"'You are from Nancy?'

"The man appeared in the door, impassible, like all the deaf.

"She resumed:

"'It doesn't make any difference. He can't hear.'

"Then, at the end of several seconds:

"'So you know people at Nancy?'

"'Oh yes, nearly everybody.'

"'The family of SainteAllaize?'

"'Yes, very well; they were friends of my father.'

"'What are you called?'

"I told her my name. She regarded me fixedly, then said, in that low voice which is roused by memories:

"'Yes, yes; I remember well. And the Brisemares, what shall become of them?'

"'They are all dead.'

"'Ah! And the Sirmonts, do you know them?'

"'Yes, the last of the family is a general.'

"Then she said, trembling with emotion, with anguish, with I do not know what, feeling confused, powerful, and holy, with I do not know how great a need to confess, to tell all, to talk of those things which she had hitherto kept shut in the bottom of her heart, and to speak of those people whose name distracted her soul:

"'Yes, Henri de Sirmont. I know him well. He is my brother.'

"And I lifted my eyes at her, aghast with surprise. And of all a sudden my memory of it came back.

"It had caused, once, a great scandal among the nobility of Lorraine. A young girl, beautiful and rich, Suzanne de Sirmont had run away with an underofficer in the regiment of hussars commanded by her father.

"He was a handsome fellow, the son of a peasant, but he carried his blue dolman very well, this soldier who had captivated his colonel's daughter. She had seen him, noticed him, fallen in love with him, doubtless while watching the squadrons filing by. But how she had got speech of him, how they had managed to see one another, to hear from one another; how she had dared to let him understand she loved him -- that was never known.

"Nothing was divined, nothing suspected. One night when the soldier had just finished his time of service, they disappeared together. Her people looked for them in vain. They never received tidings, and they considered her as dead.

"So I found her in this sinister valley.

"Then in my turn I took up the word:

"'Yes, I remember well. You are Mademoiselle Suzanne.'

"She made the sign 'yes,' with her head. Tears fell from her eyes. Then with a look showing me the old man motionless on the threshold of his hut, she said:

"'That is he.'

"And I understood that she loved him yet, that she still saw him with her bewitched eyes.

"I asked:

"'Have you at least been happy?'

"She answered with a voice which came from her heart:

"'Oh yes! very happy. He has made me very happy. I have never regretted.'

"I looked at her, sad, surprised, astounded by the sovereign strength of love! That rich young lady had followed this man, this peasant. She was become herself a peasant woman. She made for herself a life without charm, without luxury, without delicacy of any kind, she had stooped to simple customs. And she loved him yet. She was become the wife of a rustic, in a cap, in a cloth skirt. Seated on a strawbottomed chair, she ate from an earthenware dish, at a wooden table, soup of potatoes and of cabbages with lard. She slept on a mattress by his side.

"She had never thought of anything but of him. She had never regretted her jewels, nor her fine dresses, nor the elegancies of life, nor the perfumed warmth of the chambers hung with tapestry, nor the softness of the downbeds where the body sinks in for repose. She had never had need of anything but him; provided he was there, she desired nothing.

"Still young, she had abandoned life and the world and those who had brought her up, and who had loved her. She had come, alone with him, into this savage valley. And he had been everything to her, all that one desires, all that one dreams of, all that one waits for without ceasing, all that one hopes for without end. He had filled her life with happiness from the one end to the other.

"She could not have been more happy.

"And all the night, listening to the hoarse breathing of the old soldier stretched on his pallet beside her who had followed him so far, I thought of this strange and simple adventure, of this happiness so complete, made of so very little.

"And I went away at sunrise, after having pressed the hands of that aged pair."

The storyteller was silent. A woman said:

"All the same, she had ideals which were too easily satisfied, needs which were too primitive, requirements which were too simple. She could only have been a fool."

Another said, in a low, slow voice, "What matter! she was happy."

And down there at the end of the horizon, Corsica was sinking into the night, returning gently into the sea, blotting out her great shadow, which had appeared as if in person to tell the story of those two humble lovers who were sheltered by her coasts.

The Piazza

Herman Melville

Herman Melville (1819-1891), novelist, short story writer, and poet, is best known for *Moby Dick, The Piazza Tales*, and *Billy Budd*.

Born into a well-to-do New York family, his father's bankruptcy and death left the family with financial difficulties when Melville was twelve years old. At nineteen he became a merchant sailor on the *St. Lawrence*. His sea experiences, his travels, and his exposure to the sordid corners of Liverpool heightened his awareness of the darker side of man. This theme came alive in much of his work. In 1841 after trying his hand at teaching and writing, he returned to the sea upon the whaler *Acushnet* bound for the Pacific. Deserting the ship in the Marquesas Islands, he gathered material for his novels *Typee* (1846), *Omoo* (1847), *Redburn* (1849), and *White-Jacket* (1850), which brought him literary success.

In 1850 he settled on a farm at Arrowhead near Pittsfield, Massachusetts. There he wrote *Moby Dick* (1851). In 1856 he completed *The Piazza Tales,* which included *The Piazza, Bartelby the Scrivener, The Encantadas,* and *Benito Cereno*. By 1857 he had lost favor with the public, and although he continued to write he no longer published fiction.

By 1866 he was a customs inspector in New York. He wrote *Battle Pieces and Aspects of the War*, a volume of poetry about the Civil War, and *Billy Budd*, published posthumously in 1924.

"With fairest flowers,
Whilst summer lasts, and I live here, fidele--"

WHEN I REMOVED into the country, it was to occupy an old-fashioned farmhouse, which had no piazza--a deficiency the more regretted because not only did I like piazzas, as somehow combining the coziness of indoors with the freedom of outdoors, and it is so pleasant to inspect your thermometer there, but the country round about was such a picture that in berry time no boy climbs hill or crosses vale without coming upon easels planted in every nook, and sunburnt painters painting there. A very

186

paradise of painters. The circle of the stars cut by the circle of the mountains. At least, so looks it from the house; though, once upon the mountains, no circle of them can you see. Had the site been chosen five rods off, this charmed ring would not have been.

The house is old. Seventy years since, from the heart of the Hearth Stone Hills, they quarried the Kaaba, or Holy Stone, to which, each Thanksgiving, the social pilgrims used to come. So long ago that, in digging for the foundation, the workmen used both spade and ax, fighting the troglodytes of those subterranean parts--sturdy roots of a sturdy wood, encamped upon what is now a long landslide of sleeping meadow, sloping away off from my poppybed. Of that knit wood but one survivor stands-- an elm, lonely through steadfastness.

Whoever built the house, he builded better than he knew, or else Orion in the zenith flashed down his Damocles' sword to him some starry night and said, "Build there." For how, otherwise, could it have entered the builder's mind, that, upon the clearing being made, such a purple prospect would be his?--nothing less than Greylock, with all his hills about him, like Charlemagne among his peers.

Now, for a house, so situated in such a country, to have no piazza for the convenience of those who might desire to feast upon a view, and take their time and ease about it, seemed as much of an omission as if a picture gallery should have no bench; for what but picture galleries are the marble halls of these same limestone hills?--galleries hung, month after month anew, with pictures ever fading into pictures ever fresh. And beauty is like piety--you cannot run and read it; tranquillity and constancy, with, nowa- days, an easy chair, are needed. For though, of old, when reverence was in vogue and indolence was not, the devotees of Nature doubtless used to stand and adore--just as, in the cathedrals of those ages, the worshipers of a higher Power did--yet, in these times of failing faith and feeble knees, we have the piazza and the pew.

During the first year of my residence, the more leisurely to witness the coronation of Charlemagne (weather permitting, they crown him every sunrise and sunset), I chose me, on the hillside bank near by, a royal lounge of turf--a green velvet lounge, with long, mosspadded back; while at the head, strangely enough, there grew (but, I suppose, for heraldry) three tufts of blue violets in a field argent of wild strawberries; and a trellis, with honeysuckle, I set for canopy. Very majestical lounge, indeed. So much so that here, as with the reclining majesty of Denmark in his orchard, a sly earache invaded me. But, if damps abound at times in

Westminster Abbey because it is so old, why not within this monastery of mountains, which is older?

A piazza must be had.

The house was wide, my fortune narrow, so that, to build a panoramic piazza, one round and round, it could not be-- although, indeed, considering the matter by rule and square, the carpenters, in the kindest way, were anxious to gratify my furthest wishes, at I've forgotten how much a foot.

Upon but one of the four sides would prudence grant me what I wanted. Now, which side?

To the east, that long camp of the Hearth Stone Hills, fading far away towards Quito, and every fall, a small white flake of something peering suddenly, of a coolish morning, from the topmost cliff--the season's newdropped lamb, its earliest fleece; and then the Christmas dawn, draping those dun highlands with redbarred plaids and tartans--goodly sight from your piazza, that. Goodly sight; but, to the north is Charlemagne--can't have the Hearth Stone Hills with Charlemagne.

Well, the south side. Apple trees are there. Pleasant, of a balmy morning in the month of May, to sit and see that orchard, whitebudded, as for a bridal; and, in October, one green arsenal yard, such piles of ruddy shot. Very fine, I grant; but, to the north is Charlemagne.

The west side, look. An upland pasture, alleying away into a maple wood at top. Sweet, in opening spring, to trace upon the hillside, otherwise gray and bare--to trace, I say, the oldest paths by their streaks of earliest green. Sweet, indeed, I can't deny but, to the north is Charlemagne.

So Charlemagne, he carried it. It was not long after 1848, and, somehow, about that time, all round the world these kings, they had the casting vote, and voted for themselves.

No sooner was ground broken than all the neighborhood, neighbor Dives, in particular, broke, too--into a laugh. Piazza to the north! Winter piazza! Wants, of winter midnights, to watch the Aurora Borealis, I suppose; hope he's laid in good store of polar muffs and mittens.

That was in the lion month of March. Not forgotten are the blue noses of the carpenters, and how they scouted at the greenness of the cit, who would build his sole piazza to the north. But March don't last forever; patience, and August comes. And then, in the cool elysium of my northern bower, I, Lazarus in Abraham's bosom, cast down the hill a pitying glance on poor old Dives, tormented in the purgatory of his piazza to the south.

But, even in December, this northern piazza does not repel-- nipping cold and gusty though it be, and the north wind, like any miller, bolting by the snow in finest flour--for then, once more, with frosted beard, I pace the sleety deck, weathering Cape Horn.

In summer, too, Canutelike, sitting here, one is often reminded of the sea. For not only do long ground swells roll the slanting grain, and little wavelets of the grass ripple over upon the low piazza, as their beach, and the blown down of dandelions is wafted like the spray, and the purple of the mountains is just the purple of the billows, and a still August noon broods upon the deep meadows as a calm upon the Line, but the vastness and the lonesomeness are so oceanic, and the silence and the sameness, too, that the first peep of a strange house, rising beyond the trees, is for all the world like spying, on the Barbary coast, an unknown sail.

And this recalls my inland voyage to fairyland. A true voyage, but, take it all in all, interesting as if invented.

From the piazza, some uncertain object I had caught, mysteriously snugged away, to all appearance, in a sort of purpled breast pocket, high up in a hopperlike hollow or sunken angle among the northwestern mountains--yet, whether, really, it was on a mountainside or a mountaintop could not be determined; because, though, viewed from favorable points, a blue summit, peering up away behind the rest, will, as it were, talk to you over their heads, and plainly tell you, that, though he (the blue summit) seems among them, he is not of them (God forbid!), and, indeed, would have you know that he considers himself--as, to say truth, he has good right--by several cubits their superior, nevertheless, certain ranges, here and there double-filed, as in platoons, so shoulder and follow up upon one another, with their irregular shapes and heights, that, from the piazza, a nigher and lower mountain will, in most states of the atmosphere, effacingly shade itself away into a higher and further one; that an object, bleak on the former's crest, will, for all that, appear nested in the latter's flank. These mountains, somehow, they play at hideandseek, and all before one's eyes.

But, be that as it may, the spot in question was, at all events, so situated as to be only visible, and then but vaguely, under certain witching conditions of light and shadow.

Indeed, for a year or more, I knew not there was such a spot, and might, perhaps, have never known, had it not been for a wizard afternoon in autumn--late in autumn--a mad poet's afternoon, when the turned maple woods in the broad basin below me, having lost their first vermilion tint, dully smoked, like smoldering towns, when flames expire upon their prey; and rumor had it that this smokiness in the general air was not all Indian summer--which was not used to be so sick a thing, however mild--but, in great part, was blown from far-off forests, for weeks on fire, in Vermont; so that no wonder the sky was ominous as Hecate's caldron--and two sportsmen, crossing a red stubble buckwheat field, seemed guilty Macbeth and foreboding Banquo; and the hermit sun, hutted in an Adullum cave, well towards the south, according to his season did little else but, by indirect reflection of narrow rays shot down a Simplon Pass among the clouds, just steadily paint one small, round strawberry mole upon the wan cheek of northwestern hills. Signal as a candle. One spot of radiance, where all else was shade.

Fairies there, thought I; some haunted ring where fairies dance.

Time passed, and the following May, after a gentle shower upon the mountains--a little shower islanded in misty seas of sunshine; such a distant shower--and sometimes two, and three, and four of them, all visible together in different parts--as I love to watch from the piazza, instead of thunderstorms as I used to, which wrap old Greylock like a Sinai, till one thinks swart Moses must be climbing among scathed hemlocks there; after, I say, that gentle shower, I saw a rainbow, resting its further end just where, in autumn, I had marked the mole. Fairies there, thought I; remembering that rainbows bring out the blooms, and that, if one can but get to the rainbow's end, his fortune is made in a bag of gold. Yon rainbow's end, would I were there, thought I. And none the less I wished it, for now first noticing what seemed some sort of glen, or grotto, in the mountainside; at least, whatever it was, viewed through the rainbow's medium it glowed like the Potosi mine. But a workaday neighbor said no doubt it was but some old barn--an abandoned one, its broadside beaten in, the acclivity its background. But I, though I had never been there, I knew better.

A few days after, a cheery sunrise kindled a golden sparkle in the same spot as before. The sparkle was of that vividness, it seemed as if it could only come from glass. The building, then--if building, after all, it was-- could, at least, not be a barn, much less an abandoned one, stale hay ten years musting in it. No; if aught built by mortal, it must be a cottage;

perhaps long vacant and dismantled, but this very spring magically fitted up and glazed.

Again, one noon, in the same direction, I marked, over dimmed tops of terraced foliage, a broader gleam, as of a silver buckler held sunwards over some croucher's head; which gleam, experience in like cases taught, must come from a roof, newly shingled. This, to me, made pretty sure the recent occupancy of that far cot in fairyland.

Day after day, now, full of interest in my discovery, what time I could spare from reading the *Midsummer Night's Dream*, and all about Titania, wishfully I gazed off towards the hills; but in vain. Either troops of shadows, and imperial guard, with slow pace and solemn, defiled along the steeps, or, routed by pursuing light, fled broadcast from east to west--old wars of Lucifer and Michael; or the mountains, though unvexed by these mirrored sham fights in the sky, had an atmosphere otherwise unfavorable for fairy views. I was sorry, the more so because I had to keep my chamber for some time after--which chamber did not face those hills.

At length, when pretty well again, and sitting out in the September morning upon the piazza and thinking to myself, when, just after a little flock of sheep, the farmer's banded children passed, anutting, and said, "How sweet a day"--it was, after all, but what their fathers call a weather-breeder--and, indeed, was become so sensitive through my illness as that I could not bear to look upon a Chinese creeper of my adoption, and which, to my delight, climbing a post of the piazza, had burst out in starry bloom, but now, if you removed the leaves a little, showed millions of strange, cankerous worms, which, feeding upon those blossoms, so shared their blessed hue as to make it unblessed evermore--worms whose germs had doubtless lurked in the very bulb which, so hopefully, I had planted: in this ingrate peevishness of my weary convalescence was I sitting there, when, suddenly looking off, I saw the golden mountain window, dazzling like a deep-sea dolphin. Fairies there, thought I, once more, the queen of fairies at her fairywindow, at any rate, some glad mountain girl; it will do me good, it will cure this weariness, to look on her. No more; I'll launch my yawl--ho, cheerly, heart!--and push away for fairyland, for rainbow's end, in fairyland.

How to get to fairyland, by what road, I did not know, nor could any one inform me, not even one Edmund Spenser, who had been there--so he wrote me--further than that to reach fairyland it must be voyaged to, and with faith. I took the fairy-mountain's bearings, and the first fine day, when strength permitted, got into my yawl--highpommeled, leather one-cast off the fast, and away I sailed, free voyager as an autumn leaf. Early dawn, and, sallying westward, I sowed the morning before me.

Some miles brought me nigh the hills, but out of present sight of them. I was not lost, for roadside goldenrods, as guideposts, pointed, I doubted not, the way to the golden window. Following them, I came to a lone and languid region, where the grassgrown ways were traveled but by drowsy cattle, that, less waked than stirred by day, seemed to walk in sleep. Browse they did not--the enchanted never eat. At least, so says Don Quixote, that sagest sage that ever lived.

On I went, and gained at least the fairymountain's base, but saw yet no fairy ring. A pasture rose before me. Letting down five moldering bars--so moistly green they seemed fished up from some sunken wreck--a wigged old Aries, longvisaged and with crumpled horn, came snuffing up, and then, retreating, decorously led on along a milkyway of whiteweed, past dimclustering Pleiades and Hyades, of small forgetme-nots, and would have led me further still his astral path but for golden flights of yellow-birds--pilots, surely, to the golden window, to one side flying before me, from bush to bush, toward deep woods--which woods themselves were luring-- and somehow, lured, too, by their fence, banning a dark road, which, however dark, led up. I pushed through, when Aries, renouncing me now for some lost soul, wheeled, and went his wiser way. Forbidding and forbidden ground--to him.

A winter wood road, matted all along with wintergreen. By the side of pebbly waters--waters the cheerier for their solitude; beneath swaying fir boughs, petted by no season but still green in all, on I journeyed--my horse and I; on, by an old sawmill bound down and hushed with vines that his grating voice no more was heard; on, by a deep flume clove through snowy marble, vernaltinted, where freshet eddies had, on each side, spun out empty chapels in the living rock; on, where Jacksin-thepulpit like their Baptist namesake, preached but to the wilderness; on, where a huge crossgrain block, fernbedded,showed where, in forgotten times, man after man had tried to split it, but lost his wedges for his pains--which wedges yet rusted in their holes; on, where, ages past, in steplike ledges of a cascade, skullhollow pots had been churned out by ceaseless whirling of a flintstone--ever wearing, but itself unworn; on, by wild rapids pouring into a secret pool, but, soothed by circling there awhile, issued forth serenely; on, to less broken ground and by a little ring, where, truly, fairies must have danced or else some wheeltire been heated--for all was bare;

still on, and up, and out into a hanging orchard, where maidenly looked down upon me a crescent moon, from morning.

My horse hitched low his head. Red apples rolled before him--Eve's apples, seeknofurthers. He tasted one, I another; it tasted of the ground. Fairyland not yet, thought I, flinging my bridle to a humped old tree, that crooked out an arm to catch it. For the way now lay where path was none, and none might go but by himself, and only go by daring. Through blackberry brakes that tried to pluck me back, though I but strained toward fruitless growths of mountain laurel, up slippery steeps to barren heights, where stood none to welcome. Fairyland not yet, thought I, though the morning is here before me.

Footsore enough and weary, I gained not then my journey's end, but came erelong to a craggy pass, dipping towards growing regions still beyond. A zigzag road, half overgrown with blueberry bushes, here turned among the cliffs. A rent was in their ragged sides; through it a little track branched off, which, upwards threading that short defile, came breezily out above, to where the mountaintop, part sheltered northward by a taller brother, sloped gently off a space ere darkly plunging; and here, among fantastic rocks, reposing in a herd, the foot track wound, half beaten, up to a little, lowstoried, grayish cottage, capped, nunlike, with a peaked roof.

On one slope the roof was deeply weatherstained, and, nigh the turfy eavestrough, all velvetnapped; no doubt the snailmonks founded mossy priories there. The other slope newly shingled. On the north side, doorless and windowless, the clapboards, innocent of paint, were yet green as the north side of lichened pines, or copperless hulls of Japanese junks becalmed. The whole base, like those of the neighboring rocks, was rimmed about with shaded streaks of richest sod; for, with hearthstones in fairyland, the natural rock, though housed preserves to the last, just as in open fields, its fertilizing charm only, by necessity, working now at a remove, to the sward without. So, at least, says Oberon, grave authority in fairy lore. Though, setting Oberon aside, certain it is that, even is the common world, the soil close up to farmhouses, as close up to pasture rocks, is, even though untended, ever richer than it is a few rods off--such gentle, nurturing heat is radiated there.

But with this cottage the shaded streaks were richest in front and about its entrance, where the groundsill, and especially the doorsill, had, through long eld, quietly settled down.

No fence was seen, no inclosure. Near by--ferns, ferns ferns; further--woods, woods, woods; beyond--mountains, mountains, mountains; then--sky, sky, sky. Turned out in aerial commons, pasture for the mountain moon. Nature, and but nature, house and all; even a low crosspile of silver birch, piled openly, to season; up among whose silvery sticks, as through the fencing of some sequestered grave, sprang vagrant raspberry bushes--willful assertors of their right of way.

The foot track, so dainty narrow, just like a sheep track, led through long ferns that lodged. Fairyland at last, thought I; Una and her lamb dwell here. Truly, a small adobe--mere palanquin, set down on the summit, in a pass between two worlds, participant of neither.

A sultry hour, and I wore a light hat, of yellow sinnet, with white duck trousers--both relics of my tropic seagoing. Clogged in the muffling ferns, I softly stumbled, staining the knees a sea green.

Pausing at the threshold, or rather where threshold once had been, I saw, through the open doorway, a lonely girl, sewing at a lonely window. A palecheeked girl and flyspecked window, with wasps about the mended upper panes. I spoke. She shyly started, like some Tahiti girl, secreted for a sacrifice, first catching sight, through palms, of Captain Cook. Recovering, she bade me enter; with her apron brushed off a stool; then silently resumed her own. With thanks I took the stool; but now, for a space, I, too, was mute. This, then, is the fairy-mountain house, and here the fairy queen sitting at her fairy-window.

I went up to it. Downwards, directed by the tunneled pass, as through a leveled telescope, I caught sight of a faroff, soft, azure world. I hardly knew it, though I came from it.

"You must find this view very pleasant," said I, at last.

"Oh, sir," tears starting in her eyes, "the first time I looked out of this window, I said 'never, never shall I weary of this.'"

"And what wearies you of it now?"

"I don't know," while a tear fell; "but it is not the view, it is Marianna."

Some months back, her brother, only seventeen, had come hither, a long way from the other side, to cut wood and burn coal, and she, elder sister, had accompanied him. Long had they been orphans, and now sole inhabitants of the sole house upon the mountain. No guest came, no traveler passed. The zigzag, perilous road was only used at seasons by the coal wagons. The brother was absent the entire day, sometimes the entire night. When, at evening, fagged out, he did come home, he soon left his bench, poor fellow, for his bed, just as one, at last, wearily quits that, too, for still deeper rest. The bench, the bed, the grave.

Silent I stood by the fairywindow, while these things were being told.

"Do you know," said she at last, as stealing from her story, "do you know who lives yonder?--I have never been down into that country--away off there, I mean; that house, that marble one," pointing far across the lower landscape; "have you not caught it? there, on the long hillside: the field before, the woods behind; the white shines out against their blue; don't you mark it? the only house in sight."

I looked, and, after a time, to my surprise, recognized, more by its position than its aspect or Marianna's description, my own abode, glimmering much like this mountain one from the piazza. The mirage haze made it appear less a farmhouse than King Charming's palace.

"I have often wondered who lives there; but it must be some happy one; again this morning was I thinking so."

"Some happy one," returned I, starting; "and why do you think that? You judge some rich one lives there?"

"Rich or not, I never thought, but it looks so happy, I can't tell how, and it is so far away. Sometimes I think I do but dream it is there. You should see it in a sunset."

"No doubt the sunset gilds it finely, but not more than the sunrise does this house, perhaps."

"This house? The sun is a good sun, but it never gilds this house. Why should it? This old house is rotting. That makes it so mossy. In the morning, the sun comes in at this old window, to be sure--boarded up, when first we came; a window I can't keep clean, do what I may--and half burns, and nearly blinds me at my sewing, besides setting the flies and wasps astir--such flies and wasps as only lone mountain houses know. See, here is the curtain--this apron--I try to shut it out with then. It fades it, you see. Sun gild this house? not that ever Marianna saw."

"Because when this roof is gilded most, then you stay here within."

"The hottest, weariest hour of day, you mean? Sir, the sun gilds not this roof. It leaked so, brother newly shingled all outside. Did you not see it? The north side, where the sun strikes most on what the rain has wetted. The sun is a good sun, but this roof, it first scorches, and then rots. An old house. They went West, and are long dead, they say, who built it. A mountain house. In winter no fox could den in it. That chimney-place has been blocked up with snow, just like a hollow stump."

"Yours are strange fancies, Marianna."

"They but reflect the things."

"Then I should have said, 'These are strange things,' rather than, 'Yours are strange fancies.'"

"As you will," and took up her sewing.

Something in those quiet words, or in that quiet act, it made me mute again; while, noting through the fairywindow a broad shadow stealing on, as cast by some gigantic condor floating at brooding poise on outstretched wings. I marked how, by its deeper and inclusive dusk, it wiped away into itself all lesser shades of rock or fern.

"You watch the cloud," said Marianna.

"No, a shadow; a cloud's, no doubt--though that I cannot see. How did you know it? Your eyes are on your work."

"It dusked my work. There, now the cloud is gone, Tray comes back."

"How?"

"The dog, the shaggy dog. At noon, he steals off, of himself, to change his shape--returns, and lies down awhile, nigh the door. Don't you see him? His head is turned round at you, though when you came he looked before him."

"Your eyes rest but on your work; what do you speak of?"

"By the window, crossing."

"You mean this shaggy shadow--the nigh one? And, yes, now that I mark it, it is not unlike a large, black Newfoundland dog. The invading shadow gone, the invaded one returns. But I do not see what casts it."

"For that, you must go without."

"One of those grassy rocks, no doubt."

"You see his head, his face?"

"The shadow's? You speak as if *you* saw it, and all the time your eyes are on your work."

"Tray looks at you," still without glancing up; "this is his house; I see him."

"Have you, then, so long sat at this mountain window, where but clouds and vapors pass, that to you shadows are as things, though you speak of

them as of phantoms; that, by familiar knowledge working like a second
sight, you can, without looking for them, tell just where they are, though,
as having mice-like feet, they creep about, and come and go; that to you
these lifeless shadows are as living friends, who, though out of sight, are
not out of mind, even in their faces--is it so?"

"That way I never thought of it. But the friendliest one, that used to
soothe my weariness so much, coolly quivering on the ferns, it was taken
from me, never to return, as Tray did just now. The shadow of a birch. The
tree was struck by lightning, and brother cut it up. You saw the crosspile
outdoors--the buried root lies under it, but not the shadow. That is flown,
and never will come back, nor ever anywhere stir again."

Another cloud here stole along, once more blotting out the dog, and
blackening all the mountain; while the stillness was so still deafness might
have forgot itself, or else believed that noiseless shadow spoke.

"Birds, Marianna, singing birds, I hear none; I hear nothing. Boys and
bobolinks, do they never come aberrying up here?"

"Birds I seldom hear; boys, never. The berries mostly ripe and fall--few
but me the wiser."

"But yellowbirds showed me the way--part way, at least."

"And then flew back. I guess they play about the mountainside but
don't make the top their home. And no doubt you think that, living so
lonesome here, knowing nothing, hearing nothing--little, at least, but
sound of thunder and the fall of trees--never reading, seldom speaking, yet
ever wakeful, this is what gives me my strange thoughts--for so you call
them-- this weariness and wakefulness together. Brother, who stands and
works in open air, would I could rest like him; but mine is mostly but dull
woman's work--sitting, sitting, restless sitting."

"But do you not go walk at times? These woods are wide."

"And lonesome; lonesome, because so wide. Sometimes, 'tis true, of
afternoons, I go a little way, but soon come back again. Better feel lone
by hearth than rock. The shadows hereabouts I know--those in the woods
are strangers."

"But the night?"

"Just like the day. Thinking, thinking--a wheel I cannot stop; pure want
of sleep it is that turns it."

"I have heard that, for this wakeful weariness, to say one's prayers, and
then lay one's head upon a fresh hop pillow----"

"Look!"

Through the fairywindow, she pointed down the steep to a small garden patch near by--mere pot of rifled loam, half rounded in by sheltering rocks--where, side by side, some feet apart, nipped and puny, two hopvines climbed two poles, and, gaining their tip ends, would have then joined over in an upward clasp, but the baffled shoots, groping awhile in empty air, trailed back whence they sprung.

"You have tried the pillow, then?"

"Yes."

"And prayer?"

"Prayer and pillow."

"Is there no other cure, or charm?"

"Oh, if I could but once get to yonder house, and but look upon whoever the happy being is that lives there! A foolish thought: why do I think it? Is it that I live so lonesome, and know nothing?"

"I, too, know nothing, and therefore cannot answer; but for your sake, Marianna, well could wish that I were that happy one of the happy house you dream you see; for then you would behold him now, and, as you say, this weariness might leave you."

--Enough. Launching my yawl no more for fairyland, I stick to the piazza. It is my boxroyal, and this amphitheater, my theater of San Carlo. Yes, the scenery is magical--the illusion so complete. And Madam Meadow Lark, my prima donna, plays her grand engagement here; and, drinking in her sunrise note, which, Memnonlike, seems struck from the golden window, how far from me the weary face behind it.

But every night when the curtain falls, truth comes in with darkness. No light shows from the mountain. To and fro I walk the piazza deck, haunted by Marianna's face, and many as real a story.

To Domitius Apollinaris

Pliny the Younger

Pliny the Younger (A.D. 62?-A.D. 113?), whose full Latin name was Caius Plinius Caecilius Secundus, was born in Comum (Como). He was the nephew and adopted son of Pliny the Elder. Pliny belonged to a wealthy family and received an excellent education in Rome.

At eighteen Pliny began to practice law and was extremely successful in his profession. He rose to a high and respected rank in imperial society. He established a reputation as a prosecutor in civil and political courts and was an outstanding speaker.

Pliny is known for his ten books of *Letters (Epistulae)*, which were published in groups possibly arranged by Pliny himself. The letters demonstrate Pliny's strong regard for literary style and it is believed that Pliny edited some of his correspondence to meet the rules of the literary letter, a popular genre in the Latin literature of his period.

Each of the letters examines a single historical, social, moral, or literary subject and are invaluable to the historical reconstruction of the period. Only two Roman writers before Pliny are known to have had their letters published, Cicero and Seneca.

Pliny recounted many of his experiences in public service and wrote on the theory and practice of oratory. He also recorded the darker side of Roman life, such as the murder of a cruel slave owner, and produced two books of light verse.

THE KIND CONCERN you expressed when you heard of my design to pass the summer at my villa in Tuscany, and your obliging endeavours to dissuade me from going to a place which you think unhealthy, is extremely agreeable to me. I confess, indeed, the air of that part of Tuscany, which lies towards the coast, is thick and unwholesome: but my house is situated at a great distance from the sea, and at the foot of the Apennine range, so much esteemed for salubrity. But that you may lay aside all apprehensions on my account, I will give you a description of the mildness of the climate, the situation of the country, and the beauty of my villa, which I am persuaded you will hear with as much pleasure as I shall relate.

The winters are severe and cold, so that myrtles, olives, and other trees which delight in constant warmth, will not flourish here; but bay trees can grow, and even in great perfection; yet sometimes, though indeed not oftener than in the neighbourhood of Rome, they are killed by the sharpness of the seasons. The summers are exceedingly temperate; currents of air are continually stirring, though breezes are more frequent than high winds. Hence old men abound; if you were to come here and see the numbers who have adult grandchildren and great-grandchildren, and hear the stories they can entertain you with of their ancestors, you would fancy yourself born in some former age.

The aspect of the country is the most beautiful possible; figure to yourself an immense amphitheatre, such as the hand of nature could alone form. Before you lies a vast extended plain bounded by a range of mountains, whose summits are crowned with lofty and venerable woods, which supply abundance and variety of game; from hence as the mountains decline, they are adorned with under-woods. Intermixed with these are little hills of so loamy and fat a soil, that it would be difficult to find a single stone upon them; their fertility is nothing inferior to the lowest grounds; and though their harvest indeed is something later, their heavy crops are as well matured. At the foot of these hills the eye is presented, wherever it turns, with one unbroken view of numberless vineyards, which are terminated below by a border, as it were, of shrubs. From thence extend meadows and fields. The soil of the latter is so extremely stiff, upon the first poughing it rises in such vast clods, that it is necessary to go over it nine several times with the largest oxen and the strongest ploughs, before they can be thoroughly broken. The flower-enamelled meadows produce trefoil and other kinds of herbage as fine and tender as if it were but just sprung up, being everywhere refreshed by never-failing rills. But though the country abounds with great plenty of water, there are no marshes; for as the ground is sloping, whatever water it receives without absorbing, runs off into the Tiber. This river, which winds through the middle of the meadows, is navigable only in the winter and spring, when it transports the produce of the lands to Rome; but its contracted channel is so extremely low in summer, that it resigns the name of a *great river* which, however, it resumes in autumn.

You would be most agreeably entertained by taking a view of the face of this country from the mountains: you would imagine that not a real, but some painted landscape lay before you, drawn with the most exquisite beauty and exactness; such an harmonious and regular variety charms the eye which way soever it throws itself. My villa, though situated at the foot of the mountain, commands as wide a prospect as the summit affords; you go up to it by so gentle and insensible a rise, that you find yourself upon an elevation without perceiving you ascended. Behind, but at a great distance, stand the Apennine mountains; in the calmest days breezes reach us from thence, but so spent and weakened by the long tract of land they travel over, that they are entirely divested of all their strength and violence.

The exposure of the main part of the house is full south; thus it seems to invite the sun, from midday in summer (but something earlier in winter), into a wide and proportionably long portico, containing many divisions, one of which is an atrium, built after the manner of the ancients. In front of the portico is a terrace divided into a great number of geometrical figures, and bounded with a box-hedge. The descent from the terrace is a sloping bank, adorned with a double row of box-trees cut in the shape of animals; the level ground at the foot of the bank is covered with the soft, I had almost said, the liquid acanthus: this lawn is surrounded by a walk enclosed with dense evergreens, trimmed into a variety of forms. Beyond is an *allée* laid out in the form of a circus, which encircles a plantation of box-trees cut in numberless different figures, and of small shrubs, either low-growing or prevented by the shears from running up too high. The whole is fenced in with a wall masked by box-trees, which rise in graduated ranks to the top. Beyond the wall lies a meadow that owes as many beauties to nature, as all I have been describing *within* does to art; at the end of which are several other meadows and fields interspersed with thickets.

At the extremity of the portico stands a grand dining-room, which through its folding-doors looks upon one end of the terrace; while beyond there is a very extensive prospect over the meadows up into the country; from the windows you survey on the one hand the side of the terrace and such parts of the house which project forward, on the other, with the woods enclosing the adjacent hippodrome. Opposite almost to the centre of the portico stands a *suite* of apartments something retired, which encompasses a small court, shaded by four plane-trees, in the midst of which a foundation rises, from whence the water running over the edges of a marble basin gently refreshes the surrounding plane-trees and the ground underneath them. This *suite* contains a bed-chamber free from

every kind of noise, and which the light itself cannot penetrate; together
with my ordinary dining-room that I use too when I have none but familiar
friends with me; this looks upon the little court I just now described, also
upon the portico and the whole prospect thence. There is, besides, another
room, which, being situated close to the nearest plane-tree, enjoys a
constant shade and verdure; its sides are covered with marble up to the
cornice: on the frieze above a foliage is painted, with birds perched among
the branches, which has an effect altogether as agreeable as that of the
marble. In this room is placed a little fountain, that, playing several small
pipes into a vase, produces a most pleasing murmur.

From a wing of the portico you enter into a very spacious chamber
opposite to the grand dining-room, which from some of its windows has
a view of the terrace, and from others of the meadow, while those in the
front dominate an ornamental basin just beneath them, which entertains
at once both the eye and the ear; for the water falling from a great height,
foams round its marble receptacle. This room in extremely warm in
winter, being much exposed to the sun, and in a cloudy day the hot air
from an adjoining stove very well supplies his absence. From hence you
pass through a spacious and pleasant undressing-room into the cold-bath-
room, in which is a large, gloomy bath: but if you are disposed to swim
more at large, or in warmer water, there is a pool for that purpose in the
court, and near it a reservoir from whence you may be supplied with cold
water to brace yourself again, if you should perceive you are too much
relaxed by the warm. Contiguous to the cold-bath is a tepid one, which
enjoys the kindly warmth of the sun, but not so intensely as that of the
hot-bath, which projects from the house. This last consists of three several
divisions, each of different degrees of heat; the two former lie open to the
full sun, the latter, though not so much exposed to its heat, receives an
equal share of its light.

Over the undressing-room is built the ball-court, which is large enough
to admit of several different kinds of games being played at once, each
with its own circle of spectators. Not far from the baths is a stair-case
which leads to a gallery, and to three apartments on the way; one of these
looks upon the little court with the four plane-trees round it; another has
a sight of the meadows; the third abuts upon the vineyard, and command
a prospect of opposite quarters of the heavens. At one end of the gallery,
and indeed taken off from it, is a chamber that looks upon the hippodrome,
the vineyard and the mountains; adjoining is a room which has a full

exposure to the sun, especially in winter: from hence runs an apartment that connects the hippodrome with the house.

Such are the villa's beauties and conveniences on the front. On the side is a summer gallery which stands high, and has not only a prospect of the vineyard, but seems almost to touch it. Midway it contains a dining-room cooled by the wholesome breezes which come from the Apennine valleys: the back-windows, which are extremely large, let in, as it were, the vineyards, as do the folding-doors, but you get the latter view through the gallery. Along that side of this dining-room where there are no windows; runs a private stair-case for the greater conveniency of serving at entertainments; at the farther end is a chamber from whence the eye is entertained with a view of the vineyards, and (what is equally agreeable) of the gallery. Underneath this room is a gallery resembling a crypt, which in the midst of summer heats retains its pentup chilliness, and, enjoying its own atmosphere, neither admits nor wants the refreshment of external breezes.

Behind both these galleries, at the end of the dining-room, stands a portico, which as the day is more or less advanced, serves either for winter or summer use. It leads to two different apartments, one containing four chambers, the other three, which enjoy, as the day progresses, alternately sun and shade. In the front of these agreeable buildings lies a very spacious hippodrome, entirely open in the middle, by which means the eye, upon your first entrance, takes in its whole extent at one view. It is encompassed on every side with plane-trees covered with ivy, so that while their heads flourish with their own green, their bodies enjoy a borrowed verdure; and the ivy twining round the trunk and branches, spreads from tree to tree, and connects them together. Between each plane-tree are planted box-trees, and behind these, bay-trees, which blend their shade with that of the planes. The raised path around the hippodrome, which here runs straight, bends at the farther end into a semi-circle and takes on a new aspect, being embowered in cypress-trees and obscured by their denser and more gloomy shade; while the inward circular alleys (for there are several) enjoy the full sun. Farther on, there are roses too along the path, and the cool shade is pleasantly alternated with sunshine.

Having passed through these manifold winding alleys, the path resumes a straight course, and at the same time divides into several tracks, separated by box-hedges. In one place you have a little meadow; in another the box is interposed in groups, and cut into a thousand different forms; sometimes into letters, expressing the name of the master, or again that of the artificer: whilst here and there little obelisks rise intermixed alternately with fruit-trees: when on a sudden, in the midst of this elegant regularity, you are surprised with an imitation of the negligent beauties of rural nature; in the centre of which lies a spot surrounded with a knot of dwarf plane-trees. Beyond these are interspersed clumps of the smooth and twining acanthus; then come a variety of figures and names cut in box.

At the upper end is a semicircular bench of white marble, shaded with a vine which is trained upon four small pillars of Carystian marble. Water gushing through several little pipes from under this bench, as if it were pressed out by the weight of the persons who repose themselves upon it, falls into a stone cistern underneath, from whence it is received into a fine polished marble basin, so artfully contrived that it is always full without ever overflowing. When I sup here, the tray of whets and larger dishes are placed around the margin, while the smaller ones swim about in the form of little ships and water-fowl. Opposite this is a fountain which is incessantly emptying and filling: for the water, which it throws up a great height, falling back again into it, is by means of connected openings returned as fast as it is received.

Fronting the bench (and which reflects as great an ornament to it, as it borrows from it) stands a chamber of lustrous marble, whose doors project and open into a lawn; from its upper and lower windows the eye ranges upward or downward over other spaces of verdure. Next to this is a little private closet (which though it is distinct may be laid into the same room) furnished with a couch; and notwithstanding it has windows on every side, yet it enjoys a very agreeable gloominess, by means of a flourishing vine which climbs to the top, and entirely overshades it. Here you may lie and fancy yourself in a wood, with this difference only, that you are not exposed to the rain. Here, too, a fountain rises and instantly disappears. In different quarters are disposed several marble seats, which serve, no less than the chamber, as so many reliefs after one is wearied with walking. Near each seat is a little fountain; and throughout the whole hippodrome small rills conveyed through pipes run murmuring along, wheresoever the hand of art has thought proper to conduct them; watering here and there different spots of verdure, and in their progress bathing the whole.

I should have avoided ere this the appearance of being too minute in detail, if I had not proposed to lead you by this letter into every corner of my house and gardens. But I am not afraid you will think it a trouble to read of a place, which you would think it none to survey; especially as you can take a rest whenever you please, sit down as it were, by laying aside my letter. Besides I have indulged the fondness which I confess I feel for what was mostly either put in hand, or, carried to perfection, by myself. To sum up (for why should I conceal from my friends my sentiments whether right or wrong?) I hold it the first duty of an author to con his title-page, and frequently ask himself what he set out to write; and he may be assured if he closely pursues his subject he cannot be tedious; whereas if he drags in extraneous matters, he will be tedious to the last degree.

You see how many lines Homer and Virgil devote respectively to describing the arms of Achilles and the arms of Aeneas; yet each poet is succinct, because he carries out his original design. Aratus, you see, keeps due proportion, though he traces and groups the minutest stars; for this digression on his part, but his main subject. In the same manner (to compare small things with great), if endeavouring to bring my whole villa before your eyes, I have not wandered into any thing foreign, or, as it were, devious, it is not my letter, which describes, but the villa, which is described, that is to be deemed large.

But not to dwell any longer upon this digression lest I should myself be comdemned by the maxim I have just laid down; I have now informed you why I prefer my Tuscan villa, to those which I possess at Tusculum, Tiber, and Praeneste. Besides the advantages already mentioned, I there enjoy a securer, as it is a more profound leisure; I never need put on full dress; nobody calls from next door on urgent business. All is calm and composed; which contributes, no less than its clear air and unclouded sky, to the salubrity of the spot. There I am peculiarly blessed with health of body and cheerfulness of mind, for I keep my mind in proper exercise by study and my body by hunting. And indeed there is no place which agrees better with all my household; I am sure, at least, I have not yet lost one (under favour be it spoken) of all those I brought with me hither. May the gods continue this happiness to *me*, and this glory to my *villa* ! Farewell.

The Fall of the House of Usher

Edgar Allan Poe

Edgar Allan Poe's (1809-1849) short stories reflect traditional European symbolism, a style of writing which was most common in France. *The Fall of the House of Usher,* one of Poe's most popular stories, is a fine example of his Gothic writing.

Poe was born in Boston to parents who were actors. By the age of three his father David had deserted him. His mother Elizabeth died during a tour. He was taken in and educated by John Allan, a well-to-do tobacco exporter and his wife. From 1815 to 1820 he attended preparatory school in England and Scotland, and then returned to Virginia where he attended the University of Virginia.

Following his education he was offerred a position by Allan. Poe refused and left for Boston, where he published *Tamerlane and Other Poems* (1827). He entered West Point in 1830, but discovered that he was unsuited for military life and provoked his own dismissal in March of 1831. The same year he published *Poems* (1831).

After working on several magazines and publishing some of his work he married his thirteen year old cousin Virginia, who succumbed to tuberculosis. Distraught over her death Poe became an alcoholic.

Poe's contributions to the literary canon include his symbolic poetry, the invention of the first detective story, *Murders in the Rue Morgue*, new fiction of psychological analysis and symbolism, and the development of important critical theory, which he discusses in his book, *Philosophy of Composition* (1846).

> *Son coeur est un luth suspendu;*
> *Sitôt qu'on le touche il résonne.*
>> *De Béranger*

DURING THE WHOLE of a dull, dark, and soundless day in the autumn of the year, when the clouds hung oppressively low in the heavens, I had been passing alone, on horseback, through a singularly dreary tract of country, and at length found myself, as the shades of the evening drew on, within view of the melancholy House of Usher. I know not how it was--but, with the first glimpse of the building, a sense of insufferable gloom pervaded my spirit. I say insufferable; for the feeling was unrelieved by any of that half-pleasurable, because poetic, sentiment with which the mind usually receives even the sternest natural images of the desolate or terrible. I looked upon the scene before me--upon the mere house, and the simple landscape features of the domain--upon the bleak walls--upon the vacant eyelike windows--upon a few rank sedges--and upon a few white trunks of decayed trees--with an utter depression of soul which I can compare to no earthly sensation more properly than to the afterdream of the reveller upon opium--the bitter lapse into everyday life--the hideous dropping off of the veil. There was an iciness, a sinking, a sickening of the heart--an unredeemed dreariness of thought which no goading of the imagination could torture into aught of the sublime. What was it--I paused to think--what was it that so unnerved me in the contemplation of the House of Usher? It was a mystery all insoluble; nor could I grapple with the shadowy fancies that crowded upon me as I pondered. I was forced to fall back upon the unsatisfactory conclusion, that while, beyond doubt, there *are* combinations of very simple natural objects which have the power of thus affecting us, still the analysis of this power lies among considerations beyond our depth. It was possible, I reflected, that a mere different arrangement of the particulars of the scene, of the details of the picture, would be sufficient to modify, or perhaps to annihilate its capacity for sorrowful impression; and, acting upon this idea, I reined my horse to the precipitous brink of a black and lurid tarn that lay in unruffled lustre by the dwelling, and gazed down-- but with a shudder even more thrilling than before--upon the remodelled and inverted images of the gray sedge, and the ghastly treestems, and the vacant and eyelike windows.

Nevertheless, in this mansion of gloom I now proposed to myself a sojourn of some weeks. Its proprietor, Roderick Usher, had been one of my boon companions in boyhood; but many years had elapsed since our last meeting. A letter, however, had lately reached me in a distant part of the country--a letter from him--which, in its wildly importunate nature, had admitted of no other than a personal reply. The MS. gave evidence of nervous agitation. The writer spoke of acute bodily illness-- of a mental disorder which oppressed him--and of an earnest desire to see me, as his best and indeed his only personal friend, with a view of attempting, by the cheerfulness of my society, some alleviation of his malady. It was the

manner in which all this, and much more, was said-- it was the apparent
heart that went with his request--which allowed me no room for hesitation; and I accordingly obeyed forthwith what I still considered a very
singular summons.

Although, as boys, we had been even intimate associates, yet I really
knew little of my friend. His reserve had been always excessive and
habitual. I was aware, however, that his very ancient family had been
noted, time out of mind, for a peculiar sensibility of temperament, dis-
playing itself, through long ages, in many works of exalted art, and
manifested, of late, in repeated deeds of munificent yet unobtrusive
charity, as well as in a passionate devotion to the intricacies, perhaps even
more than to the orthodox and easily recognizable beauties, of musical
science. I had learned, too, the very remarkable fact, that the stem of the
Usher race, all timehonoured as it was, had put forth, at no period, any
enduring branch; in other words, that the entire family lay in the direct
line of decent, and had always, with very trifling and very temporary
variation, so lain. It was this deficiency, I considered, while running over
in thought the perfect keeping of the character of the premises with the
accredited character of the people, and while speculating upon the possible influence which the one, in the long lapse of centuries, might have
exercised upon the other--it was this deficiency, perhaps, of collateral
issue, and the consequent undeviating transmission, from sire to son, of
the patrimony with the name, which had, at length, so identified the two
as to merge the original title of the estate in the quaint and equivocal
appellation of the "House of Usher"--an appellation which seemed to
include, in the minds of the peasantry who used it, both the family and the
family mansion.

I have said that the sole effect of my somewhat childish experiment--
that of looking down within the tarn--had been to deepen the first singular
impression. There can be no doubt that the consciousness of the rapid
increase of my superstition--for why should I not so term it?-- served
mainly to accelerate the increase itself. Such, I have long known, is the
paradoxical law of all sentiments having terror as a basis. And it might
have been for this reason only, that, when I again uplifted my eyes to the
house itself, from its image in the pool, there grew in my mind a strange
fancy--a fancy so ridiculous, indeed, that I but mention it to show the vivid
force of the sensations which oppressed me. I had so worked upon my
imagination as really to believe that aboutthe whole mansion and domain
there hung an atmosphere peculiar to themselves and their immediate

vicinity--an atmosphere which had no affinity with the air of heaven, but which had reeked up from the decayed trees, and the gray wall, and the silent tarn--a pestilent and mystic vapour, dull, sluggish, faintly discernible, and leadenhued.

Shaking off from my spirit what *must* have been a dream, I scanned more narrowly the real aspect of the building. Its principal feature seemed to be that of an excessive antiquity. The discoloration of ages had been great. Minute fungi overspread the whole exterior, hanging in a fine tangled webwork from the eaves. Yet all this was apart from any extraordinary dilapidation. No portion of the masonry had fallen; and there appeared to be a wild inconsistency between its still perfect adaptation of parts, and the crumbling condition of the individual stones. In this there was much that reminded me of the specious totality of old woodwork which has rotted for long years in some neglected vault, with no disturbance from the breath of the external air. Beyond this indication of extensive decay, however, the fabric gave little token of instability. Perhaps the eye of a scrutinizing observer might have discovered a barely perceptible fissure, which, extending from the roof of the building in front, made its way down the wall in a zigzag direction, until it became lost in the sullen waters of the tarn.

Noticing these things, I rode over a short causeway to the house. A servant in waiting took my horse, and I entered the Gothic archway of the hall. A valet, of stealthy step, thence conducted me, in silence, through many dark and intricate passages in my progress to the *studio* of his master. Much that I encountered on the way contributed, I know not how, to heighten the vague sentiments of which I have already spoken. While the objects around me--while the carvings of the ceilings, the sombre tapestries of the walls, the ebon blackness of the floors, and the phantasmagoric armorial trophies which rattled as I strode, were but matters to which, or to such as which, I had been accustomed from my infancy--while I hesitated not to acknowledge how familiar was all this --I still wondered to find how unfamiliar were the fancies which ordinary images were stirring up. On one of the staircases, I met the physician of the family. His countenance, I thought, wore a mingled expression of low cunning and perplexity. He accosted me with trepidation and passed on. The valet now threw open a door and ushered me into the presence of his master.

The room in which I found myself was very large and lofty. The windows were long, narrow, and pointed, and at so vast a distance from the black oaken floor as to be altogether inaccessible from within. Feeble gleams of encrimsoned light made their way through the trellissed panes, and served to render sufficiently distinct the more prominent objects around; the eye, however, struggled in vain to reach the remoter angles of the chamber, or the recesses of the vaulted and fretted ceiling. Dark draperies hung upon the walls. The general furniture was profuse, comfortless, antique, and tattered. Many books and musical instruments lay scattered about, but failed to give any vitality to the scene. I felt that I breathed an atmosphere of sorrow. An air of stern, deep, and irredeemable gloom hung over and pervaded all.

Upon my entrance, Usher arose from a sofa on which he had been lying at full length, and greeted me with a vivacious warmth which had much in it, I at first thought, of an overdone cordiality--of the constrained effort of the *ennuyé* man of the world. A glance, however, at his countenance convinced me of his perfect sincerity. We sat down, and for some moments, while he spoke not, I gazed upon him with a feeling half of pity, half of awe. Surely, man had never before so terribly altered, in so brief a period, as had Roderick Usher! It was with difficulty that I could bring myself to admit the identity of the man being before me with the companion of my early boyhood. Yet the character of his face had been at all times remarkable. A cadaverousness of complexion; an eye large, liquid, and luminous beyond comparison; lips somewhat thin and very pallid, but of a surpassingly beautiful curve; a nose of a delicate Hebrew model, but with a breadth of nostril unusual in similar formations; a finely moulded chin, speaking, in its want of prominence, of a want of moral energy; hair of a more than weblike softness and tenuity; these features, with an inordinate expansion above the regions of the temple, made up altogether a countenance not easily to be forgotten. And now in the mere exaggeration of the prevailing character of these features, and of the expression they were wont to convey, lay so much of change that I doubted to whom I spoke. The now ghastly pallor of the skin, and the now miraculous lustre of the eye, above all things startled and even awed me. The silken hair, too, had been suffered to grow all unheeded, and as, in its wild gossamer texture, it floated rather than fell about the face, I could not, even with effort, connect its Arabesque expression with any idea of simple humanity.

In the manner of my friend I was at once struck with an incoherence --an inconsistency; and I soon found this to arise from a series of feeble and futile struggles to overcome an habitual trepidancy--an excessive

nervous agitation. For something of this nature I had indeed been prepared, no less by his letter, than by reminiscences of certain boyish traits,
and by conclusions deduced from his peculiar physical conformation and
temperament. His action was alternately vivacious and sullen. His voice
varied rapidly from a tremulous indecision (when the animal spirits
seemed utterly in abeyance) to that species of energetic concision--that
abrupt, weighty, unhurried, and hollowsounding enunciation--that leaden,
selfbalanced, and perfectly modulated guttural utterance, which may be
observed in the lost drunkard, or the irreclaimable eater of opium, during
the periods of his most intense excitement.

It was thus that he spoke of the object of my visit, of his earnest desire
to see me, and of the solace he expected me to afford him. He entered, at
some length, into what he conceived to be the nature of his malady. It was,
he said, a constitutional and a family evil, and one for which he despaired
to find a remedy--a mere nervous affection, he immediately added, which
would undoubtedly soon pass off. It displayed itself in a host of unnatural
sensations. Some of these, as he detailed them, interested and bewildered
me; although, perhaps, the terms and the general manner of their narration
had their weight. He suffered much from a morbid acuteness of the senses;
the most insipid food was alone endurable; he could wear only garments
of certain texture; the odours of all flowers were oppressive; his eyes were
tortured by even a faint light; and there were but peculiar sounds, and
these from stringed instruments, which did not inspire him with horror.

To an anomalous species of terror I found him a bounden slave. "I shall
perish," said he, "I *must* perish in this deplorable folly. Thus, thus, and not
otherwise, shall I be lost. I dread the events of the future, not in themselves, but in their results. I shudder at the thought of any, even the most
trivial, incident, which may operate upon this intolerable agitation of soul.
I have, indeed, no abhorrence of danger, except in its absolute effect--in
terror. In this unnerved--in this pitiable condition--I feel that the period
will sooner or later arrive when I must abandon life and reason together,
in some struggle with the grim phantasm, FEAR."

I learned, moreover, at intervals, and through broken and equivocal
hints, another singular feature of his mental condition. He was enchained
by certain superstitious impressions in regard to the dwelling which he
tenanted, and whence, for many years, he had never ventured forth in
regard to an influence whose supposititious force was conveyed in terms
too shadowy here to be re-stated--an influence which some peculiarities
in the mere form and substance of his family mansion had, by dint of long

sufferance, he said, obtained over his spirit--an effect which the *physique* of the gray walls and turrets, and of the dim tarn into which they all looked down, had, at length, brought about upon the *morale* of his existence.

He admitted, however, although with hesitation, that much of the peculiar gloom which thus afflicted him could be traced to a more natural and far more palpable origin--to the severe and longcontinued illness-- indeed to the evidently approaching dissolution--of a tenderly beloved sister, his sole companion for long years, his last and only relative on earth. "Her decease," he said, with a bitterness which I can never forget, "would leave him (him, the hopeless and the frail) the last of the ancient race of the Ushers." While he spoke, the lady Madeline (for so was she called) passed slowly through a remote portion of the apartment, and, without having noticed my presence, disappeared. I regarded her with an utter astonishment not unmingled with dread; and yet I found it impossi- ble to account for such feelings. A sensation of stupor oppressed me, as my eyes followed her retreating steps. When a door, at length, closed upon her, my glance sought instinctively and eagerly the countenance of the brother--but he had buried his face in his hands, and I could only perceive that a far more than ordinary wanness had overspread the emaciated fingers through which trickled many passionate tears.

The disease of the lady Madeline had long baffled the skill of her physicians. A settled apathy, a gradual wasting away of the person, and frequent although transient affections of a partially cataleptical character were the unusual diagnosis. Hitherto she had steadily borne up against the pressure of her malady, and had not betaken herself finally to bed; but on the closing in of the evening of my arrival at the house, she succumbed (as her brother told me at night with inexpressible agitation) to the prostrating power of the destroyer; and I learned that the glimpse I had obtained of her person would thus probably be the last I should obtain-- that the lady, at least while living, would be seen by me no more.

For several days ensuing, her name was unmentioned by either Usher or myself: and during this period I was busied in earnest endeavours to alleviate the melancholy of my friend. We painted and read together, or I listened, as if in a dream, to the wild improvisations of his speaking guitar. And thus, as a closer and still closer intimacy admitted me more unre- servedly into the recesses of his spirit, the more bitterly did I perceive the futility of all attempt at cheering a mind from which darkness, as if an inherent positive quality, poured forth upon all objects of the moral and physical universe in one unceasing radiation of gloom.

I shall ever bear about me a memory of the many solemn hours I thus spent alone with the master of the House of Usher. Yet I should fail in any attempt to convey an idea of the exact character of the studies, or of the occupations, in which he involved me, or led me the way. An excited and highly distempered ideality threw a sulphureous lustre over all. His long improvised dirges will ring forever in my ears. Among other things, I hold painfully in mind a certain singular perversion and amplification of the wild air of the last waltz of Von Weber. From the paintings over which his elaborate fancy brooded, and which grew, touch by touch, into vaguenesses at which I shuddered the more thrillingly, because I shuddered knowing not why;--from these paintings (vivid as their images now are before me) I would in vain endeavour to educe more than a small portion which should lie within the compass of merely written words. By the utter simplicity, by the nakedness of his designs, he arrested and overawed attention. If ever mortal painted an idea, that mortal was Roderick Usher. For me at least, in the circumstances then surrounding me, there arose out of the pure abstractions which the hypochondriac contrived to throw upon his canvas, an intensity of intolerable awe, no shadow of which felt I ever yet in the contemplation of the certainly glowing yet too concrete reveries of Fuseli.

One of the phantasmagoric conceptions of my friend, partaking not so rigidly of the spirit of abstraction, may be shadowed forth, although feebly, in words. A small picture presented the interior of an immensely long and rectangular vault or tunnel, with low walls, smooth, white, and without interruption or device. Certain accessory points of the design served well to convey the idea that this excavation lay at an exceeding depth below the surface of the earth. No outlet was observed in any portion of its vast extent, and no torch or other artificial source of light was discernible; yet a flood of intense rays rolled throughout, and bathed the whole in a ghastly and inappropriate splendour.

I have just spoken of that morbid condition of the auditory nerve which rendered all music intolerable to the sufferer, with the exception of certain effects of stringed instruments. It was, perhaps, the narrow limits to which he thus confined himself upon the guitar which gave birth, in great measure, to the fantastic character of his performances. But the fervid *facility* of his *impromptus* could not be so accounted for. They must have been, and were, in the notes, as well as in the words of his wild fantasias (for he not unfrequently accompanied himself with rhymed verbal improvisations), the result of that intense mental collectedness and concen-

tration to which I have previously alluded as observable only in particular
moments of the highest artificial excitement. The words of one of these
rhapsodies I have easily remembered. I was, perhaps, the more forcibly
impressed with it as he gave it, because, in the under or mystic current of
its meaning, I fancied that I perceived, and for the first time, a full
consciousness on the part of Usher of the tottering of his lofty reason upon
her throne. The verses, which were entitled "The Haunted Palace," ran
very nearly, if not accurately, thus:

In the greenest of our valleys,

By good angels tenanted,

Once a fair and stately palace--

Radiant palace--reared its head.

In the monarch Thought's dominion--

It stood there!

Never seraph spread a pinion

Over fabric half so fair.

Banners yellow, glorious, golden,

On its roof did float and flow

(Thisall this--was in the olden

Time long ago)

And every gentle air that dallied,

In that sweet day,

Along the ramparts plumed and pallid,

A winged odour went away.

Wanderers in that happy valley

Through two luminous windows saw

Spirits moving musically

To a lute's well tuned law,

Round about a throne, where sitting

(Porphyrogene!)

In state his glory well befitting,

The ruler of the realm was seen.

And all with pearl and ruby glowing
Was the fair palace door,
Through which came flowing, flowing, flowing
And sparkling evermore,
A troop of Echoes whose sweet duty
Was but to sing,
In voices of surpassing beauty,
The wit and wisdom of their king.

But evil things, in robes of sorrow,
Assailed the monarch's high estate;
(Ah, let us mourn, for never morrow
Shall dawn upon him, desolate!)
And, round about his home, the glory
That blushed and bloomed
Is but a dimremembered story
Of the old time entombed.

And travellers now within that valley,
Through the redlitten windows see
Vast forms that move fantastically
To a discordant melody;
While, like a rapid ghastly river,
Through the pale door,
A hideous throng rush out forever,
And laugh--but smile no more.

I well remember that suggestions arising from this ballad, led us into a train of thought, wherein there became manifest an opinion of Usher's which I mention not so much on account of its novelty, (for other men have thought thus,) as on account of the pertinacity with which he maintained it. This opinion, in its general form, was that of the sentience of all vegetable things. But, in his disordered fancy, the idea had assumed a more daring character, and trespassed, under certain conditions, upon the kingdom of inorganization. I lack words to express the full extent, or the earnest *abandon* of his persuasion. The belief, however, was connected (as I have previously hinted) with the gray stones of the home of his forefathers. The conditions of the sentence had been here, he imagined, fulfilled in the method of collocation of these stones--in the order of their arragenment, as well as in that of the many *fungi* which overspread them, and of the decayed trees which stood around--above all, in the long undisturbed endurance of this arrangement, and in its reduplication in the still waters of the tarn. Its evidence--the evidence of the sentience--was to be seen, he said (and I here started as he spoke), in the gradual yet certain condensation of an atmosphere of their own about the waters and the walls. The result was discoverable, he added, in that silent yet importunate and terrible influence which for centuries had moulded the destinies of his family, and which made *him* what I now saw him--what he was. Such opinions need no comment, and I will make none.

Our books--the books which, for years, had formed no small portion of the mental existence of the invalid--were, as might be supposed, in strict keeping with this character of phantasm. We pored together over such works as the Ververt et Chartreuse of Gresset; the Belphegor of Machilvelli; the Heaven and Hell of Swedenborg; the Subterranean Voyage of Nicholas Klimm of Holberg; the Chiromancy of Robert Flud, of Jean D'Indaginé, and of De la Chambre; the Journey into the Blue Distance of Tieck; and the City of the Sun of Campanella. One favourite volume was a small octavo edition of the *Directorium Inquisitorum* , by the Dominican Eymeric de Gironne; and there were passages in Pomponius Mela, about the old African Satyrs and Ægipans, over which Usher would sit dreaming for hours. His chief delight, however, was found in the perusal of an exceedingly rare and curious book in quarto Gothic--the manual of a forgotten church--the *Vigilioe Mortuorum secundum Chorum Ecclesioe Maguntinoe.*

I could not help thinking of the wild ritual of this work, and of its probable influence upon the hypochondriac, when, one evening, having informed me abruptly that the lady Madeline was no more, he stated his intention of preserving her corpse for a fortnight, (previously to its final interment,) in one of the numerous vaults within the main walls of the building. The worldly reason, however, assigned for this singular proceeding, was one which I did not feel at liberty to dispute. The brother had been led to his resolution (so he told me) by consideration of the unusual character of the malady of the deceased, of certain obtrusive and eager inquiries on the part of her medical men, and of the remote and exposed situation of the burialground of the family. I will not deny that when I called to mind the sinister countenance of the person whom I met upon the staircase, on the day of my arrival at the house, I had no desire to oppose what I regarded as at best but a harmless, and by no means an unnatural, precaution.

At the request of Usher, I personally aided him in the arrangements for the temporary entombment. The body having been encoffined, we two alone bore it to its rest. The vault in which we placed it (and which had been so long unopened that our torches, half smothered in its oppressive atmosphere, gave us little opportunity for investigation) was small, damp, and entirely without means of admission for light; lying, at great depth, immediately beneath that portion of the building in which was my own sleeping apartment. It had been used, apparently, in remote feudal times, for the worst purposes of a donjonkeep, and, in later days, as a place of deposit for powder, or some other highly combustible substance, as a portion of its floor, and the whole interior of a long archway through which we reached it, were carefully sheathed with copper. The door, of massive iron, had been, also, similarly protected. Its immense weight caused an unusually sharp grating sound, as it moved upon its hinges.

Having deposited our mournful burden upon tressels within this region of horror, we partially turned aside the yet unscrewed lid of the coffin, and looked upon the face of the tenant. A striking similitude between the brother and sister now first arrested my attention; and Usher, divining, perhaps, my thoughts, murmured out some few words from which I learned that the deceased and himself had been twins, and that sympathies of a scarcely intelligible nature had always existed between them. Our glances, however, rested not long upon the dead--for we could not regard her unawed. The disease which had thus entombed the lady in the maturity of youth, had left, as usual in all maladies of a strictly cataleptical character, the mockery of a faint blush upon the bosom and the face, and that suspiciously lingering smile upon the lip which is so terrible in death. We replaced and screwed down the lid, and, having secured the door of iron, made our way, with toil, into the scarcely less gloomy apartments of the upper portion of the house.

And now, some days of bitter grief having elapsed, an observable change came over the features of the mental disorder of my friend. His ordinary manner had vanished. His ordinary occupations were neglected or forgotten. He roamed from chamber to chamber with hurried, unequal, and objectless step. The pallor of his countenance had assumed, if possible, a more ghastly hue--but the luminousness of his eye had utterly gone out. The once occasional huskiness of his tone was heard no more; and a tremulous quaver, as if of extreme terror, habitually characterized his utterance. There were times, indeed, when I thought his unceasingly agitated mind was labouring with some oppressive secret, to divulge which he struggled for the necessary courage. At times, again, I was obliged to resolve all into the mere inexplicable vagaries of madness, for I beheld him gazing upon vacancy for long hours, in an attitude of the profoundest attention, as if listening to some imaginary sound. It was no wonder that his condition terrified--that it infected me. I felt creeping upon me, by slow yet certain degrees, the wild influences of his own fantastic yet impressive superstitions.

It was, especially, upon retiring to bed late in the night of the seventh or eighth day after the placing of the lady Madeline within the donjon, that I experienced the full power of such feelings. Sleep came not near my couch--while the hours waned and waned away. I struggled to reason off the nervousness which had dominion over me. I endeavoured to believe that much, if not all of what I felt, was due to the bewildering influence of the gloomy furniture of the room--of the dark and tattered draperies, which, tortured into motion by the breath of a rising tempest, swayed fitfully to and fro upon the walls, and rustled uneasily about the decorations of the bed. But my efforts were fruitless. An irrepressible tremour gradually pervaded my frame; and, at length, there sat upon my very heart an incubus of utterly causeless alarm. Shaking this off with a gasp and a struggle, I uplifted myself upon the pillows, and, peering earnestly within the intense darkness of the chamber, hearkened--I know not why, except that an instinctive spirit prompted me--to certain low and indefinite sounds which came, through the pauses of the storm, at long intervals, I knew not whence. Overpowered by an intense sentiment of horror, unaccountable yet unendurable, I threw on my clothes with haste, (for I felt that I should sleep no more during the night,) and endeavoured to arouse myself from the pitiable condition into which I had fallen, by pacing rapidly to and fro through the apartment.

I had taken but few turns in this manner, when a light step on an adjoining staircase arrested my attention. I presently recognized it as that of Usher. In an instant afterward he rapped, with a gentle touch, at my door, and entered, bearing a lamp. His countenance was, as usual, cadaverously wan--but, moreover, there was a species of mad hilarity in his eyesan evidently restrained *hysteria* in his whole demeanour. His air appalled me--but anything was preferable to the solitude which I had so long endured, and I even welcomed his presence as a relief.

"And you have not seen it?" he said abruptly, after having stared about him for some moments in silence--"you have not then seen it?--but, stay! you shall." Thus speaking, and having carefully shaded his lamp, he hurried to one of the casements, and threw it freely open to the storm.

The impetuous fury of the entering gust nearly lifted us from our feet. It was, indeed, a tempestuous yet sternly beautiful night, and one wildly singular in its terror and its beauty. A whirlwind had apparently collected its force in our vicinity; for there were frequent and violent alterations in the direction of the wind; and the exceeding density of the clouds (which hung so low as to press upon the turrets of the house) did not prevent our perceiving the lifelike velocity with which they flew careering from all points against each other, without passing away into the distance. I say that even their exceeding density did not prevent our perceiving this--yet we had no glimpse of the moon or stars--nor was there any flashing forth of the lightning. But the under surfaces of the huge masses of agitated vapour, as well as all terrestrial objects immediately around us, were glowing in the unnatural light of a faintly luminous and distinctly visible gaseous exhalation which hung about and enshrouded the mansion.

"You must not--you shall not behold this!" said I, shuddering, to Usher, as I led him, with a gentle violence, from the window to a seat. "These appearances, which bewilder you, are merely electrical phenomena not uncommon--or it may be that they have their ghastly origin in the rank miasma of the tarn. Let us close this casement;--the air is chilling and dangerous to your frame. Here is one of your favourite romances. I will read, and you shall listen;--and so we will pass away this terrible night together."

The antique volume which I had taken up was the "Mad Trist" of Sir Launcelot Canning; but I had called it a favourite of Usher's more in sad jest than in earnest; for, in truth, there is little in its uncouth and unimaginative prolixity which could have had interest for the lofty and spiritual ideality of my friend. It was, however, the only book immediately at hand;

and I indulged a vague hope that the excitement which now agitated the hypochondriac, might find relief (for the history of mental disorder is full of similar anomalies) even in the extremeness of the folly which I should read. Could I have judged, indeed, by the wild overstrained air of vivacity with which he hearkened, or apparently hearkened, to the words of the tale, I might well have congratulated myself upon the success of my design.

I had arrived at that wellknown portion of the story where Ethelred, the hero of the Trist, having sought in vain for peaceable admission into the dwelling of the hermit, proceeds to make good an entrance by force. Here, it will be remembered, the words of the narrative run thus:

"And Ethelred, who was by nature of a doughty heart, and who was now mighty withal, on account of the powerfulness of the wine which he had drunken, waited no longer to hold parley with the hermit, who, in sooth, was of an obstinate and maliceful turn, but, feeling the rain upon his shoulders, and fearing the rising of the tempest, uplifted his mace outright, and, with blows, made quickly room in the plankings of the door for his gauntleted hand; and now pulling therewith sturdily, he so cracked, and ripped, and tore all asunder, that the noise of the dry and hollowsounding wood alarumed and reverberated throughout the forest."

At the termination of this sentence I started and, for a moment, paused; for it appeared to me (although I at once concluded that my excited fancy had deceived me)--it appeared to me that, from some very remote portion of the mansion, there came, indistinctly, to my ears, what might have been, in its exact similarity of character, the echo hut a stifled and dull one certainly) of the very cracking and ripping sound which Sir Launcelot had so particularly described. It was, beyond doubt, the coincidence alone which had arrested my attention; for, amid the rattling of the sashes of the casements, and the ordinary commingled noises of the still increasing storm, the sound, in itself, had nothing, surely, which should have interested or disturbed me. I continued the story:

"But the good champion Ethelred, now entering within the door, was sore enraged and amazed to perceive no signal of the maliceful hermit; but, in the stead thereof, a dragon of a scaly and prodigious demeanour, and of a fiery tongue, which sate in guard before a palace of gold, with a floor of silver; and upon the wall there hung a shield of shining brass with this legend enwritten--

Who entereth herein, a conqueror hath bin; Who slayeth the dragon, the shield he shall win.

And Ethelred uplifted his mace, and struck upon the head of the dragon, which fell before him, and gave up his pesty breath, with a shriek so horrid and harsh, and withal so piercing, that Ethelred had fain to close his ears with his hands against the dreadful noise of it, the like whereof was never before heard."

Here again I paused abruptly, and now with a feeling of wild amazement--for there could be no doubt whatever that, in this instance, I did actually hear (although from what direction it proceeded I found it impossible to say) a low and apparently distant, but harsh, protracted, and most unusual screaming or grating sound--the exact counterpart of what my fancy had already conjured up for the dragons unnatural shriek as described by the romancer.

Oppressed, as I certainly was, upon the occurrence of this second and most extraordinary coincidence, by a thousand conflicting sensations, in which wonder and extreme terror were predominant, I still retained sufficient presence of mind to avoid exciting, by any observation, the sensitive nervousness of my companion. I was by no means certain that he had noticed the sounds in question; although, assuredly, a strange alteration had, during the last few minutes, taken place in his demeanour. From a position fronting my own, he had gradually brought round his chair, so as to sit with his face to the door of the chamber; and thus I could but partially perceive his features, although I saw that his lips trembled as if he were murmuring inaudibly. His head had dropped upon his breast-- yet I knew that he was not asleep, from the wide and rigid opening of the eye as I caught a glance of it in profile. The motion of his body, too, was at variance with this idea--for he rocked from side to side with a gentle yet constant and uniform sway. Having rapidly taken notice of all this, I resumed the narrative of Sir Launcelot, which thus proceeded:

"And now, the champion, having escaped from the terrible fury of the dragon, bethinking himself of the brazen shield, and of the breaking up of the enchantment which was upon it, removed the carcass from out of the way before him, and approached valorously over the silver pavement of the castle to where the shield was upon the wall; which in sooth tarried not for his full coming, but fell down at his feet upon the silver floor, with a mighty great and terrible ringing sound."

No sooner had these syllables passed my lips, than--as if a shield of brass had indeed, at the moment, fallen heavily upon a floor of silver--I became aware of a distinct, hollow, metallic, and clangorous, yet apparently muffled, reverberation. Completely unnerved, I leaped to my feet; but the measured rocking movement of Usher was undisturbed. I rushed to the chair in which he sat. His eyes were bent fixedly before him, and throughout his whole countenance there reigned a stony rigidity. But, as I placed my hand upon his shoulder, there came a strong shudder over his whole person; a sickly smile quivered about his lips; and I saw that he spoke in a low, hurried, and gibbering murmur, as if unconscious of my presence. Bending closely over him, I at length drank in the hideous import of his words.

"Not hear it?--yes, I hear it, and *have* heard it. Long--long--long--many minutes, many hours, many days, have I heard it--yet I dared not --oh, pity me, miserable wretch that I am!--I dared not--I *dared* not speak! *We have put her living in the tomb!* Said I not that my senses were acute? I *now* tell you that I heard her first feeble movements in the hollow coffin. I heard them--many, many days ago--yet I dared not--I *dared not speak!* And now--tonight--Ethelred--ha! ha!--the breaking of the hermit's door, and the deathcry of the dragon, and the clangour of the shield!--say, rather, the rending of her coffin, and the grating of the iron hinges of her prison, and her struggles within the coppered archway of the vault! Oh whither shall I fly? Will she not be here anon? Is she not hurrying to upbraid me for my haste? Have I not heard her footstep on the stair? Do I not distinguish that heavy and horrible beating of her heart? MADMAN!" --here he sprang furiously to his feet, and shrieked out his syllables, as if in the effort he were giving up his soul--" MADMAN! I TELL YOU THAT SHE NOW STANDS WITHOUT THE DOOR!"

As if in the superhuman energy of his utterance there had been found the potency of a spell, the huge antique panels to which the speaker pointed threw slowly back, upon the instant, their ponderous and ebony jaws. It was the work of the rushing gust--but then without those doors there DID stand the lofty and enshrouded figure of the lady Madeline of Usher. There was blood upon her white robes, and the evidence of some bitter struggle upon every portion of her emaciated frame. For a moment she remained trembling and reeling to and fro upon the threshold, then, with a low moaning cry, fell heavily inward upon the person of her brother, and in her violent and now final deathagonies, bore him to the floor a corpse, and a victim to the terrors he had anticipated.

From that chamber, and from that mansion, I fled aghast. The storm was still abroad in all its wrath as I found myself crossing the old causeway. Suddenly there shot along the path a wild light, and I turned to see whence a gleam so unusual could have issued; for the vast house and its shadows were alone behind me. The radiance was that of the full, setting, and bloodred moon, which now shone vividly through that once barely discernible fissure, of which I have before spoken as extending from the roof of the building, in a zigzag direction, to the base. While I gazed, this fissure rapidly widened--there came a fierce breath of the whirlwind --the entire orb of the satellite burst at once upon my sight--my brain reeled as I saw the mighty walls rushing asunder--there was a long tumultuous shouting sound like the voice of a thousand waters--and the deep and dank tarn at my feet closed sullenly and silently over the fragments of the "HOUSE OF USHER."

The Princess and the Vagabone

Ruth Sawyer

Ruth Sawyer (1880 - 1970) was born in Boston but spent her early years on New York City's Upper East Side. Through her Irish nurse, she was instilled with a love of folk tales and storytelling.

After training in Boston and at Teachers College in New York, she was hired by the *Sunday Sun* in 1905 to travel to Ireland and write a series of feature articles about Irish folk tales. Much of the material for her later stories was gathered during this trip. In 1910, at the invitation of Anne Carroll Moore of The New York Public Library, she began telling stories to children in all parts of the city. In 1911 she married and settled in Ithaca, New York.

Her most enduring work is the autobiographical novel *Roller Skates* (1936) which was awarded the Newbery Medal in 1937 by the American Library Association. Several collections of holiday folk tales, particularly *The Long Christmas* (1941) and *Joy to the World* (1961), have a lasting appeal to children. She articulated her philosophy of storytelling in *The Way of the Storyteller* (1942) which also includes a selection of traditional Irish folk tales.

Sawyer died in June 1970 while summering in Hancock, Maine. Her faith in God, love of life, and confidence in the goodness of people mark all her writings. She is widely regarded as a seminal figure in American storytelling.

If you would hear a tale in Ireland, you must first tell one. So it happened, as we sat in the Hegartys' cabin on a late fall night after a crossroads dance, that I, the stranger, found myself beginning the story-telling. The cabin was overflowing with neighbors from the hills about: girls and lads stretched tiredlimbed beside the hearth, elders sitting in an outer circle. The men smoked, the women were busy with their knitting, and the old gray piper--hidden in the shadow of the chimney-corner--sat with his pipes across his knees, fingering the stops with tenderness as unconsciously as a parent's hand goes out to stroke a much loved child. From between the curtains of the outshot bed peered the children, slee-plesseyed and laughing. The kettle hung, freshly filled, over the fire; the empty griddle stood beside it, ready for a late baking, for there would be tea and currantbread at the end of the evening.

I remember I told the legend of the Catskills, dwelling long on Rip's shrewish wife and the fame of her sharp tongue. They liked the story; I knew well that they would, for the supernatural lies close to the Irish heart; and before ever it was finished Michael Hegarty was knocking the ashes from his pipe that he might be ready with the next tale.

"That's grand," he said at the conclusion. "Do ye know, ye've given me a great consolation? I was afther thinkin' that Ireland had the exclusive rights to all the sharptongued, pestherin' wives," and he shook his head teasingly at the wife who sat across the firelight from him.

"Did ye, now?" she answered, her face down into an expression of mock solemnity. "Sure, was it because ye knew we had the run o' vagabone husbands?"

The children gurgled with appreciative merriment, but Michael pulled me gently by the sleeve.

"I have a tale--do ye know Willie Shakespeare?"

I nodded, surprised at the question.

"Well, ye may not be knowin' this: he was afther writin' a play a few hundthred years ago which he took sthraight out of a Connaught tale. Like as not he had it from an Irish nurse, or maybe he heard it from a rovin' tinker that came to his town."

"Which play do you mean?"

"Faith, I haven't the name by me handy, just, but your story put me in mind of it. I was readin' it myself once, so it's the truth I am tellin' ye. He has it changed a wee bit--turned it an' patched it an' made it up in a sthrange fashion; but 'tis the same tale, for all o' that. Sure, did ye ever know an Englishman yet that would let on to anything he'd took from an Irishman?"

A joyful murmur greeted the last.

"Tell us the tale," I said.

There was a long pause; the burning turf sifted down into "faery gold" upon the hearth and the kettle commenced to sing. Michael Hegarty smiled foolishly--

"I am afther wishin' ye had the Gaelic so as I could tell it to ye right. Ye see, I'm not good at givin' a tale in English--I haven't the words, just"; and he fumbled uneasily with his empty pipe.

"Ye can do it," said the wife, proudly.

"I can make the try," he answered, simply; and then he added, regretfully, "But I wish ye had the Gaelic."

Thus did Michael Hegarty begin the story of the Princess and the Vagabone. I marveled at first that the poetry and beauty of language should come so readily yet so unconsciously to his lips; and then I remembered that his people had once been the poets of the world, and men had come from far away to be taught by them.

This is the tale as he told it that night by the hearth--save that the soft Donegal brogue is missing, and nowhere can you hear the rhythmic click of the knitters' needles or the singing of the kettle on the crook making accompaniment.

Once, in the olden time, when an Irish king sat in every province and plenty covered the land, so that fat wee pigs ran free on the highroad, crying "Who'll eat us?" there lived in Connaught a grand old king with one daughter. She was as tall and slender as the reeds that grow by Loch Erne, and her face was the fairest in seven counties. This was more the pity, for the temper she had did not match it at all, at all; it was the blackest and ugliest that ever fell to the birthlot of a princess. She was proud, she was haughty; her tongue had the length and the sharpness of the thorns on a sidheog bush; and from the day she was born till long after she was a woman grown she was never heard to say a kind word or known to do a kind deed to a living creature.

As each year passed, the King would think to himself, "'Tis the New Year will see her better." But it was worse instead of better she grew, until one day the King found himself at the end of his patience, and he groaned aloud as he sat alone, drinking his poteen.

"Faith, another man shall have her for the next eighteen years, for, by my soul, I've had my fill of her!"

So it came about, as I am telling ye, that the King sent word to the nobles of the neighboring provinces that whosoever would win the consent of his daughter in marriage should have the half of his kingdom and the whole of his blessing. On the day that she was eighteen they came: a wonderful procession of earls, dukes, princes, and kings, riding up to the castle gate, acourting. The air was filled with the ring of the silver trappings on their horses, and the courtyard was gay with the colors of their bratas and the long cloaks they wore, riding. The King made each welcome according to his rank; and then he sent a servingman to his daughter, bidding her come and choose her suitor, the time being ripe for her to marry. It was a courteous message that the King sent, but the Princess heard little of it. She flew into the hall on the heels of the servingman, like a fowl hawk after a bantam cock. Her eyes burned with the anger that was hot in her heart, while she stamped her foot in the King's face until the rafters rang with the noise of it.

"So ye will be giving me away for the asking--to any one of these blithering fools who have a rag to their backs or a castle to their names?"

The King grew crimson at her words. He was ashamed that they should all hear how sharp was her tongue; moreover, he was fearsome lest they should take to their heels and leave him with a shrew on his hands for another eighteen years. He was hard at work piecing together a speech made up of all the grand words he knew, when the Princess strode past him on to the first suitor in the line.

"At any rate, I'll not be choosin' ye, ye long legged corncrake," and she gave him a sound kick as she went on to the next. He was a large man with a shaggy beard; and, seeing how the first suitor had fared, he tried a wee bit of a smile on her while his hand went out coaxingly. She saw, and the anger in her grew three-fold.

She sprang at him, digging the two of her hands deep in his beard, and then she wagged his foolish head back and forth, screaming:

"Take that, and that, and that, ye old whiskered rascal!"

It was a miracle that any beard was left on his face the way that she pulled it. But she let him go free at last, and turned to a thin, sharp-faced prince with a monstrous long nose. The nose took her fancy, and gave it a tweak, telling the prince to take himself home before he did any damage with it. The next one she called "pudding-face" and slapped his fat cheeks until they were purple, and the poor lad groaned with the sting of it.

"Go back to your trough, for I'll not marry a grunter, i' faith," said she.

She moved swiftly down the line in less time than it takes for the telling. It came to the mind of many of the suitors that they would be doing a wise thing if they betook themselves off before their turn came; so as many of them as were not fastened to the floor with fear started away. There happened to be a fat, crooked-legged prince from Leinster just making for the door when the Princess looked around. In a trice she reached out for the tongs that stood on the hearth near by, and she laid it across his shoulders, sending him spinning into the yard.

"Take that, ye old gander, and good riddance to ye!" she cried after him.

It was then that she saw looking at her a great towering giant of man; and his eyes burned through hers, deep down into her soul. So great was he that he could have picked her up with a single hand and thrown her after the gander; and she knew it, and yet she felt no fear. He was as handsome as Nuada of the Silver Hand; and not a mortal fault could she have found with him, not if she had tried for a hundred years. The two of them stood facing each other, glaring, as if each would spring at the other's throat the next moment; but all the while the Princess was thinking how wonderful he was, from the top of his curling black hair, down the seven feet of him, to the golden clasps on his shoes. What the man was thinking I cannot be telling. Like a breath of wind on smoldering turf, her liking for him set her anger fierceburning again. She gave him a sound cuff of the ear; then turned, and with a sob in her throat she went flying from the room, the serving-men scattering before her as if she had been a hundred million robbers on a raid.

And the King? Faith, he was dumb with rage. But when he saw the blow that his daughter had given to the finest gentleman in all Ireland, he went after her as if he had been two hundred million constables on the trail of the robbers.

"Ye are a disgrace and a shame to me," said he, catching up with her and holding firmly to her two hands; "and, what's more, ye are a disgrace and a blemish to my castle and my kingdom; I'll not keep ye in it a day longer. The first traveling vagabone who comes begging at the door shall have ye for his wife."

"Will he?" and the Princess tossed her head in the King's face and went to her chamber.

The next morning a poor singing *sthronshuch* came to the castle to sell a song for a penny or a morsel of bread. The song was sweet that he sang, and the Princess listened as Oona, the tirewoman, was winding strands of her long black hair with golden thread:

The gay young wran sang over the moor.

"I'll build me a nest," sang he.

"'Twill have a thatch and a wee latched door,

For the wind blows cold from the sea.

And I'll let no one but my true love in,

For she is the mate for me."

Sang the gay young wran.

The wee brown wran by the hedgerow cried--

"I'll wait for him here," cried she.

"For the way is far and the world is wide,

And he might miss the way to me.

Long is the time when the heart is shut,

But I'll open to none save he,"

Sang the wee brown wran.

A strange throb came to the heart of the Princess when the song was done. She pulled her hair free from the hands of the tirewoman.

"Get silver," she said; "I would throw it to him." And when she saw the wonderment grow in Oona's face, she added: "The song pleased me. Can I not pay for what I like without having ye look at me as if, ye feared my wits had flown? Go, get the silver!"

But when she pushed open the grating and leaned far out to throw it, the *sthronsuch* had gone.

For the King had heard the song as well as the Princess. His rage was still with him, and when he saw who it was, he lost no time, but called him quickly inside.

"Ye are as fine a vagabone as I could wish for," he said. "Maybe ye're not knowing it, but ye are a bridegroom this day." And the King went on to tell him the whole tale. The tale being finished, he sent ten strong men to bring the Princess down.

A king's word was law in those days. The Vagabone knew this; and, what's more, he knew he must marry the Princess, whether he liked it or no. The Vagabone had great height, but he stooped so that it shortened the length of him. His hair was long, and it fell, uncombed and matted, about his shoulders. His brogues were patched, his hose were sadly worn, and with his rags he was the sorriest cut of a man that a maid ever laid her two eyes on. When the Princess came, she was dressed in a gown of gold, with jewels hanging from every thread of it, and her cap was caught with a jeweled brooch. She looked as beautiful as a May morning--with a thundercloud rising back of the hills; and the Vagabone held his breath for a moment, watching her. Then he pulled the King gently by the arm.

"I'll not have a wife that looks grander than myself. If I marry your daughter, I must marry her in rags--the same as my own."

The King agreed 'twas a good idea, and sent for the worst dress of rags in the whole countryside. The rags were fetched, the Princess dressed, the priest brought, and the two of them married; and, though she cried and she kicked and she cuffed and she prayed, she was the Vagabone's wife--hard and fast.

"Now take her, and good luck good with ye," said the King. Then his eyes fell on the tongs on the hearth. "Here, take these along--they may come in handy on the road; but, whatever ye do, don't let them out of your hands, for your wife is very powerful with them herself."

Out of the castle gate, across the gardens, and into the country that lay beyond went the Princess and the Vagabone. The sky was blue over their heads and the air was full of spring; each wee creature that passed them on the road seemed bursting with the joy of it. There was naught but anger in the Princess' heart, however; and what was in the heart of the Vagabone I cannot be telling. This I know--that he sang the "Song of the Wran" as they went. Often and often the Princess turned back on the road or sat down, swearing she would go no farther;

and often and often did she feel the weight of the tongs across her shoulders that day.

At noon the two sat down by the crossroads to rest.

"I am hungry," said the Princess; " not a morsel of food have I tasted this day. Ye will go get me some."

"Not I, my dear," said the Vagabone; "ye will go beg for yourself."

"Never," said the Princess.

"Then ye'll go hungry," said the Vagabone; and that was all. He lighted his pipe and went to sleep with one eye open and the tongs under him.

One, two, three hours passed, and the sun hung low in the sky. The Princess sat there until hunger drove her to her feet. She rose wearily and stumbled to the road. It might have been the sound of wheels that had startled her, I cannot be telling; but as she reached the road a great coach drawn by six black horses came galloping up. The Princess made a sign for it to stop; for though she was in rags, yet she was still so beautiful that the coachman drew in the horses and asked her what she was wanting.

"I am near to starving;" and as she spoke the tears started to her eyes, while a new soft note crept into her voice. "Do ye think your master could spare me a bit of food--or a shilling?" and the hand that had been used to strike went out for the first time to beg.

It was a prince who rode inside the coach that day, and he heard her. Reaching out a fine, big hamper through the window, he told her she was hearty welcome to whatever she found in it, along with his blessing. But as she put up her arms for it, just, she looked--and saw that the Prince was none other than the fat suitor whose face she had slapped on the day before. Then anger came back to her again, for the shame of begging from him. She emptied the hamper--chicken pasty, jam, currant bread, and all--on top of his head, peering through the window, and threw the empty basket at the coachman. Away drove the coach; away ran the Princess, and threw herself, sobbing, on the ground near the Vagabone.

"Twas a good dinner that ye lost," said the Vagabone; and that was all.

But the next coach that passed she stopped. This time it was the shaggy-bearded rascal that rode inside. She paid no heed, however, and begged again for food; but her cheeks grew crimson when he looked at her, and she had to be biting her lips fiercely to keep the sharp words back.

"Ye are a lazy good-for-naught to beg. Why don't ye work for your food?" called the rascal after her.

And the Vagabone answered: "Ye are right entirely. 'Tis a sin to beg, and tomorrow I'll be teaching her a trade, so she need never be asking charity again upon the highroad."

That night they reached a wee scrap of a cabin on the side of a hill. The Vagabone climbed the steps and opened the door. "Here we are at home, my dear," said he.

"What kind of a home do ye call that?" and the Princess stamped her foot. "Faith, I'll not live in it."

"Then ye can live outside; it's all the same to me." The Vagabone went in and closed the door after him; and in a moment he was whistling merrily the song of "The Wee Brown Wran."

The Princess sat down on the ground and nursed her poor tired knees. She had walked many a mile that day, with a heavy heart and an empty stomach--two of the worst traveling companions ye can find. The night came down, black as a raven's wing; the dew fell, heavy as rain, wetting the rags and chilling the Princess to the marrow. The wind blew fresh from the sea, and the wolves began their howling in the woods near by, and at last, what with the cold and the fear and the loneliness of it, she could bear it no longer, and she crept softly up to the cabin and went in.

"There's the creepy-stool by the fire, waiting for ye," said the Vaga-bone; and that was all. But late in the night he lifted her from the chimney-corner where she had dropped asleep and laid her gently on the bed, which was freshly made and clean. And he sat by the hearth till dawn, keeping the turf piled high on the fire, so that the cold would not waken her. Once he left the hearth; coming to the bedside, he stood a moment to watch her while she slept, and he stopped and kissed the wee pink palm of her hand that lay there like a half-closed loch lily.

Next morning the first thing the Princess asked was where was the breakfast, and where were the servants to wait on her, and where were some decent clothes.

"Your servants are your own two hands, and they will serve ye well when ye teach them how," was the answer she got.

"I'll have neither breakfast nor clothes if I have to be getting them myself. And shame on ye for treating a wife so," and the Princess caught up a piggin and threw it at the Vagabone.

He jumped clear of it, and it struck the wall behind him. "Have your own way, my dear," and he left her to go out on the bogs and cut turf.

That night the Princess hung the kettle and made stir-about and griddle bread for the two of them.

"'Tis the best I have tasted since I was a lad and my mother made the baking," said the Vagabone, and that was all. But often and often his lips touched the braids of her hair as she passed him in the dark; and again he sat through the night, keeping the fire and mending her wee leather brogues, that they might be whole against the morrow.

Next day he brought some sally twigs and showed her how to weave them into creels to sell on coming market-day. But the twigs cut her fingers until they bled, and the Princess cried, making the Vagabone white with rage. Never had she seen such a rage in another creature. He threw the sally twigs about the cabin, making them whirl and eddy like leaves before an autumn wind; he stamped upon the half-made creel, crushing it to pulp under his feet; and, catching up the table, he tore it to splinters, throwing the fragments into the fire, where they blazed.

"By St. Patrick, 'tis a bad bargain that ye are! I will take ye this day to the castle in the next county, where I hear they are reeding a scullery-maid, and there I'll apprentice ye to the King's cook."

"I will not go," said the Princess; but even as she spoke fear showed in her eyes and her knees began to tremble under her.

"Aye, but ye will, my dear;" and the Vagabone took up the tongs quietly from the hearth.

For a month the Princess worked in the castle of the King, and all that time she never saw the Vagabone.

Often and often she said to herself, fiercely, that she was well rid of him; but often, as she sat alone after her work in the cool of the night, she would wish for the song of "The Wee Brown Wran," while a new loneliness crept deeper and deeper into her heart.

She worked hard about the kitchen, and as she scrubbed the pots and turned the spit and cleaned the floor with fresh white sand she listened to the wonderful tales the other servants had to tell of the King. They had it that he was the handsomest, aye, and the strongest, king in all Ireland; and every man and child and little creature in his kingdom worshiped him. And after the tales were told the Princess would say to herself: "If I had not been so proud and free with my tongue, I might have married such a king, and ruled his kingdom with him, learning kindness."

Now it happened one day that the Princess was told to be unusually spry and careful about her work; and there was a monstrous deal of it to be done; cakes to be iced and puddings to be boiled, fat ducks to be roasted, and a whole sucking pig put on the spit to turn.

"What's the meaning of all this?" asked the Princess.

Ochone, ye poor feebleminded girl!" and the cook looked at her pityingly. "Haven't ye heard the King is to be married this day to the fairest Princess in seven counties?"

"One that was I," thought the Princess, and she sighed.

"What makes ye sigh?" asked the cook.

I was wishing, just, that I could be having a peep at her and the King."

"Faith, that's possible. Do your work well, and maybe I can put ye where ye can see without being seen."

So it came about, as I am telling ye, at the end of the day, when the feast was ready and the guests come, that the Princess was hidden behind the broidered curtains in the great hall. There, where no one could see her, she watched the hundreds upon hundreds of fair ladies and fine noblemen in their silken dresses and shining coats, all silver and gold, march back and forth across the hall, laughing and talking and making merry among themselves. Then the pipes began to play, and everybody was still. From the farthest end of the hall came two-and-twenty lads in white and gold; these were followed by two-and-twenty pipers in green and gold and two-and-twenty bowmen in saffron and gold and, last of all, the King.

A scream, a wee wisp of a cry, broke from the Princess, and she would have fallen had she not caught one of the curtains. For the King was as tall and strong and beautiful as Nuada of the Silver Hand; and from the top of his curling black hair down the seven feet of him to the golden clasps of his shoes he was every whit as handsome as he had been that day when she had cuffed him in her father's castle.

The King heard the cry and stopped the pipers. "I think," said he, "there's a scullery-maid behind the curtains. Someone fetch her to me."

A hundred hands pulled the Princess out; a hundred more pushed her across the hall to the feet of the King, and held her there, fearing lest she should escape. "What were ye doing there?" the King asked.

"Looking at ye, and wishing I had the undoing of things I have done," and the Princess hung her head and sobbed piteously.

"Nay, sweetheart, things are best as they are," and there came a look into the King's eyes that blinded those watching, so that they turned away and left the two alone.

"Heart of mine," he went on, softly, "are ye not knowing me?"

"Ye are putting more shame on me because of my evil tongue and the blow my hand gave ye that day."

"I' faith, it is not so. Look at me."

Slowly the eyes of the Princess looked into the eyes of the King. For a moment she could not be reading them; she was as a child who pores over a strange tale after the light fades and it grows too dark to see. But bit by bit the meaning of it came to her, and her heart grew glad with the wonder of it. Out went her arms to him with the cry of loneliness that had been hers so long.

"I never dreamed that it was ye; never once."

"Can ye ever love and forgive?" asked the King.

"Hush ye!" and the Princess laid her finger on his lips.

The tirewomen were called, and she was led away. Her rags were changed for a dress that was spun from gold and woven with pearls, and her beauty shone about her like a great light.

They were married again that night, for none of the guests were knowing of that first wedding long ago.

Late o' that night a singing *sthronshuch* came under the Princess' window, and very softly the words of his song came to her:

The gay young wran sang over the moor.

"I'll build me a nest," sang he.

"'T'will have a thatch and a wee latched door,

For the wind blows cold from the sea.

And I'll let no one but my true love in,

For she is the mate for me,

Sang the gay young wran.

The wee brown wran by the hedgerow cried--

"I'll wait for him here," cried she.

"For the way is far and the world is wide,

And he might miss the way to me.

Long is the time when the heart is shut,

But I'll open to none save he,"

Sang the wee brown wran.

The grating opened slowly; the Princess leaned far out, her eyes like stars in the night, and when she spoke there was naught but gentleness and love in her voice.

"Here is the silver I would have thrown ye on a day long gone by. Shall I throw it now, or will ye come for it?"

And that was how a princess of Connaught was won by a king who was a vagabone.

The Snow Story

Chauncey Thomas

Chauncey Thomas (1872 - 1941) was a writer of Western fiction who depicted an unromanticized view of the West. He wrote from first hand experience as a cowboy and a rancher in the Western Rocky Mountains. He was also a skilled pistol shot and an expert on ballistics. In addition to writing fiction he wrote numerous articles for newspapers and magazines.

The story presented in this volume is based on Thomas' mountain climbing experiences in the Rockies. This story caught the attention of many well known readers including Rudyard Kipling. A peak in the Rockies has been named Mt. Chauncey in honor of this story. *The Snow Story* first appeared in the November 1901 issue of McClure's Magazine under the title *Why the Hot Sulphur Mail Was Late.*

One touch of Nature makes the whole world kin.--SHAKESPEARE.

Berthoud Pass is a mighty pass. It is the crest of a solid wave of granite two miles high, just at timber line. Berthoud is a vertebra in the backbone of the continent. It is the gigantic aerial gateway to Middle Park, Colorado--a park onefifth as large as all England. The mail for this empire is carried by one man--my friend Mason.

On Berthoud is a pebble. One summer a raindrop fell upon that pebble, splashed in two and each half rolled away; one danced down the Platte-MissouriMississippi, the longest river on the globe, to the Atlantic; the other tumbled down the Fraser, rolled along the Grand, thence through the greatest gorge on earth, the Grand Cañon of the Colorado, where the stars shine by day, to the Pacific. In the clasp of the Berthoudborn raindrop there were Europe and Asia one way, two oceans and the two Americas the other. Then from the two oceans the nebulized half-drops arose, sundrawn, miles into the zenith and rode the upper winds straight back to Berthoud Pass. There they united and crystallized into a snowflake. And with it came the Cold. There, far above the Pass, the frost spirit hung in

Damoclean deadliness over a creeping speck below--Mason, the mail carrier.

The rising sun glorified the snowflake; but away down there in Clear Creek cañon, where other waters gurgled and strangled under the ice, it was still a blue dark. Mason and the sun began to climb. The morning light started down Berthoud just as Mason started up. The snow-flake watched the crawling atom, then blew across the Pass, and from all along the range gathered unto itself the storm. On Berthoud was all the power of the Arctic. But the intelligent dot climbed on.

Eleven months of every year there is snow on Berthoud; only in July are the flowers safe. Even then, in shades that the sun cannot reach--packed by the centuries--is snow that fell on the rocks before they were cold. How black, how sharp the shadows are on the heights--and how cold! In them for ages has lurked ice from the continent-grinding glaciers of the North. Silent Christmas finds Berthoud hung with avalanches. At Easter these white thunderbolts come to life; and, leaning over the valleys, are so exquisitely held that they are launched even by an echo touch. Up there in long, wavering lines and tiny whirls the gritty snow blows like sugar. Shrublike, the tops of pines bend under locks and beards of alabaster moss, their trunks frigid for seventy feet in the crusted depths. Airy crystals float as on the breath of Polar fairies; the sunlight is alive with blue sparkles; the twig splitting in the cold sends a puff of frosty feathers; in the gale white shot sings in level volleys. Nature on Berthoud in winter is not dead, but alive. She is congealed into a new life. The very air seeming to snap, is thinner as if about to solidify. A mist, frozen to a transparent blue, quivers with its own chill. Water is not ice, but glass. When the black, solid lakes burst and shatter in the awful cold, ice splinters fly and burn like slivers of whitehot iron. Ice powder, hard, dry and sharp, grinds the web of snowshoes like steel filings. On Berthoud at night the stars are near; they silently crackle and spit colors like electric sparks.

In the valley just then the morning star paled as if frozen, and with a spiteful snap winked out. The line of sunlight, halfway down the Pass, met Mason, halfway up. The bluegray cold melted to a flood of heaven's own warmth. It would be warmer soon, then hot, then blistering there on the snow. Mason stopped to rest, panting steam; peeled off his coat and put on his veil.

To climb Berthoud in winter is the work of a man. It is too much for an engine. The man was at his work. Up, slowly up, the east side, around the Big Bend, up to the now deserted mail barn, labored the mail carrier. The summit was a mile farther on and a quarter of mile farther up. No arranged postal car, warm, light and convenient, was the lot of Mason. The car was on his back, a bag of mail. Contrary to regulations, devised by easychair postal officials in faroff Washington, the papers and packages had been held at Empire. Only the letters went over.

"They'll keep," had said the Empire postmaster, a man of vast common sense, as he filled his pipe from Mason's pouch. Then he and Mason had hidden the bag of 2nd class under the hay in the manger of the mail team back in Empire until the thaw was over. So Mason traveled light--only sixtyfour pounds on his back and twenty pounds of wet snow on each web a foot beneath the surface. By the bleak, now empty, halfway station slouched Mason.

"Only zero! Hot. Wheeww!" he gasped, as he wiped the sweat from his eyes with his shirtsleeve. Mason meant it. Twelve feet of frigid white was between him and the earth; in the shadow the mercury was solid in the split tubes, yet in the sunlight the surface was slush. Mason was in his shirtsleeves with fur mittens on his hands. Icicles hung from his eye-lashes, yet his cheeks were frying. His nose was a blister, though his face was veiled as heavily as Milady's on an escapade. In the sun the snow was mush--in the shadow it was marble. Such is sunlight and shade on the southeastern snow banks at timberline. No wind. And the air was thin. Silence. The only sound was the carrier's bellowsed breath, and the sockraspsplosh of the shoes. And Mason came to the summit--and the shadow. Noon. Here the mercury falls a degree a minute when the sun goes down. A hundred and four at noon, an inch of ice at sundown. The ground is frozen for five hundred and forty feet. Such is the summer summit.

But this was winter. Up the south gorge of the Fraser, from the Pacific side of the Pass, like the burst of a volcano, so cold that the smoke was snowdust, roared the storm. Mason saw it--looked with the indifferent interest of long experience, and put on his short fur coat. As he retied his snowshoes he looked back--and down. Below him lay the west fork of Clear Creek, green in the coming spring. Mason stood on the rampart of winter. On either side the Pass towered pinnacles of stormeaten rock, bleak as the Poles themselves. From their tops white powder streamed in the wind like crests, and floured down on the back-turned pigmy at their feet. The carrier was taking with his eyes from the Atlantic side a swift, silent goodbye of the infant summer. Straight to the south flamed the sun, so low in the clear sky that Mason, standing on Berthoud, felt that it was below him--infernal--and that he stood alone on the tip of the Universe. Behind him the swirling heavens were murky. The world was black, white and thin blue-- silent, motionless, and cold, lit, but unwarmed, by the open furnacedoor of hell.

But the cold was creeping for Mason's heart, and he flung his arms.

"Good for the legs," he remarked to a stump that in summer was a dead pine tree. "Track looks like a hobbled elephant's. Well--here goes." And down into the gorge went Mason.

That gale had started in Alaska and swept twothirds of a continent to the southwest. In Montana it had torn the anemometer, the official whirling, from the signal station, but left the register, and the needle pointed to eightyfive miles an hour. It was faster now. Caught by the wide mouth of the south fork of the Fraser and jammed into the upright narrowing of the rocky defile, the white fiend roared straight into the air a league and back over itself--chaos with flying chains. Into this walked Mason.

A single snowflake, a bunch of frozen needle points, struck his forehead, but glanced away into the white pandemonium. Snowsand cut his veil as if blown from a gun. Instantly his breath was sucked from his lungs and sent twenty thousand feet--four miles above the sea. Mason whirled, his back to the flinty sleet, and the storm fell upon the United States mail. But no snow storm can stop the United States mail. With a belly-jerk Mason wrenched a breath from the torrent.

"Quite a Colorado zephyr," he yelled, but could not hear himself. There was almost perfect silence around him, because he could hear nothing--only a leaden roar. No slush here; the surface was sand paper. Zip-zip-zip, with his head low, Mason butted down the gulch. Then it eased up. The wind dropped to a mile a minute, and cleared greatly. Mason could see ten feet ahead. Easier now, he loped over the crust, down, down, down, leaving no track--not even a whiff of snow was blown from the trail. The snow was as hard, sharp, and glittering in the white night as the surface of broken steel. A blast of snow-sand caught the flying, dropping carrier square in the face. The ground ice cut like powdered glass shot from a battery. Mason, his arms before his head, ran into and leaned against a crackling pine. Amid these convulsions of the Wilderness he seemed like a frightened child.

Suddenly the pine straightened with a snap, quivering as if tired. Mason lowered his arms; all was still, quiet, pleasant. The snow was smiling; the sun was shining; there was no wind. But a mile--now two--boiling in the air--white hell churned.

Lovely, ain't it? Snow slide gone off wrong end up," said a voice.

Mason jumped. A quick sweep of the near distance showed nothing human but himself.

"Did I say that?" he muttered. "This bucking snow is about as good on a man's savey as herding sheep. I'll be as locoed as a swell-necked buck if I keep this up--Hello! "

"Howdy?" answered the voice, and from under a sheltering ledge, crusted over but filled soft and dry with ice down as if banked from a featherbed, heaved a sheeted figure and shook itself. It fairly rattled.

"Nice little blow, wasn't it? I had an idea I was the only pack animal of the longeared breed on the Range--but I see I have company; baggage and all. Glad to see you, though. Bytheway, sorry to trouble you, but I'll have to ask you for those shoes--and that coat; also any spare change you've got, your ticker, and that mail bag. Now don't go off halfcocked and empty, or we'll have trouble."

He of the voice had leveled a long sixshooter, white with frost and snow, at the mail carrier.

Mason was not startled. What was the use? But he was annoyed--this lack of mountain courtesy. Then he grinned.

"Not this trip, pardner. Your artillery's as full of snow as the Arctic circle; while this instrument I have--"

A burst of flame, smoke and steam exploded between the two men. As it floated upward Mason saw the stranger bend double and squeeze his right hand between his knees. Blood was dripping over his felt boots and overshoes. A splintered sixshooter rang on the ice twenty feet away.

"I told you you'd have fireworks if you turned that ice jam loose. No wonder she exploded. What'd you expect? You're too experienced a man by the looks of you to throw such a kid trick as that. Thought I wasn't heeled, hey? And you'd work a bluff on me, did you? Going to spear me on an icicle. Now, you fool"--Mason's tone became dry, metallic-- "you wiggle a hair and I'll kill you. My gun has not been out all winter; it is ready for business. Just off the hip; hot as buckwheat. Now don't do the stageeye act on me, nor try any football dives--and leave that sticker of yours alone. You might cut somebody with it. No, thank you, I'll help myself. Straighten up now; and turn your back. See here-- Are you going to do as I tell you, or shall I fix your hide so that they'll tan it for chair bottoms? Jump lively now, or I'll fill you so full of lead that you'll assay for Georgetown ore and it'll take the coroner's jury twentyfour hours to count the holes. Still I don't want to kill you. It's a dirty job, and I would rather walk you into town than haul you there on your back. Oh, don't go frothing now and sass me back like that. Of course I'm festive. Who wouldn't be with a five-thousand-dollar winner--Hold on there. Fivethousanddollar gold mine, as I was a say'en, in your own self as a standing reward for Salarado --N-No. My dear sir, a single jump into my latitude and I'll plug you. Postoffice robber, ugh? And gathered in by Uncle Sam himself in the person of your humble striker. Lord. I ain't talked so much since speechmakin' over good luck come into fashion. Oh, yes; I know you. No; it isn't any lie, either. I have your circular description here in my pocket, right next my heart, to tack up in every mail window in Empire and Hot Sulphur. You're wanted, wanted bad; five thousand dollars' worth of bad, too; and I've got you--and incidentally I intend to keep you. Now drop that cleaver of your'n and shinny on down the trail there, or we'll have troub--"

A mile above a concussion jolted the cliff; a terrific echo to the pistolshot. Down came the slide--gently at first--so far away it seemed only as wide as one's hand. In an instant the snow shot from under the two men. A mile of snow bristling hairlike with roottorn pines, thundered down the slope. Mason and Salarado, forgetful of each other, were whirled into the air, and fell back on a huge slab of ice that crashed down the tumbling mountainside unbroken by the mass of fighting logs around it. This piece of ice on which they lay was thick and solid, laced and interlaced with tough brushwood frozen in. This woven acre rode the avalanche like a sled. A crag a quarter of a mile, ten feet, ahead, passed with a roar. A huge pine whipped by faster yet. That rocky spur half a mile down--now behind--was a pain in the ear. Faster, faster, dropping, falling, sailingthey are standing still; but on either side, up from below, the air and the mountains pour--then blackness.

An hour later a mountain lion sneaked over the wreck. A hill of snow, ice, broken stone and splintered logs dammed the gulch. Away to the top of the Range the track of the slide lay like a scald. Miles away, high in the air, a cloud of white dust was floating. An eighth of a mile up the opposing slope had shot a huge piece of ice, and lay half buried in the debris. All Nature was hushed as if frightened. A screeching eagle went flapping far away. From under the ruin a wolf howled dismally; then weaker and weaker--a piteous whineand silence. The frozen wind went up a gulch of naked, fire-blackened pines crooning a requiem. But the music from that wild cathedral breathed not of eternal rest and peace; it chilled the heart in icy triumph. Berthoud had struck a mountainous blow; and humanity--Where were the men?

The panther was hunting; his nose had found them, but not his jaws. Settling himself, he dug. As the famished brute raked a log to one side with his gaunt jaw, he heard a groan within an inch of his ear--whirling he flashed up the mountainside a streak of yellow. But his work was done.

From the shallow hole reared the mail sack, and the head and arms of Mason, all chalk white but his face, which was a ghastly blue. He struggled carefully, then desperately, to free himself; but when he stopped exhausted, only his head and shoulders appeared above the snow.

"Pinned down--dead--my last trip--and yet not hurt. Freeze like a cockroach in the icehouse. Cool, my boy, cool--keep cool. Don't lose your head--don't get rattled, or you're a dead man. Now's when you need all your brains. Keep cool--though you will be cool enough all too soon."

Mason's head disappeared in the panther-dug hole. Slowly the end of a small log ten feet away rose into the air and fell aside. Upstraightened the grizzly head of Salarado, one side daubed with a red slush.

"Well--I--be--damned. This don't look much like hell; still it's a pretty good imitation," growled the desperado as he gazed around the piled confusion. He noticed the straining mailsack. Salarado waited silently till Mason's haggard face again came above the rim. The two men looked into each other's eyes.

"Hurt?" asked Mason.

"Don't think so. Both feet fast. How's yourself?" answered Salarado.

"One leg in a vise--can't move it. What d'you think?"

"We're done for."

"Guess you're right. How's the snow 'round you?"

"None 't all--all ice. Solid."

"Hold still. I've got one foot a little loose," and Mason stamped on a log far below.

"Same log," said the thief. "Got us both."

Nothing more was said. They went to work. Mason unslung the mailsack and laid it carefully aside. For an hour both men strained, pulled, twisted, and dug at their white irons with bare fingers till the purple ends were raw. Great red finger scratches stained the snow around them. Human fingers are not panther claws. Both men were packed tight up to their armpits in solid snow. Four feet below the surface of the ruin their legs were fast between two parallel logs as in a steel trap. An inch closer and their ankles would have cracked like pipestems; an inch wider and the two men would have been free. They were not hurt; merely held. Berthoud had been kind only to be cruel.

"No use," panted Mason. "My trail ends here."

"Mine don't. I wish it did," murmured Salarado. The hard tone was gone; the voice was almost gentle. "Hell's ahead of me. You are an honest man, Señor, and have nothing to fear from death; while I"-- and there was silence for many minutes. "Many's the time I've faced it, but not when I had to think it over--like this," he continued to himself.

Then they waited. A camprobber, that bird of winter timberline, came like the blue angel of death, and hopped and scolded within a yard of them, and mocked them.

"Lucky jay; you've got what I would give the world for," mused Salarado. Mason said nothing. He was thinking of a little rawhide dugout down in the hot sands of New Mexico where Mexie lay basking in the sun; and over this picture like a haze crept the scene of a great fire in the night, with Indians about it, and a cauldron of boiling water steaming furiously. With a start Mason looked about him and recognized where he was. This was the cañon where so many years before he had fought the Colorow Utes.

"What is it, Señor?" asked Salarado.

"Nothing," answered Mason.

Mason was brave; yet he did not want to die. Life held so much for him to live and to work for, yet he waited calmly, his brain as cold as his freezing foot. At intervals the men struggled, wrenched their muscles with no hope of getting out to keep warm. The thirstfever that comes from pain had dried Mason's tongue. He longed for water. A mouthful of snow burned like hot cinders; he spat it out and pressed his rigid jaw with stiff, bare hands to warm the aching teeth. He looked about for water. Fifty feet up the mountain, in the lee of a boulder, was a spring, but it was solid ink banked with crystal milk. The breeze was gently keen. Mason's clothes grew cold. He felt nude and shrank from them. His skin became small and tight, and smarted as though blistered. A chill shook him. Blunt pains worked along the bones and met in the joints. Each particular finger and toe seemed about to burst. His scalp stiffened. His chin was numb. The cold, gnawing between his shoulders, was biting for his heart. Only the wedged foot was warm, and strangely comfortable. Webs of spidery ice floated and vanished in the cheerful sunlight. Flashing wiggles swarmed before the man's angular eyes like joyous worms, and disappeared only to come again. Mason was freezing. Away in the sky loomed Berthoud Pass hoary with ice ermine and wrapped in fleecy clouds. To Mason's hopeless eyes the wreath-veils seemed smoke and steam, curiously warm. He shuddered, locked his rattling jaws and grimly faced the end.

Up there on the summit the clouds of gold; the very top was red. In oblivions majesty eternal rose the Pass; but over and about the two heads sticking in the snow a living spangle, a single snow-flake, flashing dazzling, glittering, wafted like a dancing diamond. It tickled the cold flesh of Mason's face, then tumbled into the air in a very ecstasy of whirls. The man's head drooped, drooped, dipped, jerked back; drooped again; and hung pendulous. Mason was asleep, warm and comfortable. With a dull yell of pain he awoke. Salarado had hit him in the ear with a snowball.

"Hang on, Señor. Keep a scrape'n. Don't give up," were the rough words of cheer.

Mason knotted his muscles, shook off the torpor as if it were the tightening coils of a cold snake, and rubbed his burning ear.

"What's the use?" We'll both be stiff in three hours. Might as well have it over with," replied Mason as if speaking of a card game.

Aroused he freed his feet of the webs and pulled some feeling into the clutched one. From his pocket he took his lunch, until now forgotten, and silently tossed half to his fellow prisoner. The camprobber captured a piece of meat in the air and flew squawking to a limb. Salarado swore at the bird in profane amusement. Mason redivided his piece of pork and threw it over. The holdup protested, raked it in, and tossed it back. Mason chewed down his own share, but this piece of meat he put back in his pocket. Salarado looked at him:

"Say, pardner, you're a man."

The fires of life, rekindled, flamed up anew in the desperado. "I will get loose," he snarled with set teeth as he tore frightfully at the snow around his waist.

"Try this; my hands are too stiff to use it," and Mason threw his watch to Salarado.

"Ah, Señor, a regular snowplough," grunted the other as he sprang open the lid with his teeth and began to scrape.

"Saay"--the yell rang up the Pass--"here's my knife."

Buried tight in the snow was the knife--Life itself--within easy reach, yet frozen fast. Mason did not answer, but waited. Just then Salarado's dead hands dropped the watch. It vanished along his leg into the black hole that held him, and then faintly clinked on a stone under the log-jam. With a curse the lifelong criminal clawed viciously at the snow with scarlet fingers. Ten minutes of bloody scratching cleared the handle and hilt of the heavy bowie; and Salarado's head and shoulders arose triumphant, his gory right hand flourishing the priceless steel. The light from that blade flashed to the very top of Berthoud. Mason writhed to keep warm.

The shadows were growing longer now. In another two hours the sun would be down, and their lives would go out like candles. Salarado jabbed, ripped, strained and from his burrow hurled ice, snow and splintered wood. Iron against water, with men for stakes! In thirty minutes he was free all but his feet. Both ankles were held between two logs; one thick as his waist, the other a mere pole. Hack, slice, split. In five minutes more Salarado crawled painfully, sweating and breathless, from the hole.

He tried to stand, but tottered and fell as if on stilts. He rubbed, he pounded, he rolled and twisted his numbed calves and feet; the thick, black blood turned bright and throbbed again. Salarado stood erect, danced sorely, and except for his skinless fingers and a scalp wound, now staunched with a frozen plaster of bloody hair, he was as well as ever. The bruised shoulder was unheeded. A lusterless snowflake dropped weakly at the man's feet. He stepped on it as he picked up the knife and clambered over the snow and logs to Mason.

Salarado looked at Mason, and Mason looked at Salarado. Mason's lips were without motion, but in his eyes was the look of a pawfast grizzly. The multimurderer seated himself on a broken spruce branch not six feet from Mason, rested his hands on his knees and thought. He stared at the carrier. Here was a man whom two hours before he had tried to kill who in turn stood ready to kill him; and even started him at the muzzle of his sixshooter on that short, sure road to a living death, the penitentiary for life, or the noose. Leave him there--why not? No crime--he had not put him there. What if it were a crime? Who would know? And what if they did? Far from being his first. In the spring--perhaps not for years--they would find the skeleton; and fleshless jaws say little. Dig him out--then what? Was it not to set free a messenger sure to start all the machinery of the law to land the rescuer in a cage--a cage--where nothing could come but insanity and death? Why again seek from what he has just escaped? And entirely by his own efforts, too-- The watch? But the other's hands had been--still were--to cold to use it; so it could have done him no good. Salarado thought these things, seated there on the logend in the snowslide that frigid February day, facing his enemy--that enemy now harmless; but all-powerful when free. Why reverse their positions? Salarado looked at the Range ahead. In the setting sun the Pass was banked high with frozen blood. Hard, almost fatal it was. Why add a vindictive posse from behind? It was good just to be alive--and free. Then he looked once more at Mason, silent, waiting Mason--then at the empty hole, splotched with his own blood. Why not kill him quickly? One thrust and the cold-tortured man would be out of his misery--surely an act of mercy. Was not this enough? The stagerobber, murderer, desperado--reckless, careless of life and death, hunted by thirty millions, a bounty on his head--thoroughly understood the situation. So did his victim. The camp-robber flickered into the air and away homeward to a distant ranch. This winged freedom fascinated the criminal. He watched the bird float beyond the pine tops, looked again at the Range, stiffened to his feet, picked up the bowie, glanced behind him, and gazed down at the helpless freezing man.

"I would not trade places with you," curled from Mason's lips, but Salarado was looking, at the pocketed piece of meat. Then Salarado took the knife by the blade and handed it to Mason.

The Light in Mason's eyes cannot be put into words. He tried to speak. Salarado smiled, and with wooden fingers tried to roll a cigarette. Mason bent into his dead-fall to hide his tears--and to work. A half hour and Salarado pulled Mason from the hole. A minute more and the two men, the morally white with black spots, the morally black with white spots, stood face to face. Mason put out his hand. Salarado took it--still smoking.

"Pardner, you're a square man. Thanks. Here--" Mason peeled off his fur jacket, his cap and his overshoes, "take these, and this," he added, as he handed the desperado two bills and some silver. Then he hesitated--but with a jerk unbuckled his cartridge belt and, with its dangling holster full of snow, handed to Salarado. "You'll find the gun in the hole; I felt it with my foot. Don't use it unless you have to. She's sighted to a hair and has a soft trigger--but I want this knife. Good-bye. Mexico is the place for you. Less snow there." Both men smiled grimly. "Take straight down the gulch on the other side--it'll be frozen by the time you get there--and a freight is due at Empire at two in the morning--usually late, though. You can make it if you hump yourself. The shoes are in the hole there. I kicked them off. Eat that bacon when you get on top. It'll limber up your legs. Leave the tracks at the mouth of the cañon--she slows up there for the switch--for Golden is right ahead, and your picture is in the Post Office there. Cut to your right across the saddleback you'll see about four miles to the southeast; then straight on southeast fifteen or twenty miles till you cross the Platte, and you'll hit the Santa Fe tracks going south. Jump 'em, and a week from now you'll cross the Rio Grande--*quien sabe?* Go to the Three Triangle outfit in Chihuahua; tell the foreman, Pete Miller, he is known down there, I sent you and he'll give you a job punching. He'll do it 'cause I snaked him out of the Republican two years ago with his chaps on, and she was a boomin'--runnin' ice. I'd help you fish out those webs, but I got a case of cold feet and guess I'll have to quit ya."

Salarado breathed a slow curl of smoke and murmured, "Your foot's frozen, Señor? Maybeso I go with you--part way?"

"No. No need of that; only frosted; all right now. I can stump it in all right. These dutch socks'll last me till I reach Chipmunk's. You've no time to lose, pardner, so *adios*. Good luck to you. And--" Mason stopped, embarrassed--"and--if I were you, I'd quit this business. Don't pay."

"Si, Señor, you're right. I made up my mind to that in that hole there--just before I found the knife. If I hadn't--you--" Salarado left the sentence as it was; but Mason knew. He gripped the desperado's hand again, but its five bloody fingers made him think of five one-thousand dollar bills and half a score of murdered men.

"Well, be good to yourself. The mail must go through," Mason replied as he swung the sack to his shoulders. Then with the knife held like a sword, Mason saluted the other and left him. Salarado's face gave a whitefanged smile, but said nothing.

On darkening Berthoud the snow had turned to ashes. At the edge of the timber Mason turned and once more waved the bowie. Salarado swung his cap. Then Mason passed beneath the pines. Looking back between the trunks, now out of the other's sight, he saw a puff of snow and a piece of brush go into the air from the hole. It was Salarado digging for the shoes.

Three hours late Mason limped into Chipmunk's. Ten feet on the level had buried the station in December. Only the plumed chimney showed.

During that tramp Mason had been thinking; the inevitable reaction had set in, and he staggered under his load, for it seemed to him as if that sack held the mail of the nation; his brain was boiling with conflicting thoughts and warring emotions; and his conscience was divided against itself, for Mason was an honest man and Salarado was everything that was bad. One word to those in the cabin he was approaching and by midnight Salarado, the most dangerous criminal in the West, would be behind the bars--or lynched. Lynched? Mason shivered, and pushed open the hingecomplaining door. Gansen was swearing--had been for two hours.

"What's the trouble?" he demanded. "Think I'm going to hold the team here a week and drive it all night? With the spirit thermometer fifty-two below at the Springs this morning? If I miss the Coulter connection, Glenn won't do a thing but come up the line with a meatax for the whole outfit. The mails has got to go through. What's the trouble? You look as if you and a mowing machine had been havin' an argument."

"Oh nothing," said Mason, "bucked into a little slide just above High Bridge. We mixed, and I lost my goods and chattels, but acquired a whole museum of bumps and such things, besides a choice set of refrigerated toes. But here's the mail. No. No secondclass at Empire at all. Guess it's delayed in Denver, or else good people don't mail papers in the winter time."

"Where did you get that bowie?" grinned Gansen. "Regular yearling sword--some toothpick. Fine can opener. Will it cut anything? Overgrown rooster spur, isn't it? Going to mow some hay? Better wait till the snow pulls out, and the grass comes up."

"Ugh. Maybeso," and Mason thumbed the still frosted edge. "Swapped my sixgun for it some time ago. Nothing to shoot on the Range now. Better to chop wood with. Might use it for a sawmill sometime. Or dig a prospect hole while I'm taking a siesta and letting the snowshoes cool off, or let the wind out of something. Questions break friendships, and comments are worse. That's why angels go on the warpath."

Gansen eyed that foot of chilled steel quizzically, opened his mouth to say something, then closed it.

"No noise," chuckled old Chipmunk into his whiskers.

"See here, Chipmunk, you old gorilla," continued Mason as he sheathed the knife, "I want you to let up on trappin' along my trail. I don't like it. Found a marten in one of your infernal machines, and I turned him loose. Threw the Newhouse about forty miles somewheres off into the timber. I don't want any more of it. Savey?

Well?, *addios*, Jim. Give my apologies to the folks in Hot Sulphur 'cause their mail is late. It won't happen next time--perhaps not for a thousand years. Tell Mark I'll be down to the dance sure. Ask the Coulter school-marm to save me a waltz. Sure, now. Ta-ta."

"Say Chip! Get a wiggle on ya. Got any coffee? I'm tired. W-whew." And Mason lifted the pot off the stove. On the fire he put a bunch of circulars. They soon had the coffee boiling.

Extract from Captain Stormfield's Visit to Heaven

Mark Twain

Samuel Langhorne Clemen's (1835-1910) pseudonym, Mark Twain, a boat pilot's call, reflects his love of the river life. Best remembered for his works *The Adventures of Tom Sawyer*, (1876), *Life on the Mississippi*, (1883), *The Adventures of Huckleberry Finn*, (1884), his satirical short stories are a social commentary on Southern regionalism in nineteenth century America.

Growing up in Hannibal, Missouri Twain's observation of the activity along the river banks of the Mississippi provided him with a reservoir of material that would later appear in his work. At eighteen, after a brief education, he left for Philadelphia, New York and Washington to begin newspaper work. During this period Twain's travel letters were published by his brother Orion in his *Mescatine Journal*. He eventually joined the staff of a newspaper, lectured, and engaged in entreprenurial ventures on the side. He received national attention as a writer with his short story collection, *The Notorious Jumping Frog of Calaveras County and Other Sketches* published in 1867.

A trip to Europe, funded by a commission from Alta, California, inspired him to write the best-seller *Innocents Abroad* in 1869. His first novel, *The Gilded Age,* written in collaboration with Charles Dudley Warner, was completed in 1873.

Twain's other works include *The American Claimant* (1892), *The L1,000,000 Bank-Note* (1893), *The Tragedy of Pudd'nhead Wilson* (1894), *Personal Recollection of Joan of Arc* (1896), and *Following the Equator* (1897), the last of the travel works.

WELL, WHEN I HAD been dead about thirty years, I begun to get a little anxious. Mind you, I had been whizzing through space all that time, like a comet. *Like* a comet! Why, Peters, I laid over the lot of them! Of course there warn't any of them going my way, as a steady thing, you know, because they travel in a long circle like the loop of a lasso, whereas I was pointed as straight as a dart for the Hereafter; but I happened on one every now and then that was going my way for an hour or so, and then we had a bit of a brush together. But it was generally pretty one-sided, because I sailed by them the same as if they were standing still. An ordinary comet don't make more than about 200,000 miles a minute. Of course when I came across one of that sort--like Encke's and Haley's comets, for instance it warn't anything but just a flash and a vanish, you see. You couldn't rightly call it a race. It was as if the comet was a gravel-train and I was a telegraph despatch. But after I got outside of our astronomical system, I used to flush a comet occasionally that was something *like*. We haven't got any such comets--ours don't begin. One night I was swinging along at a good round gait, everything taut and trim, and the wind in my favor--I judged I was going about a million miles a minute--it might have been more, it couldn't have been less--when I flushed a most uncommonly big one about three points off my starboard bow. By his stern lights I judged he was bearing about northeast-and-by-north-half-east. Well, it was so near my course that I wouldn't throw away the chance; so I fell off a point, steadied my helm, and went for him. You should have heard me whiz, and seen the electric fur fly! In about a minute and a half I was fringed out with an electrical nimbus that flamed around for miles and miles and lit up all space like broad day. The comet was burning blue in the distance, like a sickly torch, when I first sighted him, but he begun to grow bigger and bigger as I crept up on him. I slipped up on him so fast that when I had gone about 150,000,000 miles I was close enough to be swallowed up in the phosphorescent glory of his wake, and I couldn't see anything for the glare. Thinks I, it won't do to run into him, so I shunted to one side an tore along. By and by I closed up abreast of his tail. Do you know what it was like? It was like a gnat closing up on the continent of America. I forged along. By and by I had sailed along his coast for a little upwards of a hundred and fifty million miles, and then I could see by the shape of him that I hadn't even got up to his waistband yet. Why, Peters, *we* don't know anything about comets, down here. If you want to see comets that *are* comets, you've got to go outside of our solar system--where there's room for them, you understand. My friend, I've seen comets out there that couldn't even lay down inside the *orbits* of our noblest comets without their tails hanging over.

Well, I boomed along another hundred and fifty million miles, and got up abreast his shoulder, as you may say. I was feeling pretty fine, I tell you; but just then I noticed the officer of the deck come to the side and hoist his glass in my direction. Straight off I heard him sing out--

"Below there, ahoy! Shake her up, shake her up! Heave on a hundred million billion tons of brimstone!"

"Ay--ay, sir!"

"Pipe the starboard watch! All hands on deck!"

"Ay--ay, sir!"

"Send two hundred thousand million men aloft to shake out royals and skyscrapers!"

"Ay--ay, sir!"

"Hand the stuns'ls! Hang out every rag you've got! Clothe her from stem to rudder-post!"

"Ay--ay, sir!"

In about a second I begun to see I'd woke up a pretty ugly customer, Peters. In less than ten seconds that comet was just a blazing cloud of red-hot canvas. It was piled up into the heavens clean out of sight--the old thing seemed to swell out and occupy all space; the sulphur smoke from the furnaces--oh, well, nobody can describe the way it rolled and tumbled up into the skies, and nobody can half describe the way it smelt. Neither can anybody begin to describe the way that monstrous craft begun to crash along. And such another powwow--thousands of bo's'n's whistles screaming at once, and a crew like the populations of a hundred thousand worlds like ours all swearing at once. Well, I never heard the like of it before.

We roared and thundered along side by side, both doing our level best, because I'd never struck a comet before that could lay over me, and so I was bound to beat this one or break something. I judged I had some reputation in space, and I calculated to keep it. I noticed I wasn't gaining as fast, now, as I was before, but still I was gaining. There was a power of excitement on board the comet. Upwards of a hundred billion passengers swarmed up from below and rushed to the side and begun to bet on the race. Of course this careened her and damaged her speed. My, but wasn't the mate mad! He jumped at that crowd, with his trumpet in his hand, and sung out--

"Amidships! amidships, you------! or I'll brain the last idiot of you!"

Well, sir, I gained and gained, little by little, till at last I went skimming sweetly by the magnificent old conflagration's nose. By this time the captain of the comet had been rousted out, and he stood there in the red glare for'ard, by the mate, in his shirtsleeves and slippers, his hair all rats' nests and one suspender hanging, and how sick those two men did look! I just simply couldn't help putting my thumb to my nose as I glided away and singing out:

"Tata! tata! Any word to send to your family?"

Peters, it was a mistake. Yes, sir, I've often regretted that--it was a mistake. You see, the captain had given up the race, but that remark was too tedious for him--he couldn't stand it. He turned to the mate, and says he--

"Have we got brimstone enough of our own to make the trip?"

"Yes, sir."

"Sure?"

"Yes, sir--more than enough."

"How much have we got in cargo for Satan?"

"Eighteen hundred thousand billion quintillions of kazarks."

"Very well, then, let his boarders freeze till the next comet comes. Lighten ship! Lively, now, lively, men! Heave the whole cargo overboard!"

Peters, look me in the eye. and be calm. I found out, over there, that a kazark is exactly the bulk of a *hundred and sixty-nine worlds like ours!* They hove all that load overboard. When it fell it wiped out a considerable raft of stars just as clean as if they'd been candles and somebody blowed them out. As for the race, that was at an end. The minute she was lightened the comet swung along by me the same as if I was anchored. The captain stood on the stern, by the afterdavits, and put his thumb to his nose and sung out--

"Tata! tata! Maybe *you've* got some message to send your friends in the Everlasting Tropics!"

Then he hove up his other suspender and started for'ard, and inside of threequarters of an hour his craft was only a pale torch again in the distance. Yes, it was a mistake, Peters--that remark of mine. I don't reckon I'll ever get over being sorry about it. I'd 'a' beat the bully of the firmament if I'd kept my mouth shut.

But I've wandered a little off the track of my tale; I'll get back on my course again. Now you see what kind of speed I was making. So, as I said, when I had been tearing along this way about thirty years I begun to get uneasy. Oh, it was pleasant enough, with a good deal to find out, but then it was kind of lonesome, you know. Besides, I wanted to get somewhere. I hadn't shipped with the idea of cruising forever. First off, I liked the delay, because I judged I was going to fetch up in pretty warm quarters when I got through; but towards the last I begun to feel that I'd rather go to--well, most any place, so as to finish up the uncertainty.

Well, one night--it was always night, except when I was rushing by some star that was occupying the whole universe with its fire and its glare--light enough then, of course, but I necessarily left it behind in a minute or two and plunged into a solid week of darkness again. The stars ain't so close together as they look to be. Where was I? Oh yes; one night I was sailing along, when I discovered a tremendous long row of blinking lights away on the horizon ahead. As I approached, they begun to tower and swell and look like mighty furnaces. Says I to myself--

"By George, I've arrived at last--and at the wrong place, just as I expected!"

Then I fainted. I don't know how long I was insensible, but it must have been a good while, for, when I came to, the darkness was all gone and there was the loveliest sunshine and the balmiest, fragrantest air in its place. And there was such a marvelous world spread out before me--such a glowing, beautiful, bewitching country. The things I took for furnaces were gates, miles high, made all of flashing jewels, and they pierced a wall of solid gold that you couldn't see the top of, nor yet the end of, in either direction. I was pointed straight for one of these gates, and a-coming like a house afire. Now I noticed that the skies were black with millions of people, pointed for those gates. What a roar they made, rushing through the air! The ground was as thick as ants with people, too--billions of them, I judge.

I lit. I drifted up to a gate with a swarm of people, and when it was my turn the head clerk says, in a businesslike way--

"Well, quick! Where are you from?"

"San Francisco," says I.

"San Fran--*what?*" says he.

"San Francisco."

He scratched his head and looked puzzled, then he says--

"Is it a planet?"

By George, Peters, think of it! *"Planet?"* says I; "it's a city. And moreover, it's one of the biggest and finest and--"

"There, there!" says he, "no time here for conversation. We don't deal in cities here. Where are you from in a *general* way?"

"Oh," I says, "I beg your pardon. Put me down for California."

I had him *again,* Peters! He puzzled a second, then he says, sharp and irritable--

I don't know any such planet--is it a constellation?"

"Oh, my goodness!" says I. "Constellation, says you? No--it's a State."

"Man, we don't deal in States here. *Will* you tell me where you are from *in general--at large,* don't you understand?"

"Oh, now I get your idea," I says, "I'm from America,--the United States of America."

Peters, do you know I had him *again?* If I hadn't I'm a clam! His face was as blank as a target after a militia shootingmatch. He turned to an under clerk and says--

"Where is America? *What* is America?"

The under clerk answered up prompt and says--

"There ain't any such orb."

"Orb?" says I. "Why, what are you talking about, young man? It ain't an orb; it's a country; it's a continent. Columbus discovered it; I reckon likely you've heard of *him,* anyway. America--why, sir, America--"

"Silence!" says the head clerk. "Once for all, where--are--you--*from?*"

"Well," says I, "I don't know anything more to say--unless I lump things, and just say I'm from the world."

"Ah," says he, brightening up, "now that's something like! *What* world?"

Peters, he had *me,* that time. I looked at him, puzzled, he looked at me, worried. Then he burst out--

"Come, come, what world?"

Says I, "Why, *the* world, of course."

"The world!" he says. "H'm! there's billions of them! . . . Next!"

That meant for me to stand aside. I done so, and a skyblue man with seven heads and only one leg hopped into my place. I took a walk. It just occurred to me, then, that all the myriads I had seen swarming to that gate, up to this time, were just like that creature. I tried to run across somebody I was acquainted with, but they were out of acquaintances of mine just then. So I thought the thing all over and finally sidled back there pretty meek and feeling rather stumped, as you may say.

"Well?" said the head clerk.

"Well, sir," I says, pretty humble, "I don't seem to make out which world it is I'm from. But you may know it from this--it's the one the Saviour saved."

He bent his head at the Name. Then he says, gently--

"The worlds He has saved are like to the gates of heaven in number-- none can count them. What astronomical system is your world in?--perhaps that may assist."

"It's the one that has the sun in it--and the moon--and Mars"--he shook his head at each name--hadn't ever heard of them, you see-- "and Neptune--and Uranus--and Jupiter--"

"Hold on!" says he--"hold on a minute! Jupiter . . . Jupiter . . . Seems to me we had a man from there eight or nine hundred years ago--but people from that system very seldom enter by this gate." All of a sudden he begun to look me so straight in the eyes that I thought he was going to bore through me. Then he says, very deliberate, "Did you come *straight here* from your system?"

"Yes, sir," I says--but I blushed the least little bit in the world when I said it.

He looked at me very stern, and says--

"That is not true; and this is not the place for prevarication. You wandered from your course. How did that happen?"

Says I, blushing again--

"I'm sorry, and I take back what I said, and confess. I raced a little with a comet one day--only just the least little bit--only tiniest lit--"

"So--so," says he--and without any sugar in his voice to speak of.

I went on, and says--

"But I only fell off just a bare point, and I went right back on my course again the minute the race was over."

"No matter--that divergence has made all this trouble. It has brought you to a gate that is billions of leagues from the right one. If you had gone to your own gate they would have known all about your world at once and there would have been no delay. But we will try to accommodate you." He turned to an under clerk and says--

"What system is Jupiter in?"

"I don't remember, sir, but I think there is such a planet in one of the little new systems away out in one of the thinly worlded corners of the universe. I will see."

He got a balloon and sailed up and up and up, in front of a map that was as big as Rhode Island. He went on up till he was out of sight, and by and by he came down and got something to eat and went up again. To cut a long story short, he kept on doing this for a day or two, and finally he came down and said he thought he had found that solar system, but it might be fly-specks. So he got a microscope and went back. It turned out better than he feared. He had rousted out our system, sure enough. He got me to describe our planet and its distance from the sun, and then he says to his chief--

"Oh, I know the one he means, now, sir. It is on the map. It is called the Wart."

Says I to myself, "Young man, it wouldn't be wholesome for you to go down *there* and call it the Wart."

Well, they let me in, then, and told me I was safe forever and wouldn't have any more trouble.

Then they turned from me and went on with their work, the same as if they considered my case all complete and shipshape. I was a good deal surprised by this, but I was diffident about speaking up and reminding them. I did so hate to do it, you know; it seemed a pity to bother them, they had so much on their hands. Twice I thought I would give up and let the thing go; so twice I started to leave, but immediately I thought what a figure I should cut stepping out amongst the redeemed in such a rig, and that made me hang back and come to anchor again. People got to eying me--clerks, you know--wondering why I didn't get under way. I couldn't stand this long--it was too uncomfortable. So at last I plucked up courage and tipped the head clerk a signal. He says--

"What! you here yet? What's wanting?"

Says I, in a low voice and very confidential, making a trumpet with my hands at his ear--

"I beg pardon, and you mustn't mind my reminding you, and seeming to meddle, but hain't you forgot something?"

He studied a second, and says--

"Forgot something? . . . No, not that I know of."

"Think," says I.

He thought. Then he says--

"No, I can't seem to have forgot anything. What is it?"

"Look at me," says I, "look me all over."

He done it.

"Well?" says he.

"Well," says I. "you don't notice anything? If I branched out amongst the elect looking like this, wouldn't I attract considerable attention?--wouldn't I be a little conspicuous?"

"Well," he says, "I don't see anything the matter. What do you lack?"

"Lack! Why, I lack my harp, and my wreath, and my halo, and my hymnbook, and my palm branch--I lack everything that a body naturally requires up here, my friend."

Puzzled? Peters, he was the worst puzzled man you ever saw. Finally he says--

"Well, you seem to be a curiosity every way a body takes you. I never heard of these things before;"

I looked at the man awhile in solid astonishment: then I says--

"Now, I hope you don't take it as an offence, for I don't mean any, but really, for a man that has been in the Kingdom as long as I reckon you have, you do seem to know powerful little about its customs."

"Its customs!" says he. "Heaven is a large place, good friend. Large empires have many and diverse customs. Even small dominions have, as you doubtless knew by what you have seen of the matter on a small scale in the Wart. How can you imagine I could ever learn the varied customs of the countless kingdoms of heaven? It makes my head ache to think of it. I know the customs that prevail in those portions inhabited by peoples that are appointed to enter by my own gate--and hark ye, that is quite enough knowledge for one individual to try to pack into his head in the thirtyseven millions of years I have devoted night and day to that study. But the idea of learning the customs of the whole appalling expanse of heaven--O man, how insanely you talk! Now I don't doubt that this odd costume you talk about is the fashion in that district of heaven you belong to, but you won't be conspicuous in this section without it."

I felt all right, if that was the case, so I bade him goodday and left. All day I walked towards the far end of a prodigious hall of the office, hoping to come out into heaven any moment, but it was a mistake. That hall was built on the general heavenly plan--it naturally couldn't be small. At last I got so tired I couldn't go any farther; so I sat down to rest, and began to tackle the queerest sort of strangers and ask for information, but I didn't get any; they couldn't understand my language, and I could not understand theirs. I got dreadfully lonesome. I was so downhearted and homesick I wished a hundred times I never had died. I turned back, of course. About noon next day, I got back at last and was on hand at the bookingoffice once more. Says I to the head clerk--

"I begin to see that a man's got to be in his own heaven to be happy."

"Perfectly correct," says he. "Did you imagine the same heaven would suit all sorts of men?"

"Well, I had that idea--but I see the foolishness of it. Which way am I to go to get to my district?"

He called the under clerk that had examined the map, and he gave me general directions. I thanked him and started; but he says--

"Wait a minute; it is millions of leagues from here. Go outside and stand on that red wishingcarpet; shut your eyes, hold your breath, and wish yourself there."

"I'm much obliged," says I; "why didn't you dart me through when I first arrived?"

"We have a good deal to think of here; it was your place to think of it and ask for it. Goodby; we probably sha'n't see you in this region for a thousand centuries or so."

"In that case, *o revoor*," says I.

I hopped onto the carpet and held my breath and shut my eyes and wished I was in the bookingoffice of my own section. The very next instant a voice I knew sung out in a business kind of a way--

"A harp and a hymnbook, pair of wings and a halo, size 13, for Cap'n Eli Stormfield, of San Francisco!--make him out a clean bill of health, and let him in."

I opened my eyes. Sure enough, it was a Pi Ute Injun I used to know in Tulare County; mighty good fellow--I remembered being at his funeral, which consisted of him being burnt and the other Injuns gauming their faces with his ashes and howling like wild-cats. He was powerful glad to see me, and you may make up your mind I was just as glad to see him, and felt that I was in the right kind of a heaven at last.

Just as far as your eye could reach, there was swarms of clerks, running and bustling around, tricking out thousands of Yanks and Mexicans and English and Arabs, and all sorts of people in their new outfits; and when they gave me my kit and I put on my halo and I took a look in the glass, I could have jumped over a house for joy, I was so happy. "Now *this* is something like!" says I. "Now," says I, "I'm all right--show me a cloud."

Inside of fifteen minutes I was a mile on my way towards the cloud-banks and about a million people along with me. Most of us tried to fly, but some got crippled and nobody made a success of it. So we concluded to walk, for the present, till we had had some wing practice.

We begun to meet swarms of folks who were coming back. Some had harps and nothing else; some had hymnbooks and nothing else; some had nothing at all; all of them looked meek and uncomfortable; one young fellow hadn't anything left but his halo, and he was carrying that in his hand, all of a sudden he offered it to me and says--

"Will you hold it for me a minute?"

Then he disappeared in the crowd. I went on. A woman asked me to hold her palm branch, and then *she* disappeared. A girl got me to hold her harp for her, and by George, *she* disappeared; and so on and so on, till I was about loaded down to the guards. Then comes a smiling old gentle-man and asked me to hold *his* things. I swabbed off the perspiration and says, pretty tart--

"I'll have to get you to excuse me, my friend,--*I* ain't no hat-rack."

About this time I begun to run across piles of those traps, lying in the road. I just quietly dumped my extra cargo along with them. I looked around, and, Peters, that whole nation that was following me were loaded down the same as I'd been. The return crowd had got them to hold their things a minute, you see. They all dumped their loads, too, and we went on.

When I found myself perched on a cloud, with a million other people, I never felt so good in my life. Says I, "Now this is according to the promises; I've been having my doubts, but now I *am* in heaven, sure enough." I gave my palm branch a wave or two, for luck, and then I tautened up my harp-strings and struck in. Well, Peters, you can't imagine anything like the row we made. It was grand to listen to, and made a body thrill all over, but there was considerable many tunes going on at once, and that was a drawback to the harmony, you understand; and then there was a lot of Injun tribes, and they kept up such another war-whooping that they kind of took the tuck out of the music. By and by I quit performing, and judged I'd take a rest. There was quite a nice mild old gentleman sitting next me, and I noticed he didn't take a hand; I encouraged him, but he said he was naturally bashful, and was afraid to try before so many people. By and by the old gentleman said he never could seem to enjoy music somehow. The fact was, I was beginning to feel the same way; but I didn't say anything. Him and I had a considerable long silence, then, but of course it warn't noticeable in that place. After about sixteen or seventeen hours, during which I played and sung a little, now and then--always the same tune, because I didn't know any other--I laid down my harp and begun to fan myself with my palm branch. Then we both got to sighing pretty regular. Finally, says he--

"Don't you know any tune but the one you've been pegging at all day?"

"Not another blessed one," says I.

"Don't you reckon you could learn another one?" says he.

"Never," says I; "I've tried to, but I couldn't manage it."

"It's a long time to hang to the one--eternity, you know."

"Don't break my heart," says I; "I'm getting lowspirited enough already."

After another long silence, says he--

"Are you glad to be here?"

Says I, "Old man, I'll be frank with you. This *ain't* just as my near idea of bliss as I thought it was going to be, when I used to go to church."

Says he, "What do you say to knocking off and calling it half a day?"

"That's me," says I. "I never wanted to get off watch so bad in my life."

So we started. Millions were coming to the cloudbank all the time, happy and hosannahing; millions were leaving it all the time, looking mighty quiet, I tell you. We laid for the newcomers, and pretty soon I'd got them to hold all my things a minute, and then I was a free man again and most outrageously happy. Just then I ran across old Sam Bartlett, who had been dead a long time, and stopped to have a talk with him. Says I--

"Now tell me--is this to go on forever? Ain't there anything else for a change?"

Says he--

"I'll set you right on that point very quick. People take the figurative language of the Bible and the allegories for literal, and the first thing they ask for when they get here is a halo and a harp, and so on. Nothing that's harmless and reasonable is refused a body here, if he asks it in the right spirit. So they are outfitted with these things without a word. They go and sing and play just about one day, and that's the last you'll ever see them in the choir. They don't need anybody to tell them that that sort of thing wouldn't make a heaven--at least not a heaven that a sane man could stand a week and remain sane. That cloudbank is placed where the noise can't disturb the old inhabitants, and so there ain't any harm in letting everybody get up there and cure himself as soon as he comes.

"Now you just remember this--heaven is as blissful and lovely as it can be; but it's just the busiest place you ever heard of. There ain't any idle people here after the first day. Singing hymns and waving palm branches through all eternity is pretty when you hear about it in the pulpit, but it's as poor a way to put in valuable time as a body could contrive. It would just make a heaven of warbling ignoramuses, don't you see? Eternal Rest sounds comforting in the pulpit, too. Well, you try it once, and see how heavy time will hang on your hands. Why, Stormfield, a man like you, that had been active and stirring all his life would go mad in six months in a heaven where he hadn't anything to do. Heaven is the very last place to come to *rest* in,--and don't you be afraid to bet on that!"

Says I--

"Sam, I'm as glad to hear it as I thought I'd be sorry. I'm glad I come, now."

Says he--

"Cap'n, ain't you pretty physically tired?"

Says I--

"Sam, it ain't my name for it! I'm dog-tired."

"Just so--just so. You've earned a good sleep, and you'll get it. You've earned a good appetite, and you'll enjoy your dinner. It's the same here as it is on earth--you've got to earn a thing, square and honest, before you enjoy it. You can't enjoy first and earn afterwards. But there's this difference, here: you can choose your own occupation, and all the powers of heaven will be put forth to help you make a success of it, if you do your level best. The shoemaker on earth that had the soul of a poet in him won't have to make shoes here."

"Now that's all reasonable and right," says I. "Plenty of work, and the kind you hanker after; no more pain, no more suffering--"

"Oh, hold on; there's plenty of pain here--but it don't kill. There's plenty of suffering here, but it don't last. You see, happiness ain't a *thing in itself*--it's only a *contrast* with something that ain't pleasant. That's all it is. There ain't a thing you can mention that is happiness in its own self--it's only so by contrast with the other thing. And so, as soon as the novelty is over and the force of the contrast dulled, it ain't happiness any longer, and you have to get something fresh. Well, there's plenty of pain and suffering in heaven--consequently there's plenty of contrasts, and just no end of happiness."

Says I, "It's the sensiblest heaven I've heard of, yet, Sam, though it's about as different from the one I was brought up on as a live princess is different from her own wax figger."

Along in the first months I knocked around about the Kingdom, making friends and looking at the country, and finally settled down in a pretty likely region, to have a rest before taking another start. I went on making acquaintances and gathering up information. I had a good deal of talk with an old bald-headed angel by the name of Sandy McWilliams. He was from somewhere in New Jersey. I went about with him, considerable. We used to lay around, warm afternoons, in the shade of a rock, on some meadow-ground that was pretty high and out of the marshy slush of his cranberry-farm, and there we used to talk about all kinds of things, and smoke pipes. One day, says I--

"About how old might you be, Sandy?"

"Seventytwo."

"I judged so. How long you been in heaven?"

"Twenty-seven years, come Christmas."

"How old was you when you come up?"

"Why, seventy-two, of course."

"You can't mean it!"

"Why can't I mean it?"

"Because, if you was seventy-two then, you are naturally ninety-nine now."

"No, but I ain't. I stay the same age I was when I come."

"Well," says I, "come to think, there's something just here that I want to ask about. Down below, I always had an idea that in heaven we would all be young, and bright, and spry."

"Well, you *can* be young if you want to. You've only got to wish."

"Well, then, why didn't you wish?"

"I did. They all do. You'll try it, some day, like enough; but you'll get tired of the change pretty soon."

"Why?"

"Well, I'll tell you. Now you've always been a sailor; did you ever try some other business?"

"Yes, I tried keeping grocery, once, up in the mines; but I couldn't stand it; it was too dull--no stir, no storm, no life about it; it was like being part dead and part alive, both at the same time. I wanted to be one thing or t'other. I shut up shop pretty quick and went to sea."

"That's it. Grocery people like it, but you couldn't. You see you wasn't used to it. Well, I wasn't used to being young, and I couldn't seem to take any interest in it. I was strong, and handsome, and had curly hair,--yes, and wings, too!--gay wings like a butterfly. I went to picnics and dances and parties with the fellows, and tried to carry on and talk nonsense with the girls, but it wasn't any use; I couldn't take to it--fact is, it was an awful bore. What I wanted was early to bed and early to rise, and something to *do;* and when my work was done, I wanted to sit quiet, and smoke and think--not tear around with a parcel of giddy young kids. You can't think what I suffered whilst I was young."

"How long was you young?"

"Only two weeks. That was plenty for me. Laws, I was so lonesome! You see, I was full of the knowledge and experience of seventytwo years; the deepest subject those young folks could strike was only *abc* to me. And to hear them argue--oh, my! it would have been funny, if it hadn't been so pitiful. Well, I was so hungry for the ways and the sober talk I was used to, that I tried to ring in with the old people, but they wouldn't have it. They considered me a conceited young up-start, and gave me the cold shoulder. Two weeks was a-plenty for me. I was glad to get back my bald head again, and my pipe, and my old drowsy reflections in the shade of a rock or a tree."

"Well," says I, "do you mean to say you're going to stand still at seventy-two, forever?"

"I don't know, and I ain't particular. But I ain't going to drop back to twenty-five any more--I know that, mighty well. I know a sight more than I did twenty-seven years ago, and I enjoy learning, all the time, but I don't seem to get any older. That is, bodily--my mind gets older, and stronger, and better seasoned, and more satisfactory."

Says I, "If a man comes here at ninety, don't he ever set himself back?"

"Of course he does. He sets himself back to fourteen: tries it a couple of hours, and feels like a fool; sets himself forward to twenty; it ain't much improvement; tries thirty, fifty, eighty, and finally ninety--finds he is more at home and comfortable at the same old figure he is used to than any other way. Or, if his mind begun to fail him on earth at eighty, that's where he finally sticks up here. He sticks at the place where his mind was last at its best, for there's where his enjoyment is best, and his ways most set and established."

"Does a chap of twentyfive stay always twenty-five, and look it?"

"If he is a fool, yes. But if he is bright, and ambitious and industrious, the knowledge he gains and the experience he has, change his ways and thoughts and likings, and make him find his best pleasure in the company of people above that age; so he allows his body to take on that look of as many added years as he needs to make him comfortable and proper in that sort of society; he lets his body go on taking the look of age, according as he progresses, and by and by he will be bald and wrinkled outside, and wise and deep within."

"Babies the same?"

"Babies the same. Laws, what asses we used to be, on earth, about these things! We said we'd be always young in heaven. We didn't say *how* young--we didn't think of that, perhaps--that is, we didn't all think alike, anyway. When I was a boy of seven, I suppose I thought we'd all be twelve, in heaven; when I was twelve, I suppose I thought we'd all be eighteen or twenty in heaven; when I was forty, I begun to go back; I remember I hoped we'd all be about *thirty* years old in heaven. Neither a man nor a boy ever thinks the age he *has* is exactly the best one--he puts the *right* age a few years older or a few years younger than he is. Then he makes the ideal age the general age of the heavenly people. And he expects everybody to *stick* at that age--stand stock-still--and expects them to enjoy it!--Now just think of the idea of standing still in heaven! Think of a heaven made up entirely of hoop-rolling, marble-playing cubs of seven years!--or of awkward, diffident, sentimental immaturities of nineteen!--or of vigorous people of thirty, healthy-minded, brimming with ambition, but chained hand and foot to that one age and its limitations like so many helpless galley-slaves! Think of the dull sameness of a society made up of people all of one age and one set of looks, habits, tastes and feelings. Think how superior to it earth would be, with its variety of types and faces and ages, and the enlivening attrition of the myriad interests that come into pleasant collision in such a variegated society."

"Look here," says I, "do you know what you're doing?"

"Well, what am I doing?"

"You are making heaven pretty comfortable in one way, but you are playing the mischief with it in another."

"How d'you mean?"

"Well," I says, "take a young mother that's lost her child, and--"

"'Sh!" he says. "Look!"

It was a woman. Middle-aged, and had grizzled hair. She was walking slow, and her head was bent down, and her wings hanging limp and droopy; and she looked ever so tired, and was crying, poor thing! She passed along by, with her head down, that way, and the tears running down her face, and didn't see us. Then Sandy said, low and gentle, and full of pity:

"*She's* hunting for her child! No. *found* it, I reckon. Lord, how she's changed! But I recognized her in a minute, though it's twenty-seven years since I saw her. A young mother she was, at about twenty-two or four, or along there; and blooming and lovely and sweet--oh, just a flower! And all her heart and all her soul was wrapped up in her child, her little girl, two years old. And it died, and she went wild with grief, just wild! Well, the only comfort she had was that she'd see her child again, in heaven--'never more to part,' she said, and kept on saying it over and over, 'never more to part.' And the words made her happy; yes, they did; they made her joyful; and when I was dying, twentyseven years ago, she told me to find her child the first thing, and say she was coming--'soon, soon, *very* soon, she hoped and believed!'"

"Why, it's pitiful, Sandy."

He didn't say anything for a while, but sat looking at the ground, thinking. Then he says, kind of mournful:

"And now she's come!"

"Well? Go on."

"Stormfield, maybe she hasn't found the child, but *I* think she has. Looks so to me. I've seen cases before. You see, she's kept that child in her head just the same as it was when she jounced it her arms a little chubby thing. But here it didn't elect to *stay* a child. No, it elected to grow up, where it did. And in these twentyseven years it has learned all the deep scientific learning there is to learn, and is studying and studying and learning and learning more and more, all the time, and don't give a damn for anything *but* learning; just learning, and discussing gigantic problems with people like herself."

"Well?"

"Stormfield, don't you see? Her mother knows *cranberries,* and how to tend them, and pick them, and put them up, and market them; and not another blamed thing! Her and her daughter can't be any more company for each other *now* than mud turtle and bird o' paradise. Poor thing, she was looking for a baby to jounce; *I* think she's struck a disappointment."

"Sandy, what will they do--stay unhappy forever in heaven?"

"No, they'll come together and get adjusted by and by. But this year, and not next. By and by."

I had been having considerable trouble with my wings. The day after I helped the choir I made a dash or two with them, but was not lucky. First off, I flew thirty yards, and then fouled an Irishman and brought him down--brought us both down, in fact. Next, I had a collision with a Bishop--and bowled him down of course. We had some sharp words, and I felt pretty cheap to come banging into a grave old person like that, with a million strangers looking on and smiling to themselves.

I saw I hadn't got the hang of the steering, and so couldn't rightly tell where I was going to bring up when I started. I went afoot the rest of the day, and let my wings hang. Early next morning I went to a private place to have some practice. I got up on a pretty high rock, and got a good start, and went swooping down, aiming for a bush a little over three hundred yards off; but I couldn't seem to calculate for the wind, which was about two points abaft my beam. I could see I was going considerable to looard of the bush, so I worked my starboard wing slow and went ahead strong on the port one, but it wouldn't answer; I could see I was going to broach to, so I slowed down on both, and lit. I went back to the rock and took another chance at it. I aimed two or three points to starboard of the bush--yes, more than that--enough so as to make it nearly a head-wind. I done well enough, but made pretty poor time. I could see, plain enough, that on a head-wind, wings was a mistake. I could see that a body could sail pretty close to the wind, but he couldn't go in the wind's eye. I could see that if I wanted to go a-visiting any distance from home, and the wind was ahead, I might have to wait days, maybe, for a change; and I could see, too, that these things could not be any use at all in a gale; if you tried to run before the wind, you would make a mess of it, for there isn't any way to shorten sail--like reefing, you know--you have to take it *all* in--shut your feathers down flat to your sides. That would *land* you, of course. You could lay to, with your head to the wind--that is the best you could do, and right hard work you'd find it, too. If you tried any other game, you would founder, sure.

I judge it was about a couple of weeks or so after this that I dropped old Sandy McWilliams a note one day--it was a Tuesday--and asked him to come over and take his manna and quails with me next day; and the first thing he did when he stepped in was to twinkle his eye in a sly way, and say,--

"Well, Cap, what you done with your wings?"

I saw in a minute that there was some sarcasm done up in that rag somewheres, but I never let on. I only says,--

"Gone to the wash."

"Yes," he says, in a dry sort of way, "they mostly go to the wash--about this time--I've often noticed it. Fresh angels are powerful neat. When do you look for 'em back?"

"Day after to-morrow," says I.

He winked at me, and smiled.

Says I,--

"Sandy, out with it. Come--no secrets among friends. I notice you don't ever wear wings--and plenty others don't. I've been making an ass of myself--is that it?"

"That is about the size of it. But it is no harm. We all do it at first. It's perfectly natural. You see, on earth we jumped to such foolish conclusions as to things up here. In the pictures we always saw the angels with wings on--and that was all right; but we jumped to the conclusion that that was their way of getting around--and that was all wrong. The wings ain't anything but a uniform, that's all. When they are in the field--so to speak--they always wear them; you never see an angel going with a message anywhere without his wings, any more than you would see a military officer presiding at a court-martial without his uniform, or a postman delivering letters, or a policeman walking his beat, in plain clothes. But they ain't to *fly* with! The wings are for show, not for use. Old experienced angels are like officers of the regular army--they dress plain, when they are off duty. New angels are like the militia--never shed the uniform--always fluttering and floundering around in their wings, butting people down, flapping here, and there, and everywhere, always imagining they are attracting the admiring eye--well, they just think they are the very most important people in heaven. And when you see one of them come sailing around with one wing tipped up and t'other down, you make up your mind he is saying to himself: 'I wish Mary Ann in Arkansaw could see me now. I reckon she'd wish she hadn't shook me.' No, they're just for show, that's all--only for show."

I judge you've got it about right, Sandy," says I.

"Why, look at it yourself," says he. "You ain't built for wings--no man is. You know what a grist of years it took you to come here from the earth--and yet you were booming along faster than any cannon-ball could go. Suppose you had to fly that distance with your wings--wouldn't eternity have been over before you got here? Certainly. Well, angels have to go to the earth every day--millions of them--to appear in visions to dying children and good people, you know--it's the heft of their business. They appear with their wings, of course, because they are on official service, and because the dying persons wouldn't know they were angels if they hadn't wings--but do you reckon they fly with them? It stands to reason they don't. The wings would wear out before they got half-way: even the pinfeathers would be gone; the wing frames would be as bare as kite sticks before the paper is pasted on. The distances in heaven are billions of times greater; angels have to go all over heaven every day; could they do it with their wings alone? No, indeed; they wear the wings for style, but they travel any distance in an instant by *wishing*. The wishing-carpet of the Arabian Nights was a sensible idea--but our earthly idea of angels flying these awful distances with their clumsy wings was foolish.

"Our young saints, of both sexes, wear wings all the time--blazing red ones, and blue and green, and gold, and variegated, and rainbowed, and ring-streaked-and-striped ones and nobody finds faults. It is suitable to their time of life. The things are beautiful, and they set the young people off. They are the most striking and lovely part of their outfit--a halo don't *begin.*"

"Well," says I, "I've tucked mine away in the cupboard, and I allow to let them lay there till there's mud."

"Yes--or a reception."

"What's that?"

"Well, you can see one to-night if you want to. There's a barkeeper from Jersey City going to be received."

"Go on--tell me about it."

"This barkeeper got converted at a Moody and Sankey meeting, in New York, and started home on the ferryboat, and there was a collision and he got drowned. He is of a class that thinks all heaven goes wild with joy when a particularly hard lot like him is saved; they think all heaven turns out hosannahing to welcome them; they think there isn't anything talked about in the realms of the blest but their case, for that day. This barkeeper thinks there hasn't been such another stir here in years, as his coming is going to raise.-- And I've always noticed this peculiarity about a dead barkeeper--he not only expects all hands to turn out when he arrives, but he expects to be received with a torch-light procession."

"I reckon he is disappointed, then."

"No, he isn't. No man is allowed to be disappointed here. Whatever he wants, when he comes--that is, any reasonable and unsacrilegious thing--he can have. There's always a few millions or billions of young folks around who don't want any better entertainment than to fill up their lungs and swarm out with their torches and have a high time over a barkeeper. It tickles the barkeeper till he can't rest, it makes a charming lark for the young folks, it don't do anybody any harm, it don't cost a rap, and it keeps up the place's reputation for making all comers happy and content."

"Very good. I'll be on hand and see them land the barkeeper."

"It is manners to go in full dress. You want to wear your wings, you know, and your other things."

"Which ones?"

"Halo, and harp, and palm branch, and all that."

"Well," says I, "I reckon I ought to be ashamed of myself but the fact is I left them laying around that day I resigned from the choir. I haven't got a rag to wear but this robe and the wings."

"That's all right. You'll find they've been raked up and saved for you. Send for them."

"I'll do it, Sandy. But what was it you was saying about unsacrilegious things, which people expect to get, and will be disappointed about?"

"Oh, there are a lot of such things that people expect and don't get. For instance, theres a Brooklyn preacher by the name of Talmage, who is laying up a considerable disappointment for himself. He says, every now and then in his sermons, that the first thing he does when he gets to heaven, will be to fling his arms around Abraham, Isaac and Jacob, and kiss them and weep on them. There's millions of people down there on earth that are promising themselves the same thing. As many as sixty thousand people arrive here every single day, that want to run straight to Abraham, Isaac and Jacob, and hug them and weep on them. Now mind you, sixty thousand a day is a pretty heavy contract or those old people. If they were a mind to allow it, they wouldn't ever have anything to do, year in and year out, but stand up and be hugged and wept on thirty-two hours in the twenty-four. They would be tired out and as wet as muskrats all the time. What would heaven be, to *them?* It would be a mighty good place to get out of--you know that, yourself. Those are kind and gentle old Jews, but they ain't any fonder of kissing the emotional high-lights of Brooklyn than you be. You mark my words, Mr. T.'s endearments are going to be declined, with thanks. There are limits to the privileges of the elect, even in heaven. Why, if Adam was to show himself to every new comer that wants to call and gaze at him and strike him for his autograph, he would never have time to do anything else but just that. Talmage has said he is going to give Adam some of his attention, as well as A., I. and J. But he will have to change his mind about that."

"Do you think Talmage will really come here?"

"Why, certainly, he will; but don't you be alarmed; he will run with his own kind, and there's plenty of them. That is the in charm of heaven--there's all kinds here--which wouldn't be the case if you let the preachers tell it. Anybody can find the sort he prefers, here, and he just lets the others alone, and they let him alone. When the Deity builds a heaven, it is built right, and on a liberal plan."

Sandy sent home for his things, and I sent for mine, and about nine in the evening we begun to dress. Sandy says.--

"This is going to be a grand time for you, Stormy. Like as not some of the patriarchs will turn out."

"No, but will they?"

"Like as not. Of course they are pretty exclusive. They hardly ever show themselves to the common public. I believe they never turn out except for an eleventh-hour convert. They wouldn't do it then, only earthly tradition makes a grand show pretty necessary on that kind of an occasion."

"Do they all turn out, Sandy?"

"Who?--all the patriarchs? Oh, no--hardly ever more than a couple. You will be here fifty thousand years--maybe more--before you get a glimpse of all the patriarchs and prophets. Since I have been here, Job has been to the front once, and once Ham and Jeremiah both at the same time. But the finest thing that has happened in my day was a year or so ago; that was Charles Peace's reception--him they called 'the Bannercross Murderer'--and Englishman. There were four patriarchs and two prophets on the Grand Stand that time--there hasn't been anything like it since Captain Kidd came; Abel was there--the first time in twelve hundred years. A report got around that Adam was coming; well, of course, Abel was enough to bring a crowd, all by himself, but there is nobody that can draw like Adam. It was a false report, but it got around, anyway, as I say, and it will be a long day before I see the like of it again. The reception was in the English department, of course, which is eight hundred and eleven million miles from the New Jersey line. I went, along with a good many of my neighbors, and it was a sight to see, I can tell you. Flocks came from all the departments. I saw Esquimaux there, and Tartars, Negroes, Chinamen--people from everywhere. You see a mixture like that in the Grand Choir, the first day you land here, but you hardly ever see it again. There were billions of people; when they were singing or hosannahing, the noise was wonderful; and even when their tongues were still the drumming of the wings was nearly enough to burst your head, for all the sky was as thick as if it was snowing angels. Although Adam was not here, it was a great time anyway, because we had three archangels on the Grand Stand--it is a seldom thing that even one comes out."

"What did they look like. Sandy?"

"Well, they had shining faces, and shining robes, and wonderful rainbow wings, and they stood eighteen feet high, and wore swords, and held their heads up in a noble way, and looked like soldiers."

"Did they have halos?"

"No--anyway, not the hoop kind. The archangels and the upper-class patriarchs wear a finer thing than that. It is a round, solid, splendid glory of gold, that is blinding to look at. You have often see a patriarch in a picture, on earth, with that thing on--you remember it?--he looks as if he had his head in a brass platter. That don't give you the right idea of it at all--it is much more shining and beautiful."

"Did you talk with those archangels and patriarchs, Sandy?

"Who *I*? Why, what can you be thinking about, Stormy? I ain't worthy to speak to such as they."

"Is Talmage?"

"Of course not. You have got the same mixed-up idea about these things that everybody has down there. I had it once, but I got over it. Down there they talk of the heavenly King--and that is right--but then they go right on speaking as if this was a republic and everybody was on a dead level with everybody else, and privileged to fling his arms around anybody he comes across, and be hail-fellow-well-met with all the elect, from the highest down. How tangled up and absurd that is! How are you going to have a republic under a king? How are you going to have a republic at all, where the head of the government is absolute, holds his place forever, and has no parliament, no council to meddle or make in his affairs, nobody voted for, nobody elected, nobody in the whole universe with a voice in the government, nobody asked to take a hand in its matters, and nobody *allowed* to do it? Fine republic, ain't it?"

"Well, yes--it is a little different from the idea I had--but I thought I might go around and get acquainted with the grandees, anyway--not exactly splice the main-brace with them, you know, but shake hands and pass the time of day."

"Could Tom, Dick and Harry call on the Cabinet of Russia and do that?--on Prince Gortschakoff, for instance?"

"I reckon not, Sandy."

"Well, this is Russia--only more so. There's not the shadow of a republic about it anywhere. There are ranks, here. There are viceroys, princes, governors, sub-governors, sub-sub-governors, and a hundred orders of nobility, grading along down from grand-ducal archangels, stage by stage, till the general level is struck, where there ain't any titles. Do you know what a prince of the blood is, on earth?"

"No."

"Well, a prince of the blood don't belong to the royal family exactly, and he don't belong to the mere nobility of the kingdom; he is lower than the one, and higher than t'other. That's about the position of the patriarchs and prophets here. There's some mighty high nobility here--people that you and I ain't worthy to polish sandals for--and *they* ain't worthy to polish sandals for the patriarchs and prophets. That gives you a kind of an idea of their rank, don't it? You begin to see how high up they are, don't you? Just to get a two-minute glimpse of one of them is a thing for a body to remember and tell about for a thousand years. Why, Captain, just think of this: if Abraham was to set his foot down here by this door, there would be a railing set up around that foot-track right away, and a shelter put over it, and people would flock here from all over heaven, for hundreds and hundreds of years, to look at it. Abraham is one of the parties that Mr. Talmage, of Brooklyn, is going to embrace, and kiss, and weep on, when he comes. He wants to lay in a good stock of tears, you know, or five to one he will go dry before he gets a chance to do it."

"Sandy," says I, "I had an idea that *I* was going to be equal with everybody here, too, but I will let that drop. It don't matter, and I am plenty happy enough anyway."

"Captain, you are happier than you would be, the other way. These old patriarchs and prophets have got ages the start of you; they know more in two minutes than you know in year. Did you ever try to have a sociable improving-time discussing winds, currents and variations of compass with an undertaker?"

"I get your idea, Sandy. He couldn't interest me. He would be an ignoramus in such things--he would bore me, and I would bore him."

"You have got it. You would bore the patriarchs when you talked, and when they talked they would shoot over your head. By and by you would say, "Good morning, your Eminence, I will call again"--but you wouldn't. Did you ever ask the slush-boy to come up in the cabin and take dinner with you?"

"I get your drift again, Sandy. l wouldn't be used to such grand people as the patriarchs and prophets, and I would be sheepish and tongue-tied in their company, and mighty glad to get out of it. Sandy, which is the highest rank, patriarch or prophet?"

"Oh, the prophets hold over the patriarchs. The newest prophet, even, is of a sight more consequence than the oldest patriarch. Yes, sir, Adam himself has to walk behind Shakespeare."

"Was Shakespeare a prophet?"

"Of course he was; and so was Homer, and heaps more. But Shakespeare and the rest have to walk behind a common tailor from Tennessee, by the name of Billings; and behind a horse-doctor named Sakka, from

Afghanistan. Jeremiah, and Billings and Buddah walk together, side by side, right behind a crowd from planets not in our astronomy; next come a dozen or two from Jupiter and other worlds; next come Daniel, and Sakka and Confucius; next a lot from systems outside of ours; next come Ezekiel, and Mahomet, Zoroaster, and a knife-grinder from ancient Egypt; then there is a long string, and after them, away down toward the bottom, come Shakespeare and Homer, and a shoemaker named Marais, from the back settlements of France."

"Have they really rung in Mahomet and all those other heathens?"

"Yes--they all had their message, and they all get their reward. The man who don't get his reward on earth, needn't bother--he will get it here, sure."

"But why did they throw off on Shakespeare, that way, and put him away down there below those shoemakers and horse-doctors and knife-grinders--a lot of people nobody ever heard of?"

"That is the heavenly justice of it--they warn't rewarded according to their deserts, on earth, but here they get their rightful rank. That tailor Billings, from Tennessee, wrote poetry that Homer and Shakespeare couldn't begin to come up to; but nobody would print it, nobody read it but his neighbors, an ignorant lot, and they laughed at it. Whenever the village had a drunken frolic and a dance, they would drag him in and crown him with cabbage leaves, and pretend to bow down to him; and one night when he was sick and nearly starved to death, they had him out and crowned him, and then they rode him on a rail about the village, and everybody followed along, beating tin pans and yelling. Well, he died before morning. He wasn't ever expecting to go to heaven, much less that there was going to be any fuss made over him, so I reckon he was a good deal surprised when the reception broke on him."

"Was you there, Sandy?"

"Bless you, no!"

"Why? Didn't you know it was going to come off?"

"Well, I judge I did. It was the talk of these realms--not for a day, like this barkeeper business, but for twenty years before the man died."

"Why the mischief didn't you go, then?"

"Now how you talk! The like of me go meddling around at the reception of a prophet? A mudsill like me trying to push in and help receive an awful grandee like Edward J. Billings? Why, I should have been laughed at for a billion miles around. I shouldn't ever heard the last of it."

"Well, who did go, then?"

"Mighty few people that you and I will ever get a chance to see, Captain. Not a solitary commoner ever has the luck to see a reception of a prophet, I can tell you. All the nobility, and all the patriarchs and prophets--every last one of them and all the archangels, and all the princes and governors and viceroys, were there,--and *no* small fry--not a single one. And mind you, I'm not talking about only the grandees from *our* world, but the princes and patriarchs and so on from *all* the worlds that shine in our sky, and from billions more that belong in systems upon systems away outside of the one our sun is in. There were some prophets and patriarchs there that ours ain't a circumstance to, for rank and illustriousness and all that. Some were from Jupiter and other worlds in our own system, but the most celebrated were three poets, Saa, Bo and Soof, from great planets in three different and very remote systems. These three names are common and familiar in every nook and corner of heaven, clear from one end of it to the other--fully as well known as the eighty Supreme Archangels, in fact--whereas our Moses, and Adam, and the rest, have not been heard of outside of our world's little corner of heaven, except by a few very learned men scattered here and there--and they always spell their names wrong, and get the performances of one mixed up with the doings of another and they almost always locate them simply *in our solar system,* and think that is enough without going into little details such as naming the particular world they are from. It is like a learned Hindoo showing off how much he knows by saying Longfellow lived in the United States--as if he lived all over the United States, and as if the country was so small you couldn't throw a brick there without hitting him. Between you and me, it does gravel me, the cool way people from those monster worlds outside our system snub our little world, and even our system. Of course we think a good deal of Jupiter, because our world is only a potato to it, for size; but then there are worlds in other systems that Jupiter isn't even a mustard-seed to--like the planet Goobra, for instance, which you couldn't squeeze inside the orbit of Haley's comet without straining the rivets. Tourists from Goobra (I mean parties that lived and died there--natives) come here, now and then, and inquire about our world, and when they find out it is so little that a streak of lightning can flash clear around it in the eighth of a second, they have to lean up against something to laugh. Then they screw a glass into their eye and go to examining *us*, as if we were a curious kind of foreign bug, or something of that sort. One of them asked me how long our day was; and when I told him it was twelve hours long, as a general thing, he asked me if people where I was from considered it worth while to get up and wash for such a day as that. That is the way with those Goobra people--they can't seem to let a chance go by to throw it in your face that their day is three hundred and twenty-two of our years long. This young snob was just of age--he was six or seven thousand of his days old--say two million of our years--and he had all the puppy airs that belong to that time of life--that turning-point when a person has got over being a boy and yet ain't quite a man exactly. If it had been anywhere else but in heaven, I would have given him a piece of my mind. Well, anyway, Billings had the grandest reception that has been seen in thousands of centuries, and I think it will have a good effect. His name will be carried pretty far, and it will make our system talked about, and maybe our world, too, and raise us in the respect of the general public of heaven. Why, look here--Shakespeare walked backwards before that tailor from Tennessee, and scattered flowers for him to walk on, and Homer stood behind his chair and waited on him at the banquet. Of course that didn't go for much *there,* amongst all those big foreigners from other systems, as they hadn't heard of Shakespeare or Homer either, but it would amount to considerable down there on our little earth if they could know about it. I wish there was something *in* that miserable spiritualism, so we could send them word. That Tennessee village would set up a monument to Billings, then, and his autograph would outsell Satan's. Well, they had grand times at that reception--a small-fry noble from Hoboken told me all about it--Sir Richard Duffer, Baronet."

"What, Sandy, a nobleman from Hoboken? How is that?"

"Easy enough. Duffer kept a sausageshop and never saved a cent in his life because he used to give all his spare meat to the poor, in a quiet way. Not tramps,--no, the other sort--the sort that will starve before they will beg--honest square people out of work. Dick used to watch hungry-looking men and women and children, and track them home, and find out all about them from neighbors, and then feed them and find them work. As nobody ever *saw* him give anything to anybody, he had the reputation of being mean: he died with it, too, and everybody said it was a good riddance; but the minute he landed here, they made him a baronet, and the very first words Dick the sausage-maker of Hoboken heard when he stepped upon the heavenly shore were, "Welcome, Sir Richard Duffer!" It surprised him some, because he thought he had reasons to believe he was pointed for a warmer climate than this one."

All of a sudden the whole region fairly rocked under the crash of eleven hundred and one thunder blasts, all let off at once, and Sandy says,--

"There, that's for the barkeep."

I jumped up and says,--

"Then let's be moving along, Sandy; we don't want to miss any of this thing, you know."

"Keep your seat," he says; "he is only just telegraphed, that is all."

" How?"

"That blast only means that he has been sighted from the signal-station. He is off Sandy Hook. The committees will go down to meet him, now, and escort him in. There will be ceremonies and delays; they won't be coming up the Bay for a considerable time, yet. It is several billion miles away, anyway."

"*I* could have been a barkeeper and a hard lot just as well as not," says I, remembering the lonesome way I arrived, and how there wasn't any committee nor anything.

"I notice some regret in your voice," says Sandy. "and it is natural enough; but let bygones be bygones; you went according to your lights, and it is too late now to mend the thing."

"No, let it slide, Sandy, I don't mind. But you've got a Sandy Hook *here,* too, have you?"

"We've got everything here, just as it is below. All the States and Territories of the Union, and all the kingdoms of the earth and the islands of the sea are laid out here just as they are on the globe--all the same shape they are down there, and all graded to the relative size, only each State and realm and island is a good many billion times bigger here than it is below. There goes another blast."

"What is that one for?"

"That is only another fort answering the first one. They each have eleven hundred and one thunder blasts at a single dash--it is the usual salute for an eleventh-hour guest, a hundred for each hour and an extra one for the guest's sex; if it was a woman we would know it by their leaving off the extra gun."

"How do we know there's eleven hundred and one, Sandy, when they all go off at once?--and yet we certainly do know."

"Our intellects are a good deal sharpened up, here, in some ways, and that is one of them. Numbers and sizes and distances are so great, here, that we have to be made so we can *feel* them--our old ways of counting and measuring and ciphering wouldn't ever give us an idea of them, but would only confuse us and oppress us and make our heads ache."

After some more talk about this, I says: "Sandy, I notice that I hardly ever see a white angel; where I run across one white angel, I strike as many as a hundred million copper-colored ones--people that can't speak English. How is that?"

"Well, you will find it the same in any State or Territory of the American corner of heaven you choose to go to. I have shot along, a whole week on a stretch, and gone millions and millions of miles, through perfect swarms of angels, without ever seeing a single white one, or hearing a word I could understand. You see, America was occupied a billion years and more, by Indians and Aztecs, and that sort of folks, before a white man ever set his foot in it. During the first three hundred years after Columbus's discovery, there wasn't ever more than one good lecture audience of white people, all put together, in America--I mean the whole thing, British Possessions and all; in the beginning of our century there were only 6,000,000 or 7,000,000--say seven; 12,000,000 or 14,000,000 in 1825; say 23,000,000 in 1850; 40,000,000 in 1875. Our death-rate has always been 20 in 1000 per annum. Well, 140,000 died the first year of the century; 280,000 the twenty-fifth year, 500,000 the fiftieth year; about a million the seventy-fifth year. Now I am going to be liberal about this thing, and consider that fifty million whites have died in America from the beginning up to to-day--make it sixty, if you want to; make it a hundred million--it's no difference about a few millions one way or t'other. Well, now, you can see, yourself, that when you come to spread a little dab of people like that over these hundreds of billions of miles of American territory here in heaven, it is like scattering a ten-cent box of homoeopathic pills over the Great Sahara and expecting to find them again. You can't expect us to amount to anything in heaven, and we *don't*--now that is the simple fact, and we have got to do the best we can with it. The learned men from other planets and other systems come here and hang around a while, when they are touring around the Kingdom, and then go back to their own section of heaven and write a book of travels, and they give America about five lines in it. And what do they say about us? They say this wilderness is populated with a scattering few hundred thousand billions of red angels, with now and then a curiously complected *diseased* one. You see, they think we whites and the occasional nigger are Injuns that have been ached out or blackened by some leprous disease or other--for some peculiarly rascally *sin,* mind you. It is a mighty sour pill for us all, my friend--even the modestest of us, let alone the other kind, that think they are going to be received like a long-lost government bond, and hug Abraham into the bargain. I haven't asked you any of the particulars, Captain, but I judge it goes without saying--if my experience is worth anything--that there wasn't much of a hooraw made over you when you arrived-- now was there?"

"Don't mention it, Sandy," said I, coloring up a little "I wouldn't have had the family see it for any amount you are a mind to name. Change the subject, Sandy, change the subject."

"Well, do you think of settling in the California department of bliss?"

"I don't know. I wasn't calculating on doing anything really definite in that direction till the family come. I Thought I would just look around, meantime, in a quiet way, and make up my mind. Besides, I know a good many dead people, and I was calculating to hunt them up and swap a little gossip with them about friends, and old times, and one thing or another, and ask them how they like it here, as far as they have got. I reckon my wife will want to camp in the California range, though, because most all her departed will be there, and she likes to be with folks she knows."

"Don't you let her. You see what the Jersey district of heaven is for whites; well, the California district is a thousand times worse. It swarms with a mean kind of leather-headed mud-colored angels--and your nearest white neighbors is likely to be a million miles away. *What a man mostly misses, in heaven, is company*--company of his own sort and color and language. I have come near settling in the European part of heaven once or twice on that account."

"Well, why didn't you, Sandy?"

"Oh, various reasons. For one thing, although you see plenty of whites there, you can't understand any of them hardly, and so you go about as hungry for talk as you do here. I like to look at a Russian or a German or an Italian--I even like to look at a Frenchman if I ever have the luck to catch him engaged in anything that ain't indelicate--but *looking* don't cure the hunger--what you want is talk."

"Well, there's England, Sandy--the English district of heaven."

"Yes, but it is not so very much better than this end of the heavenly domain. As long as you run across Englishmen born this side of three hundred years ago, you are all right; but the minute you get back to Elizabeth's time the language begins to fog up, and the further back you go the foggier it gets. I had some talk with one Langland and a man by the name of Chaucer--old-time poets--but it was no use. I couldn't quite understand them and they couldn't quite understand me. I have had letters from them since, but it is such broken English I can't make it out. Back of those men's time the English are just simply foreigners, nothing more, nothing less; they talk Danish, German, Norman French, and sometimes a mixture of all three; back of *them,* they talk Latin, and ancient British, Irish, and Gaelic; and then back of these come billions and billions of pure savages that talk a gibberish that Satan himself couldn't understand. The fact is, where you strike one man in the English settlements that you can understand, you wade through awful swarms that talk something you can't make head nor tail of. You see, every country on earth has been overlaid so often, in the course of a billion years, with different kinds of people and different sorts of languages, that this sort of mongrel business was bound to be the result in heaven."

"Sandy," says I, "did you see a good many of the great people history tells about?"

"Yes--plenty. I saw kings and all sorts of distinguished people."

"Do the kings rank just as they did below?"

"No; a body can't bring his rank up here with him. Divine right is a good-enough earthly romance, but it don't go, here. Kings drop down to the general level as soon as they reach the realms of grace. I knew Charles the Second very well--one of the most popular comedians In the English section--draws first rate. There are better, of course--people that were never heard of on earth--but Charles is making a very good reputation indeed, and is considered a rising man. Richard the Lionhearted is in the prize-ring, and coming into considerable favor. Henry the Eighth is a tragedian, and the scenes where he kills people are done to the very life. Henry the Sixth keeps a religious-book stand."

"Did you ever see Napoleon, Sandy?"

"Often--sometimes in the Corsican range, sometimes in the French. He always hunts up a conspicuous place, and goes frowning around with his arms folded and his field-glass under his arm, looking as grand, gloomy and peculiar as his reputation calls for, and very much bothered because he don't stand as high, here, for a soldier, as he expected to."

"Why, who stands higher?"

"Oh, a *lot* of people *we* never heard of before the shoe-maker and horse-doctor and knife-grinder kind, you know--Clodhoppers from goodness knows where, that never handled a sword or fired a shot in their lives--but the soldiership was in them, though they never had a chance to show it. But here they take their right place, and Cæsar and Napoleon and Alexander have to take a back seat. The greatest military genius our world ever produced was a bricklayer from somewhere back of Boston--died during the Revolution--by the name of Absalom Jones. Wherever he goes, crowds flock to see him. You see, everybody knows that if he had had a chance he would have shown the world some generalship that would have made all generalship before look like child's play and 'prentice work. But he never got a chance; he tried heaps of times to enlist as a private, but he had lost both thumbs and a couple of front teeth, and the recruiting sergeant wouldn't pass him. However, as I say, everybody knows, now, what he *would* have been, and so they flock by the million to get a glimpse of him whenever they hear he is going to be anywhere. Cæsar, and Hannibal, and Alexander, and Napoleon are all on his staff, and ever so many more great generals; but the public hardly care to look at *them* when *he* is around. Boom! There goes another salute. The barkeeper's off quarantine now."

Sandy and I put on our things. Then we made a wish, and in a second we were at the reception-place. We stood on the edge of the ocean of space, and looked out over the dimness, but couldn't make out anything. Close by us was the Grand Stand--tier on tier of dim thrones rising up toward the zenith. From each side of it spread away the tiers of seats for the general public. They spread away for leagues and leagues--you couldn't see the ends. They were empty and still, and hadn't a cheerful look, but looked dreary, like a theater before anybody comes--gas turned down. Sandy says,--

"We'll sit down here and wait. We'll see the head of the procession come in sight away off yonder pretty soon, now."

Says I,--

"It's pretty lonesome. Sandy; I reckon there's a hitch somewheres. Nobody but just you and me--it ain't much of a display for the barkeeper."

"Don't you fret, it's all right. There'll be one more gunfire--then you'll see."

In a little while we noticed a sort of a lightish flush, away off on the horizon.

"Head of the torchlight procession." says Sandy.

It spread, and got lighter and brighter; soon it had a strong glare like a locomotive headlight; it kept on getting brighter and brighter till it was like the sun peeping above the horizon-line at sea--the big red rays shot high up into the sky.

"Keep your eyes on the Grand Stand and the miles of seats--sharp!" says Sandy, "and listen for the gun-fire."

Just then it burst out. "Boomboomboom!" like a million thunderstorms in one, and made the whole heavens rock. Then there was a sudden and awful glare of light all about us, and in that very instant every one of the millions of seats was occupied, and as far as you could see, in both directions, was just a solid pack of people, and the place was all splendidly lit up! It was enough to take a body's breath away. Sandy says,--

"That is the way we do it here. No time fooled away; nobody straggling in after the curtain's up. Wishing is quicker work than traveling. A quarter of a second ago these folks were millions of miles from here. When they heard the last signal, all they had to do was to wish, and here they are."

The prodigious choir struck up,--

We long to hear thy voice,
To see thee face to face.

It was noble music, but the uneducated chipped in and spoilt it, just as the congregations used to do on earth.

The head of the procession begun to pass, now, and it was a wonderful sight. It swept along, thick and solid, five hundred thousand angels abreast, and every angel carrying a torch and singing--the whirring thunder of the wings made a body's head ache. You could follow the line of the procession back, and slanting upward into the sky, far away in a glittering snakyrope, till it was only a faint streak in the distance. The rush went on and on, for a long time, and at last, sure enough, along comes the barkeeper, and then everybody rose, and a cheer went up that made the heavens shake, I tell you! He was all smiles, and had his halo tilted over one ear in a cocky way, and was the most satisfied-looking saint I ever saw. While he marched up the steps of the Grand Stand, the choir struck up.--

The whole wide heaven groans,

And waits to hear that voice.

There were four gorgeous tents standing side by side in the place of honor, on a broad railed platform in the center of the Grand Stand, with a shining guard of honor round about them. The tents had been shut up all this time. As the barkeeper climbed along up, bowing and smiling to everybody, and at last got to the platform, these tents were jerked up aloft all of a sudden, and we saw four noble thrones of gold, all caked with jewels, and in the two middle ones sat old white-whiskered men, and in the two others a couple of the most glorious and gaudy giants, with platter halos and beautiful armor. All the millions went down on their knees, and stared, and looked glad, and burst out into a joyful kind of murmurs. They said,--

"Two archangels!--that is splendid. Who can the others be?"

The archangels gave the barkeeper a stiff little military bow; the two old men rose; one of them said, "Moses and Esau welcome thee!" and then all the four vanished, and the thrones were empty.

The barkeeper looked a little disappointed, for he was calculating to hug those old people, I judge; but it was the gladdest and proudest multitude you ever saw--because they had seen Moses and Esau. Everybody was saying, "Did you see them?--I did--Esau's side face was to me, but I saw Moses full in the face, just as plain as I see you this minute!"

The procession took up the barkeeper and moved on with him again, and the crowd broke up and scattered. As we went along home, Sandy said it was a great success, and the barkeeper would have a right to be proud of it forever. And he said *we* were in luck. too; said we might attend receptions for forty thousand years to come, and not have a chance to see a brace of such grand moguls as Moses and Esau. We found afterwards that we had come near seeing another patriarch, and likewise a genuine prophet besides, but at the last moment they had sent regrets. Sandy said there would be a monument put up there, where Moses and Esau had stood, with the date and circumstances, and all about the whole business, and travelers would come for thousands of years and gawk at it, and climb over it, and scribble their names on it.

Micromegas

Voltaire

Francois-Marie Arouet (1694-1778) was born into a well-to-do family in Paris. He began writing at an early age using the pseudonym Voltaire.

Voltaire's family belonged to a Puritan sect that taught humility, the word of the scriptures, and a creed of other worldliness. Voltaire's father insisted he follow the rigors of religion and pursue an education, but his godfather Abbe de Chateauneuf, a noted poet and free thinker, encouraged Voltaire's creativity. His father's attempt to have him enter the field of law and diplomacy was unsuccessful. Voltaire was more interested in socializing and writing poetry.

Voltaire did not fear offending the aristocracy, but his self-assuredness resulted in the burning of his books and imprisonment in the Bastille. He eventually left his youthful hedonism behind to become a philosopher. He studied the philosophical teachings of John Locke, Sir Isaac Newton, and the Royal Society and was intrigued by the new cause and effect theories of science.

Voltaire became an historian of France and wrote several biographies of European kings. His histories include *The Century of Louis XIV* (1751), a classic of French literature, and *The Essay on the Customs and Genius of Nations*, which encompasses a history of the Occident and the Orient.

Among his works were the tragedies *Zaire* (1732) and *Alzire* (1736), the philosophical novels *Zadig* (1747) and *Candide* (1759), and the *Dictionnaire Philosophique* (1764).

IN ONE OF THOSE planets which revolve round the star named Sirius there was a young man of much wit with whom I had the honour to be acquainted during the last journey he made on our little ant-hill. He was called Micromegas, a name very well suited to all big men. His height was eight leagues: by eight leagues I mean twenty-four thousand geometrical paces of five feet each.

Some of the mathematicians, persons of unending public utility, will at once seize their pens and discover that since Mr. Micromegas, inhabitant of the land of Sirius, measures from head to foot twenty-four thousand paces (which make one hundred and twenty thousand royal feet), and since we other citizens of the earth measure barely five feet, and our globe has a circumference of nine thousand leagues--they will discover, I say, that it follows absolutely that the globe which produced Mr. Micromegas must have exactly twenty-one million six hundred thousand times more circumference than our little earth. Nothing in nature is simpler or more ordinary. The states of certain German and Italian sovereigns, round which one may travel completely in half an hour, compared with the empires of Turkey, Muscovy or China, are but a very feeble example of the prodigious differences which nature contrives everywhere.

His Excellency's stature being as I have stated, all our sculptors and all our painters will agree without difficulty that he is fifty thousand royal feet round the waist; which makes him very nicely proportioned.

As regards his mind, it is one of the most cultured we possess. He knows many things, and has invented a few. He had not yet reached the age of two-hundredandfifty, and was studying, according to custom, at the Jesuit college in his planet, when he solved by sheer brain power more than fifty of the problems of Euclid. That is eighteen more than Blaise Pascal who, after solving thirtytwo to amuse himself, by what his sister says, became a rather mediocre geometer and a very inferior metaphysician.

Towards the age of four hundred and fifty, when his childhood was past, he dissected many of those little insects which, not being a hundred feet across, escape the ordinary microscope. He wrote about them a very singular book which, however, brought him some trouble. The mufti of his country, a hairsplitter of great ignorance, found in it assertions that were suspicious, rash, offensive, unorthodox and savouring of heresy, and prosecuted him vigorously. The question was whether the bodies of Sirian fleas were made of the same substance as the bodies of Sirian slugs. Micromegas defended himself with spirit, and brought all the women to his way of thinking. The case lasted two hundred and twenty years, and ended by the mufti having the book condemned by some jurists who had not read it, and by the author being banished from the court for eight hundred years.

Micromegas was only moderately distressed at being banished from a court which was such a hotbed of meannesses and vexations. He wrote a very droll song against the mufti, which barely troubled that dignitary, and set forth on a journey from planet to planet in order to finish forming his heart and mind as the saying is.

Those who travel only in postchaise and coach will be astonished, doubtless, at the methods of transport in the world above, for we on our little mudheap cannot imagine anything outside the range of our ordinary experience. Our traveller had a marvellous knowledge of the laws of gravitation, and of the forces of repulsion and attraction. He made such good use of them that sometimes by the good forces of a comet, and at others by the help of a sunbeam, he and his friend went from globe to globe as a bird flutters from branch to branch. He traversed the Milky Way in no time, and I am forced to confess that he never saw across the stars with which it is sown the beautiful paradise that the illustrious and revered Mr. Derham boasts of having seen at the end of his spyglass. Not that I claim that Mr. Derham's eyesight is bad: God forbid! but Micromegas was on the spot, he is a sound observer, and I do not wish to contradict anyone.

After making a long tour round, Micromegas reached the globe of Saturn. Although he was accustomed to see new things, he could not, on beholding the littleness of the globe and its inhabitants, refrain from that superior smile to which even the wisest men are sometimes subject. For Saturn, after all, is hardly more than nine hundred times bigger than the earth, and its citizens are dwarfs only about a thousand fathoms tall. He and his friends laughed at them at first, much as an Italian musician, when he comes to France, laughs at Lulli's music. The Sirian had good brains, however, and understood quickly that a thinking being may very well not be ridiculous merely because his height is only six thousand feet. Having started by amazing the Saturnians, he finished by becoming intimate with them. He engaged in a close friendship with the secretary of the Academy of Saturn, a man of much wit who, although he had indeed invented nothing himself, yet has a very good idea of the inventions of others, and had produced quite passable light verses and weighty computations.

I will record here for the benefit of my readers an odd conversation which Micromegas had with Mr. Secretary.

When his Excellency had laid himself down, and the secretary had drawn near to his face, Micromegas spoke. "It must be admitted," he said, "that there is plenty of variety in nature."

"Yes", agreed the Saturnian, "nature is like a flowerbed of which the flowers . . ."

"Enough of your flowerbed," said the other.

"Nature," resumed the secretary "is like a company of fair women and dark women whose apparel. . ."

"What do I have to do with your dark women?" said the other.

"Well, then, nature is like a gallery of pictures whose features. . ."

"Oh, no!" said the traveller. " I tell you once more--nature is like nature. Why speak to compare it with anything?"

"To please you," answered the secretary.

"I do not want people to please me," replied the traveller. "I want them to teach me. Begin by telling me how many senses men in your world have."

"We have seventy-two," said the academician, "and we complain every day that we have not more. Our imagination surpasses our needs. We find that with our seventy-two senses, our ring and our five moons, we are too limited; and despite all our curiosity and the fairly large numbers of emotions arising from our seventy-two senses, we have plenty of time to be bored.

"That I can quite understand," said Micromegas, "for although in our world we have nearly a thousand senses, we still have an indescribable, vague yearning, an inexpressible restlessness, which warns us incessantly that we are of small account, and that there exist beings far more perfect. I have travelled a little, and I have seen mortals much below our level: I have also seen others for superior: but I have not seen any who have not more appetites than real needs, and more needs than contentment. One day, maybe, I shall reach the country where nobody lacks anything, but up to now no one has given me definite news of that country."

The Saturnian and the Sirian proceeded to tire themselves out with conjectures, but after many very ingenious and very uncertain arguments, they were forced to return to facts.

"How long do you live?" asked the Sirian.

"Ah! a very short time," replied the small man of Saturn.

"Just as with us," said the Sirian. "We are always complaining how short life is. It must be one of the universal laws of nature."

"Alas!" sighed the Saturnian. "We live for only five hundred complete revolutions of the sun. (That makes fifteen thousand years, or thereabouts, according to our reckoning.) As you can see, that means dying almost as soon as one is born. Our existence is a point, our duration a flash, our globe an atom. Hardly has one started to improve one's self a little than death arrives before one has any experience. For my part, I dare make no plans; I am like a drop of water in an immense ocean. I am ashamed, particularly before you, of the ridiculous figure I cut in this world."

"If you were not a philosopher," returned Micromegas, "I should fear to distress you by telling you that our life is seven hundred times as long as yours, but you know too well that when a man has to return his body to the earth whence it sprang, to bring life again to nature in another form--which is called dying--it is precisely the same thing, when the time for this metamorphosis arrives, whether he has lived a day or an eternity. I have been in countries where the people lived a thousand times longer than my people, and they still grumbled. But everywhere there are persons who know how to accept their fate and thank the author of nature. He has spread over this universe variety in profusion, coupled with a kind of wonderful uniformity. For instance, all thinking beings are different, and yet at bottom all resemble each other in their possession of the gifts of thought and aspiration. Matter is found everywhere, but in each globe it has different properties. How many of these properties do you count your matter as having?"

"If you speak of those properties," said the Saturnian, "without which we believe our globe could not exist in its present form, we count three hundred, such as extension, impenetrability, mobility, gravitation, divisibility, and so on."

"It appears," said the traveller, "that for the Creator's purposes regarding your insignificant abode that small number suffices. I admire His wisdom in everything. I see differences everywhere, but everywhere also I see proportion. Your world is small and so are its occupants; you have few sensations; your matter has few properties: all that is the work of Providence. Of what colour does your sun prove to be if you examine it closely?"

"Of a very yellowish-white," said the Saturnian; "and when we split up one of its rays we find it contains seven colours."

"Our sun," remarked the Sirian, "is reddish, and we have thirtynine primary colours. Of all the suns I have approached there are no two which are alike, just as with you there is no face which does not differ from all the other faces."

After several questions of this kind, he inquired how many essentially different substances they counted in Saturn. He learned that they counted only about thirty, such as God, Space, Matter, substances which have Extension and Feeling, substances which have Extension, Feeling and

Thought, substances which have Thought and no Extension; those which are self-conscious, those which are not selfconscious, and the rest. The Sirian, in whose world they counted three hundred, and who had discovered in his travels three thousand others, staggered the philosopher of Saturn. At last, after acquainting each other with a little of what they did know and a great deal of what they did not, after arguing during a complete revolution of the sun, they decided to make together a little philosophical journey.

Our two philosophers were ready to set forth into the atmosphere of Saturn, with a nice supply of mathematical instruments, when the Saturnian's mistress, who had heard of their approaching departure, came in tears to protest. She was a pretty little dark girl who stood only six hundred and sixty fathoms; but she made amends for her small stature by many other charms. "Ah! cruel man," she cried, "when after resisting you for fifteen hundred years I was beginning at last to give way, when I have passed barely a hundred years in your arms, you leave me to go on a journey with a giant from another world. Away with you! your intentions are not serious, you have never had any love: if you were a real Saturnian you would be faithful. Where are you going to gad about? What do you seek? Our five moons are less errant than you, our ring is less variable. One thing is certain! I shall never love anyone else."

The philosopher kissed her, wept with her, for all that he was a philosopher, and the lady swooned. After which she went and consoled herself with one of the dandies of the land.

Meanwhile, our two seekers after knowledge departed. First they jumped on the ring; they found it to be fairly flat, as an illustrious inhabitant of our little globe has very well guessed. Thence they journeyed from moon to moon. A comet passed quite close to the last one they visited; with their servants and instruments they hurled themselves on it. When they had covered about a hundred and fifty million leagues they came upon the satellites of Jupiter. They passed right into Jupiter and stayed there a year, during which time they learned some very wonderful secrets that would now be in the hands of the printers, had not my lords the inquisitors found some of the propositions rather tough. But I read the manuscript in the library of the illustrious archbishop of . . ., who with a generosity and kindness which cannot be sufficiently praised, allowed me to see his books.

But let us return to our travellers. When they left Jupiter they crossed a space about a hundred million leagues wide, and passed along the coast of Mars which, as we know, is five times smaller than our little globe. They saw two moons which serve this planet, and which have escaped the attention of our astronomers. I am well aware that Father Castel will decry, even with humour, the existence of these two moons, but I take my stand on those who reason by analogy. Those good philosophers know how difficult it would be for Mars, which is so far from the sun, to do without at least two moons. Whatever the facts are, our friends found Mars so small that they feared they might not have room enough to lay themselves down, and so they continued on their road like two travellers who scorn a miserable village inn, and push on to the nearest town. But the Sirian and his companion soon repented, for they travelled a long while without finding anything. At last they perceived a small glimmer: it was the earth, and it stirred the pity of the people coming from Jupiter. However, fearing that they might have to repent a second time, they decided to land. They passed along the tail of the comet and, finding an aurora borealis handy, climbed inside it, and touched land on the northern coast of the Baltic Sea, the fifth of July, seventeen hundred and thirtyseven, new style.

After a short rest, they ate for lunch two mountains which their attendants served up for them quite nicely, and then had a mind to explore the minute country in which they found themselves. They went first from north to south. The usual pace of the Sirian and his people measured about thirtythousand king's feet. The dwarf from Saturn followed at a distance, panting, for he had to take twelve paces to each of the other's strides. Picture to yourself (if such a comparison be permitted) a very small lap dog following a captain of the King of Prussia's Guards.

As these foreigners moved rather quickly, they circled the world in thirtysix hours, The sun, or rather the earth, it is true, does a like journey in a day, but it must be remembered that it is easier to travel on one's axis than on one's feet. Here they are, then, returned to the point whence they started. They have seen the puddle, almost imperceptible to them, which we call the " Mediterranean," and that other little pond which under the name of the "Great Ocean," surrounds the molehill. The water had never come above the dwarf's knees, and the other had scarcely wet his heels. Moving above and below, they did their best to discover whether or no this globe was inhabited. They stooped, laid themselves down flat, and sounded everywhere; but as their eyes and their hands were in nowise adapted to the diminutive beings which crawl here, they perceived nothing which might make them suspect that we and our colleagues, the other dwellers on this earth, have the honour to exist.

The dwarf, who sometimes judged a little too hastily, decided at once that there was no one on the earth, his first reason being that he had seen no one. Micromegas politely made him feel that it was a poor enough reason. "With your little eyes," he said, "you do not see certain stars of the fiftieth magnitude, which I perceive very distinctly. Do you conclude from your blindness that these stars do not exist?"

"But," said the dwarf, "I have searched well."

"But," replied the other, "you have seen badly."

"But," said the dwarf, "this globe is so badly constructed and so irregular; it is of a form which to me seems ridiculous! Everything here is in chaos, apparently. Do you see how none of those little brooks runs straight? And those ponds which are neither round, square, oval, nor of any regular form? Look at all those little pointed things with which this world is studded; they have taken the skin off my feet! (He referred to the mountains.) Do you not observe the shape of the globe, how flat it is at the poles, and how clumsily it turns round the sun, with result that the climate at the poles is necessarily bitter? What really makes me think there is no one on the earth is that I cannot imagine any sensible people wanting to live here."

"Well, well!" said Micromegas, "perhaps the people who live here are not sensible after all. But anyway there is an indication that the place was not made for nothing. You say that everything here looks irregular, because in Jupiter and Saturn everything is arranged in straight lines. Perhaps it is for that very reason there is something of a jumble here. Have I not told you that in my travels I have always observed variety?"

The Saturnian replied to all these arguments, and the discussion might never have finished, had not Micromegas become excited with talking, and by good luck broken the string of his diamond necklace. The diamonds fell to the ground. They were pretty little stones, but rather unequal; the biggest weighed four hundred pounds, the smallest fifty. The dwarf picked some of them up, and perceived when he put them to his eye that from the way they were cut they made firstrate magnifyingglasses. He took, therefore, one of these small magnifyingglasses, a hundred and sixty feet in diameter, and put it to his eye: Micromegas selected one of two thousand five hundred feet. They were excellent, but at first nothing could be seen by their aid; an adjustment was necessary. After a long time, the inhabitant of Saturn saw something almost imperceptible under water in the Baltic Sea: it was a whale. Very adroitly he picked it up with his little finger and, placing it on his thumbnail, showed it to the Sirian, who started laughing at the extreme smallness of the inhabitants of our globe. The Saturnian, satisfied that our world was inhabited after all, assumed immediately that all the inhabitants were whales, and as he was a great reasoner wished to ascertain how so small an atom moved, if it had ideas, a will, self direction. Micromegas was very embarrassed by his questions. He examined the animal with great patience, and finished by thinking it impossible that a soul lodged there. The two travellers were disposed to think, therefore, that there was no spirituality in our earthly abode. While they were considering the matter, they noticed with the aid of the magnifyingglass something bigger than a whale floating on the Baltic Sea.

It will be remembered that at that very time a bevy of philosophers were on their way back from the Arctic Circle, where they had gone to make observations of which nobody up to then had taken any notice. The papers said that their ship foundered on the shores of Bothnia, and that the philosophers had a very narrow escape. But in this world one never knows what goes on behind the scenes. What really happened I will relate quite simply and without adding one word of my own. And that is no small effort for a historian.

Micromegas stretched forth his hand very gently towards the spot where the object appeared, and put out two fingers; withdrew them for fear of making a mistake, then opening and closing them, very adroitly took hold of the ship carrying these gentlemen, and placed it on his nail, without squeezing too much for fear of crushing it.

"This animal is quite different from the first one," said the dwarf from Saturn, while the Sirian deposited the supposed animal in the hollow of his hand.

The passengers and the crew, who thought they had been swept up by a cyclone and cast on a kind of rock, started bustling. The sailors took some casks of wine, threw them overboard on Micromegas' hand, and hurled themselves down after them. The geometers took their quadrants, their sectors, and two Lapp girls, and climbed down to the Sirian's fingers. They made such a commotion that finally he felt something tickling him. It was an iron shod pole which the philosophers were driving a foot deep into his forefinger. From the itching he judged that something had issued from the little animal he held, but at first he did not suspect anything further. The magnifyingglass which could scarcely discern a whale and a ship had perforce no cognisance of such diminutive creatures as men, I do not wish to offend here anyone's vanity, but I feel obliged to ask selfimportant persons to note with me that, if the average height of a man be taken as five feet, we do not cut a better figure on this earth than would an animal about one sixhundredthousandth of an inch high on a ball ten feet in circumference. Imagine a being which could hold the earth in its hand and which had organs in proportion to ours--and it is very likely there would be a great number of these beings: then conceive, I ask you, what they would think of those battles which let a conqueror win a village only to lose it in the sequel. I do not doubt that if some captain of giant Grenadiers ever reads this work, he will increase by at least two feet the height of his soldiers' foragecaps, but it will be in vain, I warn him: he and his will never be anything but infinitely little.

What marvellous perspicacity would not our Sirian philosopher need, then, to descry the atoms of which I have just spoken? When Leuwenhock and Hartsoeker were the first to see, or think that they saw, the germ of which we are fashioned, they did not, by a long way, make such an astonishing discovery. What pleasure Micromegas experienced in seeing these little machines move, in examining all their tricks, in following all their performances! How he cried out with glee! With what joy did he hand one of his magnifyingglasses to his travelling companion! "I see them!" they exclaimed in concert, "Do you not see them carrying bundles, stooping and standing up again?" As they spoke, their hands trembled, both in delight at seeing such novel objects and in fear of loving them. The Saturnian, passing rapidly from an excess of doubt to an excess of credulousness, thought he observed them to be propagating their species. "Ah!" he said "I have caught nature redhanded." But he was deceived by appearance--which happens only too often, whether one uses a magnifyingglasses or not.

Micromegas, who was a much closer observer than his dwarf, saw clearly that the atoms were talking to each other, and drew his companion's attention thereto. The dwarf, ashamed at having been mistaken on the subject of procreation, was not disposed to believe that such species had the power of intercommunication of ideas. With the Sirian he enjoyed the gift of tongues; he had not heard our atoms speak at all, and he assumed they did not speak. Besides, how should such diminutive creatures have organs of speech, and what should they have to talk about? In order to speak, one must think, or very nearly; but if they thought, they would have the equivalent of a soul; attribute to this species the equivalent of a soul? it seemed absurd.

"But," said the Sirian, "you thought just now they were making love to each other; do you think it possible to make love without thinking and without uttering a word, or at least without making one's self understood? Do you suppose, further, that it is more difficult to produce an argument than an infant?"

"To me," replied the dwarf, "they both appear great mysteries, and I dare no longer either believe or disbelieve. I cease to have an opinion. We must try to examine these insects: we will argue afterwards."

"That is well said," returned Micromegas, and pulled out a pair of scissors with which he cut his nails. With a paring from his thumbnail he made on the spot a kind of huge speakingtrumpet, like an immense funnel, and placed the small end in his ear. The outer edge of the funnel surrounded the ship and all the crew. The faintest sound entered the circular fibres of the nail, with result that thanks to his ingenuity the philosopher of the world above heard perfectly the buzzing of our insects in this world below. In a very short time he managed to distinguish words, and finally to understand French. As did the dwarf, although with greater difficulty.

The travellers' astonishment increased with each moment. They heard maggots talking tolerably good sense, and this trick of nature seemed inexplicable to them. You can well believe that the Sirian and his dwarf burned with impatience to engage the atoms in conversation. The dwarf feared that the thunder of his voice, and particularly of the voice of Micromegas, might deafen the maggots without their understanding that it was a voice. The strength must be reduced. They put in their mouths a sort of small toothpick of which the very fine end reached close to the ship. The Sirian held the dwarf on his knees and the ship with its crew on one of his nails. He bent his head, and spoke in a low voice. At last, with the help of all these precautions and many others beside, he started to speak; and this is what he said:

"Invisible insects who the Creator has pleased should be born in this abyss of the infinitely little, I thank Him for having deigned to let me discover secrets which seemed unfathomable. At my court, maybe, they would not condescend to look at you, but I despise no one, and I offer you my protection."

If ever anyone was astonished, it was the people who heard these words. They could not imagine whence they came. The ship's chaplain repeated the prayers for casting out devils, the sailors cursed, and the philosophers on board propounded hypotheses; but no matter what hypothesis they propounded they could never guess who was speaking to them. The dwarf from Saturn, whose voice was softer than Micromegas', then told them briefly with what sort of people they had to deal. He related the journey from Saturn, made them aware who Mr. Micromegas was, and, after sympathising with them for being so small, asked if they had always enjoyed this miserable state so close to complete nonexistence, what their function was in a world which appeared to belong to whales, if they were happy, if they multiplied, it they had souls, and a hundred other questions of a like nature.

One reasoner in the party, bolder than the others, and shocked that anyone should doubt he had a soul, sighted his interlocutor through the eyelethole on a quadrant, made two observations, and at the third said: "You assume, sir, that because you measure a thousand fathoms from head to foot you are a . . ."

"A thousand fathoms!" cried the dwarf. "Holy Heaven! How can he know my height? A thousand fathoms! he is not an inch out! What, this atom has measured me! He is a mathematician, he knows my height! And I who cannot see him at all save through a magnifyingglass, I do not yet know his!"

"Yes, I have measured you," said the physicist, "and what is more I shall measure your big friend too.

The suggestion was accepted, and his Excellency stretched himself out at full length: which was necessary because, if he had remained standing, his head would have been too far above the clouds. Our philosophers planted in him a big tree on a spot which Dr. Swift would specify, but which I refrain from calling by name out of respect for the ladies. Then, by forming a network of triangles they came to the conclusion that what they saw was in reality a young man one hundred and twenty thousand royal feet long.

At this point micromegas spoke. "I see more than ever," he said, "that nothing must be judged by its apparent size, O God, who has given intelligence to beings which appear so contemptible, the infinitely small costs Thee as little effort as the infinitely great, and if there can possibly be creatures smaller than these, they may still have souls superior to those of the splendid animals I have seen in the sky, whose foot alone would cover the world to which I have come."

One of the philosophers answered him that he might indeed believe that there were intelligent creatures smaller than man, and he related for his benefit not the fables which Virgil told about the bees, but all that Swammerdam discovered and Réaumur dissected. He made him understand in short, that there are animals which to the bee are what the bee is to man, what the Sirian himself was to the prodigious animals he had mentioned, and what these animals are to other things compared with which they seem but atoms.

By degrees the conversation became interesting, and Micromegas spoke as follows:

"O intelligent atoms in whom the Eternal Being has been pleased to manifest His dexterity and His might, the joys you taste on your globe are doubtless very pure, for as you are so immaterial, and seem to be all spirit, your lives must be passed in Love and in Thought: that, indeed, is the true life of spirts. Nowhere yet have I found real happiness, but that you have it here I cannot doubt."

At these words all the philosophers shook their heads and one of them, more frank than the rest, candidly admitted that, apart from a small number of people who were little esteemed, the rest of the inhabitants of the world were a crowd of madmen, miscreants and unfortunates. "If evil be a property of matter," he said, "we have more matter than is necessary for the doing of much evil, and too much spirit if evil be a property of the spirit. Do you realise, for instance, that at this moment there are a hundred thousand madmen of our species wearing hats killing, or being killed by, a hundred thousand other animals wearing turbans, and that over almost all the face of the earth this has been the custom from time immemorial?"

The Sirian shuddered and asked what could be the ground for these horrible quarrels between such puny beasts.

"The matter at issue," replied the philosopher, "is some mudheap as large as your heel. It is not that any single man of all these millions who slaughter each other claims one straw on the mudheap. The point is--shall the mudheap belong to a certain man called 'Sultan' or to another called, I know not why, 'Cæsar'? Neither of them has ever seen or will ever see the little bit of land in dispute, and barely one of these animals which slaughter each other has ever seen the animal for which he is slaughtered."

"Wretch!" cried the Sirian indignantly. "Such a riot of mad fury is inconceivable! I am tempted to take three steps and with three blows of my foot to crush out of existence this anthill of absurd cutthroats."

"Do not trouble," answered the philosopher; "they wreak their own ruin. Know that after ten years not a hundredth part of these miscreants is ever left. Know that, even when they have not drawn the sword, hunger, exhaustion or debauchery carries them nearly all off. Besides, it is not they who should be punished, but the stayathome barbarians who, after a good meal, order from their remote closets the massacre of a million men, and then have solemn prayers of gratitude for the event offered up to God."

The traveller was stirred with pity for the little human race, in which he discovered such amazing contrasts, "Since you are of the small number of the wise," he said to these gentlemen, "and that apparently you do not kill people for money, tell me, I pray, how you employ yourselves."

"We dissect flies," answered the philosopher, "we measure lines, we gather mathematical data. We agree on the two or three points we understand, and we argue about the two or three thousand we do not."

Immediately a fancy took the Sirian and the Saturnian to question these thinking atoms, in order to find out on what things they were agreed. "What do you reckon to be the distance," asked the latter, between the Dogstar and Gemini?"

" Thirtytwo and a half degrees," they all replied in concert.

"And from here to the moon?"

"In round numbers, sixty times the radius of the earth."

"What does your air weigh?" he continued, thinking to catch them. He did not succeed, however, for they all told him that the air weighs about nine hundred times less than an equal volume of the lightest water, and nineteen thousand times less than ducat gold. The little dwarf from Saturn, astounded at their replies, was tempted to take for sorcerers their same people to whom a quarter of an hour before he bad refused a soul.

Finally, Micromegas put in a word. "Since you are so well acquainted with what is outside you," he said, "you doubtless know still better what is inside. Tell me what your soul is, and how you form your ideas."

As before, the philosophers replied in concert--but each held a different opinion. The oldest quoted Aristotle, another pronounced the name of Descartes, a third the name of Malebranche, a fourth that of Leibniz, a fifth that of Locke. An aged Peripatetic said loudly and confidently--"The soul is an entelechy and a proof of its power to be what it is." That is what Aristotle states expressly, page 653 of the Louvre edition. He quoted the passage--Éfæ£¥, etc.

"I do not understand Greek too well," remarked the giant.

"No more do I," said the philosophical maggot.

"Why then," asked the Sirian, "do you quote Aristotle in Greek?"

"Because," replied the scholar, "one should always quote what one does not comprehend at all in the language one understands least."

It was the Cartesian's turn. "The soul," he said, "is a pure spirit which has received in its mother's womb all metaphysical ideas and which, on leaving it, has to go to school to learn over again what it knew so well, and will never know again."

"It was not worth while," observed the animal eight leagues long, "for your soul to be so wise in your mother's womb if it had to become so ignorant by the time your chin could grow a beard. But what do you mean by a spirit?"

"What a question!" said the man of abstractions. "I have not the remotest idea. A spirit, it is said, is not matter."

"But do you know at least what matter is?"

"Very well," replied the man. "For example, this stone is grey, has a certain shape and three dimensions, is heavy and divisible."

"Well," said the Sirian, "this thing which appears to you to be divisible, heavy and grey, will you kindly tell me what it is? You perceive some of its attributes, but do you know what it is fundamentally?"

"No," answered the other.

"Then you do not know at all what matter is."

Mr. Micromegas then asked another of the wise men he held on his thumb what his soul was, and what it did.

"Nothing at all," replied the disciple of Malebranche. "God does everything for me. I see everything in Him, I do everything in Him. It is He who does everything without my interfering."

"It would be as well worth while not to exist," said the sage from Sirius. "And you, my friend," he continued to a Leibnizian who was there, "what is your soul?"

"My soul," answered the Leibnizian, "is a hand which points the hours while my body ticks: or, if you prefer it, it is my soul which ticks while my body points the hour: or again, my soul is the mirror of the universe, and my body is the frame of the mirror. That is quite clear."

A humble partisan of Locke stood near by, and when he was spoken to at last, replied: "I do not know how I think, but I do know that I have never thought save by virtue of my senses. That there are immaterial and intelligent beings I do not doubt: but that it is impossible for God to endow matter with mind I doubt very much. I hold the power of God in veneration: I am not free to set bounds to it: I predicate nothing: I am content to believe that more things are possible than we think."

The animal from Sirius smiled. He did not think the last speaker the least wise. The dwarf from Saturn would have embraced the follower of Locke had it not been for the difference in their proportions.

But, unluckily, there was present a minute animalcule in a clerical hat who interrupted the other animalcule philosophers. He said he understood the whole mystery; that the explanation was to be found in the "Summation of St. Thomas." He looked the two celestial inhabitants up and down, and asserted that their persons, worlds, suns and stars were created solely for man.

At this speech the two travellers fell on top of each other, suffocating with that inextinguishable laughter which, according to Homer, is the lot of the gods.

Their shoulders and stomachs heaved, and amid these convulsions the ship which the Sirian held on his thumb fell into one of the Saturnian's trousers pockets. These two good people tried to find it for a long time and, having recovered it at last, set everything very nicely in order. The Sirian picked the maggots up again and spoke to them once more with much kindness, although at the bottom of his heart he was rather angry that such infinitely small creatures should be possessed of an arrogance almost infinitely great. He promised to prepare for them a fine volume of philosophy, written very small so that they might be able to read it, and that in the volume they would find an explanation for everything. And to be sure, he did give them this book before he left them. They took it to Paris to the Academy of Science: but when the aged secretary opened it he found nothing but blank pages. "Ah!" said he. "I thought as much."

The Eyes

Edith Wharton

Edith Newbold Wharton (1862-1937) [nee Jones] was born into one of New York's socially prominent families. Wharton was an astute observer of society, and chronicled the changing moral attitudes during the turn of the Twentieth Century in America.

Edith Wharton was educated at home with private tutors. In 1885 she married Edward Robbins Wharton and moved to Boston. After a few years of marriage her husband sufferred a nervous breakdown. The resulting strain led to their divorce.

Wharton wrote novels, short fiction, and poetry. Much of her fiction focuses on the conflicts that arise between moral and economic values and the supernatural. She was extremely devoted to her writing and published fifty volumes of work. Wharton left behind several unpublished manuscripts when she died.

Wharton's early stories were collected in *The Greater Inclination* (1899), *Crucial Instances* (1901), and *The Descent of Man* (1904). The novella *Ethan Frome* was published in 1911. Her most important works are *The House of Mirth* (1905), and *The Age of Innocence* (1920), for which she received a Pulitzer Prize in 1921. Her last published work was *Ghosts* (1937).

WE HAD BEEN put in the mood for ghosts, that evening, after an excellent dinner at our old friend Culwin's, by a tale of Fred Murchard's--the narrative of a strange personal visitation.

Seen through the haze of our cigars, and by the drowsy gleam of a coal fire, Culwin's library, with its oak walls and dark old bindings, made a good setting for such evocations; and ghostly experiences at first hand being, after Murchard's opening, the only kind acceptable to us, we proceeded to take stock of our group and tax each member for a contribution. There were eight of us, and seven contrived, in a manner more or less adequate, to fulfill the condition imposed. It surprised us all to find that we could muster such a show of supernatural impressions, for none of us, excepting Murchard himself and young Phil Frenham--whose story was the slightest of the lot--had the habit of sending our souls into the invisible. So that, on the whole, we had every reason to be proud of our seven "exhibits," and none of us could have dreamed of expecting an eighth from our host.

Our old friend, Mr. Andrew Culwin, who had sat back in his armchair, listening and blinking through the smoke circles with the cheerful tolerance of a wise old idol, was not the kind of man likely to be favored with such contacts, though he had imagination enough to enjoy, without envying, the superior privileges of his guests. By age and by education he belonged to the stout Positivist tradition, and his habit of thought had been formed in the days of the epic struggle between physics and metaphysics. But he had been, then and always, essentially a spectator, a humorous detached observer of the immense muddled variety show of life, slipping out of his seat now and then for a brief dip into the convivialities at the back of the house, but never, as far as one knew, showing the least desire to jump on the stage and do a "turn."

Among his contemporaries there lingered a vague tradition of his having, at a remote period, and in a romantic clime, been wounded in a duel; but this legend no more tallied with what we younger men knew of his character than my mother's assertion that he had once been "a charming little man with nice eyes" corresponded to any possible reconstitution of his physiognomy.

"He never can have looked like anything but a bundle of sticks," Murchard had once said of him. "Or a phosphorescent log, rather," someone else amended; and we recognized the happiness of this description of his small squat trunk, with the red blink of the eyes in a face like mottled bark. He had always been possessed of a leisure which he had nursed and protected, instead of squandering it in vain activities. His carefully guarded hours had been devoted to the cultivation of a fine intelligence and a few judiciously chosen habits; and none of the disturbances common to human experience seemed to have crossed his sky. Nevertheless, his dispassionate survey of the universe had not raised his opinion of that costly experiment; and his study of the human race seemed to have resulted in the conclusion that all men were superfluous, and women necessary only because someone had to do the cooking. On the importance of this point his convictions were absolute, and gastronomy was the only science which he revered as a dogma. It must be owned that his little dinners were a strong argument in favor of this view, besides being a reason--though not the main one--for the fidelity of his friends.

Mentally he exercised a hospitality less seductive but no less stimulating. His mind was like a forum, or some open meeting place for the exchange of ideas: somewhat cold and drafty, but light, spacious and orderly--a kind of academic grove from which all the leaves have fallen. In this privileged area a dozen of us were wont to stretch our muscles and expand our lungs; and, as if to prolong as much as possible the tradition of what we felt to be a vanishing institution, one or two neophytes were now and then added to our band.

Young Phil Frenham was the last, and the most interesting, of these recruits, and a good example of Murchard's somewhat morbid assertion that our old friend "liked 'em juicy." It was indeed a fact that Culwin, for all his dryness, specially tasted the lyric qualities in youth. As he was far too good an Epicurean to nip the flowers of soul which he gathered for his garden, his friendship was not a disintegrating influence: on the contrary, it forced the young idea to robuster bloom. And in Phil Frenham he had a good subject for experimentation. The boy was really intelligent, and the soundness of his nature was like the pure paste under a fine glaze. Culwin had fished him out of a fog of family dullness, and pulled him up to peak in Darien; and the adventure hadn't hurt him a bit. Indeed, the skill with which Culwin had contrived to stimulate his curiosities without robbing them of their bloom of awe seemed to me a sufficient answer to Murchard's ogreish metaphor. There was nothing hectic in Frenham's efflorescence, and his old friend had not laid even a finger tip on the sacred stupidities. One wanted no better proof of that than the fact that Frenham still reverenced them in Culwin.

"There's a side of him you fellows don't see. I believe that story about the duel!" he declared; and it was of the very essence of this belief that it should impel him--just as our little party was dispersing--to turn back to our host with the joking demand: "And now you've got to tell us about *your* ghost!"

The outer door had closed on Murchard and the others; only Frenham and I remained; and the devoted servant who presided over Culwin's destinies, having brought a fresh supply of soda water, had been laconically ordered to bed.

Culwin's sociability was a nightblooming flower, and we knew that he expected the nucleus of his group to tighten around him after midnight. But Frenham's appeal seemed to disconcert him comically, and he rose from the chair in which he had just reseated himself after his farewells in the hall.

"My ghost? Do you suppose I'm fool enough to go to the expense of keeping one of my own, when there are so many charming ones in my friends' closets? Take another cigar," he said, revolving toward me with a laugh.

Frenham laughed too, pulling up his slender height before the chimney piece as he turned to face his short bristling friend.

"Oh," he said, "you'd never be content to share if you met one you really liked."

Culwin had dropped back into his armchair, his shock head embedded in the hollow of worn leather, his little eyes glimmering over a fresh cigar.

"Liked--*liked?* Good Lord!" he growled.

"Ah, you *have,* then!" Frenham pounced on him in the same instant, with a side glance of victory at me; but Culwin cowered gnomelike among his cushions, dissembling himself in a protective cloud of smoke.

"What's the use of denying it? You've seen everything, so of course you've seen a ghost!" his young friend persisted, talking intrepidly into the cloud. "Or, if you haven't seen one, it's only because you've seen two!"

The form of the challenge seemed to strike our host. He shot his head out of the mist with a queer tortoiselike motion he sometimes had, and blinked approvingly at Frenham.

"That's it," he flung at us on a shrill jerk of laughter; "it's only because I've seen two!"

The words were so unexpected that they dropped down and down into a deep silence, while we continued to stare at each other over Culwin's head, and Culwin stared at his ghosts. At length Frenham, without speaking, threw himself into the chair on the other side of the hearth, and leaned forward with his listening smile. ... "Oh, of course they're not show ghosts--a collector wouldn't think anything of them. ... Don't let me raise your hopes ... their one merit is their numerical strength: the exceptional fact of their being *two*. But, as against this, I'm bound to admit that at any moment I could probably have exorcised them both by asking my doctor for a prescription, or my oculist for a pair of spectacles. Only, as I never could make up my mind whether to go to the doctor or the oculist-- whether I was afflicted by an optical or a digestive delusion--I left them to pursue their interesting double life, though at times they made mine exceedingly uncomfortable. ...

Yes--uncomfortable; and you know how I hate to be uncomfortable! But it was part of my stupid pride, when the thing began, not to admit that I could be disturbed by the trifling matter of seeing two.

And then I'd no reason, really, to suppose I was ill. As far as I knew I was simply bored--horribly bored. But it was part of my boredom--I remember--that I was feeling so uncommonly well, and didn't know how on earth to work off my surplus energy. I had come back on a long journey--down in South America and Mexico--and had settled down for the winter near New York with an old aunt who had known Washington Irving and corresponded with N.P. Willis. She lived, not far from Irvington, in a damp Gothic village overhung by Norway spruces and looking exactly like a memorial emblem done in hair. Her personal appearance was in keeping with this image, and her own hair--of which there was little left--might have been sacrificed to the manufacture of the emblem.

"I had just reached the end of an agitated year, with considerable arrears to make up in money and emotion; and theoretically it seemed as though my aunt's mild hospitality would be as beneficial to my nerves as to my purse. But the deuce of it was that as soon as I felt myself safe and sheltered my energy began to revive; and how was I to work it off inside of a memorial emblem? I had, at that time, the illusion that sustained intellectual effort could engage a man's whole activity; and I decided to write a great book--I forget about what. My aunt, impressed by my plan, gave up to me her Gothic library, filled with classics bound in black cloth and daguerreotypes of faded celebrities; and I sat down at my desk to win myself a place among their number. And to facilitate my task she lent me a cousin to copy my manuscript.

"The cousin was a nice girl, and I had an idea that a nice girl was just what I needed to restore my faith in human nature, and principally in myself. She was neither beautiful nor intelligent--poor Alice Nowell!--but it interested me to see any woman content to be so uninteresting, and I wanted to find out the secret of her content. In doing this I handled it rather rashly, and put it out of joint--oh, just for a moment! There's no fatuity in telling you this, for the poor girl had never seen anyone but cousins. ...

"Well, I was sorry for what I'd done, of course, and confoundedly bothered as to how I should put it straight. She was staying in the house, and one evening, after my aunt had gone to bed, she came down to the library to fetch a book she'd mislaid, like any artless heroine, on the shelves behind us. She was pinknosed and flustered, and it suddenly occurred to me that her hair, though it was fairly thick and pretty, would look exactly like my aunt's when she grew older. I was glad I had noticed this, for it made it easier for me to decide to do what was right; and when I had found the book she hadn't lost I told her I was leaving for Europe that week.

"Europe was terribly far off in those days, and Alice knew at once what I meant. She didn't take it in the least as I'd expected--it would have been easier if she had. She held her book very tight, and turned away a moment to wind up the lamp on my desk--it had a groundglass shade with vine leaves, and glass drops around the edge, I remember. Then she came back, held out her hand, and said: 'Goodbye.' And as she said it she looked straight at me and kissed me. I had never felt anything as fresh and shy and brave as her kiss. It was worse than any reproach, and it made me ashamed to deserve a reproach from her. I said to myself: "I'll marry her, and when my aunt dies she'll leave us this house, and I'll sit here at the desk and go on with my book; and Alice will sit over there with her embroidery and look at me as she's looking now. And life will go on like that for any number of years.' The prospect frightened me a little, but at the time I didn't frighten me as much as doing anything to hurt her; and ten minuted later she had my seal ring on her finger, and my promise that when I went abroad she should go with me.

"You'll wonder why I'm enlarging on this incident. It's because the evening on which it took place was the very evening on which I first saw the queer sight I've spoken of. Being at that time an ardent believer in a necessary sequence between cause and effect, I naturally tried to trace some kind of link between what had just happened to me in my aunt's library, and what was to happen a few hours later on the same night; and so the coincidence between the two events always remained in my mind.

"I went up to bed with rather a heavy heart, for I was bowed under the weight of the first good action I had ever consciously committed; and young as I was, I saw the gravity of my situation. Don't imagine from this that I had hitherto been an instrument of destruction. I had been merely a harmless young man, who had followed his bent and declined all collaboration with Providence. Now I had suddenly undertaken to promote the moral order of the world, and I felt a good deal like the trustful spectator who has given his gold watch to the conjurer, and doesn't know in what shape he'll get it back when the trick is over. ... Still, a glow of self-frighteousness tempered my fears, and I said to myself as I undressed that when I'd got used to being good it probably wouldn't make me as nervous as it did at the start. And by that time I was in bed, and had blown out my candle, I felt that I really *was* getting used to it, and that, as far as I'd got, it was not unlike sinking down into one of my aunt's very softest wool mattresses.

"I closed my eyes on this image, and when I opened them it must have been a good deal later, for my room had grown cold, and intensely still. I was waked by the queer feeling we all know--the feeling that there was something in the room that hadn't been there when I fell asleep. I sat up and strained my eyes into the darkness. The room was pitch black, and at first I saw nothing; but gradually a vague glimmer at the foot of the bed turned into two eyes staring back at me. I couldn't distinguish the features attached to them, but as I looked the eyes grew more and more distinct: they gave out a light of their own.

"The sensation of being thus gazed at was far from pleasant, and you might suppose that my first impulse would have been to jump out of bed and hurl myself on the invisible figure attached to the eyes. But it wasn't--my impulse was simply to lie still. ... I can't say whether this was due to an immediate sense of the uncanny nature of the apparition--to the certainty that if I did jump out of bed I should hurl myself on nothing--or merely to the benumbing effect of the eyes themselves. They were the very worst eyes I've ever seen: a man's eyes--but what a man! My first thought was that he must be frightfully old. The orbits were sunk, and the thick redlined lids hung over the eyeballs like blinds of which the cords are broken. One lid drooped a little lower than the other, with the effect of a crooked leer; and between these folds of flesh, with their scant bristle of lashes, the eyes themselves, small glassy disks with an agatelike rim, looked like sea pebbles in the grip of a starfish.

"But the age of the eyes was not the most unpleasant thing about them. What turned me sick was their expression of vicious security. I don't know how else to describe the fact that they seemed to belong to a man who had done a lot of harm in his life, but had always kept just inside the danger lines. They were not the eyes of a coward, but of someone much too clever to take risks; and my gorge rose at their look of base astuteness. Yet even that wasn't the worst; for as we continued to scan each other I saw in them a tinge of derision, and felt myself to be its object.

"At that I was seized by an impulse of rage that jerked me to my feet and pitched me straight at the unseen figure. But of course there wasn't any figure there, and my fists struck at emptiness. Ashamed and cold, I groped about for a match and lit the candles. The room looked just as usual--as I had known it would; and I crawled back to bed, and blew out the lights.

"As soon as the room was dark again the eyes reappeared; and I now applied myself to explaining them on scientific principles. At first I thought the illusion might have been caused by the glow of the last embers in the chimney; but the fireplace was on the other side of my bed, and so placed that the fire could not be reflected in my toilet glass, which was the only mirror in the room. Then it struck me that I might have been tricked by the reflection of the embers in some polished bit of wood or metal; and though I couldn't discover any object of the sort in my line of vision, I got up again, groped my way to the hearth, and covered what was left of the fire. But as soon as I was back in the bed the eyes were back at its foot.

"They were an hallucination, then: that was plain. But the fact that they were not due to any external dupery didn't make them a bit pleasanter. For if they were a projection of my inner consciousness, what the deuce was the matter with that organ? I had gone deeply enough into the mystery of morbid pathological states to picture the conditions under which an exploring mind might lay itself open to such a midnight admonition; but I couldn't fit it to my present case. I had never felt more normal, mentally and physically; and the only unusual fact in my situation--that of having assured the happiness of an amiable girl--did not seem of a kind to summon unclean spirits about my pillow. But there were the eyes still looking at me.

"I shut mine, and tried to evoke a vision of Alice Nowell's. They were not remarkable eyes, but they were as wholesome as fresh water, and if she had had more imagination--or longer lashes--their expression might have been interesting. As it was, they did not prove very efficacious, and in a few moments I perceived that they had mysteriously changed into the eyes at the foot of the bed. It exasperated me more to feel these glaring at me through my shut lids than to see them, and I opened my eyes again and looked straight into their hateful stare. ...

"And so it went on all night. I can't tell you what that night was like, nor how long it lasted. Have you ever lain in bed, hopelessly wide awake and tried to keep your eyes shut, knowing that if you opened 'em you'd see something you dreaded and loathed? It sounds easy, but it's devilishly hard. Those eyes hung there and drew me. I had the *vertige de l'abîme*, and their red lids were the edge of my abyss. ... I had known nervous hours before: hours when I'd felt the wind of danger on my neck; but never this kind of strain. It wasn't that the eyes were awful; they hadn't the majesty of the powers of darkness. But they had--how shall I say?--a physical effect that was the equivalent of a bad smell: their look left a smear like a snail's. And I didn't see what business they had with me, anyhow--and I stared and stared, trying to find out.

"I don't know what effect they were trying to produce; but the effect they *did* produce was that of making me pack my portmanteau and bolt to town early the next morning. I left a note for my aunt, explaining that I was ill and had gone to see my doctor; and as a matter of fact I did feel uncommonly ill--the night seemed to have pumped all the blood out of me. But when I reached town I didn't go to the doctor's. I went to a friend's rooms, and threw myself on a bed, and slept for ten heavenly hours. When I woke it was the middle of the night, and I turned cold at the thought of what might be waiting for me. I sat up, shaking, and stared into the darkness; but there wasn't a break in its blessed surface, and when I saw that the eyes were not there I dropped back into another long sleep.

"I had left no word for Alice when I fled, because I meant to go back the next morning. But the next morning I was too exhausted to stir. As the day went on the exhaustion increased, instead of wearing off like the fatigue left by an ordinary night of insomnia: the effect of the eyes seemed to be cumulative, and the thought of seeing them again grew intolerable. For two days I fought my dread; and on the third evening I pulled myself together and decided to go back the next morning. I felt a good deal happier as soon as I'd decided, for I knew that my abrupt disappearance, and the strangeness of my not writing, must have been very distressing to poor Alice. I went to bed with an easy mind, and fell asleep at once; but in the middle of the night I woke, and there were the eyes. ...

"Well, I simply couldn't face them; and instead of going back to my aunt's I bundled a few things into a trunk and jumped aboard the first steamer for England. I was so dead tired when I got on board that I crawled straight into my berth, and slept most of the way over; and I can't tell you the bliss it was to wake from those long dreamless stretches and look fearlessly into the dark, *knowing* that I shouldn't see the eyes. ...

"I stayed abroad for a year, and then I stayed for another: and during that time I never had a glimpse of them. That was enough reason for prolonging my stay if I'd been on a desert island. Another was, of course, that I had perfectly come to see, on the voyage over, the complete impossibility of my marrying Alice Nowell. The fact that I had been so slow in making this discovery annoyed me, and made me want to avoid explanations. The bliss of escaping at one stroke from the eyes, and from this other embarrassment, gave my freedom an extraordinary zest; and the longer I savored it the better I liked its taste.

"The eyes had burned such a hole in my consciousness that for a long time I went on puzzling over the nature of the apparition, and wondering if it would ever come back. But as time passed I lost this dread, and retained only the precision of the image. Then that faded in its turn.

"The second year found me settled in Rome, where I was planning, I believe, to write another great book--a definitive work on Etruscan influences in Italian art. At any rate, I'd found some pretext of the kind for taking a sunny apartment in the Piazza di Spagna and dabbling about in the Forum; and there, one morning, a charming youth came to me. As he stood there in the warm light, slender and smooth and hyacinthine, he might have stepped from a ruined altar--one to Antinous, say; but he'd come instead from New York, with a letter from (of all people) Alice Nowell. The letter--the first I'd had from her since our break--was simply a line introducing her young cousin, Gilbert Noyes, and appealing to me to befriend him. It appeared, poor lad, that he 'had talent,' and 'wanted to write'; and, an obdurate family having insisted that his calligraphy should take the form of double entry, Alice had intervened to win him six months' respite, during which he was to travel abroad on a meager pittance, and somehow prove his ability to increase it by his pen. The quaint conditions of the test struck me first: it seemed about as conclusive as a medieval 'ordeal.' Then I was touched by her having sent him to me. I had always wanted to do her some service, to justify myself in my own eyes rather than hers; and here was a beautiful occasion.

"I imagine it's safe to lay down the general principle that predestined geniuses don't, as a rule, appear before one in the spring sunshine of the Forum looking like one of its banished gods. At any rate, poor Noyes wasn't a predestined genius. But he *was* beautiful to see, and charming as a comrade. It was only when he began to talk literature that my heart failed me. I knew all the symptoms so well--the things he had 'in him,' and the things outside him that impinged! There's the real test, after all. It was always--punctually, inevitably, with the inexorableness of mechanical law--it was *always* the wrong thing that struck him. I grew to find a certain fascination in deciding in advance exactly which wrong thing he'd select; and I acquired an astonishing skill at the game. ..

"The worst of it was that his *bêtise* wasn't of the too obvious sort. Ladies who met him at picnics thought him intellectual; and even at dinners he passed for clever. I, who had him under the microscope, fancied now and then that he might develop some kind of a slim talent, something that he could make 'do' and be happy on; and wasn't that, after all, what I was concerned with? He was so charming--he continued to be so charming--that he called forth all my charity in support of this argument; and for the first few months I really believed there was a chance for him. ...

"Those months were delightful. Noyes was constantly with me, and the more I saw of him the better I liked him. His stupidity was a natural grace--it was as beautiful, really, as his eyelashes. And he was so gay, so affectionate, and so happy with me, that telling him the truth would have been about as pleasant as slitting the throat of some gentle animal. At first I used to wonder what had put into that radiant head the detestable delusion that it held a brain. Then I began to see that it was simply protective mimicry--an instinctive ruse to get away from family life and an office desk. Not that Gilbert didn't--dear lad!--believe in himself. There wasn't a trace of hypocrisy in him. He was sure that his 'call' was irresistible, while to me it was the saving grace of his situation that it *wasn't,* and that a little money, a little leisure, a little pleasure would have turned him into an inoffensive idler. Unluckily, however, there was no hope of money, and with the alternative of the office desk before him he couldn't postpone his attempt at literature. The stuff he turned out was deplorable, and I see now that I knew it from the first. Still, the absurdity of deciding a man's whole future on a first trial seemed to justify me in withholding my verdict, and perhaps even in encouraging him a little, on the ground that the human plant generally needs warmth to flower.

"At any rate, I proceeded on that principal, and carried it to the point of getting his term of probation extended. When I left Rome he went with me, and we idled away a delicious summer between Capri and Venice. I said to myself: "if he has anything in him, it will come out now,' and it *did.* He was never more enchanting and enchanted. There were moments of our pilgrimage when beauty born of murmuring sound seemed actually to pass into his face--but only to issue forth into a flood of the palest ink.
...

"Well, the time came to turn off the tap; and I knew there was no hand but mine to do it. We were back in Rome, and I had taken him to stay with me, not wanting him to be alone in his *pension* when he had to face the necessity of renouncing his ambition. I hadn't, of course, relied solely on my own judgment in deciding to advise him to drop literature. I had sent his stuff to various people--editors and critics--and they had always sent it back with the same chilling lack of comment. Really there was nothing on earth to say.

"I confess I never felt more shabby than did on the day when I decided to have it out with Gilbert. It was well enough to tell myself that it was my duty to knock the poor boy's hopes into splinters--but I'd like to know what act of gratuitous cruelty hasn't been justified on that plea? I've always shrunk from usurping the functions of Providence, and when I have to exercise them I decidedly prefer that it shouldn't be on an errand of destruction. Besides, in the last issue, who was I to decide, even after a year's trial, if poor Gilbert had it in him or not?

The more I looked at the part I'd resolved to play, the less I liked it; and I liked it still less when Gilbert sat opposite me, with his head thrown back in the lamplight, just as Phil's is now. ... I'd been going over his last manuscript, and he knew it, and he knew that his future hung on my verdict--we'd tacitly agreed to that. The manuscript lay between us, on my table--a novel, his first novel, if you please!--and he reached over and laid his hand on it, and looked up at me with all his life in the look.

I stood up and cleared my throat, trying to keep my eyes away from his face and on the manuscript.

"'The fact is, my dear Gilbert,' I began--

"I saw him turn pale, but he was up and facing me in an instant.

"'Oh, look here, don't take on so, my dear fellow! I'm not so awfully cut up as all that!' His hands were on my shoulders, and he was laughing down on me from his full height, with a kind of mortally stricken gaiety that drove the knife into my side.

"He was too beautifully brave for me to keep up any humbug about my duty. And it came over me suddenly how I should hurt others in hurting him: myself first, since sending him home meant losing him; but more particularly poor Alice Nowell, to whom I had so longed to prove my good faith and my desire to serve her. It really seemed like failing her twice to fail Gilbert.

"But my intuition was like one of those lightning flashes that encircle the whole horizon, and in the same instant I saw what I might be letting myself in for if I didn't tell the truth. I said to myself: 'I shall have him for life'--and I'd never yet seen anyone, man or woman, whom I was quite sure of wanting on those terms. Well, this impulse of egotism decided me. I was ashamed of it, and to get away from it I took a leap that landed me straight in Gilbert's arms.

"'The thing's all right, and you're all wrong!' I shouted up at him; and as he hugged me, and I laughed and shook in his clutch, I had for a minute the sense of selfcomplacency that is supposed to attend the footsteps of the just. Hang it all, making people happy *has* its charms.

"Gilbert, of course, was for celebrating his emancipation in some spectacular manner; but I sent him away alone to explode his emotions, and went to bed to sleep off mine. As I undressed I began to wonder what their aftertaste would be--so many of the finest don't keep! Still, l wasn't sorry, and I meant to empty the bottle, even if it *did* turn a trifle flat.

"After I got into bed I lay for a long time smiling at the memory of his eyes--his blissful eyes. ... Then I fell asleep, and when I woke the room was deathly cold, and I sat up with a jerk--and there were *the other eyes*. ...

"It was three years since I'd seen them, but I'd thought of them so often that I fancied they could never take me unawares again. Now, with their red sneer on me, I knew that I had never really believed they would come back, and that I was as defenceless as ever against them. ... As before, it was the insane irrelevance of their coming that made it so horrible. What the deuce were they after, to leap out at me at such a time? I had lived more or less carelessly in the years since I'd seen them, though my worst indiscretions were not dark enough to invite the searchings of their infernal glare; but at this particular moment I was really in what might have been called a state of grace; and I can't tell you how the fact added to their horror. ...

"But it's not enough to say they were as bad as before: they were worse. Worse by just so much as I'd learned of life in the interval; by all the damnable implications my wider experience read into them. I saw now what I hadn't seen before: that they were eyes which had grown hideous gradually, which had built up their baseness coralwise bit by bit, out of a series of small turpitudes slowly accumulated through the industrious years. Yes--it came to me that what made them so bad was that they'd grown bad so slowly. ...

"There they hung in the darkness, their swollen lids dropped across the little watery bulbs rolling loose in the orbits, and the puff of flesh making a muddy shadow underneath--and as their stare moved with my move-ments, there came over me a sense of their tacit complicity, of a deep hidden understanding between us that was worse than the first shock of their strangeness. Not that I understood them; but that they made it so

clear that someday I should.... Yes, that was the worst part of it, decidedly; and it was the feeling that became stronger each time they came back. ...
"For they got into the damnable habit of coming back. They reminded me of vampires with a taste for young flesh, they seemed so to gloat over the taste of a good conscience. Every night for a month they came to claim their morsel of mine: since I'd made Gilbert happy they simply wouldn't loosen their fangs. The coincidence almost made me hate him, poor lad, fortuitous as I felt it to be. I puzzled over it a good deal, but couldn't find any hint of an explanation except in the chance of his association with Alice Nowell. But then the eyes had let up on me the moment I had abandoned her, so they could hardly be the emissaries of a woman scorned, even if one could have pictured poor Alice charging such spirits to avenge her. That set me thinking, and I began to wonder if they would let up on me if I abandoned Gilbert. The temptation was insidious, and I had to stiffen myself against it; but really, dear boy! he was too charming to be sacrificed to such demons. And so, after all, I never found out what they wanted. ..." The fire crumbled, sending up a flash which threw into relief the narrator's gnarled face under its grey-black stubble. Pressed into the hollow of the chair back, it stood out an instant like an intaglio of yellowish red-veined stone, with spots of enamel for the eyes; then the fire sank and it became once more a dim Rembrandtish blur.

Phil Frenham, sitting in a low chair on the opposite side of the hearth, one long arm propped on the table behind him, one hand supporting his thrownback head, and his eyes fixed on his old friend's face had not moved since the tale began. He continued to maintain his silent immobility after Culwin had ceased to speak, and it was I who, with a vague sense of disappointment at the sudden drop of the story, finally asked: "But how long did you keep on seeing them?"

Culwin, so sunk into his chair that he seemed like a heap of his own empty clothes, stirred a little, as if in surprise at my question. He appeared to have halfforgotten what he had been telling us.

"How long? Oh, off and on all that winter. It was infernal. I never got used to them. I grew really ill."

Frenham shifted his attitude, and as he did so his elbow struck against a small mirror in a bronze frame standing on the table behind him. He turned and changed its angle slightly; then he resumed his former attitude, his dark head thrown back on his lifted palm, his eyes intent on Culwin's face. Something in his silent gaze embarrassed me, and as if to divert attention from it I pressed on with another question:

"And you never tried sacrificing Noyes?"

"Oh, no. The fact is I didn't have to. He did it for me, poor boy!"

"Did it for you? How do you mean?"

"He wore me out--wore everybody out. He kept on pouring out his lamentable twaddle, and hawking it up and down the place till he became a thing of terror. I tried to wean him from writing--oh, ever so gently, you understand, by throwing him with agreeable people, giving him a chance to make himself felt, to come to a sense of what he *really* had to give. I'd foreseen this solution from the beginning--felt sure that, once the first ardor of authorship was quenched, he'd drop into his place as a charming parasitic thing, the kind of chronic Cherubino for whom, in old societies, there's always a seat at the table, and a shelter behind the ladies' skirts. I saw him take his place as 'the poet': the poet who doesn't write. One knows the type in every drawing room. Living in that way doesn't cost much--I'd worked it all out in my mind, and felt sure that, with a little help, he could manage it for the next few years; and meanwhile he'd be sure to marry. I saw him married to a widow, rather older, with a good cook and a wellrun house. And I actually had my eye on the widow. ... Meanwhile I did everything to help the transition--lent him money to ease his conscience, introduced him to pretty women to make him forget his vows. But nothing would do him: he had but one idea in his beautiful obstinate head. He wanted the laurel and not the rose, and he kept on repeating Gautier's axiom, and battering and filing at his limp prose till he'd spread it out over Lord knows how many hundred pages. Now and then he would send a barrelful to a publisher, and of course it would always come back.

"At first it didn't matter--he thought he was 'misunderstood.' He took the attitudes of genius, and whenever an opus came home he wrote another to keep it company. Then he had a reaction of despair, and accused me of deceiving him, and Lord knows what. I got angry at that, and told him it was he who had deceived himself. He'd come to me determined to write, and I'd done my best to help him. That was the extent of my offence, and I'd done it for his cousin's sake, not his.

"That seemed to strike home, and he didn't answer for a minute. Then he said: 'My time's up and my money's up. What do you think I'd better do?'

"'I think you'd better not be an ass,' I said.

"'What do you mean by being an ass?' he asked.

"I took a letter from my desk and held it out to him.

"'I mean refusing this offer of Mrs. Ellinger's: to be her secretary at a salary of five thousand dollars. There may be a lot more in it than that.'

"He flung out his hand with a violence that struck the letter from mine. 'Oh, I know well enough what's in it!' he said, red to the roots of his hair.

"And what's the answer, if you know?' I asked.

"He made none at the minute, but turned away slowly to the door. There, with his hand on the threshold, he stopped to say, almost under his breath: 'Then you really think my stuff's no good?'

"I was tired and exasperated, and I laughed. I don't defend my laugh--it was in wretched taste. But I must plead in extenuation that the boy was a fool, and that I'd done my best for him--I really had.

"He went out of the room, shutting the door quietly after him. That afternoon I left for Frascati, where I'd promised to spend the Sunday with some friends. I was glad to escape from Gilbert, and by the same token, as I learned that night, I had also escaped from the eyes. I dropped into the same lethargic sleep that had come to me before when I left off seeing them; and when I woke the next morning in my peaceful room above the ilexes, I felt the utter weariness and deep relief that always followed on that sleep. I put in two blessed nights at Frascati, and when I got back to my rooms in Rome I found that Gilbert had gone. ... Oh, nothing tragic had happened--the episode never rose to *that*. He'd simply packed his manuscripts and left for America--for his family and the Wall Street desk. He left a decent enough note to tell me of his decision, and behaved altogether, in the circumstances, as little like a fool as it's possible for a fool to behave. ..."

Culwin paused again, and Frenham still sat motionless, the dusky countour of his young head reflected in the mirror at his back.

"And what became of Noyes afterward?" I finally asked, still disquieted by a sense of incompleteness, by the need of some connecting thread between the parallel lines of the tale.

Culwin twitched his shoulders. "Oh, nothing became of him--because he became nothing. There could be no question of 'becoming' about it. He vegetated in an office, I believe, and finally got a clerkship in a consulate, and married drearily in China. I saw him once in Hong Kong, years afterward. He was fat and hadn't shaved. I was told he drank. He didn't recognize me."

"And the eyes?" I asked, after another pause which Frenham's continued silence made oppressive.

Culwin, stroking his chin, blinked at me meditatively through the shadows. "I never saw them after my last talk with Gilbert. Put two and two together if you can. For my part, I haven't found the link."

He rose, his hands in his pockets, and walked stiffly over to the table on which reviving drinks had been set out.

"You must be parched after this dry tale. Here, help yourself, my dear fellow. Here, Phil--" He turned back to the hearth.

Frenham made no response to his host's hospitable summons. He still sat in his low chair without moving, but as Culwin advanced toward him, their eyes met in a long look; after which the young man, turned suddenly, flung his arms across the table behind him, and dropped his face upon them.

Culwin, at the unexpected gesture, stopped short, a flush on his face.

"Phil--what the deuce? Why, have the eyes scared *you*? My dear boy--my dear fellow--I never had such a tribute to my literary ability, never!"

He broke into a chuckle at the thought, and halted on the hearthrug, his hands still in his pockets, gazing down at the youth's bowed head. Then, as Frenham still made no answer, he moved a step or two nearer.

"Cheer up, my dear Phil! It's years since I've seen them--apparently I've done nothing lately bad enough to call them out of chaos. Unless my present evocation of them has made you see them; which would be their worst stroke yet!"

His bantering appeal quivered off into an uneasy laugh, and he moved nearer, bending over Frenham, and laying his gouty hands on the lad's shoulders.

"Phil, my dear boy, really--what's the matter? Why don't you answer? *Have* you seen the eyes?"

Frenham's face was still hidden, and from where I stood behind Culwin saw the latter, as if under the rebuff of this unaccountable attitude, draw back slowly from his friend. As he did so, the light of the lamp on the table fell full on his congested face, and I caught its reflection in the mirror behind Frenham's head.

Culwin saw the reflection also. He paused, his face level with the mirror, as if scarcely recognizing the countenance in it as his own. But as he looked his expression gradually changed, and for an appreciable space of time he and the image in the glass confronted each other with a glare of slowly gathering hate. Then Culwin let go of Frenham's shoulders, and drew back a step. ...

Frenham, his face still hidden, did not stir.

The Book of Ruth

Bible, Old Testament

The Book of Ruth (ca.450 B.C.) was probably composed in the post-exilic period of the Israelites although it may be based upon a more ancient tale. Some Bibilcal scholars believe it was written as pure entertainment. Others think it developed from an ancient fertility myth. One school holds that it was written in protest against the narrow nationalism that prevailed in ancient Israel. They see it as a plea for a wider interpretation of the laws of marriage. Whatever its historical background may be, students of literature have long been captivated by its charm.

It tells how Naomi, a Judean, returns to Bethlehem after the deaths of her husband and two sons in the land of Moab. Her Moabite daughter-in-law, Orpah, returns to her family but Ruth loyally remains with Naomi. After a nearer kinsman refuses to marry her, she is wed for a second time to Boaz and subsequently bears a son Obed. There are no real villains in the story. Ruth shows great loyalty to her mother-in-law and her adopted nation. Naomi and Boaz are portrayed as completely admirable characters.

The Book of Ruth pre-dates the modern short story by some two thousand years yet many critics would cite it as the perfect example of the genre.

Now it came to pass in the days when the judges ruled, that there was a famine in the land. And a certain man of Beth-lehem-judah went to sojourn in the country of Moab, he, and his wife, and his two sons. And the name of the man was Elimelech, and the name of his wife Naomi, and the name of his two sons Mahlon and Chilion, Ephrathites of Beth-lehem-judah. And they came into the country of Moab, and continued there.

And Elimelech Naomi's husband died; and she was left, and her two sons. And they took them wives of the women of Moab; the name of the one was Orpah, and the name of the other Ruth: and they dwelled there about ten years. And Mahlon and Chilion died also both of them; and the woman was left of her two sons and her husband.

319

Then she arose with her daughters in law, that she might return from
the country of Moab: for she had heard in the country of Moab how that
the Lord had visited His people in giving them bread. Wherefore she went
forth out of the place where she was, and her two daughters in law with
her; and they went on the way to return unto the land of Judah. And Naomi
said her unto her two daughters in law:-- "Go, return each to her mother's
house: the Lord deal kindly with you, as ye have dealt with the dead, and
with me. The Lord grant you that ye may find rest, each of you in the
house of her husband." Then she kissed them; and they lifted up their
voice, and wept. And they said unto her:-- "Surely we will return with thee
unto thy people."

And Naomi said:-- "Turn again, my daughters: why will ye go with
me? are there yet any more sons in my womb, that they may be your
husbands? Turn again, my daughters, go your way; for I am too old to
have an husband. If I should say, I have hope, if I should have an husband
also to-night, and should also bear sons; would ye tarry for them till they
were grown? would ye stay for them from having husbands? nay, my
daughters; for it grieveth me much for your sakes the hand of the Lord is
gone out against me."

And they lifted up their voice, and wept again: and Orpah kissed her
mother in law; but Ruth clave unto her. And she said:-- "Behold, thy sister
in law is gone back unto her people, and unto her gods: return thou after
thy sister in law." And Ruth said:-- "Intreat me not to leave thee, or to
return from following after thee: for whither thou goest, I will go; and
where thou lodgest, I will lodge: thy people shall be my people, and thy
God my God: where thou diest, will I die, and there will I be buried: the
Lord do so to me, and more also, if ought but death part thee and me."

When she saw that she was stedfastly minded to go with her, then she
left speaking unto her. So they two went until they came to Beth-lehem.
And it came to pass, when they were come to Beth-lehem, that all the city
was moved about them, and they said:-- "Is this Naomi?" And she said
unto them:-- "Call me not Naomi, call me Mara: for the Almighty hath
dealt very bitterly with me. I went out full, and the Lord hath brought me
home again empty: why then call ye me Naomi, seeing the Lord hath
testified against me, and the Almighty hath afflicted me?"

So Naomi returned, and Ruth the Moabitess, her daughter in law, with
her, which returned out of the country of Moab: and they came to
Beth-lehem in the beginning of barley harvest. And Naomi had a kinsman
of her husband's, a mighty man of wealth, of the family of Elimelech; and

his name was Boaz. And Ruth the Moabitess said unto Naomi:-- "Let me now go to the field, and glean ears of corn after him in whose sight I shall find grace." And she said unto her:-- "Go, my daughter." And she went, and came, and gleaned in the field after the reapers: and her hap was to light on a part of the field belonging unto Boaz, who was of the kindred of Elimelech.

And, behold, Boaz came from Beth-lehem, and said unto the reapers:-- "The Lord be with you." And they answered him:-- "The Lord bless thee." Then said Boaz unto his servant that was set over the reapers:-- "Whose damsel is this?" And the servant that was set over the reapers answered and said:-- "It is the Moabitish damsel that came back with Naomi out of the country of Moab: and she said, I pray you, let me glean and gather after the reapers among the sheaves: so she came, and hath continued even from the morning until now, that she tarried a little in the house." Then said Boaz unto Ruth:-- "Hearest thou not, my daughter? Go not to glean in another field, neither go from hence, but abide here fast by my maidens: let thine eyes be on the field that they do reap, and go thou after them: have I not charged the young men that they shall not touch thee? and when thou art athirst, go unto the vessels, and drink of that which the young men have drawn." Then she fell on her face, and bowed herself to the ground, and said unto him:-- "Why have I found grace in thine eyes, that thou shouldest take knowledge of me, seeing I am a stranger?" And Boaz answered and said unto her:-- "It hath fully been shewed me, all that thou hast done unto thy mother in law since the death of thine husband: and how thou hast left thy father and thy mother, and the land of thy nativity, and art come unto a people which thou knewest not heretofore. The Lord recompense thy work, and a full reward be given thee of the Lord God of Israel, under whose wings thou art come to trust."

Then she said:-- "Let me find favour in thy sight, my lord; for that thou hast comforted me, and for that thou hast spoken friendly unto thine handmaid, though I be not like unto one of thine handmaidens." And Boaz said unto her:-- "At mealtime come thou hither, and eat of the bread, and dip thy morsel in the vinegar." And she sat beside the reapers: and he reached her parched corn, and she did eat, and was sufficed, and left. And when she was risen up to glean, Boaz commanded his young men, saying:-- "Let her glean even among the sheaves, and reproach her not: and let fall also some of the handfuls of purpose for her, and leave them, that she may glean them, and rebuke her not."

So she gleaned in the field until even, and beat out; that she had gleaned: and it was about an ephah of barley. And she took it up, and went into the city: and her mother in law saw what she had gleaned: and she brought forth, and gave to her that she had reserved after she was sufficed. And her mother in law said unto her:-- "Where hast thou gleaned to-day? and where wroughtest thou? blessed be he that did take knowledge of thee." And she shewed her mother in law with whom she had wrought, and said:-- "The man's name with whom I wrought to-day is Boaz. " And Naomi said unto her daughter in law:-- "Blessed be he of the Lord, who hath not left off His kindness to the living and to the dead." And Naomi said unto her:-- "The man is near of kin unto us, one of our next kinsmen." And Ruth the Moabitess said:-- "He said unto me also, Thou shalt keep fast by my young men, until they have ended all my harvest. " And Naomi said unto Ruth her daughter in law:-- "It is good, my daughter, that thou go out with his maidens, that they meet thee not in any other field." So she kept fast by the maidens of Boaz to glean unto the end of barley harvest and of wheat harvest; and dwelt with her mother in law.

Then Naomi her mother in law said unto her:-- "My daughter, shall I not seek rest for thee, that it may be well with thee? And now is not Boaz of our kindred, with whose maidens thou wast? Behold, he winnoweth barley to-night in the threshing-floor. Wash thyself therefore, and anoint thee, and put thy raiment upon thee, and get thee down to the floor: but make not thyself known unto the man, until he shall have done eating and drinking. And it shall be, when he lieth down, that thou shalt mark the place where he shall lie, and thou shalt go in, and uncover his feet, and lay thee down; and he will tell thee what thou shalt do." And said unto her:-- "All that thou sayest unto me I will do."

And she went down unto the floor, and did according to all that her mother in law bade her. And when Boaz had eaten and drunk, and his heart was merry, he went to lie down at the end of the heap of corn: and she came softly, and uncovered his feet, and laid her down. And it came to pass at midnight, that the man was afraid, and turned himself: and, behold, a woman lay at his feet. And he said:-- "Who art thou?" And she answered:-- "I am Ruth thine handmaid: spread therefore thy skirt over thine handmaid; for thou art a near kinsman." And he said:-- "Blessed be thou of the Lord, my daughter: for thou hast shewed more kindness in the latter end than at the beginning, inasmuch as thou followedst not young men, whether poor or rich. And now, my daughter, fear not; I will do to thee all that thou requirest: for all the city of my people doth know that thou art a virtuous woman. And now it is true that I am thy near kinsman: howbeit there is a kinsman nearer than I. Tarry this night, and it shall be in the morning, that if he will perform unto thee the part of a kinsman, well; let him do the kinman's part: but if he will not do the part of a man to thee, then will I do the part of a kinsman to thee, as the Lord liveth: lie down until the morning."

And she lay at his feet until the morning: and she rose up before one could know another. And he said:-- "Let it not be known that a woman came into the floor." Also he said:-- "Bring the vail that thou hast upon thee, and hold it." And when she held it, he measured six measures of barley, and laid it on her: and she went into the city. And when she came to her mother in law, she said:-- "Who art thou, my daughter?" And she told her all that the man had done to her. And she said:-- "These six measures of barley gave he me; for he said to me, Go not empty unto thy mother in law." Then said she:-- "Sit still, my daughter, until thou know how the matter will fall: for the man will not be in rest, until he have finished the thing this day."

Then went Boaz up to the gate, and sat him down there: and, behold, the kinsman of whom Boaz spake came by; unto whom he said:-- "Ho, such a one! turn aside, sit down here." And he turned aside, and sat down. And he took ten men of the elders of the city, and said:-- "Sit ye down here." And they sat down. And he said unto the kinsman:-- "Naomi, that is come again out of the country of Moab, selleth a parcel of land, which was our brother Elimelech's: and I thought to advertise thee, saying, Buy it before the inhabitants, and before the elders of my people. If thou wilt redeem it, redeem it: but if thou wilt not redeem it, then tell me, that I may know: for there is none to redeem it beside thee; and I am after thee." And he said:-- "I redeem it." Then said Boaz:-- "What day thou buyest the field of the hand of Naomi, thou must buy it also of Ruth the Moabitess, the wife of the dead, to raise up the name of the dead upon his inheritance." And the kinsman said:-- "I cannot redeem it for myself, lest I mar mine own inheritance: redeem thou my right to thyself; for I cannot redeem it." Now this was the manner in former time in Israel concerning redeeming and concerning changing, for to confirm all things; a man plucked off his shoe, and gave it to his neighbour: and this was a testimony in Israel. Therefore the kinsman said unto Boaz:-- "Buy it for thee." So he drew off his shoe.

And Boaz said unto the elders, and unto all the people:-- "Ye are witnesses this day, that I have bought all that was Elimelech's, and all that was Chilion's and Mahlon's, of the hand of Naomi. Moreover Ruth the Moabitess, the wife of Mahlon, have I purchased to be my wife, to raise up the name of the dead upon his inheritance, that the name of the dead be not cut off from among his brethren, and from the gate of his place: ye are witnesses this day." And all the people that were in the gate, and the elders, said:-- "We are witnesses. The Lord make the woman that is come into thine house like Rachel and like Leah, which two did build the house of Israel: and do thou worthily in Ephratah, and be famous in Beth-lehem: and let thy house be like the house of Pharez, whom Tamar bare unto Judah, of the seed which the Lord shall give thee of this young woman."

So Boaz took Ruth, and she was his wife: and when he went in unto her, the Lord gave her conception, and she bare a son. And the women said unto Naomi:-- "Blessed be the Lord, which hath not left thee this day without a kinsman, that his name may be famous in Israel. And he shall be unto thee a restorer of thy life, and a nourisher of thine old age: for thy daughter in law, which loveth thee, which is better to thee than seven sons, hath born him. " And Naomi took the child, and laid it in her bosom, and became nurse unto it. And the women her neighbours gave it a name, saying:-- "There is a son born to Naomi;" and they called his name Obed: he is the father of Jesse, the father of David.

Now these are the generations of Pharez: Pharez begat Hezron, and Hezron begat Ram, and Ram begat Amminadab, and Amminadab begat Nahshon, and Nahshon begat Salmon, and Salmon begat Boaz, and Boaz begat Obed, and Obed begat Jesse, and Jesse begat David.

Index to Volumes I - VIII

A Cumulative index to authors and stories